M000203989

Wraiths of the Broken Land

S. Craig Zahler

RAW DOG SCREAMING PRESS

Published by Raw Dog Screaming Press
Bowie, MD

First Edition

Cover Design: Nathan Rosen
Book Design: Jennifer Barnes

Printed in the United States of America

ISBN: 978-1-935738-35-0

Library of Congress Control Number: 2013935107

www.RawDogScreaming.com

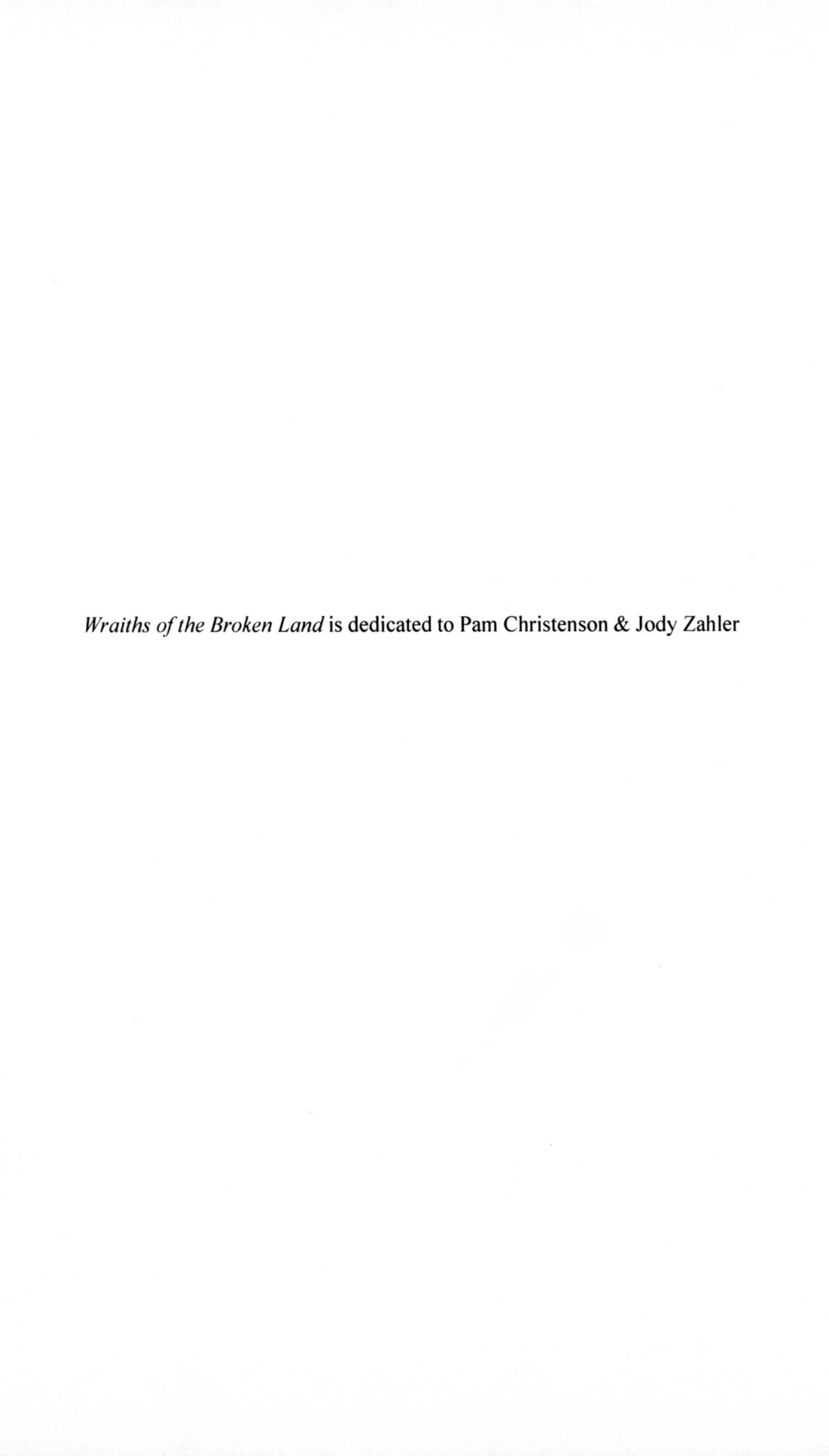

Wraiths of the Broken Land is dedicated to Pam Christenson & Jody Zahler

Summer, 1902

Part I

This Ain't No Sojourn

Chapter I
Shaking Hands

The woman who had forgotten her name shifted upon the damp mattress, and the raw sores across her back, buttocks and arms sang out in a chorus of pain. She turned onto her left side to relieve the wounds. As her legs closed, something hard and unfamiliar press against her vaginal walls, and she said, "Lord..." The woman slid her right hand to her pelvis, poked her fingertips inside, touched a hemispherical lump and withdrew it like a pearl from an oyster. After a moment of lightheadedness, she opened her eyes and looked at the thing pinched in-between her right thumb and index finger and saw that it was a dead baby turtle.

The sight of the deceased creature should have shocked her, but the woman who had forgotten her name felt only a detached curiosity regarding the extracted inhabitant, as if she were listening to nearby strangers discuss a topic of mild interest.

Beside her bed and nestled within small cubbyholes were two candles that yielded the overripe smells of flowers, cinnamon and vanilla and a small amount of amber light. In this cloying luminance, the woman appraised the dead baby turtle that had been inserted into her for some obscure purpose by a man whom she thankfully could not remember. The creature had died with its head and legs withdrawn into its shell, wholly isolated from the world, and she envied it.

Far fouler things had intruded upon her during the past eight months of her subterranean perdition.

For no reason that she understood, the woman set the circular corpse upon her pillow, beside tangled locks of her long blonde hair, and ran a fingertip gently across its crenulate shell. The baby turtle's head slid from the front aperture and dangled, flaccid.

"Reina!" The voice was male, and it penetrated wood and stone.

The woman looked away from the tiny corpse and across the chamber, at the thick, iron-braced wooden door set in the far wall.

"Foods," announced the man.

Unable to locate her nightgown, the woman pulled a blanket that was coarse with dried semen over her bare body.

A line of yellow light appeared at the edge of the door and grew into a seven-foot tall oblong. Within the rectangle of luminance stood the man with the wooden nose, the hombre who brought the canister. The candle flames glinted upon his rubber slicker.

The woman said, "Not hungry," and shook her head. "No food. No comida para mi."

The man with the wooden nose ignored her statements and rolled the canister into the room, steering it by the lever that jutted from its top. The wheels beneath the vessel squeaked like tortured rodents, and the abused woman felt the shrill sounds within the fluids of her eyeballs.

"Foods," announced the man with the wooden nose as he parked the canister beside her bed. He leaned over and unwound a corporeal tube from the side of the device.

Repulsed by the thought of eating, the woman said, "No food." Her quavering body needed something else.

The man with the wooden nose brought the dripping end of the pig's intestine toward the woman's mouth, but she pursed her lips and turned her head away. The tube dribbled viridescent drops onto the blanket.

"Reina must eat and keep beautiful." Air whistled through the nostrils that had been drilled into the man's false nose, and his small obsidian eyes stared. He raised the end of the pig's intestine to his mouth, licked a drop of soup from the tip, smiled and nodded. "Bueno. Is good."

The woman pointed to the dark marks upon her bony arms and said, "I need more."

"No more medicine."

Like a fire throughout desiccated woodlands, fear consumed her interiors. "I…I need more." Her mouth dried up. "I need more medicine, it's been days since—"

"No more." The man with the wooden nose raised the dripping tip of the pig intestine. "Por favor reina, tu—"

"I won't eat until I get medicine."

A fist slammed into the woman's stomach. She gasped for air, and the pig intestine entered her mouth. The man with the wooden nose clamped her jaw shut and pumped the canister lever with his right foot. Soup that tasted like garlic, mildew and rotten chicken flooded down the woman's throat and into her stomach. She tried to call out, but instead sputtered sour broth through her nostrils.

"Bueno."

The man with the wooden nose pumped another sour burst of soup into her, watched her swallow, withdrew the tube and began to coil it around the canister. "You needs sleep. In three days is big fiesta. You have muy important customers, and the boss wants—"

"Get me medicine," demanded the woman.

"No more medicine. It is making you sick. Customers complain that you have cold hands and your hairs is falling out."

Without the opiate's protection, the woman could not endure another fiesta. "I'll make trouble if you don't get me medicine. I'll mess the bed again."

"No." The man with the wooden nose frowned. "No do that."

"You get me medicine or I'll mess the bed when a client is here. Make big trouble for everyone."

The man with the wooden nose whistled through his nostrils, turned away from the recumbent woman, rolled his canister from the room, shut the door and twisted the key.

Alone and full of foul food, the prisoner grew drowsy and fell asleep. In her dream, she was a happily-married choirmaster who lived in San Francisco. Her name was Yvette.

Yvette awakened. Her negligee (which she did not remember donning), face and hair were damp with the sweat of withdrawal. She opened her eyes and saw less. The bedside candles had guttered while she slept, and the room was dark, excepting the small amount of light that crept beneath the oaken door. At the foot of her bed she descried a vaguely triangular shape, like that of a cloaked figure, and felt fear.

The intruder wheezed.

"Who's there?" asked Yvette.

The intruder breathed, clicked his tongue and sneezed explosively. Yvette gasped and released a small amount of urine.

A wet tongue slid across the bottom of her right foot, and she hastily retracted the appendage. The triangular shape sniffed thrice, orbited the bed, paused beside her pillow and panted. The smells that reached the woman's nostrils were those of meat and marrow.

Yvette placed her right hand upon a damp snout. The dog whimpered with pleasure at her touch, unfurled its meaty tongue and licked the salt that had dried upon her wrist.

After she emptied her bladder into the metal pot that she kept beneath her mattress, Yvette struck a match, shared the flame with a candlewick and snuffed the phosphorous head inside a crack in the wall.

The dog was a rusty, fifty-pound male mongrel with pointy ears, wise eyebrows and a big beard that sprouted in all directions from its long snout. The guileless animal stared at her directly, as would an innocent child or a lover.

It had been many months since Yvette had looked into the eyes of anyone that she did not loathe, and she felt tears track down her cheeks. The drops lingered at the edge of her chin and dripped onto the sodden mattress.

Unimpressed by its surroundings, the distinguished dog scratched its side and inspected a toenail.

"Howdy," Yvette said to the creature.

The dog's mouth opened and shut, as if the animal had intended to speak, but then decided against so doing. It sat upon its haunches and lifted its right paw.

"You know how to shake hands?"

The beast eyed her imperiously.

Yvette leaned forward to clasp the proffered appendage, but was seized by the sickness of withdrawal in a horrible flood. She reached beneath her bed, retrieved the metal pot and violently dislodged the major part of the soup that had been forced into her earlier that evening. Sweat coated her flush, down-turned face and she heaved again.

For a ponderous and inert moment, she dripped.

Yvette pulled tangled twines of hair from her mouth, spat sour detritus into the collected excreta and did her best not to inhale the mephitic odors that would certainly bring about another round of retching.

She replaced the pot, laid back and stared up at the cracked ceiling. When strangers slobbered upon her breasts, as if she were their mother and could somehow return them to a state of ecstatic infancy, or entered her canal, she gazed up at the riven stone and imagined that she was a bug crawling across its coarse surface. Some fellows wanted her to look at them and playact affections, but not until the man with the wooden nose had given her medicine had she been able to render these services.

The hope that she would be saved from her terrible perdition had dwindled each month, and although it had not yet disappeared, it was a miniscule mote of dust. Whenever she spoke to the Lord, Yvette asked Him to send rescuers or call her up to be at His side. She had suffered for far too long. Perhaps the dog was a friend sent by Him to comfort her as her life came to its miserable conclusion?

Yvette sat up, felt a wave of pain, pulled her bony ankles across the bed and set the soles of her feet upon the carpet. Trembling, she reached out and said, “Shake hands.”

The dog sneezed and yawned, but did not proffer a paw.

Yvette pondered the animal’s reluctance and said, “Mano,” which was the Spanish word for ‘hand.’

As if it were about to take a solemn oath, the distinguished canine raised its right paw.

The captive woman shook the appendage and released it. “So you’re a Mexican?”

The dog sneezed.

“I won’t hold it against you.” Yvette ruminated for a moment and remembered the Spanish word for ‘talk.’ “Habla.”

The dog woofed, and the burst of loud air made its beard flap.

Metal squeaked on the far side of the room. Yvette and her distinguished roommate looked at the door. Beyond the open portal and silhouetted by a torch that was ensconced in the hallway stood the man with the wooden nose. Instead of his usual slicker, he wore brown trousers and a fancy burgundy shirt. His small eyes caught the candle flames and shone like two distant stars.

“You like Henry?” inquired the man with the wooden nose.

Yvette felt evil creep into the room.

The man scratched his neck and pointed an index finger at the dog. “His name is Henry. You like him?”

"I sicked up the food you gave me." Yvette leaned over and retrieved the metal pot filled with her yields. "In here. Can you—"

"Henry is circus dog from Mexico City," said the man with the wooden nose. "The ringmaster die, and his daughter sells away the animals to buy him un coffin."

"I am hungry," Yvette said in an effort to redirect the conversation. "Tengo hambre. Would you—"

"Henry." The dog looked at the tiny pinpricks of light that were the man's eyes. "¡Vengaqui!" (Yvette knew that this meant 'Come here.')

The dog walked toward the man with the wooden nose.

"¡Alto!"

The dog paused.

"¡Sientate!"

The dog sat upon its haunches.

Yvette's stomach dropped. "Don't!"

The man flung the door. Wood and stone impacted the dog's skull, and it howled.

"Leave him be!" Yvette rose from her bed, grew dizzy and collapsed upon the mattress. "Don't hurt him!"

The man with the wooden nose reopened the door. The animal whimpered pitifully, staggered back a step, regained its footing and shook its head.

"¡Vengaqui!"

The dog ambled forward. The door slammed upon its snout, and something cracked.

"Stop!" yelled Yvette. "Stop, stop!"

The man with the wooden nose opened the door. Twisting its head weirdly, as if it were watching the flight of a drunken bumblebee, the dog hobbled back into the room. Blood dripped from its nostril and right ear, and a sliver of bone, white and agleam, jutted from its crooked snout.

The man with the wooden nose walked toward the captive. Atop his moccasins, ornate beads clicked like dice.

The dog collapsed upon its side, rose to its feet, walked in a circle and shook its concussed, dripping head.

One yard from the bed, the man stopped. "Reina. Mirame. Look at me!"

Yvette wiped tears from her eyes and looked up.

"You will give good lovemaking to the clients or I will make Henry suffer very bad."

"I'll be good."

"No mess the bed?"

"I won't," confirmed Yvette.

"Bueno." The man with the wooden nose turned away and strode past the stumbling dog. "Now we can be good friends."

Chapter II
A Quiet Squabble

Nathaniel Stromler strode from the stable toward the Footmans' house, ruminating upon squabbles, which were his least favorite form of communication. His mother and father had bickered throughout his childhood back in Michigan, especially during wintertime (when the heat of their verbal battles often superseded the blazing emanations of the hearth), and by the time he was ten, he had decided that such dialogues only occurred when people were unable to think clearly, speak precisely and remain rational when confronted by opposing viewpoints.

Kathleen O'Corley, Nathaniel's fiancé, had a different opinion about squabbles. She believed that such interactions were normal and cleansing, and that they proved a person was an impassioned individual. (He had courteously disagreed with her surmise.)

Nathaniel walked along the pebble pathway, toward the black square that was the house within which he and his fiancé lived, and the chill night winds of the New Mexico Territory tingled his skin. He feared that the folded advert he carried within his vest would incite Kathleen to argumentatively demonstrate her love for him, and for this reason, he had shrewdly awaited the hour when all of the Footmans were indoors and able to hear raised voices.

"Evenin' Mister Stromler," said the white-haired negro named Sir, amicably waving his four-fingered right hand.

Nathaniel absently reciprocated the gesture, but his mind was so busy arranging words for his coming discussion that he forgot to proffer any in reply.

Upon the façade, the dark living room curtains informed him that the little ones had already eaten and been sent to bed. Kathleen would not be able to raise her voice.

Nathaniel ascended two steps and landed upon the unpainted wooden porch that circumscribed the edifice's south and west sides.

The front door disappeared, and the screen swung out. From the home's amber interior strode its owner, a squat cattle rancher, clothed in workpants and a red union suit. "You missed dinner," Ezekiel Footman stated with mild concern. The forty-nine-year-old man put an ancient pipe into his mouth and tamped down the bowl's hirsute contents with a splayed thumb. "Harriet saved you some," he added as he disappeared onto the western landing, where two benches depended from sturdy iron chains so that five or six people could comfortably rock to and fro while watching the sun sink below the distant mountains.

"Thank you," said Nathaniel.

"Mmhm."

Around the corner, a match hissed and flashed, dazzling a moth that had previously fluttered unnoticed just beside Nathaniel's left ear. The opalescent creature was the size of a small bat. He puffed air at the phantom insect and sent it gently toward the stars.

Nathaniel walked through the screen door and across a checkered rug that dirt and abrasions would only improve and stopped before a substantial looking glass, which was tastefully decorated with a vine motif and golden filigree. This mirror was precisely the type of accoutrement that he had hoped to hang within each deluxe suite of Stromler's Very High Quality Hotel.

Staring back at him from the reflective glass was a tall, blonde, fully-mustachioed man of twenty-six, who was fairly handsome, but aged prematurely by his large nose, receding hairline (which had yielded an inch of territory during the last two years) and haunted blue eyes.

Nathaniel Stromler had not slept well or felt hopeful or eaten lustily since the day the storm blew down the eastern wall of his half-built hotel and killed a laborer, a young Comanche, who had fallen asleep in the adjacent alley after a long day of construction work. After the event, all of the native employees had refused to work on the edifice (they felt that the death was portentous) and all of the available Mexicans had raised their fees. Nathaniel had all but exhausted his savings to build what stood and the loss was too great to overcome with his remaining funds. Construction halted.

The gentleman and would-be hotelier from Michigan wiped dust from his lapels, put a dab of oil in his palms and slicked back his lank hair. He checked his teeth for corn skins (two salty ears were all that he had eaten that day), saw with irritation how many lines a simple grin etched into his face and returned his lips to horizontal ambivalence.

Nathaniel turned away from himself and strode up the stairwell, across an ugly spotted rug and to the enclosure that he and his fiancé had shared like prisoners for sixteen months, since the day that the winds of catastrophe had blown. Because the furthest any tenant of 'the baby's room' could be from the door was less than four yards, he rapped very gently upon the wood.

"Is that you Nathan?"

"It is I. Are you clothed?"

"I have on my nightgown."

Nathaniel thought of Orton, the eldest Footman boy, who had more than once inappropriately eyeballed Kathleen (but was good-natured whenever the dog of puberty was not barking in his groin), and he looked over his shoulder. A sparkling white eye peered out of the thirteen-year-old's darkened bedroom.

"Orton Footman," said Nathaniel.

The door closed, slowly and quietly, as if a sudden movement or telltale creak would confirm that he was indeed trying to steal a glimpse of Kathleen.

Nathaniel turned back to the baby's room, put his key into the lock, twisted it around and pressed his free palm into the wood. Seated upon the raised bed that filled most of the enclosure and dressed in a rose nightgown was Kathleen O'Corley, a tall twenty-four-year-old woman with delicate features, reluctant freckles, emerald eyes and loose black hair.

The gentleman withdrew his key from the outside lock, entered the room and shut the door.

They kissed. Kathleen tasted like Harriet Footman's apple cobbler (which was good, but contained far too much nutmeg). Nathaniel withdrew from his betrothed and readied himself for the unpleasant conversation that was a necessity.

Illuminated by the lamp that hung upon the opposite wall, the woman's eyes and teeth glowed, as did the stack of handwritten papers that rested upon her lap.

"A letter from your uncle arrived today," announced Kathleen.

Nathaniel's pulse raced—perhaps the folded advert that laid within his vest pocket could be discarded without any discussion or squabble. "Did he locate any investors?" The thought of returning to their abandoned child, the half-built hotel, caused the gentleman's blood to quicken.

"Quite possibly. He sent us the names of three men who might be interested in investing, but are currently undecided. Your uncle has recommended for us to send out letters of solicitation in order to sway them." Kathleen raised the stack of papers from her lap. "I've written the missives already—all that each requires is your signature." She became perplexed. "Aren't you pleased?"

"Certainly."

"Your face has a peculiar way of conveying that sentiment."

"I am pleased—truly, I am—but when you mentioned a letter from my uncle, I had hoped for something more substantial...more...more immediate." Nathaniel thought for a moment. "Where are these investors located?"

"Two are in Connecticut. One is in New York."

Within the gentleman's chest, the risen hopes sank. "Then it will take days—possibly weeks—to get responses from them."

"We've been lodgers for over a year." A small amount of irritation sharpened Kathleen's voice. "This is the best opportunity we've had in some time."

"It is. Indeed." Nathaniel squeezed his fiancé's shoulder and kissed her cheek. "I appreciate you taking the initiative and writing out those solicitations."

"Peruse them so that we may send them off anon."

Nathaniel nodded, sat upon the footstool, read the first letter (the solicitation was flawless), said "Perfect" and signed its nether region with the gold fountain pen that he had intended to set upon the lobby desk of Stromler's Very High Quality Hotel for guests to use in the registrar. He scribbled his name upon the other two immaculate documents, set them upon the floor to dry and turned to face his fiancé.

"I found a job."

"You have a job." Kathleen's voice was flat.

"I found a different job. One that offers far better wages than does a cobbler's assistant." The verbal articulation of this lowly profession brought a shameful flush to the gentleman's face, but the point had to be made.

"What is this new job of which you speak with so much hesitancy and circumlocution?"

Nathaniel withdrew a folded advert from his vest, and Kathleen snatched it from his hands.

"I would prefer to read it to you."

"I am a quite capable reader."

Nathaniel did not disagree with his fiancé's statement.

Kathleen unfolded the document and read it three times. She did not look up from the paper when she asked with a dry, quiet voice, "Who are these men?"

"I do not know." Fabrications often precipitated squabbles, and Nathaniel was an uncomfortable liar whenever he spoke to somebody for whom he cared.

"For what purpose do they require the services of a 'a gentleman with fancy dress who can ride long days and is fluent in Spanish?'"

"I do not know."

"How did this very wonderful opportunity come to your attention?" Kathleen's sarcasm was poisonous.

"Miss Barlone was operating the telegraph and—"

"She is meddlesome."

"Miss Barlone is aware of our predicament, and last month I fixed her son's shoes for free when her purse was light. She showed me the advert before she posted it, so that I might claim the opportunity." Nathaniel paused for a moment. "She has already wired my acceptance."

"You've already accepted?" Disbelief flashed across Kathleen's green eyes and was summarily replaced by something hotter. "You've agreed to work for men, about whom you know nothing, way out in some far-off place?"

"You are getting loud. And neither you nor I know whether the job is in a far-off location."

"The advert stipulates that the gentleman with fancy dress must able to 'ride long days.' What do you suppose that means? Ride around in great big circles!?!" Kathleen's voice would be audible to any person awake on the second floor.

After his heart had pulsed ten times, Nathaniel calmly replied, "The long ride could be out to a far-off location, as you have suggested, or away to a nearer one and then back by sunset each night."

"It seems far more likely that you'll be required to ride into Mexico, since they've stipulated that the gentleman rider must be 'fluent in Spanish.'"

"That is a realistic possibility," admitted Nathaniel. "I do not know."

"But you intend to leave me here and ride off with strangers to wherever they might lead you."

"I intend to earn four hundred and fifty dollars in one week."

Kathleen pursed her lips as if she were about to spit venom into her fiancé's eyes. "The proffered wages are substantial enough to call into question the safety of this job...and its legality."

"Unless I am required to do something unlawful or immoral, I will do what is required of me."

Incredulous, Kathleen shook her head back and forth. "And I shall have no influence upon this decision?"

"You have spoken your mind."

"At a time when you were deaf to contrary opinions—you had decided the matter long before our discussion."

"I had," agreed Nathaniel. "This is something that I must do."

The woman snorted through her nostrils. "What if I told you that I would leave the New Mexico Territory and go back east to my family if you took this job?"

"I love you deeply, but if you are no longer certain that I can be a proper husband—if you no longer believe that my actions will advance us toward a greater happiness—you are encouraged to seek out a better life with someone else. We are not yet married."

Kathleen was stunned.

Nathaniel's stomach shifted, anxiously. He did not think that Kathleen would abandon him, but the possibility existed—she was a smart, educated and attractive woman, and she had not taken a locomotive to the frontier so that she could work as a maid for the Footman family while her fiancé cobbled shoes. Like every couple, they were two separate individuals tied together by a rope with an indeterminate snapping point, and this conversation certainly strained their line. Distant animal noises and more immediate house creaks intruded upon the heavy silence.

Unable to breathe the thickening air, the gentleman said, "It would take five months to earn that much money at the shop."

"Four months." The woman's voice was sharp.

"Kathleen. If the job is hazardous or illicit, I will not go." Looking into his fiancé's doubtful face, the gentleman added, "This is a very significant sum."

"It is." The woman's voice was gentler.

Weight came off of Nathaniel's shoulders—the squabble had ended. "And," the gentleman added, "the possibility exists that these employers are simply wealthy men to whom four hundred and fifty dollars means very little."

"The diction employed in the advert doesn't intimate good breeding," the woman replied, "but I suppose it's possible."

Nathaniel traversed the room with a small step, sat upon the mattress and kissed Kathleen. She admitted him for a moment and withdrew, hastily, as if they were courting teenagers and the condemning head of a parent had just materialized in a window.

"Don't look so distraught."

"You closed the door on me," stated Nathaniel, who was very rarely shut out. He reapplied his lips to those of his fiancé, but she kept her mouth closed in firm denial. As he withdrew, the gentleman remarked, "I did better the first time."

"Not tonight," stated the woman. "My mind is too full of concerns to be present with you in a romantic way."

Nathaniel placed his right hand upon the canvas of bare skin that was framed by lace décolletage and pressed forward, gently urging Kathleen to lie down.

The woman resisted. "I'm too preoccupied by your departure."

Through a smile, the gentleman said, "Please lie down."

"Nathan. I am not of a mind to—"

"I understand. And I promise that I shall remain fully clothed." Nathaniel looked into Kathleen's emerald eyes and felt her heart beat significantly beneath the palm of his right hand. "This is wholly for your benefit."

The woman's cheeks admitted several clandestine freckles, and she nodded.

"Lie down."

Kathleen laid into the locks of her long black hair and the iridescent fabric of her rose nightgown, and was gently received by the hay-packed mattress. Nathaniel touched his lips to the soft skin just above her bare left knee and landed a second kiss beneath her nightgown, exactly where the leg joined her pelvis. He exhaled warm air upon the woman's nexus, and her entire body shuddered.

Running his fingertips along his fiancé's inner thigh, the gentleman asked, "Will you allow me to alter your humors?"

Kathleen made an allowance.

The would-be hotelier and soon-to-be traveling bilingual gentleman looked over his fiancé's recumbent body and through the window, at the effulgent gray sky, upon which neither sun nor moon trespassed. During the interstices of his three-and-a-half hours of fractured sleep, Nathaniel had pondered the east coast investors, the new job and the progress that he could make on his sundered hotel with four hundred and fifty dollars (plus the six hundred and twenty-four bills that he had saved during these last thirteen months) and was anxious. Although he was still tired, he knew that he would not again fall asleep and so decided to begin his day.

Nathaniel climbed over Kathleen's long legs, gently set the soles of his bare feet upon the ground (if trod indelicately, the floorboards imitated the previous baby tenants) and leaned forward, slowly shifting his weight until he found himself standing upright. He pulled a yellow riding outfit over his union suit, picked up his shoes, took one step east, reached out his free hand, twisted the key, exited, closed the door and departed to the attic, wherein his traveling luggage was kept while he and his fiancé were lodgers in a room built for humans who possessed nothing more substantial than diapers, pacifiers and teeth the size of rice grains.

Yawning quietly, Nathaniel strode across the second floor hallway, past the master bedroom and toward the wooden ladder that led to the attic. A door opened behind the creeping gentleman, and he turned around.

From the darkened bedroom emerged Ezekiel, scratching the back of his hirsute neck (a location that seemed to offer perpetual itches) while his healthy stomach inflated between the open wings of his plaid robe. The squat man yawned a salutation.

"Good morning," responded Nathaniel.

"It's chilly for the summer." Ezekiel looked over the lodger's shoulder and said, "Going up to the attic?"

"I need to retrieve my luggage and some garments. I will be away for one week."

The cattle rancher tilted his head sideways, possibly to allow the hand that scratched his nape some new opportunities, and inquired, "Business?"

"Indeed."

"Kathleen's staying on here?"

"She will remain here and tend to her duties."

A strange narrowing happened in the middle of the bushy aggregation of brows and whiskers that was Ezekiel's face. "Why're you sneaking around this way?"

"I did not wish to awaken anybody."

"We heard you two having some words last night." The squinting clefts that shaded Ezekiel's eyes appraised Nathaniel in a blunt and intrusive manner.

"I am not running off." The gentleman was galled by the implication, but suppressed his indignity.

"You won't do better than that woman." Ezekiel lowered one scratching hand from his nape and applied another. "I've seen her with my kids, and I've seen her haggle with shopkeepers or reprimand them if they try and cheat her. She's all there—complete and beautiful—and she even stuck by you after those winds wrecked your hotel."

"I love Kathleen and have no intention of deserting her. I apologize for disturbing you last night, but she and I have amicably resolved our differences."

Unconvinced, the cattle rancher wrinkled his mouth.

"You may rouse her if you would like to check the veracity of my words," suggested Nathaniel. It was difficult for him to keep bitterness out of this remark.

"It isn't necessary." Ezekiel returned the original hand to the back of his neck, pulled the gaping robe over his belly, turned around and strode into his bedroom. "There're plenty of successful fellows in Leesville who'd court her if you dawdled overlong or went serpentine."

No reply issued from the gentleman's pursed lips.

The bedroom door closed.

Embarrassment and anger sat hot upon Nathaniel's face as he turned away, strode to the end of the hall, climbed the ladder, entered the attic, located a large green valise and into it packed water skins, a flask, undergarments, kerchiefs, gloves, a double-breasted royal blue three-piece suit, a long-tailed black tuxedo, two white shirts, cufflinks, Italian shoes, shoe polish, two bow ties (royal blue and black), a red cravat, a royal blue derby, a black stovepipe hat and a novel entitled *La Playa de Sangre* with which he could illustrate his fluency in Spanish.

Presently, he descended from the attic and strode across the second floor hallway. When the gentleman heard a plaintive sound emanate from the closed door of the baby's room, he paused.

The couple had said goodbye the previous evening, and Kathleen had specifically asked Nathaniel to leave in the morning without rousing her, so that they might avoid an anxious farewell.

Standing in the hallway with his heavy valise in his left hand, the tall blonde gentleman from Michigan listened to his fiancé's quiet sobs. The sounds shrank his insides and made his vision hazy.

And then he left.

Chapter III
The Plugfords

Brent Plugford inhaled deeply, and with the unseasonably cool morning air came the odors that filled the hotel apartment—damp underclothes, soap, moldering wood, oiled leather, iron, stale cigar smoke and cheap bourbon. The twenty-nine-year-old cowboy opened his eyes and saw Long Clay, whose tall lean body was clothed in a black shirt and matching trousers, standing at the foot of his bed like the late day shadow of a scarecrow. The silver-haired man pointed to the person who slept next to Brent. "Wake him."

"Okay."

Long Clay walked toward the window.

Brent sat up, stretched his stiff muscles, ran a hand through his wavy brown hair and looked to his left. Prostrated upon the bed beside him was his younger brother, Stevie Plugford, dead asleep and wearing last week's long johns. "Stevie. You gotta get up. We're goin'."

The twenty-one-year-old man grunted.

"Up," ordered Brent. "Now." The cowboy shook his brother's left shoulder.

Stevie swatted his brother's hand away and pulled a blanket over his head.

"You shouldn't've drunk so much bourbon," admonished Brent. "I told you you shouldn't."

"Roast in Hell."

Long Clay withdrew a black pistol, gripped it by the barrel and walked toward the bed.

To the tall narrow man, Brent said, "I'll get him to—"

The handle of the gun impacted the lump that was Stevie's head.

The young man shouted, pulled the blanket down and rubbed his tomato-colored ear. "Goddamn that hurt!" Stevie looked up at Long Clay's triangular face, upon which sat cold blue eyes, a thin gray mustache and a lipless mouth, and declined to proffer any direct criticism.

The gunfighter turned away from the young man, holstered the black six-shooter that was one of two upon his waist, and walked across the room.

Seated upon the windowsill and silhouetted by the drear gray sky was John Lawrence Plugford, a huge man with fifty-six years, a wild beard and worn gray overalls. "You're done drinkin' until we get home." It sounded as if the man's throat were filled with dry autumn leaves.

"I didn't take that much," Stevie defended, "I only—"

"Don't make Pa repeat himself," said Brent. "This ain't no sojourn."

"I know it ain't."

Brent felt a terrible agony in his chest as he pondered the purpose of their journey.

A fist knocked thrice upon the door. Two shooting stars that were drawn pistols arced across Long Clay's black shirt.

A key tickled plaintive tumblers, and the door opened. Standing in the hallway with two lamb chops in his left hand was Patch Up, a short and pudgy gray-haired negro who was clothed in a maroon suit far finer than any garment worn by the white men. He eyed the tips of Long Clay's revolvers—one was trained upon his face and the other was pointed at his heart—and fearlessly chewed. Through a mouth full of food, the negro said, "If this is about the lamb chops, I'm willing to make a deal."

The tall narrow gunfighter holstered his weapons and turned away.

Patch Up swallowed, entered the room and closed the door. "Good morning folks."

"Mornin'," replied Brent.

"Mornin'," croaked Stevie.

The negro strode over to the window and proffered the second lamb chop to the huge patriarch. "Your favorite."

John Lawrence Plugford shook his head and returned his gaze to the gray dawn outside the window. The wild beard that sprouted from his face and neck seemed like an explosion of outrage.

"It's cooked all the way through," added the negro.

The huge man remained uninterested.

"Pa," Brent said, "you need to eat. We've got a big ride today."

John Lawrence Plugford took the proffered victual, whispered, "Thanks," and turned again to the gray window. The lamb chop sat in his thick hands like a musical instrument that he did not know how to play.

Brent stretched, set his soles upon the worn plaid carpet and walked toward the yellow dresser, upon which his washed underclothes were sprawled like flat gray men.

"Where's that Indian?" Stevie asked Patch Up.

"You forget his name?"

"No."

"People have names for a reason. Even niggers and Indians."

"Where's Deep Lake?" asked Stevie.

"It's Deep Lakes," Patch Up stated, "there's an 's' at the end."

"But there's only one of him."

"That's his name."

Stevie stood from the bed and stretched. "You tryin' to make me orn'ry?"

"You should respect what people want to be called. You want me to call you Stovie?"

"I wouldn't. Where's Deep Lakes?"

"Don't know."

Brent looked up from his damp long drawers and inquired, "He didn't stay with you in the servants' quarters?"

"The cooks wouldn't bunk with an Indian," said Patch Up. "I told them he was civilized, but they're suspicious negroes. Deep Lakes said he'd make a camp somewhere and leave town when we do."

Unhappy that the native had been ostracized, Brent said, "He should've come to me with this grievance."

"He doesn't want to force his company where he isn't wanted."

"Okay."

Brent set damp socks that still smelled like soap into his suitcase, and nearby, Stevie began to gather his belongings.

Something thudded within the closet, and was succeeded by a dimly audible moan. Brent's face darkened with anger.

"Goddamn that dumb idiot," remarked Stevie.

Long Clay walked across the room and opened the closet door. Standing upright within the enclosure and wobbling minutely was a large black trunk.

The gunfighter banged the handle of his pistol upon the wood. "Keep quiet or I'll get mean."

The man inside the trunk was silent.

Brent glanced over at his father. John Lawrence Plugford's vitriolic eyes seared the air. The uneaten lamb chop fell to the sawdust, and the huge man slapped his right hand to the grip of his black sawed-off shotgun.

"J.L.," cautioned Patch Up.

Brent hastened to the window, gripped his father's right wrist and said, "Let go of it."

Long Clay interposed himself between John Lawrence Plugford and the trunk and extricated a flask of bourbon from his rear pocket. Light shone upon the silver vessel and glared in the wild eyes of the patriarch.

"Get calm," said the gunfighter.

John Lawrence Plugford released the grip of his sawed-off shotgun, took the flask from Long Clay, spun the cap and inserted the nozzle into the thicket that surrounded his vanished mouth. He drank three draughts and summarily replaced his gaze upon the gray morning. As had often been the case for more than half a year, the huge patriarch was beyond words.

Patch Up reclaimed the fallen lamb chop, wiped sawdust from its surface and wrapped it in a piece of wax paper.

Long Clay looked at Brent and Stevie. "Drain the trunk and put it in the wagon. Now."

Chapter IV
A Ballad for the Real People

Humberto Calles walked toward the gallows that had been erected in Nueva Vida two summers ago, over fifty years after the true people of the land had yielded precious Mexican acres to pale Texicans. The punitive structure was a visibly imposing icon of justice that regularly provided onlookers with an entertaining spectacle, especially if the hanged man struggled overlong or was accidentally decapitated by the noose.

The lone walker reached the gallows, wiped beads of sweat from his head, covered his bald scalp with a sombrero, climbed steps that were decorated with artful tiles that would surely please the eye of any aesthete condemned to death and ascended toward an empty gray heaven. Winded from his climb, the fifty-four-year-old Mexican strode across the platform to the balustrade.

From the stage of death, Humberto asked the onlookers if they would like to hear a song.

"¡Por favor!" shouted eight of the twenty-four people below. Humberto scanned the gathering to see if any town officials were in attendance (they did not want their serious structure used for non-lethal entertainments), but he did not see anybody who might trouble him.

As he adjusted the four strings stretched across the bejeweled frets of his polished blue guitarrita, the balladeer surveyed the crowd. The assemblage was comprised of unhurried people—seamstresses, farmers and old men—and so Humberto decided to perform a long and melancholic song that would appeal to their sensibilities. He squeezed a chord upon his guitarrita's enameled neck and, with the thick nails that jutted from the fingertips of his right hand, sharply plucked the strings. Atop this steady arpeggio of musical raindrops, Humberto introduced the composition, a ballad entitled, "Beneath the Pebbles," which was the true story of a man who had fought in the war against the pale Texicans more than fifty years ago.

Strumming a lush augmented chord, Humberto began to sing.

Black clouds rained upon a small farming village in Mexico. In an adobe that was only three seasons old, a man named Alexzander said goodbye to his wife, Gabrielle, who was pregnant with their first child. The twenty-five-year-old man deeply regretted leaving his beloved, but the war with the pale Texicans was going poorly, and he needed to see that the true people of the land retained what was rightfully theirs. Gabrielle wept.

(Humberto played isolated high notes in the pizzicato style upon the thinnest string of his guitarrita.) Despite her sadness, the selfless Mexican woman did not protest her husband's departure because she knew that he must do his duty. They kissed.

(Humberto articulated two melodies that became one harmonized line—the refrain of their love.)

Accompanied by four of his childhood friends, Alexzander departed the small town, journeyed north and joined a failing regiment that was encamped on a Tejas hacienda that had recently been seized by the Mexican army. The gringos had won two decisive battles in the surrounding region, and Alexzander's superior, El Capitán Jesus Garcia, knew that an unorthodox gambit was needed to defeat the Texicans.

The officer's plan was simple. Alexzander and his four childhood friends were to hide themselves in a mountain pass that was used by the enemy messengers and slaughter the letter bearers before they ever reached the Texican fort. Alexzander, an educated man literate in both Spanish and English, would alter the documents in ways that would benefit the true people of the land and return the revised missives to the messengers' corpses for the gringos of the fort to find. The soldiers doubted that they would be able to complete their mission, but it was near the end of the war and such desperate gambits were commonplace.

(Humberto twice played a slow descending melody that was the declining spirit of Mexico.)

The day before the detachment was to leave, Alexzander received a week old missive from Gabrielle in which she informed him that she had miscarried their child. She had wrapped the tiny baby boy in a shawl, buried him in their backyard beside the pond and decorated the grave with smooth pebbles that she had retrieved from the bottom of the creek where she and Alexzander had once stood, twilit, and exchanged their first kiss.

(Humberto played the melody that was their love.)

Alexzander asked Capitán Jesus Garcia to grant him a two-day furlough. The wan soldier hoped to ride south to his village, console his grieving wife and conceive another child before he began his desperate and unlikely mission. The superior officer expected a troop of Texican messengers to come through the pass in the near future and denied Alexzander's request.

(The balladeer violently strummed his guitarrita and then muted the strings. Below the gallows platform stood twenty-seven spectators, each imagining a personalized and idiosyncratic version of the tale he told.)

Alexzander sent a letter to his wife in which he asked her to ride north and hide herself within the abandoned barn situated at the easternmost edge of the hacienda. He knew that she would not receive the missive for at least six days.

(Humberto flourished his long fingernails and urgently hastened the song.)

Alexzander and his four friends went to the pass wherein they would ambush the Texican messengers. Within an abandoned savage dugout, the quintet hid and waited. Two weeks later, the Texican messengers came through the defile—a group of thirty pale gringos.

(The balladeer strummed frantic triplets; the crowd of thirty-one people was still and silent.)

Although they were outnumbered six-to-one, Alexzander's detachment, armed with old pistols and knives, engaged the enemy. Half of the pale Texicans were slain in the battle, and four of the Mexicans fell dead to the soil that was rightfully theirs. Alexzander was stabbed in the stomach and shot through the left leg. (Humberto plucked his guitarrita violently and paused. Unaccompanied by his instrument, he spoke.) The mission was a failure.

(The balladeer plucked a slow and careful minor key melody.)

Alexzander rose up to his hands and knees and crawled toward the hacienda. He was cold, and he was thirsty, but he did not relent.

(The slow and careful minor key melody was repeated.)

Alexzander reached the hacienda and crawled across the grass, toward the barn wherein he hoped to rendezvous with his beloved, Gabrielle. Night fell as he proceeded, slowly and in great agony, but the Mexican was inexorable.

At dawn, Alexzander entered the barn. He crawled across the hay, past cows with ruptured udders and bloody goats that had devoured their own kind. Gabrielle called out his name, descended from her hiding place and hastened to his side.

(Humberto played the melody that was their love.)

Shortly after they had conceived the baby that would grow up to write and sing this song, Alexzander died in Gabrielle's arms.

(The audience below the gallows applauded and called out accolades while the final chord decayed.)

"Gracias," said Humberto. "Gracias."

Through this ballad, Alexzander lived, and Mexicans knew his name and thought upon the many honorable sacrifices that had been made over five decades earlier by the true people of the land against the pale Texicans. The performer warmed when he saw two octogenarians wipe moisture from their rugose cheeks.

"Bonita cantando," complimented a weathered septuagenarian who gripped the elongated necks of two dead black hens with her bronze fist.

Gold and silver pesos clinked and buried the blue-felt lining of the guitar case that Humberto had earlier placed at the foot of the gallows. To his benefactors, the balladeer said, "Gracias. Amigos, gracias."

The size of the crowd was not substantial enough to produce a significant pecuniary sum, but Humberto was not overly concerned. The riders from America would soon allay his financial troubles.

Chapter V
Gringa Madre

The man who smelled like fish guts pinched the woman's nostrils shut and clapped the palm of his other hand over her mouth. His bare belly dragged north and south along her stomach like a hirsute slug, trailing sour perspiration. In between her legs, fire burned.

The woman bucked in an effort to urge the man who smelled like fish guts toward a hasty climax, certain that once he spilled his fluids, he would release her, apologize and become remorseful. (This was not the first time he had suffocated her.) The man watched her bitten breasts sway and mumbled the word, "Madre." The woman, a gringa who was ten years his junior, knew that this was the Spanish word for 'Mother.'

A full minute without air passed.

The pain in-between the woman's legs sharpened, and the sores upon her back shrieked. Within her abused shell, she suffocated. Her heart pounded out while the man pounded in.

Although she did not relish the life that she now had, the woman did not want to die beneath a fetid wretch who would not notice her expiration until the temperature of her body matched that of the chill subterranean room. Her death should have more meaning than that.

"Gringa madre."

The woman's entire body pulsated in time with her desperate heart, and her oxygen-starved lungs burned.

"Madre." The man's breath quickened, and his oily belly squeaked across her abdomen, vacillating north and south.

The woman felt her heart pound within her throat.

"Gringa madre." The hairy belly squeaked.

The woman lost the power of sight and slapped the man's face as hard as she could.

Hot fluid streamed inside of her.

The hands that clasped her nose and mouth withdrew.

She gasped. Cold air rushed into her burning lungs. After two huge breaths, the woman's eyesight returned, blurry and with flashing orbs.

"Sorry," said the man who smelled like fish guts.

The woman began to cough.

"No germs." Concerned for his safety, the man extracted his diminishing member and rose from the bed.

"Goddamn." The woman pressed her bruised thighs together.

The man pulled on his red trousers, tied a rope belt around his waist, slid his feet into two leather-and-wood sandals, walked over to a cubbyhole, reached inside, rummaged amongst his possessions, extricated a flat bottle and brought it over to the woman. "Bebes." He set the vessel upon her stomach. "Good drink."

The woman examined the wooden flask, which was engraved with the word or name 'Coco,' removed its stopper and drank. The liquor tasted like fruity lantern oil, but she consumed it, eager to diminish everything.

After her fourth draught, she pulled a damp sheet over her sore extremities and looked at Coco's ugly face. "No sofocarse." (She did not know how to say, 'It's nice to meet you,' in Spanish, but she knew how to say, 'Don't suffocate.')

"Sorry." Upon the far corner of the wooden bed, Coco tilted his lumpy head forward and stared at his terrible toes, which looked like root vegetables arranged in two groups of five. His face was heavy with remorse.

The woman saw an opportunity.

"I am going to tell the big jefe that you did sofocarse to me." (A dead whore had even less value than a coyote carcass, and thus asphyxiation was a forbidden diversion.)

The lumpy head swiveled toward the woman. "It was accident." The root vegetables in his sandals stirred anxiously. "I tol' you I am sorry." He swallowed dryly. "No tell Gris."

"If I tell Gris you did sofocarse, he will not let you come to the big fiesta. And no more gringa madre for you ever again."

Employing whatever cogitating vapors were trapped within his skull, Coco contemplated his predicament. "I only play. I never never hurt the gringa madre for real—I was playing."

"Do something for me and I won't tell Gris what you did."

"What you wanting?" asked Coco. "I cannot get you escape from here."

"I want information. I want to know if somebody's still alive."

"Who?"

"The blonde woman they brought here with me."

"What is her name?" inquired Coco.

"Yvette."

"Ella es tu hermanita?"

"Si," Dolores responded, "she's my little sister."

Chapter VI
Unsafe and Safe Ventures

Wearing his yellow riding outfit, Nathaniel Stromler rode his tan mare along the central avenue of Leesville, toward the blacksmith's forge where he was to meet his future employers. A homogeneous blanket of gray clouds covered the vault, diffused the sun and threw the world into a drear limbo from which no person could divine the time of day. Underneath the effulgent slate, the gentleman and his horse failed to cast shadows.

A crucifix that was only slightly darker than its dull surroundings glided across ashen sky, toward the avenue. Presently, Nathaniel, a novice birdwatcher, determined that it was some type of hawk.

A thin black line sprouted from the creature's neck. Silently, the aviator plummeted from the sky and landed upon the avenue. A short man with dark skin, shoulder-length grayish-black hair, blue denim clothing, a strange bow and a lopsided gait walked toward the felled hawk.

Nathaniel neared the archer, and a third individual, a portly fellow with a green suit and a crescent of white hair surrounding his otherwise bald pate, emerged from a nearby storefront and clapped. "You sure can use that thing good," enthused the elder. "Can I fiddle with it for a moment?"

The archer, who was a native in his fifties, shook his head, a tacit refusal. He slung the strange bow over his bare left shoulder and knelt beside the bird carcass.

The portly elder inquired, "You intend to make yourself some hawk stew? Maybe some hawk tacos?" He ruminated momentarily. "Hawk a vin?"

"I'll eat its eyes and mind."

A disingenuous smile did not disguise the portly man's disquiet.

The native plucked out his arrow, slid it inside a groove upon the back of his vest and picked up the bird by its talons. The head of the animal dangled, and crimson beads dribbled from the holes in its neck. Without another word, the native departed into an alleyway with his prize.

Nathaniel glanced at the beads of blood that sat upon the dirt avenue like a game of red marbles, wiped chill sweat from his forehead and tried not to think about his fiancé, alone and crying in the baby's room of the Footman's house.

Riding east along the avenue, the gentleman passed Harding's Notable Chandler, Pocket Watches & Knick-Knacks, Dame Gertrude's Dress Shoppe, Chemist Stuff,

Baked Goods, Leesville's Butcher and We've Got Some Guns. Ambitious dust was escorted from porches by the hissing bristles of thick brooms.

Nathaniel neared a motley assemblage, the cynosure of which was a large wagon that had a tattered green canopy, which had been mended with a pair of yellow long drawers. Two tan, five foot nine-inch fellows, who wore damp beige clothes and had curly brown hair, flung blankets upon the bare backs of horses that were tied in front of the blacksmith's forge. Stretched out upon the crossbar were four other blankets that a pudgy gray-haired negro, wearing a maroon suit, beat with a fire-hardened walking stick.

It immediately occurred to Nathaniel that these were poor men to whom four hundred and fifty dollars would mean a great deal. He gently tugged upon the reins of his tan mare, and slowed the animal's gait.

The brothers adjusted the cloths that draped the animals' spines, and the negro whacked a blanket. Without looking up from his work, the older sibling maneuvered so that his torso was on the other side of his horse, hidden from Nathaniel, and hitched his right shoulder. The younger brother, whose red eyes betrayed that he had either a fever or terrible hangover, paused, leaned upon his horse and perspired. The negro had disappeared.

Nathaniel assumed that the shielded sibling held a gun behind the body of the mustang, and he stopped his tan mare. "Good morning."

Eyeballing the gentleman's hips and valise, the older brother nodded.

"I never carry any weapons," announced Nathaniel. A loud whack startled him. He looked to his right and saw that the negro had returned with his stick.

"Doesn't seem like he's got one stashed away." The colored man sneezed out a damp distillation of the dust he had wrought.

"Nope." The older sibling relaxed his right shoulder and looked up at the mounted gentleman. "Are you Nathaniel Stromler?"

"I am. Are you Brent Plugford or John Lawrence Plugford?"

"Brent." The fellow strode around his horse and toward the gentleman, openly appraising him. "Where's your fancy dress at?" His Texas accent was heavy.

"In my valise."

"Show me them garments." Brent's damp boots squeaked. "I want to see."

The brusque demands irked Nathaniel, and he decided to respond in kind. "Show me the stipend with which you intend to pay me."

Brent paused just beyond the nostrils of the gentleman's tan mare. "My pa's got the money in his wallet."

"Are you speaking of John Lawrence Plugford?"

"I am."

"Perhaps I should speak to him directly." This was not uttered as a question.

"Best to leave Pa in his quietude," recommended the younger sibling. "He's... he's bereft."

Brent worked through some inner sadness and said to the gentleman, "You'll deal with me." His voice was harder than it had been a moment ago.

Although Nathaniel would not leave Leesville until he was certain that these poor rubes could pay him, he wanted to diffuse the burgeoning tension before it turned into a squabble. "I shall show you the garments that I selected."

"Okay," said Brent.

The gentleman climbed from his saddle, landed upon the avenue, took his mare's reins, walked the beast beneath the overhang of the blacksmith's forge, pulled the lines around a post, claimed the green linen valise from the saddle nook, set it upon a bench, undid its four gold buckles, slid the straps, opened the top and popped the six buttons that secured the inner lining.

"It's like he's undressing a prude," opined the younger bother.

"Stevie," chastised Brent.

From the dark interior of the valise, Nathaniel raised the black, long-tailed tuxedo jacket.

Brent ran his fingertips along the fabric. "Okay. The other one got some color? Mex'cans like things colorful."

At that moment, Nathaniel knew that he was going to be required to ride across the border, which he had hoped would not be the case. After replacing the first garment, he raised the double-breasted royal blue jacket.

Brent took the fine coat in his hands and inspected it as if it were the pelt of an Oriental animal. "This one here's better."

"You should go show it to Long Clay and ask what he thinks," advised Stevie.

Ignoring his brother's suggestion, Brent returned the garment to its owner and disappeared into the dark interior of the blacksmith's forge. Stevie and the negro resumed their respective tasks—flinging and whacking blankets.

Nathaniel set the jacket inside his valise and withdrew the Spanish novel.

A tall narrow man with an unpleasant triangular face, which was delineated by a long narrow nose, three vertical scars and a slender gray mustache, emerged from the forge, carrying a heavy bundle upon his left shoulder. His hat, shirt and trousers were black, and his eyes were bright blue. He glanced at the gentleman from a superior altitude (it was uncommon for Nathaniel—who was six foot two—to look up at anyone) and walked past him without a word. The ponderous burden upon the fellow's left shoulder clanked metallically with each stride.

Nathaniel knew instantly that this man was Long Clay. The fellow's height matched the nickname, and it was clear that he was not the type of person who desired children or remained near accidental gets, and thus was not the siblings' father. The two long black pistols that jutted from his hips and his cold demeanor informed the world that he was a gunfighter and possibly a practitioner of less lawful trades.

Before he agreed to travel with this type of man, Nathaniel would need certain assurances.

Long Clay set his bundle inside the wagon canopy, beside a large black trunk. The wind moaned and sounded eerily like a miserable human being.

Footsteps shook the slats beneath Nathaniel's boots, and he turned back to face the doorway. A huge older man, wearing an untamed beard and gray overalls, emerged from the forge, followed by Brent.

"Pa. This here's Nathaniel Stromler. The gentleman who wired us."

Eyes that did not seem attached to anything rational stared out at the gentleman from a craggy canvas of inebriation, grief and hatred. In the leather holster that depended from John Lawrence Plugford's waist sat a wide gauge sawed-off shotgun that had been covered with black paint.

"Good morning," Nathaniel said to the bestial face.

The patriarch stared.

Brent pointed to the book in the gentleman's left hand. "What's that?"

"A Spanish novel entitled, *La Playa de Sangre*."

"You can read and understand it?"

"I can. Choose any passage, and I shall translate it for you."

"I believe you and wouldn't know if you were lyin' anyhow."

Brent extricated a weathered wallet from the breast pocket of his father's gray overalls and handed it over to Nathaniel. "Count 'em, so you know it certain true."

John Lawrence Plugford stared.

The thickness of the wallet told Nathaniel that it contained the promised amount, but he counted out the many, many small bills as he had been instructed. The bank notes were not freshly withdrawn from a bank, and the gentleman surmised that the variegated sum had been earned over a lengthy period of time and squirreled away.

"The amount that you have promised lies therein." Nathaniel handed the wallet back to Brent. "I will require half of my payment before our departure."

The older brother reached into the wallet, withdrew half of the notes and thrust them forward.

Nathaniel was surprised by how willing the man was to give so much money to a stranger, and he deliberated on the motley bills and their owners. To take the proffered stack of crisp and wrinkled and bright and discolored notes was to agree to be in their employ.

"Take it." Brent shook the bills.

John Lawrence Plugford stared terribly.

"Before I accept any wages," Nathaniel announced, "I must enquire after the details of the job for which I am being hired."

Without uttering a word, John Lawrence Plugford stormed off toward the wagon.

Brent glanced at his father and returned his gaze to the gentleman. "You're goin' to reconnoiter for us. Do some investigatin'."

Dissatisfied by the vague explanation, Nathaniel asked, "Could you please be more specific?"

"I'll handle him." The tall narrow man strode upon sharp black boots toward the forge.

Brent, Stevie and the negro were still.

Long Clay walked directly at Nathaniel, stopped when half of a yard of air hung between their faces and stared down coolly. "You won't be asked to do anything unlawful." He radiated the smells of cinders, oil and iron.

Nathaniel drummed his fingers upon the book, found his strong baritone voice and employed it when he inquired, "Shall I have any part in facilitating unlawful acts?"

"That's our business," responded Long Clay.

"I would simply like to know to what end my—"

"You work for us or you don't," stated the gunfighter. "We don't answer to you."

Long Clay turned away and strode toward a tall black mare.

In a voice that was too quiet for anybody but Nathaniel to hear, Brent said, "We're tryin' to find my sisters. They were taken. Kidnapped." Tears glimmered at the bottom of the man's brown eyes. "We're good honest folks—I'm just a cowboy foreman—but—" He strained to keep his composure. "We're all gonna do what's required to get them back. That's why Long Clay come with us."

The gentleman believed the cowboy.

Atop the black mare, Long Clay called out, "Don't gab about our business." His words were hard.

Brent extended the advance toward Nathaniel, and the motley bills trembled. "Please."

Nathaniel took the wage. "I shall return after I have deposited this sum." He put the bills inside his shirt pocket, replaced the book, tied the valise, took the mare's reins and climbed into the saddle.

By the time Nathaniel returned from depositing his advance into one of the ten small safes located within The Reputable Bank of Leesville, the gray sky had brightened minutely. The Plugfords and Long Clay were astride their horses, and the negro was seated upon a padded bench at the front of the wagon, holding a long-handled whip with which he could coax his brace of four mismatched steeds. Two healthy palfreys that wore finely-decorated women's sidesaddles were attached to lines that the huge patriarch held in a tightly clenched fist.

The quietude that had settled upon the assemblage was not peaceful, but ominous.

Nathaniel guided his horse toward the wagon that was situated at the rear of the small caravan.

Long Clay snapped tack, and his black mare started forward. The Plugfords and the negro followed the gunfighter, as did Nathaniel.

The caravan rode west along the avenue.

The portly, gray-haired negro placed the ball of his long-handled whip inside a nook, slid across the wagon bench toward Nathaniel and extended a chubby hand, but the fabric of his right sleeve tugged against his chest and he withdrew the appendage. "Nuisance." The negro undid his top jacket button and extended his hand once more. "My name's Patch Up." He sounded like a Floridian.

Nathaniel took his hand (which was the only one proffered by any member of the caravan) and shook it. "I am pleased to meet you. My name is Nathaniel Stromler."

"A pleasure to meet you, Mr. Stromler."

They shared a dip in the road and released each other.

"Very often," Patch Up stated, "folks who ride with me come back heavier than when they left."

"You are a skilled cook?"

"Your belly won't want to give up my provender."

Long Clay guided his horse off of the central avenue and onto a southerly street, and the others followed. The open terrain beyond the last buildings was a vast orange swath as homogeneous and blank as the gray sky.

"Do you have a favorite comestible item that you'd like for the cook to add to his menu?" inquired Patch Up, magniloquently employing third person.

"I am quite partial to grouse and pheasant."

"Fricasseed or pan fried?"

"You don't got no grouse or no pheasant," Stevie grumbled from his spotted colt on the far side of the wagon.

"Not yet. But Deep Lakes got us that hawk."

Stevie spit his opinion of such meat onto the road.

Nathaniel recalled the archer whom he had seen earlier that morning. "Did you purchase that bird from a native with a limp and a strange bow?"

"Deep Lakes didn't sell it to us," replied Patch Up. "He eats the parts he wants and gives us the rest."

"Is that fellow traveling with us?"

"Near us." Patch Up turned the light side of his hand up, as if he intended to catch a falling raindrop, and motioned expansively. "In our perimeters."

The eyes of the siblings flickered to Nathaniel's face, which likely betrayed some concern at the idea of traveling with a native who ate the brain and eyes of a hawk.

"He's hunted up grouse before," Patch Up added, "but prefers animals that breathe the high up air and get bigger views."

Nathaniel remarked, "Oh?" because he could not think of anything intelligent to say regarding this information.

"He ain't the kind of Indian you need to worry 'bout," clarified Brent.

"I shall not," replied the gentleman, worried.

The horses cantered, and the town of Leesville retreated. Winds that howled like a miserable man chilled the beads of sweat that clung to Nathaniel's brow, nape and mustache.

Long Clay coaxed his horse to a brisk canter, and the other riders matched his pace. The buildings at the southern edge of the town shrank.

"And if you need anything mended," Patch Up resumed, as if he and Nathaniel were in the middle of a conversation, "I can do that too."

"Thank you."

"Shirts, pants, shoes, lacerations, broken bones, dangling scalps—I've fixed them all."

Chapter VII
Saddled

Brent Plugford was impressed that the dandy had been able to return Long Clay's stare, back in Leesville. Nathaniel Stromler had been a little frightened, but it was clear that he had nerves, even facing a gunfighter who could cow any man in existence.

Beneath an ambivalent gray sky, the briskly cantering horses traversed open plains and entered terrain that begat avoidable creosote bushes and unavoidable stalks of purple three awn and black grama. The foliage harassed the beasts' legs and the riders' leather chaps, but did not break open any hides or substantially slow the caravan. Patch Up had a tough time steering his vehicle through the arid vegetation, and every few minutes Brent heard the word "Nuisance" muttered or shouted—the volume of the exclamation determined by how strongly the landscape and the wagon wheels disagreed.

The cowboy pulled right upon his reins, guided his brindled mustang in a loop around the rear of the caravan and urged his animal alongside the dandy's tan mare. Brent glanced at Long Clay and saw only the back of the tall narrow man. This lack of attention from the gunfighter meant that it was now acceptable to speak more candidly with Nathaniel Stromler.

Without preamble, Brent said, "We got a letter from a man named Ojos."

"Ojos means eyes," the dandy remarked, "and is not often given as a name."

The possibility that Ojos was fictitious had been discussed by the Plugfords, but they were desperate and had no other information upon which to act. Brent said, "It's the name he proffered, anyhow."

The dandy was quiet.

"In his letter, he wrote, 'I have identified two rich Mexican gentlemen who know one or both of your missing sisters.'" Brent had read the missive more than fifty times.

"How does Ojos know these men?" asked Nathaniel.

"Ain't sure. I s'pose he'll tell us at the rendezvous." Uttered aloud, the information that he possessed sounded quite insubstantial. "Never spoke to him yet—they don't got no wire in that town. He told us where he could be found most nights and we're goin' there to meet him."

A field of high black grama harassed the legs of the cantering horses; several beasts complained, yet they all continued apace. The tallest stalks slapped against Brent's chaps, crackling like a campfire.

The dandy inquired, "Do you think it is possible that the man who calls himself Ojos simply intends to extort money from your family?"

"Of course it's possible!" exploded Brent. "Don't you think we'd thought of that!?!" He suddenly hated the arrogant Yank.

Nathaniel was silent.

"You think we all got wooden heads!?!" shouted Brent.

The dandy declined to answer the cowboy and instead adjusted the strap of his yellow hat.

The horses' hooves rumbled, and Brent calmed himself. "That letter—it's all we got. In months and months of postin' and sendin' notices all over everywhere, it's all we heard."

"I understand," the dandy remarked, "and would do exactly the same thing if I were in your position."

Before the abductions, Brent had been a well-regarded cowboy foreman, a good, honest and thoughtful boss. For years he had fairly employed oldsters, youths, negroes, Indians, Mexicans and even Yanks who had fought on the wrong side during the War for Southern Independence, but this dreadful business with his sisters was changing him. Now, a poorly chosen word or a patronizing question brought him directly to the precipice beyond which laid only violent action.

Brent looked at the dandy and saw that the man was patiently waiting for him to continue. "Ojos said a rich gentleman who spoke good Spanish could get a talk with them Mex'cans who've seen my sisters."

"I am not rich."

"You'll have whatever pesos you need to play the part."

"I see." The dandy ruminated.

(Long Clay had earlier remarked that it would not be difficult to acquire Mexican dollars, and Brent had an idea how this sum was to be earned.)

The dandy asked, "I am to meet with these two Mexican gentlemen and ask after your sisters?"

Brent nodded. "Once we know for certain where they are, you can ride off. Or if you'd rather, you can ride back with us once we've got 'em safe."

"Throughout this business, I shall employ an alias."

"That's fine."

Nathaniel Stromler extricated a thorny bramble that had attached itself to his chaps, cast it aside and delicately inquired, "And if this proves to be a ruse…if Ojos has lied to you or if these Mexican gentlemen are unhelpful…?"

"Then you can ride off and keep your advance for time spent. Fair?"

"Very fair," said Nathaniel. "But I do hope that I can help you locate your sisters."

As the horses sped past creosote bushes, an errant limb snatched against Brent's chaps and left behind a pointy lavender-green leaf.

"Are we going to stop and eat in the near future?" asked Nathaniel.

"We've got to be at Nueva Vida by nightfall if we want to meet Ojos today."

"How far away is Nueva Vida?"

"We keep at this pace for the whole day without stoppin'," Brent said, "and we'll get there." The dandy was not pleased by this information, but to his credit, he did not complain. "Patch Up boilt some 'tatoes last night and we got jerked beef if you want it. None of us is hungry."

The blank sky smoldered somewhere between gray and black.

Shortly after the caravan traversed an open mesa, its fast progress was impeded by a vast swath of obstreperous creosotes. The dusty horses were forced to slacken their pace and wend the obstacles.

John Lawrence Plugford guided his white stallion beside the pair of cantering palfreys that were reserved for the girls, withdrew a silken rag from his overalls and wiped grit from the empty sidesaddles. He dusted the leather with such tenderness that Brent, watching, felt tears in his eyes and had to look away before he broke. It was clear to him that his father would be wholly destroyed if the girls were not safely recovered—already the huge man was a bestial being whose mind was daily devoured by the jaws of horrible contemplations.

The cowboy wiped his eyes and glanced over at Stevie, about whom he had serious concerns as well. For almost a full decade, Brent had ridden with cattle outfits, and he knew the difference between good fellows and bad fellows and good fellows who did bad things accidentally and bad fellows who did good things deceivingly. This terrible tableau in which the Plugfords were embroiled was exactly the sort of event that could turn Stevie—who already liked to drink too much and cause trouble (and call it fun)—into the sort of man who drank his way into brawls and gunfights and did not live to become twenty-two.

The lives of Brent's sisters, father and brother were at the precipice.

Beneath the rumbling of hooves and the crackling of purple three awn was an erratic noise, barely audible, that was the captive, the man in the trunk, sobbing. The dandy glanced at the wagon for a moment, but doubted his ears.

The sky became a dark gray slate, a feverish limbo untouched by any celestial body. Weary but apace, the horses galloped from a plain of wild vegetation onto a trail articulated by the hooves and wheels of those who dwelled in the region. The ruts intimated to Brent that Nueva Vida was not far off.

"This is better," Patch Up opined from the wagon bench. "Not that I mind getting kicked in the behind for eleven straight hours." He arched his back and elicited seven cracks.

Brent looked over at his brother. "Stevie."

"Yeah?'

"You're gonna be in charge of makin' camp, so keep an eye out for someplace hidden private."

"We ain't stayin' in town?" Stevie looked as if a soft pillow had just been yanked out from beneath his head.

"We don't want people knowin' all of our faces or our number," explained Brent. "Mr. Stromler and I will talk to Ojos, and Long Clay'll watch from outside, but the rest of you stay back." Stevie would not win them any advantage in this rendezvous (and it was possible that he would be truculent) and Brent well knew the affects that men like his father and Long Clay had upon people.

"Okay. I'll make camp." Stevie was apparently too tired and sore to argue.

"Patch Up will help you."

Long Clay, who had not turned around once since they left Leesville, looked at the cowboy. "Brent."

"Yeah?"

"After your meeting, you're coming with me."

A chill descended Brent's spine. Up until that moment, he had assumed that Long Clay was going to garner the needed Mexican dollars by himself.

"Your father isn't capable right now." Long Clay turned away.

John Lawrence Plugford, tightly clasping the bridle lines of the two palfreys upon which he intended to seat his saved daughters, said nothing.

"I can go," volunteered Stevie.

"No you can't," said Brent.

The cowboy knew that he had no choice.

The riders endeavored a decline that was steep enough to pull sweat-dampened hair from their brows, and ahead of them, on the southwestern horizon, a mountain range emerged from the ground. The sharp peaks swelled like the sails of approaching warships.

After a twenty-minute descent, the terrain underneath the caravan leveled out. Yucca, cacti and a few hills shaped like turtles interposed themselves between the assemblage and the rising range. Presently, the riders entered a thick copse and wended its dark vegetation.

Stevie pointed out a clearing that was concealed behind a dense cluster of yuccas. "How 'bout there?"

"Good," said Brent. "Once we eyeball the town, you come back here and throw camp."

"I will."

"Make sure Pa eats. It's been three days for him."

"I'll try to get somethin' in him."

"Stevie and I will hold him down if he refuses," added Patch Up.

"Get somethin' in." Brent ruminated for a moment. "Pour soup into his whiskey if you have to."

The caravan emerged from the woodlands, and the brothers, the negro and the dandy pulled up alongside the two senior men. Forty miles away from the riders stood the dark brown mountains that had consumed the major part of the southwestern horizon.

Brent surveyed the flat plain on the near side of the range, looking for the border town that he had hoped to descry more than an hour earlier. Several miles from his current location, he saw an unnatural ochre luminance upon the land. Relief ran down his spine like warm water squeezed from a sponge. "That's it." He pointed. "Gotta be Nueva Vida." He looked at the dandy and inquired, "What's that mean? Nueva Vida?"

"It means New Life."

Brent heard the sound of crackling tinder. He looked to his left and saw that Long Clay was laughing.

Chapter VIII
A Thoughtful Mexican

Humberto Calles leaned his guitarrita case against the wall in the back room of the bar where he regularly performed and, from his beaded, fringe-adorned vest, withdrew his pocket watch. The hands were fixed at nine seconds after eleven seventeen, the exact moment that some careless horse had compressed its mechanisms. When Humberto had found the pocket watch, a circular corpse lying upon a street in Mexico City (where he visited seven of his cousins twice a year), he had pocketed it and planned to have it repaired. Two days later, the balladeer returned home to Nueva Vida and learned that his mother, Gabrielle, had passed away alone in the night. He had mourned her for several months, and shortly afterwards, impregnated his wife Patricia with the child who was to become their first daughter, Anna.

The fifty-four-year-old Mexican believed in the Savior—and often contemplated less-renowned spirits who had not suffered quite so spectacularly—and wondered at portends and hidden significances.

Because Humberto had found the watch shortly after midnight, he was certain that it had been stomped upon in the evening, rather than at the nine seconds after eleven seventeen that occurred in the morning. (It was very unlikely that the little machine—even crushed—would sit upon a Mexico City avenue unclaimed for thirteen hours.) He knew that his mother had died on the night that he had found the watch, and he often wondered if perhaps she had passed away at the exact moment that its hands had been stopped by the misplaced hoof. He believed that this concurrency was likely, and often contemplated its significance.

Ultimately, Humberto had decided not to repair the broken machine. Nine seconds after eleven seventeen was a moment that he was meant to contemplate, frozen forever like a photograph upon a little crushed face.

Alone in the back room of the bar, Humberto clicked the long fingernails of his plucking hand upon the inert pocket watch, thinking of his deceased mother and waiting for the Americans.

A cool shadow slinked across the table and covered the tarnished metal. Marietta kissed the top of Humberto's bald head, set down a glass of red wine and said, "En la casa." (The owner of the bar always gave the performer of the night a free drink [and Marietta always gave Humberto a second one when the boss had his back turned]).

"Gracias amigita."

The thirty-year-old woman smiled, complimented his performance and asked after his associates from America.

Humberto replied that he would allow them twenty more minutes.

Marietta smiled at him, set a lingering kiss upon his right cheek (a quarter of an inch away from his mouth) and walked away.

If Humberto were not a happily married man, he would have danced an intimate duet with the buxom (and flirtatious) barmaid and revealed to her the tender and patient affections of a fifty-four-year-old artist who appreciated women far more than did any hombre her own age. He would have shown her real and selfless lovemaking…

Humberto drank a deep draught of red wine and sighed at the concepts of fidelity and monogamy to which he was shackled. He would remain faithful to his wife for the remainder of his life, and he would never caress or be caressed by a new woman ever again.

There were many reasons to hope for an afterlife.

A pale hand pulled aside the checkered cloth at the entrance of the bar, and a dusty gringo cowboy who had a brown hat, wavy hair, a gun on his right hip and a frown walked inside, followed by a tall blonde gentleman who wore a thick mustache beneath his big nose, a royal blue tuxedo and a charming little derby. They halted beneath a candelabrum, noticed the wax drippings upon the stone floor, took a step to their left and scanned the establishment.

Marietta walked over to the men and said, "You gentlemens are here to meet with Ojos?" (Humberto was pleased that she had remembered to use his alias.)

"Si, Señorita," replied the tall gentleman. He removed his hat, tilted his head forward and said, "Nosotros queremos hablar con Ojos, por favor." The gentleman's pronunciation was flawless.

Marietta pointed to the revolver that sat upon the cowboy's hip. "You pistola. I need. You can no have guns in here."

The cowboy scanned the bar, looked back at her and lifted his hands. "Take it."

The barmaid withdrew the weapon from the holster. "You ask me for the pistola when you leave. I am Marietta." She slid the gun into her red and brown dress. "I now take you to Ojos."

"Gracias amiga," said the gentleman.

Slowly, the cowboy nodded.

The woman escorted the gringos past the tenanted stone-and-tile bar, around three inebriates who threw knives at a plank that was decorated by a blue chalk drawing of an angry bear, beneath a large wooden statue of some bizarre three-headed pagan god that the owner had found in the badlands and hung like a piñata, past a table where two old men played checkers, in-between two long benches that were packed with hombres who drunkenly sang a refrain from one of the songs that the balladeer had performed two hours ago and down three steps, into the sunken backroom wherein sat the Mexicano whom the Americanos had come to Nueva Vida to meet.

Humberto stood up and extended his right hand toward the dusty cowboy. "I am Ojos. You are John Lawrence Plugford or the son?"

The cowboy clasped the proffered hand. "I'm the son. Brent."

As they shook, Humberto saw something that could have been either distrust or distaste flash across the gringo's face. They released each other.

"I am Thomas Weston," announced the gentleman, as he extended his hand.

Humberto shook with him and saw no look of distrust or distaste flash across his face.

"Me llamo Ojos."

The balladeer released the gentleman's hand and motioned to the cushioned stools that surrounded his table, which was decorated with red, brown and green tiles. "Please sit."

The gringos sat upon the stools.

Humberto looked down at the Americanos and inquired, "What would you like to drink?"

"We wouldn't," said the cowboy.

The balladeer sat upon a cushioned seat opposite the gringos and inquired, "Do you mind if I drink the wine that's already been poured for me?"

"We ain't here for any kind of social."

Humberto knew that Brent Plugford was not well-educated.

The cowboy set his hat upon the table, reached beneath his beige shirt, extricated a worn grouch bag and pulled the strap over his head. "Your gold."

Humberto took the proffered pouch, set it upon the table, loosened the purse strings, glanced inside and saw variegated scintillating nuggets.

"There's no hagglin'," the cowboy stated, "that's every crumb we got."

"This appears to be the amount promised in the poster," remarked the balladeer.

"You can put it on a scale, so you know it certain true."

"I doubt that you'd ride all the way down here and attempt to cheat me of an ounce."

"I'm honest," stated the cowboy, as if what he said were a well-established fact. "Now tell me 'bout my sisters."

"As I wrote in the letter," Humberto said, "I know the identities of two men who have had dealings with one or both of your sisters. Nine weeks—"

"How?" interrupted the cowboy, openly suspicious. "How you know that these men know my sisters?"

"Please allow me to tell a short story that will answer all of your questions."

"Go tell it."

"Nine weeks ago, when I was in Mexico City visiting my cousins, I saw the notice, your reward poster, in a post office. Shortly afterwards, I wrote a song about the missing woman."

"You wrote a song 'bout my sisters?"

"Yes."

Outrage blazed across the cowboy's face. The gentleman clapped a gloved hand to his companion's shoulder and squeezed.

"I apologize if I've upset you," said Humberto.

The cowboy smoldered, unable to speak.

"Why did you write a song about them?" inquired the gentleman.

"Their story moved me. Even though gringo Texicans killed my father and stole land that rightfully belongs to Mejico, I thought of these innocent and beautiful women and I was…" Humberto shook his head. "I sympathized—I have two daughters myself—and I became angry with the world, a place where beauty is stolen and abused rather than appreciated." He thought of his gorgeous cousin Elena, who had vanished twenty years ago and was presumed dead. To the cowboy, the balladeer said, "Your sisters are not the only women that have disappeared in this country."

The cowboy gave an empathetic nod.

A flung blade pierced the right eye of the blue chalk bear.

Humberto glanced at the drunken knife-thrower and returned his attention to the gringos. "My heart was heavy when I wrote the ballad. In English, the title means, 'That Which Cannot Be Stolen.'" The singer pointed to his guitarrita case. "I have a special guitar with four strings, which I play in bars like this one and on the street. I played the song, 'That Which Cannot Be Stolen," many times.

"Near the end of the ballad, there is a verse that describes one of the missing women in—"

"How did you know what she looked like?" inquired the gentleman.

"There were pictures on the reward poster."

"Go on," said the cowboy.

"Near the end of the ballad," Humberto repeated, "there is a verse that describes one of the missing women in great detail. After I paint her portrait, I call out her name." With ripping vibrato, Humberto sang, "Yvette!"

Tears rolled down the cowboy's face.

"Afterwards, I sing the final verse. I describe the other woman in great detail and call out her name." Humberto sang, "Dolores!"

The cowboy wiped away tears with the brim of his hat.

"I performed this song many times—in cities and in towns and twice inside locomotives. People were very moved by it." (Humberto decided not to inform the gringos that the ballad was one of his most lucrative compositions.) "A few weeks ago, I came home to Nueva Vida.

"Eleven days ago, I performed 'That Which Cannot Be Stolen' in our town square, and when I sang out the names of the women, two men in the audience reacted very strongly. They paled. Their eyes became moist. They were frightened. And I was absolutely certain that they knew one or both of the women in the song."

"Who are they?" The cowboy's words fell like a blunt axe.

Humberto hesitated for a moment. "You must promise that the gentleman will speak to them in a civilized manner. They are—"

"Don't put any goddamn terms to me," spat the cowboy. "I paid you for this information." He pointed at the grouch bag.

"It is quite possible that these men are unaware of your sisters' plight."

"You don't know that at all."

"You are correct," Humberto admitted, "I do not know how they know your sisters. But these two men are important and have done many good things for this town. You must promise that you will not hurt or kill them."

"We'll do what we need to do," said the cowboy, darkly.

Humberto closed the grouch bag and slid it across the tiled table. "You may reclaim your gold and go back to America."

Hatred shone clear and bright upon the cowboy's face.

Humberto drank from his glass of wine.

After the cowboy had calmed himself, he asked, "What if these good hombres of yours ain't so good?"

"If either of these gentlemen are hurt or killed, I will relay the names John Lawrence Plugford and Brent Plugford to many bad Mejicanos." Humberto let his threat sit in the air for a moment. "And if I should accidentally cut off my own head or carelessly stab myself twenty-nine times in the liver, there are other talkative people who will dispense this information to the banditos."

"You've told others 'bout our rendezvous?" The cowboy had a hard look in his eyes.

"Not yet—but I will if I feel unsafe when I leave this meeting or if you harm the Mexican gentlemen in any way."

"Hell." Brent snorted through his nostrils like a horse. "You're a clever Mex'can."

"One of many millions."

The cowboy considered his options.

"As for the hombres who have imprisoned your sisters…" Humberto shrugged his shoulders. The execution of men who kidnapped and abused women did not trouble the balladeer.

The cowboy slid the grouch bag across the tiled table. "We'll leave off these two that you're connectin' us with. My word's good."

"Bueno." Although Humberto did not like the cowboy, he trusted him. "I know a place where these two gentlemen gamble and have drinks—a nice establishment." The performer looked at the tall blonde gringo and said, "You will go there."

"Why did you not speak to them yourself?" inquired the gentleman.

"I do not wish to become directly involved." Humberto did not want to be involved at all, but his conscience had compelled him to say something and his family could use the money. "Gamble with one of these men and buy him some drinks. When he is relaxed, tell him the type of woman that you are looking for. He will tell you where to go. ¿Comprendes?"

"I understand." The gentleman seemed doubtful.

"Es muy facil," confirmed Humberto.

"You think my sisters are bein' kept in town?" asked the cowboy.

"I know of no brothel in Nueva Vida that would do this sort of thing, but perhaps there is a hidden place, a prison beneath a home. Or perhaps they are in another town or in a cave somewhere in the mountains."

The gentleman paled.

"You're paid to work a full week," the cowboy said to his companion.

"I am aware of that."

Brent looked at Humberto. "You ever hear of a Spaniard named Gris? Got one eye?"

"I have not."

"Okay." The cowboy seemed disappointed. "Now tell us about these Mex'can gentleman."

Chapter IX
Empty Skulls

Nathaniel Stromler walked past the checkered blanket that dangled in the front doorway and into the night. The air outside the bar was far cooler than what was trapped inside, and the chilled sweat upon the gentleman's brow and nape wrought horripulations that matched the texture of his anxious guts.

Brent exited, shoved his pistol back into its home and pulled the blanket across the portal. He touched the brim of his hat, which was a signal to the unseen man in the alleyway on the opposite side of the road, and whispered, "Don't look over."

"I shall not."

The cowboy's hand landed upon the gentleman's right shoulder and urged him forward. Nathaniel walked past a barbacao shack, two groping lovers, a burro that was tethered to half of a rusty anchor, four ziggurats of bricks that were to become a building and two whining terrier puppies marooned in an unmonitored baby carriage. The duo crossed the street, circumnavigated an open half-trailer (within which laid four people who the gentleman hoped were asleep rather than decomposing) and turned east, toward the outskirts of Nueva Vida.

Behind a house, a dark shape detached itself from the shadows and disappeared into an alleyway. Nathaniel felt a lambent spark climb his spine.

"Keep walking." Brent placed the meat of his right palm upon his gun grip.

Nathaniel's pulse quickened.

Walking abreast, the two men passed several houses, a score of interconnected shacks and a tiny wagon loaded with yucca leaves and hacked-up cactus limbs. The town grew sparse.

Brent asked, "You think you can get these gentlemen to divulge?"

"I will do everything that I can to learn—"

A perpendicular shadow appeared beside the cowboy. Nathaniel's stomach sank. Presently, he recognized that the darkness was Long Clay.

"You can find the camp from here?" Brent asked Nathaniel.

"I believe so."

The gunfighter and the cowboy disappeared behind a house.

"Damnation."

Nathaniel applied his monogrammed silk handkerchief to his damp forehead and looked northeast, across the plain toward the tangled coppice in which the Plugford crew was positioned. The woods were a hirsute black growth upon the dark gray land, and within them the camp was completely obscured.

The abandoned gentleman replaced his handkerchief and walked. His loafers wobbled upon hidden stones and unseen roots, and he considered the deeds that his companions might commit to acquire the pesos that he needed to convincingly playact the role of a wealthy whoremonger. Nathaniel did not think that Brent was a dark man, but the cowboy—in his desperation—submitted to Long Clay, a charcoal jackal with a thousand sharp teeth in his stomach. Once again, the gentleman contemplated abandoning the Plugfords, although he knew that he would not. He wanted to keep his word, earn his full wage and aid the women. The avenue of egress was more than two hundred miles behind him.

Nathaniel entered the woods.

Within the forested region, the world was bifurcate. The spiky obstacles that rose up from the earth were jet black, and the sand, the sky and the gentleman's outstretched hands were dark gray.

Cautiously, Nathaniel walked along an elusive footpath, which was demarcated by flat stones, and around him, the woods grew denser. Opaque night began to overpower that which was dark gray and discernible. Time sped up or slowed down.

He stumbled over a root and flung his arms wide. A yucca needle pricked his right palm, and he retracted his hand. The gentleman looked at his injury and saw a droplet of night traverse his dark gray palm.

"Damnation."

Nathaniel wiped black blood upon the trunk of a tree, strode three paces and ducked below a low-hanging branch that attempted to choke him.

"Damna—"

Two metallic clicks emanated from the mound of blackness directly in front of the gentleman. He froze.

"Who's there?' asked the dark pile.

"Nathaniel Stromler stands before you."

"I was hoping for something a bit tastier." There was a vertical glimmer within the darkness—light upon a gun barrel. "Is Brent there with you?"

Nathaniel recognized the speaker as Patch Up. "Brent is not with me. He has gone off on an errand with Long Clay."

"I suppose that's why you didn't employ the special signal."

"I was unaware that there was any such signal."

Several leaves rustled and a twig broke.

"Why're you over this way?" inquired Patch Up.

"I am returning from Nueva Vida."

"Is the town on wheels?"

"Pardon?"

"You're walking south."

The night concealed Nathaniel's embarrassment. "These damnable woods have… they have discomfited me." A hand landed upon the gentleman's shoulder and startled him. He turned and was barely able to discern the gray hair and sleepy eyes of the pudgy negro who stood right beside him.

"If you could navigate dark woods all by yourself," Patch Up stated, "you wouldn't be our dandy."

Nathaniel chose not to respond to the remark.

"Good news."

"That would be an anomaly."

"I'm roasting up a grouse—your highly-preferred favorite."

Nathaniel's anxieties had trumped his hunger for the last two hours, but his stomach reacted immediately to the news with a noise that an elderly and infirm housecat might make. "That is splendid information. I am famished."

"Let's chow."

Patch Up led Nathaniel down a declivity, through a trampled creosote patch limned by firelight and into a clearing. Beside the sunken campfire squatted the sinewy native who had killed the hawk earlier that morning. The longhaired man was clothed in jeans and a vest, and his hands were splattered with wet blood that dripped onto heated stones, sizzled and filled the air with the smell of copper. Firelight shone upon the waxen, reddish-purple skin that covered his right arm, and the man's eyes, fixated on the blaze, glowed like jewels.

"That's Deep Lakes," Patch Up informed Nathaniel.

"I recall him from this morning."

Very aware of his royal blue fancy dress at that moment, the gentleman strode beside the campfire and to the native said, "Greetings."

"Good evening to you, Mr. Stromler." Deep Lakes sounded like an educated man from the Northeast.

The gentleman was about to endeavor more conversation when he noticed the carcasses. At the foot of the native laid a dead bobcat and an armored, beaded, gray capsule-shaped creature that Nathaniel did not recognize from life experience, but instead from an illustrative plate in the first volume of his encyclopedia as an armadillo. The light from the fire shone inside the animals' cracked-open skulls.

Deep Lakes raised one of his dripping hands, put a pinkish-gray clump of matter into his mouth and swallowed it whole. Blood dripped onto the stones and sizzled. Sickened by the sight and the cloying odor, Nathaniel looked away.

Patch Up walked over to the far side of the campfire, wrapped his hands with damp rags, leaned down, grabbed the thick end of a long iron stake and raised an impaled, plucked and salted grouse from the hearth coals. Half of the bird had been cooked, and the remainder was completely raw.

The negro wrinkled his mouth and looked back to the area where the horses were hobbled. "Stevie!"

The crooked-nosed twenty-one-year-old emerged from behind the wagon. "What?" He was bare-chested and held something shiny in his right hand.

"Did you turn Mr. Stromler's grouse like I asked?" Patch Up whispered to Nathaniel, "He didn't."

"I did," proclaimed Stevie.

"Then exactly half of this bird is fireproof?"

"Go roast." Stevie swatted the air and raised the shiny object to his mouth.

Patch Up looked at Nathaniel. "He's in the flask."

"I am more than content to eat the cooked half of that grouse," remarked the gentleman.

"Let me give it some symmetry." Patch Up leaned the spit beside the hearth and from his left coat pocket withdrew a metal cylinder that was surmounted by a brass crank. "Got eleven spices in here. And special salt." He ground the peppermill, and multicolored motes clung to the bird's skin.

"Bravo," said Nathaniel.

"Hey!" shouted Stevie. "The dandy's back!" He gestured with his flask and drank, as if he had just concluded a toast.

From the darkness behind the wagon emerged a broad lumbering shape that Nathaniel mistook for a bear until he recognized it as John Lawrence Plugford. The powerfully-built patriarch strode past his son (who hastily secreted his liquor flask), directly toward the campfire.

Suppressing trepidations, Nathaniel said, "Good evening, Mr. Plugford."

Two red lights gleamed beneath John Lawrence Plugford's heavy brow.

"Would you like some of this grouse?" inquired Patch Up.

The patriarch shook his leonine head, arrived at the campfire and focused his terrible eyes upon the gentleman. "What happened?" The voice that emerged from the tangled silver and brown beard was a funereal rasp.

"Brent and I spoke with Ojos—the man who sent you the letter."

John Lawrence Plugford nodded. His eyes were like gun barrels.

"Ojos gave us the names of the two gentleman who saw your daughters, and—"

"What're their names?" John Lawrence Plugford reached into the chest pocket of his gray overalls, withdrew a fountain pen and unscrewed its cap with huge fingers that made the writing implement look no larger than a lollipop stick. The steel tip glared with reflected firelight.

The bestial man gazed at the gentleman.

Nathaniel hesitated.

"Don't make Pa ask twice," Stevie advised from behind his father's shoulder.

Nathaniel said, "The men are Manuel Menendez and Juan Bonito."

Upon the back of his left hand, John Lawrence Plugford wrote.

Manwell M

The tip clogged and scratched his skin. The colossal man sucked upon the steel, spat, shook the fountain pen and continued to write.

inindez. Wan Boneeto.

John Lawrence Plugford slid the cap onto his fountain pen, screwed it down, turned his back to the fire and walked toward the darkness.

Concerned that the wrathful man was going to hunt down the two Mexicans directly, Nathaniel said, "Sir."

The patriarch continued into the shadows.

"Mr. Plugford, sir."

"J.L." shouted Patch Up. "Wait a moment."

The huge man halted, but did not turn around.

To his substantial back, Nathaniel said, "Those two men are not to be harmed. They are the contacts with whom I am to meet, and they will tell me where to find your daughters."

The fire dimmed and the camp darkened. John Lawrence Plugford was silent.

"Your son guaranteed that Manuel Menendez and Juan Bonito would not be harmed," clarified Nathaniel. "He gave Ojos his word."

From the other side of the massive shoulders issued a quiet and crackling inquiry. "How do these two men know my angels?"

Stevie, Deep Lakes and Patch Up looked at Nathaniel.

The gentleman did not doubt that a poorly-worded answer would bring about violence. "I am not certain how these men came to know your daughters."

The huge hands became fists.

"J.L," said Patch Up. "We need to let the dandy talk to these Mexicans before you get involved. That's why he's here."

John Lawrence Plugford nodded his head, strode forward and vanished.

The native slid two fingers into the cleft skull of the bobcat and scooped out a pink morsel that he swallowed without chewing.

To Nathaniel, Patch Up said, "Your grouse is ready."

"Please set it aside. I may regain my appetite in a short while."

"I'll save it for you."

"Hey dandy!" Stevie staggered toward the campfire, reached into his back pocket, withdrew a balled-up paper and flung it. The projectile impacted the gentleman's chest and landed on the ground beside the pit, where it glowed bright yellow. "Brent said you gotta study that. They're pictures from the reward poster."

Nathaniel leaned over, picked up the paper, opened it and saw—backlit by pulsating firelight—the beautiful and crumpled faces of Yvette and Dolores. They were smiling.

Chapter X
Bad Men

Black toenails scrabbled upon the tiles of the trespassed den. Brent Plugford, whose face was hidden behind the rubber mask of a smoke respirator, braced the white dog, muzzled its mouth and drew a curved blade across its throat. Blood warmed his left pant leg, and he felt queasy.

Although Brent's job as a cowboy foreman had twice required him to shoot a man (a Yank named William who had tried to steal the payroll, and an ornery drunk with the same name who did not appreciate being dismissed from a riding outfit by a boss young enough to be his grandson), each fellow had pulled a pistol, and in so doing, authored his own end. Brent felt that his actions were fully justified, and he had been untroubled by remorseful sentiments when he had buried and abandoned each body beside the cattle trail. But the innocent creature that struggled in his hands was different from the men named William or any animal that would provide sustenance: The white dog was killed so that he could commit a wrongful act.

Two final paroxysms contorted the draining creature, and Brent's vision blurred. The blood that saturated his left pant leg grew cool and sticky.

In his hands, the thoughtless, dripping animal stared out blindly.

A shadow fell, and Long Clay, wearing a rubber respirator mask, pointed to the ground.

Upon the cold tiles, Brent laid the dog.

The gunfighter scratched a match. White light flared upon the glass lenses that covered the eyes of the masked men, turned orange and illuminated the enclosure. The den was large and furnished with Oriental rugs, Spanish tapestries and glossy European furniture, all of which seemed to confirm the owner's purported wealth.

A black snake descended from the ceiling. Brent froze.

An instant later, the cowboy realized that the serpent was actually dog's blood sliding down his left lens, and he wiped the gore away.

Long Clay pointed the barrel of a black pistol at a wooden doorway on the western wall. Brent nodded, confirming his readiness. The gunfighter snuffed the match.

Toward the chosen door, the trespassers stalked. Brent prayed that they would not have to hurt anyone.

Long Clay extended his right hand, clasped an ornate knob and twisted it gently. The cylinder squeaked. The tall shadow pushed the door forward, slowly and carefully, revealing a vertical line of pure night that grew wider and wider.

The space beyond the den was utterly opaque.

Staring into the inscrutable black region, Brent's apprehensions grew.

A match flared in Long Clay's right hand and revealed a long hallway, the walls of which were hung with paintings. The gunfighter snuffed the glaring head, tapped Brent's left lens and pointed at the passageway on the opposite side of the den and at the French doors through which they had entered the house.

The cowboy apprehended that he was to hold in his current position and monitor these two points of ingress. He nodded.

The gunfighter was absorbed by the black hallway.

Alone with his respirations, Brent monitored the den and the portals that led to it. The room was as still as a photographic image and the house was quiet. Upon the wall that he had not earlier surveyed hung a painting that was a family portrait. The cowboy's stomach sank when he saw a boy depicted in the image.

A man yelled and was abruptly silenced.

Brent drew his gun and looked up the hallway into which his partner had disappeared, but he saw only darkness. The cowboy was a wholly inexperienced criminal, but he had heard stories from his father and knew not to run blindly into a tableau, especially when Long Clay was the protagonist. He returned his attention to the den.

A figure emerged from the opposite hallway.

Brent pointed his pistol. On the other side of his weapon stood the eight-year-old child from the portrait, terrified.

The cowboy shoved his revolver into his holster, lunged forward, clapped a palm to the boy's mouth, threw him to the floor and pressed a knee into his stomach. Brent wanted to tell the child that he would not hurt him, but Long Clay had insisted that he remain mute unless the situation were dire—any English or one poorly-pronounced Spanish word would mark him as a gringo. Fortunately for the cowboy, the prone boy was so terrified that he did not struggle overmuch.

At the end of the hall wherein Long Clay had disappeared, a white light flashed, accompanied by a dim pop that Brent recognized as a muted gun report. The cowboy's stomach sank.

The boy looked west and saw the slain white dog for the first time. His big eyes filled with tears and his chest convulsed beneath the cowboy's knee. Brent tasted bitter self-loathing, but kept the boy pinned—he knew that things could get much worse.

Quiet footsteps sounded within the dark hallway.

Brent raised his revolver. A matched flashed thrice and was gone. Recognizing the signal, the cowboy lowered his weapon.

Long Clay emerged from the shadows, a lacquered wooden box nestled underneath his curled right arm.

Fully aware that he could neither wrangle nor defeat the gunfighter, Brent hoped that his father's old partner was not the type of man who would hurt or kill a subdued child.

The gunfighter set the wooden box upon the sofa, holstered his gun and knelt beside the youth. The boy trembled beneath Brent, as had the white dog four minutes earlier. Long Clay reached into his shirt pocket, withdrew a plum and inserted it into the boy's mouth. Relieved, the cowboy pulled a kerchief across the plugged orifice and tied it. The two men hog-tied the child, placed him upon an Oriental carpet and rolled him up like a burrito.

The rug breathed.

Long Clay tucked the wooden box underneath his right arm, strode through the French doors and disappeared into the night.

Brent glanced at the breathing rug, the butchered dog and the opaque west hall at the far end of which an innocent man might have been murdered. Poisons tainted the cowboy's blood.

He cursed silently, hurried through the French doors, stole across the backyards of four houses and entered a tall stand of creosote bushes wherein waited Long Clay. The thieves removed their rubber masks, tossed them and the wooden box inside two sealskin sacks and hastened to an adjacent dirt road. Brent was a fit man, but he was usually atop a horse when he needed to move quickly, and his thighs and buttocks burned as he matched his partner's long quick strides.

A lean dog that looked like a brindled coyote emerged from a shack and followed the thieves for twenty yards, barking continually. Long Clay thrust a gun barrel through its eye and fired. Its skull pan wholly muted the blast.

The men departed the western edge of Nueva Vida, entered the dark gray badlands and began to circle around to the east. As they walked across the gritty plain, Brent's blood-soaked pant leg alternately chaffed and stuck to his skin.

"Why'd we have to wear them perculiar masks?" asked the cowboy.

"Would you have preferred a scarf?"

Brent looked at the tall narrow man, but was unable to determine whether or not he was irritated by the question. "Scarf would've been easier."

"Do you think that a scarf—which covers half of man's face, none of his hair and can pulled off by a child—is the best way to maintain one's anonymity?"

"I don't."

After the pair had walked in silence for a few minutes, Brent said, "I've got one other question, and then I won't ask you nothin' more." The gunfighter neither accepted nor refused the inquiry. "What happened when you went up that hall? I heard a gunshot."

"You didn't do anything but kill a dog and gag a child," replied Long Clay. "That's all you need to know."

"I thought I was s'posed to know what happened—since I was your partner."

"No cowboy who cries over a dumb dog is my partner."

Brent was humiliated by the remark, but did not bother to defend himself.

A silent and brisk half-hour walk brought the two men to the footpath that led into the tangled black coppice. Brent slung his sack over his right shoulder and preceded the gunfighter inside.

Twenty strides later, the cowboy heard a distant wailing. He tensed and drew his revolver, but quickly realized that the ululation was his brother attempting to sing.

"Hush him or I will," threatened Long Clay.

Brent hastened along the winding footpath, where dark tree limbs and darker yucca spikes advanced from the opaque surroundings like the weapons of inhospitable natives. As he ran, a corner of the wooden box tattooed a bruise upon his back.

Stevie's singing grew louder.

An orange glow that Brent recognized as the sunken campfire flashed beyond two fronds that looked like a witch's hands. Oriented, the cowboy sped directly toward the camp.

Stevie sang, "The muskets flashed upon the barbican." (Five wooden thumps punctuated the line.) "The thunder of Confederate pride!" (Wood rumbled.) "A hand with a union cuff of blue, reached down like the greedy claw of the Jew. 'We are united!' they lied. 'Pay our tariff!' they cried. But to the end, we did defend, with a rebel shield of pride." (The singer inhaled deeply.) "Of Pride!" A miserable note was held for an amount of time unrelated to the (poorly) established meter.

When Brent entered the clearing, he saw the dandy, the Indian and Patch Up seated around the fire pit and looked for his brother.

"Of infantible Southern pride!" brayed Stevie, stretching the final word through ten flat notes, as if he were an opera singer, rather than a man who was completely unmusical.

From the darkness, Brent divined his wailing brother. The bare-chested young man was seated at the back of the wagon, atop the black trunk in which the captive was kept. "Stevie!" hissed the cowboy. "Get down from there and keep your mouth—"

"You're back!" Stevie thumped his heel against the trunk, leaned over and (loudly) whispered, "My brother's back from his special mission."

It was fortunate that the dandy was faced away from the drunken singer.

"Get down from there and keep your mouth shut." Brent heard Long Clay's footsteps upon the path. "Do it now."

Stevie considered his brother's suggestions. Depending upon how drunk he was, he would either obey Brent or resume his song at a louder volume.

"Of infantible Southern pride!"

Holding the barrel of a gleaming black revolver in his left hand, Long Clay emerged from the woods, ready to whip the young inebriate.

Brent ran toward his little brother, the soak.

"I believe," the dandy remarked from beside the campfire, "that the word you are attempting to sing is 'indefatigable.'"

"Yank!" berated Stevie.

Brent grabbed his brother's right arm. "Come off of there and don't say nothin' unless you want Long Clay to wallop you again."

The inebriate glanced across the campsite and was sobered by the sight of the approaching gunfighter.

"I'm tryin' to save you a beatin'," said Brent.

Stevie nodded. "Okay."

"Now get off of that trunk."

The young man leapt to the ground, landed on two feet, teetered to each compass point and stood upright.

A large shape emerged from the shadows, shuffled past the siblings and headed toward the gunfighter. Brent threw his brother a stern glance and followed after his father.

"Did you earn?" John Lawrence Plugford asked Long Clay.

"We earned."

The patriarch nodded, walked to the campfire and interposed himself between the dandy and the flames. "Get to town."

Surprised by the blunt imperative, Nathaniel reached into his trousers, withdrew a pocket watch and clicked its release button. Silver arrows glimmered in his weary blue eyes. "It is nearly ten minutes after one in the morning."

John Lawrence Plugford, a huge silhouette above the fire pit, loomed.

"Most Mex'cans stay up late." The cowboy set the plunder beside the campfire. "That's why they've got them afternoon naps."

The dandy looked at the sealskin sack and frowned, as if he were the parent of the flayed animal.

"Should be plenty for your performance," added Brent.

The dandy reached into the bag and extricated the burnished box. Firelight sparkled upon three drops of blood that sat atop the wood like ladybugs, but the tall man from Michigan did not remark upon the sanguinary keepsakes.

"It's got a latch." Brent pointed an index finger.

The dandy twisted the brass knob, pulled the bracket and raised the lid. Gold and silver coins, a large black book and bundles of paper money filled the padded, purple interior.

John Lawrence Plugford withdrew the tome and held it close to his face.

"That a bible?" asked Brent.

The patriarch nodded.

"You gonna give it to Yvette?"

"It's in Spanish." John Lawrence Plugford tossed the holy book into the fire pit. The tome curled, flashed, shriveled and blackened.

Although Brent was not a religious man, the sight of the burning bible made him feel uneasy.

Long Clay cast his shadow upon the plunder. "Use the coins."

The dandy looked up. "The banknotes are for larger denominations and more commonly carried by men of wealth."

"Paper money is locally made at a thousand banks, individualized and easy to identify. Those coins are myriad and spend all the way to China."

"I understand." The dandy yawned, nodded his head and looked at Patch Up. "Would you please extricate the ten and twenty peso coins while I tend to my toilet?"

"Certainly," said the negro.

The dandy rose to his feet and stretched.

"Mr. Stromler," said Brent.

The dandy looked at him.

"Deep Lakes is gonna follow you to town. He'll wait outside the club, hidden invisible while you wheedle Menendez and Bonito. If you go somewhere else, some other place, Deep Lakes is gonna follow you there and let us know." The dandy did not look very confident. "Once you've identified my sisters—you studied their pictures, right?

"I did."

"Once you've identified my sisters, you come outside wherever you're at and drop your hat on the ground and scratch your nose. That's your meaningful gesture. When Deep Lakes sees the meaningful gesture, he'll send up his signal and we'll all come ridin'."

"What happens then?" inquired the dandy.

"Deep Lakes will get you hid and when we meet up with you, you'll tell us what's inside and where the girls are."

"And what shall I do after I have fulfilled my obligations?"

"After you've apprised us, you can start back to the New Mexico Territory. And if they make you leave your horse behind, we'll bring her along and some water too so you can ride off north." Brent looked over at Long Clay and inquired, "That's it, right? How we discussed?"

"That's how it begins," remarked the gunfighter. "Once I've heard the layout described, I'll detail the rescue."

To the dandy, Brent said, "Go get presentable and on your mare. My sisters are waitin'."

Chapter XI
Two Lullabies

A tiny fist knocked upon the outside of the bedroom door, and a voice equally small and delicate inquired, "¿Padre?" The intertwined husband and wife hesitated.

Lodged within the canal whence the knocker had emerged ten years earlier, Humberto looked up from Patricia's flush face and over to the door. "Dos minutos, por favor."

"Si," replied his youngest daughter, Estrellita.

Humberto doubted that he could achieve his culmination in the remaining time (he was no longer in his forties), but he would certainly bring a significant smile to Patricia's face. He did not conjure the image of the luscious barmaid Marietta, but she appeared in his mind nonetheless and brought about an unexpected release that was as sharp and soothing as the tequila wrought from the special blue agave that was grown in Guanajuato.

The balladeer climbed from his satisfied wife, covered her body with a warm blanket, kissed her nose, pulled on his linen pajama pants, strode to the bedroom door and undid the lock that was only employed when he and Patricia were romantically engaged. In the hallway stood Estrellita, the little star. Her big eyes were wide with fear and he knew without asking that she had been upset by a nightmare.

Humberto stepped into the hallway, shut the bedroom door and asked his daughter if she would like a bedtime song.

Estrellita considered the proffered medication and said, "Dos cantos."

"No." Humberto would have agreed to play two songs for her (she was his most adorable patron, and she possessed a more fertile imagination than did any adult), but it was half-past one in the morning, and he felt that he must deny her request. "Un canto solamente."

The ten-year-old girl, who had inherited her considerable bartering skills from her mother, said that she would compromise and accept one-and-a-half songs.

Shaking his head, the balladeer explained that a song was a story that should be told in its entirety or not at all. (Whenever she fell asleep during a familiar lullaby, he completed the tale the very next day.)

Estrellita asked for him to play, 'The Acolytes of Saint Pedro of the Object.' (This epic ballad was as long as two normal songs.)

"Si." The balladeer was fully aware that he had been bested by his conniving little star.

Humberto took Estrellita's little hand, walked her to the hickory peg from which depended his guitarrita case and claimed the unique instrument that he adored not quite as much as his wife and two girls, but more than any of his aunts or uncles or cousins or nephews. Father and daughter walked up the hallway, passed by Anna's crutches and entered the room that the balladeer had built during Patricia's second pregnancy.

The space was dark. Neither moonlight nor starlight shone through Estrellita's window, and the mountains outside were indistinguishable from the charcoal sky. Humberto set his guitarrita case down, struck a match and lit the wick of a lantern that was hung too high for his daughter to reach. Amber light chased the shadows away.

The little girl locked the door (as if she intended to hoard every forthcoming musical note), climbed into bed and told her father that she was ready.

Humberto withdrew his guitarrita and sat upon the windowsill. Behind him, the sky and mountains were a black curtain.

A gentle melody drifted from the instrument's plucked strings and into the girl's ears. Unlike some balladeers who had to sing loudly in order to ring accurate pitches, Humberto performed adeptly at any volume.

The lyric described an imaginary South American town that was located in the bottom of a dell and surrounded by green forests and tall white mountains.

"Objeto Bendito!" Estrellita sang in concert with her father. (Humberto was pleased to hear his daughter match the pitches almost perfectly.)

The people who live in Blessed Object go to church and before each meal say grace and acknowledge His great sacrifice. They are pious. (Humberto played a melody where each note was plucked strictly on the downbeat—this refrain showed the townsfolk's steadfast devotion to the Savior.)

As is often the case with Catholics who live in rural communities, the residents of Blessed Object have augmented the Trinity with a provincial saint to whom they pay tribute.

("San Pedro del Objeto!" Estrellita sang, a little ahead of the beat because of her excitement. Humberto added a two-measure etude so that he could lean over and kiss her forehead.)

Saint Pedro of the Object is the supernal patron of the town and this is his story.

(Upon Estrellita's face was an enormous smile.)

Two hundred years ago, at exactly nine seconds after eleven seventeen at night, an infant escaped his crib. He crawled from his house, across dark cobblestones and to the craftsman's shop that was located on the far side of the settlement. When his parents found him the next day, he was covered with wet clay. His mother and father apologized to the shop owner and repaid him for the material that their child had ruined.

They took young Pedro home and—with a long ivory shoehorn that the man used to get into his knee-high boots—very gently scraped the clay off of the baby's skin. The parents put their child back into his crib and went to sleep.

The next morning, when the mother and father entered Pedro's room, they saw two babies. One baby was Pedro, and the other was made out of clay. The parents were uncertain how their six-month old child could have sculpted this second baby, and they suspected divine aid. This clay infant became the first sacred Object.

The settlement that was located in the bottom of a dell and surrounded by green forests and tall white mountains was given the name Blessed Object.

("Objeto Bendito!")

Throughout his life, Saint Pedro of the Object refined the Object that he had begun as an infant. He apprenticed with a carpenter, mastered the art of woodcraft and carved elaborate curly hair, one strand at a time, for his Object. With lapis lazuli, he made eyes for his Object. With fine pearls, he made perfect fingernails and toenails for his Object.

When he was a man of forty, Pedro studied the diagrams of anatomy and thereafter began his most time-consuming elaboration. He inserted pieces of clay, each no larger than a pea, into a tiny hole in the left shoulder of the hollow Object, and with long needles and tweezers, he sculpted bones, nerves, arteries and organs inside the boy.

Saint Pedro of the Object died when he was sixty-six years-old—exactly twice as old as the Son had been when he was betrayed by Judas Iscariot and crucified. The patron was buried in the central square and mourned by every person in Blessed Object.

(Humberto saw that his daughter was getting sleepy.)

The following day, the townsfolk went to place new flowers upon Saint Pedro's grave, and they saw the Object, prone atop the burial mound. The villagers contemplated divinity. They journeyed to Saint Pedro's house and saw that the armoire in which the Object was kept was still locked, and they knew that the patron had been buried with the only key.

The townsfolk prostrated themselves. This event was the second miracle performed by Saint Pedro, the patron of Blessed Object.

The white crescent upon Estrellita's face was engulfed by a round black yawn.

Humberto let his chord decay and announced that he would finish the song tomorrow.

"Gracias." Estrellita's eyelids drooped, resisted for a moment and yielded.

The balladeer leaned over, kissed his most sacred creation upon the forehead, adjusted her cotton blanket, took himself and his instrument to the far side of the room, opened his guitarrita case and saw the grouch bag of gold nuggets that he had received from the desperate Texan earlier that evening.

Even though he did not believe in the immediate divine intervention of which he sang, Humberto said a silent prayer for the abducted gringas. He tucked away his four-stringed child, blew the flame off of the lantern wick and felt the plaintive lump in his guts that was awarded to each good father on the day that his first daughter was born.

Chapter XII
The Reapers of Scotch and Tequila

Nathaniel Stromler adjusted his royal-blue derby and walked up the only paved road in Nueva Vida, toward a white three-story building that was surrounded by carriages, stagecoaches and horses that glistened like satin. Beneath a jutting overhang and illuminated by two glaring mirror lanterns hung a green-and-gold sign.

Castillo Elegante
de
Humo, Bebidas & Dados

To the worldly, would-be hotelier from Michigan, who had thrice visited Europe and once (accidentally) sojourned in the Orient, the establishment did not resemble the elegant castle that the sign promised, but the rectilinear specters of tobacco smoke before every window, the braying laughter and the sudden exclamations that were concurrently joyful and angry did confirm the alleged cigars, drinks and dice. Two clean-shaven men in pine green uniforms stood on either side of the mahogany front door, monitoring the gringo as he approached. They wore bright new pistols and stern faces, and Nathaniel was unsure whether they were privately contracted guards or law enforcement officials or both.

"Good evening Señor," said the man on the left with stilted, but clear English. "Welcome to Castillo Elegante."

"Gracias," Nathaniel replied, "y buenas noches a ustedes."

Both men were surprised by his precise and confident enunciation.

The gringo strode underneath the overhang and saw upon the door a pretty placard warning any poor man who thought that he might smoke, drink or gamble in Castillo Elegante that he was not welcome.

No Hay Hombres Pobres Permitido.

The sentry on the right pulled open the heavy door, exposing a luminous and smoky pine-green interior.

"Amigos." Nathaniel gifted the guards with two ten-peso eagles and saw by their bright eyes that such generosity was uncommon.

"Gracias Señor," said the one who spoke.

The other nodded appreciatively.

(Nathaniel thought it best to have the armed men favorably predisposed to him should things go unexpectedly bad during his reconnoiter.)

Feeling the weight of his predicament and a sharp pang of apprehension, the man from Michigan paused at the portal and glanced back at his tan mare, the glowering sky and the shadows that concealed his hidden accomplice Deep Lakes, whose exact location was unknown. Nathaniel steeled himself, filled his lungs with chill air and entered a sizable parlor that was decorated with pine-green wallpaper and sofas and inhabited by people who did not seem to understand that dawn was less than four hours away.

A throng of Mexicans wearing shiny blue suits converged, and the gringo's eyes stung from the potency of the cigar and cigarillo smoke that they exhaled. Serving women offered smiles and drinks to any man not focused upon their bosoms, which were coaxed into voluptuous prominence by strict lace corsets. A young mariachi, a woman with castanets and an ancient trumpeter, all of whom were outfitted with gold-fringed pine-green suits, performed unobtrusively in an alcove that was illuminated by two mirror lanterns.

As he began his first circuit of the parlor, Nathaniel considered Ojos's description of Manuel Menendez. 'Menendez is fifty, portly, five-and-a-half feet tall, has a mustache, some liver marks and some gray hair.' The orbiting gringo saw that half of the men who peopled the room could be thus described, and unless he asked a serving woman or a chance stranger to identify his quarry, he would be unable to divine the Mexican gentleman from his two score doppelgangers. Consequently, Juan Bonito, 'a five foot four-inch mestizo with a flat nose and torn right ear,' was the gentleman upon whom Nathaniel decided to focus his search, even though Ojos had warned him that the fellow was 'strange and far less approachable than Menendez'.

Three circuits of the room did not reveal the conspicuous little man to the gringo. Certain that Juan Bonito was not on the first floor, Nathaniel looked for the stairwell that led to the upper stories and saw, in a dark portal, a golden diagonal line that was a balustrade.

A serpentine limb wrapped the gringo's arm, and his breath caught.

"Hello, handsome and tall American."

Nathaniel looked to his right and saw a young Mexican woman who had wide, innocent eyes and a lascivious smirk. The girl looked eighteen years old (or younger), although perhaps she was in her twenties (like negroes and Orientals, Mexicans aged slower than other people).

"Buenas noches," Nathaniel replied a little uneasily. It had been years since he had last felt the warmth of a pretty woman who was not his fiancé.

"Did you ride into the town today? From Texas?"

"You are twice correct."

"You would like a hot bath?" The woman's painted lips framed a smile. "I will clean you well."

Nathaniel devised a polite reply. "I…did not come here for…female companionship."

The woman sharply withdrew her hand from the gringo's arm and said, "I give baths only." She took a step away and added, "You smell like horse."

"I apologize for my assumption, I was—"

The indignant woman departed.

Nathaniel, who had twice visited New York, checked his trousers to see if the bathhouse girl had acquired an illicit stipend or a new American pocket watch, but he located all of his possessions. He walked to the stairwell at the back of the room, and as he ascended, he imagined how soothing a warm bath—administered by the girl or Kathleen or himself—would feel. The musings unhelpfully recalled his weariness and many aches.

Up the steps, Nathaniel trudged. The gold rectangle above him grew, and from it emanated the sudden shouts of winners and losers engaged in the ritual of inviting chance into their wallets. Amidst the cacophony, the crystalline strings of a harp resonated.

The gringo passed through the portal and into a luxurious room that was decorated with golden wallpaper and furnished with white divans and stools that were occupied by more than a score of game players. The servers wore opalescent bodices that showed the tantalizing edges of their tan breasts (which undoubtedly helped the gamblers make wise decisions whenever they bet against the house), and a mulatto woman in a silk gown played a delicate melody upon a large golden harp in a far corner. Depending from the walls were four impressionistic oil paintings that depicted stately horses atop drear mountain peaks. (Nathaniel recognized that this room was supposed to invoke Europe, but to him it seemed designed by a man who had never traveled more than three miles from the hacienda in which he had grown up. Had the gringo seen a harpsichord, he would have laughed aloud.)

The gamblers focused their attentions upon cards, dice, drinks, female flesh and the eyes of bluffers, and thus were less interested in growing the volume of smoke than were their desultory contemporaries below. As Nathaniel made his survey of the room, his stinging eyes cooled.

Seated at a white table that had raised edges was a small man wearing a brown suit. His back was to Nathaniel, and so were his mismatched ears, one of which looked as if its top half had been shot off at close range. An anxious pulse thrilled through the gringo's chest.

Nathaniel circled the table and furtively noted his subject's flat nose, atop which sat a strong brow that suggested a mix of Mexican and native ancestry. This man was Juan Bonito.

In addition to his tight brown suit, the ugly little man wore a red derby, a matching bowtie and bright white gloves, and thus appeared like something that might accompany an organ grinder with upraised palms and a banana agendum.

Juan Bonito furiously shook dice in a golden cup that was decorated with coruscating beads, as did his three peers, all of whom fit the vague description of Manuel Menendez. The caroming ivory rattled like a hailstorm. The quartet overturned their cups and slammed them to the table. Clandestine dice settled, and gamblers glanced underneath lifted lids.

Nathaniel did not know if they played the type of Liar's Dice wherein there was one loser per round or the variation wherein a victor took the entire pot from multiple losers, but either way, the ante seemed very substantial for a game of guesses—each person had fifty pesos upon the betting circle.

The gringo knew better than to approach the table before the round had concluded, and thus watched the game from a respectful distance.

"Empezas," Juan Bonito said to a man who wore a pinstriped jacket.

The chastened fellow bid five rolls of three.

A man who chewed upon a damp, unlit cigarillo said, "Seis los tres."

The next fellow in the clockwise progression bid seven rolls of three.

"Deceiver!" exclaimed Juan Bonito.

The men raised their cups, and the revealed dice showed five threes.

With bright white gloves, the diminutive mestizo took the winnings from the gentleman at whom he had yelled, circumspectly inspected the pesos and added them to the metropolis of coins and neatly-arranged bills that stood beside his right elbow. (The other bets remained untouched.)

Nathaniel asked if he could join their game.

The man who had just lost made a space between himself and Juan Bonito, so that the gringo could sit, look at the champion's ruined ear (which looked like a burnt clam) and lose.

"Gracias Señor."

A Mexican woman who had strong arms slid a chair before the gap and placed a golden cup with dice upon the table. Nathaniel thanked her and sat down.

Fingering his ruined ear, Juan Bonito said, "We do not play for wooden nickels."

The gringo withdrew his coin pouch from his jacket, opened the strings and poured onto the whitewood table a score of high-value pesos. Juan Bonito and his contemporaries nodded.

Nathaniel decided that a man of wealth (or at least the fictitious individual whom he was portraying) would adhere to some of his inbred preferences when abroad, and would not care overly whether or not he ingratiated himself to the locals. He turned to the woman who had inserted his chair and said, "Quiero un escocés, viejo y dulce, por favor."

The server recommended Águila Azul, a particularly fine tequila that was very popular amongst the refined gentlemen who visited Castillo Elegante, but the gringo politely refused her advice. Rebuffed, the woman nodded and went to retrieve a glass of old and sweet scotch.

Nathaniel and the loser from the previous round each placed fifty pesos upon the betting circle.

"Empezamos," announced Juan Bonito.

The gamblers shuttled their dice and shook their cups, and a hailstorm of rattling ivory blotted out all other sounds. The mestizo nodded. The gamblers slammed their cups to the table and surveyed their rolls. Nathaniel's dice showed a two, two threes, a four and a six.

"Perdon." The presumptuous gringo announced that he would like to make the first bid.

Two nodding heads granted him permission.

Nathaniel said, "Seis los cuatros." (This was an uncommonly high opening bid.)

"Lying deceiver!" shouted Juan Bonito.

The gentlemen lifted their cups, and the upturned faces of their dice showed four fours—two short of Nathaniel's wager. Juan Bonito claimed the gringo's money, circumspectly inspected each coin and erected a new building at the eastern edge of his monetary metropolis.

The quintet played another round. Once again the gringo bid high and was called out by the small mestizo.

"Drat!" exclaimed Nathaniel.

Juan Bonito flashed a kind smile at the American naïf and said, "Do not begin with big numbers. With so many men playing," he swept his hand in a circle, "you will not reap."

"Gracias."

"I will begin the next time." Juan Bonito amicably patted Nathaniel's shoulder.

Gamblers rattled their dice and slammed their cups. The round began with the mestizo and ended with the gringo's bad bid.

"Drat!" exclaimed Nathaniel. (He hoped that he was not overdoing his display of ineptitude.)

The woman with strong arms placed a glass of scotch at the gringo's left elbow.

Nathaniel reached for a gold coin, but had his wrist seized by Juan Bonito.

"No," admonished the mestizo. "I am taking your money. I pay for the drink."

"Gracias."

The diminutive man handed the woman a twenty-peso piece, which was an extraordinarily generous payment.

"I think we should alter the direction of the bids," Juan Bonito suggested to the gringo, "so that I cannot call you a lying deceiver."

"Gracias."

It was difficult for Nathaniel to picture this conscientious fellow paying to violate a captive woman, but he knew that men could become something else—something that they loathed—when the wolf of lust growled within them. The mestizo might very well have some dark reservoir filled with the unkind looks and remarks that his appearance, stature and ironic name elicited.

"We go in the new direction," stated Juan Bonito.

The gentleman with the unlit cigarillo between his lips changed the corner of his mouth in which the soggy cylinder sat, as if it were a weathervane for the order of bidding.

Nathaniel set down fifty pesos.

"Empezamos."

Cups became ersatz maracas and were slammed to the whitewood. Two rounds of bids circled the table. The man with the damp unlit cigarillo called the fellow to his right a liar and lost fifty pesos when the dice were revealed. The victor (whose name was Victor) left the table with his winnings and another round was played in which Nathaniel called Juan Bonito's bluff and won back some of his money.

The night trudged.

Nathaniel bought his gambling mentor a drink and had the courtesy twice returned.

"Dishonest liar deceiver!"

The last time Nathaniel had seen a watch, its small hand was reaching toward the number five. It was difficult for him to believe that less than twenty four-hours ago, he had stood in the Footman's house, outside the door of the baby's room, listening to his fiancé's quiet anguish. That somber moment now seemed almost as remote as his childhood in Michigan.

The man with the unlit cigarillo decided that he needed to light the damp tobacco leaves that had tantalized his nostrils all evening (his wife only allowed him one smokable per day since his lungs were bad) and so he left Nathaniel and Juan Bonito alone at the table.

After three hours of gaming, the moment of inquiry had finally arrived. Nathaniel wet his mouth with a sip of scotch and turned to his quarry.

Juan Bonito, who had stopped speaking English after his third tequila (excepting when he called someone a 'dishonest liar deceiver'), announced (in mildly slurred Spanish) that he must return home.

A pang of fear lanced Nathaniel. Calmly, he suggested that they share one final round of drinks.

Juan Bonito contemplated the offer.

"Uno mas, mi amigo," insisted the naïve American. This was the first time that the gringo had called the mestizo 'friend.'

The little man ruminated upon the offer. "Si, amigo—uno mas."

"Bueno."

Juan Bonito reached beside his chair, raised a crocodile skin briefcase, rested it upon the table and said that he would clean his money.

Although Nathaniel found the proposed chore to be quite odd, he nodded nonchalantly and ordered the final round from a serving woman who had an inexhaustible supply of curls, smiles and energy.

Juan Bonito undid several steel latches and opened his heavy briefcase. Affixed to the lid were a five-shot revolver and a serrated knife. (It was clear that no brigand was going to shoot off the little man's good ear.) The mestizo spread his newly-acquired banknotes across the surface of the table, raised a perfume bottle labeled 'Agua', sprayed water onto the wrinkled bills and arranged them in four neat stacks that he covered over with a damp cloth. The little man glanced at the gringo and remarked that he liked clean money.

"The best," agreed Nathaniel.

Juan Bonito produced four candles, stood them in an empty glass, struck a match and lit each wick. He shook the phosphorous head until the fire became a zigzag of smoke, dropped the tiny tinder and withdrew from his reptilian briefcase what appeared to be a small clothing iron.

"Muy inteligente," complimented Nathaniel.

Eyes full of serious purpose, the mestizo held the underside of his small iron to the quartet of flames. The smell of heated metal overpowered the duller odors of cigarillo ashes and vanished drinks.

Casually, the gringo remarked how much he liked what he had seen of Nueva Vida.

Juan Bonito rotated his iron and recommended the pernil tamales at Casa Jorge and the barbacao shacks on the west side of the town, which were superior to their eastern siblings.

After thanking the mestizo for the advice, Nathaniel leaned forward and, in a quieter voice, mentioned that there was something else that he desired, especially while he was away from his wife.

"Bebidas por Señor Bonito y el Americano," the serving woman said as she set down a glass of tequila and a tumbler of scotch.

Nathaniel withdrew a coin from his greatly diminished purse and paid for the drinks.

"Gracias." The woman stirred a curl with a lascivious finger and departed.

Juan Bonito pressed his iron to the damp cloth that covered the bills, and water hissed. Through the vapors, the mestizo asked the gringo if he wanted a sporting woman.

Nathaniel confirmed that he indeed desired the company of such a lady.

The mestizo remarked that there were two brothels in Nueva Vida and three discreet women of luxury who received clients at their homes.

After a meaningful pause, the gringo proclaimed that he desired a type of woman who would be uncommon in this region.

"You would like…scotch…instead of tequila?" inquired Juan Bonito in slurred English.

"Yes," confirmed Nathaniel. "I prefer scotch."

Juan Bonito's expression became somber. "There is a place that has two gringa women."

Nathaniel's heart raced.

"They are…" Juan Bonito searched for the correct words. "One is filled with drugs, sick, and the other…she is a drunk and her right foot is missing—chopped off."

Sickened by the news, Nathaniel turned his head down and cleared his throat.

"These gringas," Juan Bonito added, "they…they are not happy women."

"I would pay them very well for their time, and I would be kind to them." It was hard for Nathaniel to feign any carnal interest in the described captives. "Muy, muy generoso."

Juan Bonito nodded his head. "Bueno." He gathered his banknotes and supplies, placed them inside his alligator skin briefcase, withdrew a jar half-filled with amber fluid and unscrewed its top. "Bueno," repeated the little man while his mind pictured things that brought a dolorous expression to his face.

"What is the location of the establishment in which they work?" inquired Nathaniel.

The mestizo dropped a dirty coin into the amber solution, and it clinked against the bottom of the jar, bright and clean. "Come here tomorrow night at nine and look for the crimson stagecoach. For fifty pesos, it will take you where you want to go—to Gris's place." A dirty coin struck the solution and twisted.

"Gracias amigo." Nathaniel's employment of the word 'friend' no longer seemed to please the little gentleman. "Where is Gris's establishment?'

A silver coin twisted through the solution, settled at the bottom and shone. "Through the mountains."

Suppressing his apprehensions, Nathaniel inquired, "Does it have a name?"

Juan Bonito admitted a mirthless grin. "Catacumbas."

Nathaniel was chilled by the utterance of the Spanish word for catacombs.

Part II

Catacumbas

Chapter I
A Portrait of Gris

Dawn beams sneaked past gray clouds that looked wrought in clay by brutish hands, entered the picture window of an arrogant mansion built from the stones of three Aztec temples and cleaved the seated subject of portraiture into bright and dark halves. The orb of the sun was reduced to a single brilliant pinprick in the man's lone eye. His name was Gris.

"Eres muy guapo," complimented Carlo, who stood behind his easel, opposite the man from Spain.

Gris remarked that all frivolous comments should be withheld.

The admonished artist nodded and studied the portrait that he had worked on every morning for the last five days. Some of Carlo's subjects liked to talk, while others preferred to read a book or listen to music (produced by either a phonograph or a string quartet), but Gris had thus far preferred to stare forward and ruminate in silence. Additionally, the atypical man from Spain had asked to have himself accurately depicted. Gris's scarred neck, prematurely white hair, thick feminine lips, long eyelashes, narrow nose and sunken right eyelid were to be accurately detailed. This unique and oddly handsome face was to be captured and conveyed—unaltered.

After two hours of utter silence, the Spaniard looked at his pocket watch.

Carlo informed the subject that the painting was nearly finished, excepting only the walls of the room and the still life, which required more detail.

Gris said that this was acceptable.

"Bueno." The painter asked if he should include the flies that crawled across the festering still life.

Gris told the man to render the tableau faithfully.

The putrescent emanations were partially obscured by the whisky-soaked kerchief that Carlo had tied over his nose (as if he were a bandito), but the odors had grown stronger throughout the week and were currently capable of bypassing any filtration. Untroubled by the smells of rot, Gris lazed in a brown leather chair, the heels of his knee-high leather boots resting upon a footstool that was a dead man's agonized head. From the 'X' carved into the corpse's swollen stomach spilled black oil that was decorated with blood flakes and yellow bits of congealed fat. Within the ichor lurked many gray scorpions, three of which still moved.

Carlo did not wish to know why the man had been filled with oil and scorpions. This tableau existed, and the artist felt that his only responsibility was to render it well. He eyed the nascent flies, joined dots of blue, yellow and green paint with an obsidian dollop, mixed them thrice and added a dab of linseed oil.

With iridescent black paint, the artist detailed the fly that stood upon the pierced and bitten tongue of a man who had somehow displeased the Spaniard. Two inches below the wet mark that was a two-dimensional corpse inspector sat the placard that bore the name of the portrait.

El Decreto de Gris (The Decree of Gris)

The subject had named the piece himself.

Chapter II
The Insides of Men

Brent Plugford was galvanized, and a disorienting numbness filled his head, as if he were drunkenly dreaming. He punched a tree to rouse himself, but was rebuked by reality.

"Hell."

The cowboy wiped bark and sap from his red knuckles and looked up at the dandy.

"I am sorry." Upon Nathaniel's right shoulder sat the sun, a fiery epaulette that glared directly into Brent's eyes. "I thought that you should know exactly what Mr. Bonito said to me."

"I needed to hear it accurate correct."

"I am sorry."

The cowboy looked away from the dandy and over toward the fire pit, where lazy smoke wafted up from dwindling embers, and his father, his brother and the negro slept inside moth-gnawed bedrolls. Beyond the trees that surrounded the camp stood the ten mountains referred to as Gran Manos, and somewhere within that rock were two white whores who were probably Brent's sisters. "Did the red Mex'can name them?" He wanted to believe that his sisters were not a drug user and a drunken amputee. "Maybe it's some other women."

"The place where they are being kept is owned by the man for whom you are looking."

"Gris?"

The dandy nodded.

"Okay."

Brent was not certain that he would relay the conditions of the women to his father and brother.

"I am sorry."

"Did Bonito rape them?"

The dandy hesitated for a moment. "He did not detail his assignations."

"You were there," grumbled Brent. "You played games with him for hours. You ain't got no damn opinion on what kinda fella he was, and what he done?"

"He was disturbed by their conditions and was loath to mention them to me at all."

"But he did! He knows they're pris'ners and still he went and gave out his goddamn recommendation, so you could—" Brent hated the end of his sentence too much to say it aloud. "Goddamn that little red Mex'can."

"My sympathies are with you," said the dandy, apparently out of equivocating remarks. He placed his left hand upon the cowboy's right shoulder and squeezed.

The sun disappeared behind a mountain that was John Lawrence Plugford.

Brent swatted Nathaniel's hand from his shoulder. "You don't need to go and touch me."

The dandy was perplexed by the admonition.

"Where're my angels?" asked the patriarch. His voice sounded as if it traveled across a far greater distance than three yards.

"A place called Catacumbas," replied Brent. "The dandy's goin' there tonight."

Ashes fell from his father's wild beard. "We'll follow."

"Yeah." Brent hoped that his father would not ask the dandy to repeat the purported details. "We'll follow."

The huge man strode away, but the sun, smothered by thick clouds, did not return.

Brent looked over at the dandy. "You better get some sleep for tonight. It's cooler 'neath the wagon."

The tall gentleman yawned enormously and nodded.

"But let me grab out some supplies first."

Brent and his dizzy brother removed the black trunk from the wagon, took it to the other side of a high creosote barbican and set it upon its end. Inside the prison, something thudded.

The cowboy went to the edge of the bushes, removed his phallus (which already smelled overripe from the long day in the saddle), dampened triangular leaves and said over his shoulder, "Pull the stopper."

"I'll be sick if I do—I've got dizziness and some sour tastes."

"Confound you and that whisky." Brent tucked away his extrusion, buttoned his pants and walked toward his brother. "I see you in the flask again, and I'm givin' you bruises."

"You can't lick me."

"I done it every time."

"When we was younger, okay, sure, before you became a drover boss. But I'm big now—a adult—and I see how things are. I know what kind of man I am, and I know what kind you are." Stevie smirked.

Brent did not at all like the look upon his brother's face. "And what kind of man am I?"

"Why don't you go an' ask that fiancé you used to have? Why don't you ask Janie Dill what—"

Brent slammed his fist into his brother's stomach.

Stevie doubled over, fell against the trunk and took it to the ground. Within the prison, the captive groaned.

The red-faced young man clutched at stalks of purple three awn, convulsed twice and heaved his breakfast. Pale detritus spattered flora. "Go roast." Stevie coughed. "Roast in Hell." He spat bits.

Brent was mortified that his little brother had goaded him so successfully. "You okay?"

"You're a sneak," Stevie griped, "gettin' at me...like that."

"I was right there in front of you and came at you straight."

"Well..."

Brent knelt beside the prone young man. "You didn't deserve that treatment."

"I didn't," confirmed Stevie.

"I'm sorry."

The younger sibling neither accepted nor refused the apology, which was as amenable a reaction as the cowboy could expect at that time. "C'mon." Brent helped Stevie to his feet, swatted the dust from his back and wiped detritus from his face. "Let's take care of this."

The siblings righted the trunk. Holding his breath, the cowboy slid a stick into the loop of twine that depended from the stopper and jerked his arm. The rubber plug popped out of the wood. Urine and darker substances drained through the aperture and colored the dirt.

Shielding his nose and mouth, Brent asked, "See any blood?"

Stevie rapidly shook his head.

A dismal moan sounded within the trunk and was muted by the reinsertion of the stopper.

The hidden sun climbed. The black, gray and silver clouds took on the texture of sharp volcanic rock.

Patch Up cooked a stew with turnips, carrots and potatoes (all of which had been in the wagon since Texas) and the game that Deep Lakes had recently slain.

Shortly before the crew ate supper, Long Clay returned to the site, dust covering his black garments. He walked over to the patriarch and said, "His real name is Humberto Calles."

Brent knew that the gunfighter had just identified Ojos.

John Lawrence Plugford sat upon a stone, removed the steel-tipped fountain pen from his gray overalls, unscrewed the cap and wrote upon his left pant leg.

Umbeartoe Cayez

Long Clay walked toward the dinged stew pot that Patch Up tended beside the fire. To the gunfighter, Brent said, "Ojos dealt with us fair."

"If a posse of vengeful Mexicans rides into Texas, we need to know whom to look for." Long Clay raised a spoonful of stew to his mouth and blew the steam west.

"Okay." The cowboy was relieved that the gunfighter did not plan to execute the contact, who had seemed honest.

Long Clay swallowed a spoonful of stew. "J.L."

John Lawrence Plugford looked at his old partner.

"You need your strength for tonight."

The huge man stood from his rock and strode toward the pot.

Patch Up grabbed the largest wooden bowl that he possessed, filled it with stew and pulled an aluminum spoon from his shirt pocket. "It's hot."

John Lawrence Plugford ignored the spoon, took the bowl, opened his mouth and drank the stew, chewing half as often as he swallowed. Rivulets of broth wound through his wild beard, and steam rose.

"He's really relishing the flavor," remarked Patch Up.

The patriarch set the empty bowl upon the ground.

"Give him another," Long Clay said to the negro.

Patch Up refilled the bowl and handed it to the patriarch.

The huge man gulped the contents and set down the empty vessel. "Thank you."

"It's good to see you eat," replied Patch Up. "And thanks for not swallowing the bowl."

Brent and Stevie patted their father's back, as if he were an enormous infant waiting to be burped.

The patriarch pointed to the silver, black and gray clouds that hung in the vault. "Looks like a photograph."

"It does," confirmed his sons.

The huge man reached into his left pocket and withdrew a small wooden frame that contained a photograph of the Plugford clan. He looked at it for a moment and tucked it away. "Brent?"

"Yes?"

"Would you shave off these whiskers?"

"I'd be happy to."

"I don't think my angels would recognize me like this."

Chapter III
Towards the Fire

Employing Patch Up's steel scissors, Brent Plugford sheared away the outermost inches of his father's wild beard. Oily and hard clumps fell in-between the huge man's work boots and were swept into the fire by an erratic northeast wind. The cowboy brushed leaves, seeds, fleas and agglutinated bits from the huge man's prickly face, received a bowl of lather, took a sable-haired brush and applied white foam as if it were plaster.

The dandy, roused from his five-hour nap, walked to the campfire and handed Brent a straight razor that had a mother-of-pearl handle, which was embossed with the initials 'N.J.S.' "I sharpened it yesterday morning."

The cowboy accepted the blade and opened it; the action of the hinge was smooth and silent. "This's real nice. Was it a gift?"

"Yes. From my fiancé."

"Thanks for the loan."

"You are welcome."

The lumpy clouds were cracked by tenacious rays of twilight. With a steady hand, Brent set the razor to his father's lathered neck and authored a clear swath.

The dandy adjusted his royal blue trousers, sat beside the fire, served himself a bowl of stew and ingested a spoonful. "This is very flavorful."

"I hoped I'd get an accolade from you." Patch Up looked over at Stevie. "The dandy appreciates it."

"I'm thrilled what he thinks." The sullen young man was still nauseated. "Jubilacious."

"You should try some," Patch Up said, "though I should warn you—this is a South Stew."

"What's that?"

"Only tastes good going down."

The jibe was not well received. "Go roast, nigger."

"Have a recipe for that? Roasted nigger?"

Stevie spit into the fire. "Always got somethin' clever to say, don't you?"

"I have retorts."

Brent withdrew the luminous razor from his father's face and said, "It's done."

John Lawrence Plugford's neck, chin and cheeks were pale and soft compared to the remainder of his tough bronze hide. "They'll recognize me now." The patriarch felt his exhumed skin with a broad palm.

"They will."

After Brent had finished his meal, he walked around the fire and returned the straight razor to its owner, who was wearing fresh green drawers and busy with his toilet.

"Thanks 'gain."

"You are welcome." The dandy swirled a washcloth in a wooden water bucket, raised the soapy fabric to his face and scrubbed.

Brent surveyed the man's garments. "You don't have a revolver, do you?"

"My ambition is to become a hotelier rather than a gunfighter." The washcloth squeaked upon Nathaniel's chin.

"You should be able to pertect yourself."

"I will not carry a weapon." The statement was a definitive proclamation.

"You should make a exception tonight."

"Would you shoot an unarmed man?" The dandy applied suds to his armpits and scoured.

"Not unless it were a necessity."

"Would your brother or your father or Patch Up shoot an unarmed man?" The dandy dunked the washcloth and brought suds to his nape.

"Same with them."

"A door opens whenever a man wears a gun, and I choose to keep that door shut."

"There's some wisdom in that," Brent admitted, "but we ain't dealin' with no honorable men here. These fellows...well, you know what the hell they done."

The dandy rubbed the washcloth across his hairless chest. "Many men—good and bad—have qualms about gunning down an unarmed opponent."

"Then take a little two-shot—somethin' you can hide. You don't want to be in no Mex'can catacombs without no way to protect yourself but your bowtie."

"I shall consider it." The dandy's tone was dismissive.

"I rode with some drovers who think like you, and I buried one of them. Take a little bullet-flinger."

"I shall consider it."

While the dandy dressed himself in his black tuxedo, the Plugfords, Patch Up and Long Clay gathered their possessions, put out the fire, buried the coals and saddled their horses. Presently, the family and the gunfighter mounted their steeds, and the negro clambered onto his wagon bench.

Brent guided his horse toward the dandy, who was cleaning grit from his tan mare's left eye, and reined beside him. "You get in that crimson stagecoach like Bonito said to. Deep Lakes will trail you and get us whenever you throw him a signal. You remember the meaningful gesture?"

"Drop my hat, lean over and scratch my nose."

"That's it—precise exact. Here." Brent leaned over and proffered the handle of a two-shot lady's gun.

The dandy eyed the weapon, and the tan mare took one step backward, as if proffering an opinion.

"Take it," insisted Brent. "Put it in your pocket or in your drawers."

The dandy shook his head. "No."

"Why the hell not?" The cowboy wanted to slap the tall Yank idiot.

"If a weapon of this variety is discovered on my person," the dandy said as he climbed atop his tan mare, "my character would be called into question."

"I'm questionin' it right now."

The mounted gentleman eyed the cowboy from a superior altitude. "I will not fire a gun upon a human being."

Brent heard the sound of crackling tinder that was Long Clay's ugly laugh. Stevie muttered something derisive and inaudible.

"You're a wooden fool." The cowboy coaxed his horse forward and placed the lady's gun inside the dandy's saddle pack. "In case you get a epiphany."

"I will not employ that device."

"Maybe his horse will use it to save him," remarked Stevie. "Come to his resc—"

"Be quiet," said Patch Up.

Brent looked at Nathaniel. "Try to fix in your brain what you can of the layout of them catacombs."

"I have a superior memory and will try to learn as much as possible."

"Okay." The cowboy nodded at the tall gentleman. "Good luck."

"And to you as well."

"Say a prayer if you believe in that stuff."

Long Clay said, "Let's go."

Brent pulled his horse around.

Reins snapped, and hooves rumbled. The Plugfords, Patch Up and Long Clay rode through the coppice and out onto the plain, where they began their wide circumnavigation of the town.

Atop his brindled mustang, Brent conceived a simple prayer that he would say to Jesus Christ. (The cowboy had twenty pounds of doubt for every ounce of faith, but he was not too proud to ask for help from the most popular omnipotent power.) Tightly gripping the horn for no reason that he apprehended, Brent fixed the faces of Yvette and his twin sister Dolores in his mind and said, "Please keep them from any more harm and let them know we're comin' to rescue them. Amen."

The cowboy relaxed his grip and looked up at the horizon. The sun had disappeared behind the western mountain range, and the remaining clouds were an endless wall of thick blue plaster.

He doubted that his words would transcend.

Chapter IV
Muchacho Tracks

Trailing a shroud of dust, Nathaniel Stromler rode directly toward the ochre wound in the azure gloaming that was Nueva Vida. On this dangerous night, the tall gentleman from Michigan was saddened by the fact that he and Kathleen had not yet been married, although if the reconnoiter went terribly, at least she would not become a widow.

"Enough of that line of thinking." The chastening voice (even though it was his own) calmed him.

The blue clouds that filled the horizon looked like ocean waves as seen from the deck of a steamship bound for Europe, and they beckoned Nathaniel eerily, asking him to leap overboard and fall into the sky. He returned his gaze to the ochre town.

Effulgent and squat, Nueva Vida grew and consumed the gentleman. He sped past the eastern barbacao shacks that Juan Bonito had told him to avoid, reached the main avenue, rode due west for fifteen minutes and guided his cantering mare onto the lone paved road. Shod hooves clacked noisily upon the stone and garnered unfriendly glances from people holding the hands of children or carrying bundles.

Nathaniel retarded his horse's gait.

At the end of the avenue stood Castillo Elegante, brightly illuminated by mirror lanterns. The gentleman looked at his pocket watch, saw that its little hand was just below the number nine, replaced the timepiece, dusted his black tuxedo, coaxed his horse toward a gate to which two burros were tied, swung himself from his saddle, landed upon his loafers and pulled the mare's reins around the wooden crossbar.

Nathaniel turned toward the gambling house and saw a dark figure standing directly in front of him.

"Good evening, Mr. Stromler."

Presently, the gentleman recognized the silhouetted individual. "Good evening, Deep Lakes."

A spyglass hung from the native's neck, and the two severed muskrat heads that depended from his denim vest dripped. "I'm going to trail your stagecoach. If you enter a different vehicle or mount a horse, cast one or two of these upon the ground after the transition has been made." The native handed a small silk pouch to the gentleman.

The fabric tickled Nathaniel's palms, and he started. "What is in here?"

"Fireflies."

The gentleman held the undulating pouch by its drawstrings. "They will not fly away?"

"I removed their legs and wings."

"Oh." Nathaniel was displeased to learn that his fate depended upon the lambent glow of mutilated insects.

"They are a tool," Deep Lakes said, "but I'll be able to track you whether or not you use them."

"I shall surreptitiously deploy a few should the mode of transportation change."

"May your decisions be wise." The native departed.

Nathaniel delicately placed the pouch of dismembered fireflies inside his jacket, set his black stovepipe hat atop his head and walked up the paved avenue.

Before him expanded the bright white façade of Castillo Elegante, which was attended by the same two pine green guards whom he had met the previous evening. Parked immediately beside the pair was a very large crimson stagecoach. Nathaniel was chilled by the sight of the vehicle, yet strode toward it, undaunted.

Amidst the black steeds that were harnessed to the stagecoach stood a pale man, who was clothed in a blue tuxedo and had an odd discoloration in the middle of his face. He emerged from the beasts, looked at Nathaniel and inquired, "Are you the American friend of Juan Bonito?"

The gringo replied that he had very recently become acquainted with Juan Bonito.

"Bueno. Good."

Nathaniel continued forward and soon apprehended that the fellow's nose was made out of wood and affixed to his face with metal wire. When the distance between the two men diminished to a yard, they stopped and shook hands. The pale individual was almost as tall as the gringo, and his clasp was indelicate.

"Buenas noches." Nathaniel focused his gaze upon the man's brown eyes.

"Buenas noches."

They released each other.

The gringo asked the man with the wooden nose if his name was Gris.

A smile came to the fellow's lips and his false proboscis shifted. "I working for Gris. I am called Ubaldo." His breath smelled like pungent chicken soup.

"I am Thomas Weston," replied Nathaniel. (This name belonged to a horse thief who was lynched in Michigan in eighteen forty-two.)

"You would like to go to Catacumbas?"

"Si."

"It is one hundred pesos to go."

Nathaniel told Ubaldo that Juan Bonito had stated a different price.

Ubaldo nodded and said, "The price normal is fifty pesos. Pero est—but tonight is big fiesta." He pointed to the crimson stagecoach. "You may ask them—they all pay one hundred."

Through a window, Nathaniel saw two luminous orange dots, which were the ends of cigars, and the vague shapes of four men. "I do not need to enquire with them." The gringo withdrew his wallet.

"No pay now—I do not want to hold so much moneys." Ubaldo walked over to the stagecoach, twisted a wooden handle and opened the door. "Please enter." He smiled, and his nose shifted.

Nathaniel removed his stovepipe hat, set a black loafer upon the lowermost step, ascended its superiors and entered the plush and capacious lavender interior of a stagecoach in which four men sat quietly with their lascivious imaginings. The quartet nodded cordially to the arrival, but proffered no words.

"Make yourself a seat." Ubaldo shut the door. "One more person is come and then we go."

Nathaniel pulled his tuxedo tails to his buttocks and sat upon a spring-supported velvet bench, in-between a smoking hombre and the left window. Upon his thighs, he rested his stovepipe hat.

"Buenas noches Señor Bonito," greeted Ubaldo.

Nathaniel looked through the window and saw the little mestizo walk toward the stagecoach. Although the gringo did not know how the Plugford crew would endeavor their rescue, he assumed that bystanders with varying degrees of guilt would receive a thrown fist or something invisible that was accompanied by a loud bang. Nathaniel wanted to warn the little man away from Catacumbas, but he could not think of any way to do so without arousing suspicion. And Brent's comment about the 'red Mex'can's' complicity was correct—Juan Bonito had recommended two whores whom he knew to be captives.

The mestizo wore a bright blue suit, yellow shoes and a matching bowtie, and his ruined ear was somehow whole. He shook hands with Ubaldo, and presently entered the stagecoach.

"Buenas noches, Señor Weston."

Nathaniel wished the mestizo a good evening.

The little man looked at the smoker seated beside the gringo and asked him if he would yield his seat.

Without hesitation, the hombre stood from the bench.

Juan Bonito sat beside Nathaniel. "Tonight is a fiesta, and it is more pesos to get submerged in Catacumbas."

The gringo stated that the driver had asked for one hundred pesos.

"It is the price—but for you it is free." Juan Bonito smiled.

Nathaniel understood that the little man intended to treat him. "Thank you, but I cannot accept your money."

"I should not have taken so much from you in the games last night—that was improper. Now I have the opportunity to make more fair. It is why I come along tonight."

The stagecoach sagged as hard boots thudded upon the wooden ladder that led to the top of the vehicle. "Vamos al Catacumbas," announced Ubaldo from the roof. He punctuated his proclamation with a whip crack.

Behind Juan Bonito's smiling face, Castillo Elegante and the two pine green guards slid from view.

"Gracias—eres muy generoso," Nathaniel said to the mestizo's half-rubber ear.

"I like to have friends in America for when I visit there with my childrens."

Nathaniel nodded absently.

"Do you have any childrens?" inquired Juan Bonito.

"I do not."

"You would like childrens?"

"I would."

"They are a great joy, though my third child killed my wife when he was born. And he was sick and did not live for many years."

"You have my condolences." Nathaniel did not want to hear any more personal information about Juan Bonito.

"His name was Benino. The doctors say—if Benino had growed up—he was going to be very tall." The little mestizo smiled proudly, and Nathaniel had to look away.

The western remainder of Nueva Vida disappeared, and the vista expanded. To the southwest stood the ten peaks of Gran Manos, silhouetted before moonlit clouds that were pock-marked and gray like the lunar orb itself. Three stagecoach inhabitants reclined in their seats and placed derbies over their faces.

"It is not a short travel," informed Juan Bonito.

Nathaniel leaned back and stretched his legs.

"Would you like to see pictures of my childrens?" The mestizo reached into a jacket pocket. "I have one of Benino from the last birthday fiesta—"

"I am very tired. Perhaps you will show the photographs to me on our return journey home?"

"Si. You will peruse them later." Juan Bonito withdrew an empty hand from his jacket.

After a brusque nod, Nathaniel shut his eyes so that he no longer had to look at the wounded man's face.

The horses cantered briskly. Stagecoach wheels sizzled across firm grit and clicked upon occasional roots and stones. The weary gringo would have fallen asleep were he not juggling apprehensions for his own safety, as well as concerns for the captive women, Patch Up (whom he liked), Brent (who was simple, but meant well), John Lawrence Plugford (whom he pitied and feared) and Juan Bonito.

The lanterns upon the sides of the vehicle were extinguished and the plain became a dark ocean. "¡Alto, muchachos, alto!" Ubaldo shouted at the horses. The animals whinnied and their pace slowed. "¡Alto!"

Nathaniel and the other passengers looked outside. The landscape stopped moving, and the steeds quietened. Suddenly, the gringo wondered if he were about to be robbed or executed.

Boots slammed upon the dirt, and a silhouetted figure appeared outside the stagecoach window. The man with the wooden nose told the stagecoach passengers to extinguish their cigars.

Concerned that Deep Lakes or the Plugford crew had been descried by Ubaldo, Nathaniel asked if something was amiss.

"He always check for robbers," stated Juan Bonito. "Some people knows that this stagecoach has rich mens."

Ubaldo raised a spyglass to his right eye and scanned the terrain. Nueva Vida, the plains, dark flora and clouds were slowly captured, warped and released by the bulbous glass. The driver paused, and frozen in miniature upon the iridescent lens were the northern mountain peaks, distended into the shape of a clutching hand.

Nathaniel asked Ubaldo if he had descried anything of concern.

"No." The man with the wooden nose screwed and collapsed his spyglass. "I am just cautious." He climbed the wooden ladder, disappeared onto the roof and said, "Vamos muchachos." The lanterns had not been relit, and the stagecoach became a rolling shadow.

Outside the vehicle, black protrusions that were rocks, branches, cacti and yucca glided across the dark gray plain, while opaque mountains gnawed at the horizon. Upon the expanding range appeared onyx daggers, which were huge valleys, and crushed tumbleweeds, which were arid woodlands. The mountains climbed, and Nathaniel felt as if he were shrinking.

A whip cracked. "Mas rapido," exhorted the driver.

The tattoo of the horses' hooves quickened, and black aberrations sped past, blurry and elongated. Nathaniel wondered at the wisdom of driving horses so quickly across a poorly-lit plain.

"No have concerns," the perspicacious mestizo said, "the horses could wear blindfolds and it would be safe. They know the way."

Nathaniel nodded, yet remained unconvinced that it was safe to travel at such a speed through the badlands on an unclear night. Even if the animals traversed some previously established route, a significant stone or a sinkhole could tumble a horse and heave its contemporaries and the vehicle into the air. Every anomaly in the road engendered an acute jolt that touched the gringo's stomach with a cold finger, and he suspected that his retreating hairline would yield a little more ground before he made it back to Leesville.

The mountains raced toward the front of the stagecoach.

"There is a throat," Juan Bonito informed Nathaniel. "A place where we enter."

Nathaniel nodded and leaned back in his seat. On either side of the rumbling vehicle, tilted dark flora, elongated and blurry, raced across the gray canvas.

"¡Hombres, cuidado!" cautioned the driver from above.

Hombres clasped the leather straps that dangled from the cabin ceiling, and so did the gringo. The stagecoach tilted back. Outside the windows, stone walls shot up and confined the vehicle.

A whip cracked. "¡Muchachos!"

Within the defile, gravity tugged at Nathaniel's guts.

Chapter V
Fidelity, Faith and the Black Circle

The luscious mystery within Marietta's cleavage deepened as she leaned toward Humberto Calles, and the kiss that she placed upon his bare scalp felt like a benediction.

As the barmaid stood upright, she complimented the balladeer's performance, which had ended thirty minutes earlier.

Seated at his favorite table in the sunken back room, Humberto pointed to his guitarrita and stated that his unique instrument is what gives his songs a special quality.

Marietta touched a fingertip to his throat, ran it gently to his lips and remarked that the mouth is the most important instrument of all.

Her digit lingered, suggestively.

The sounds and lights within the bar dimmed, and the balladeer saw only the face of the woman who stood over him, as if descended from Heaven directly to Nueva Vida, Mexico. His heart thudded, his phallus swelled and warm light filled his blood. The beauteous arrival leaned forward, and her luscious mystery expanded.

Anxious, the faithfully married, fifty-four-year-old man slid his chair away from the table and rose to his feet.

Marietta asked him why he had withdrawn.

Thinking about his wife and daughters, Humberto stammered.

"¿Crees que soy bonita?"

The balladeer said that she was pretty—dangerously pretty.

Marietta pressed her lips to Humberto's mouth and connected their tender interiors with her tongue. The man was eighteen years old, quick and hale, with long dark hair that ran down to his buttocks in a braided tail; he was a skilled musician who knew everything and was too smart to commit himself to one town or one woman.

"P-por favor," Humberto pleaded as he pulled away from the kiss, warmth and youth proffered by Marietta. "Por favor." He looked at her befuddled eyes, apologized, took his guitarrita case, retreated and plunged through the checkered blanket into the night, where cool air turned the perspiration that covered his face into clammy oil.

Humberto looked up at the smoldering plaster that hid the heavens and asked the Lord why the barmaid had behaved so aggressively this evening.

During the silence that followed his inquiry, the balladeer removed a linen kerchief from his blue shirt, wiped his chilled face and felt a soft warm kiss upon his neck. His heart pounded.

"Por favor, mi amor." Marietta pressed her breasts into Humberto's back, slid her palms across his stomach, interlaced her strong fingers and held him tightly.

Firmly, the married man pulled away.

The barmaid stated that she had watched the balladeer perform for nearly twenty years.

Retreating from temptation, Humberto thanked her for her patronage.

Marietta confessed that she had longed to share a bed with him throughout the duration of her womanhood.

From a distance of five yards, Humberto announced that he was a faithful husband.

"Por favor—hacer una excepción."

"No." The man explained that even one indiscretion would sunder the vow of marriage.

Defeated, Marietta told Humberto that he was an excellent man in every way imaginable.

The balladeer tapped an index finger upon his bald scalp and said that he possessed a flaw.

Marietta laughed. "Por favor, vuelve dentro de la barra."

Humberto thanked the woman, but declined her invitation and said that he intended to go home and spend some time with his family before they were all asleep.

The barmaid kissed the balladeer's left cheek, presented her round buttocks and walked through the checkered sheet. Pondering wondrous treasures refused, Humberto began his journey home.

Beneath imposto lunar clouds sat the sturdy and unchanging house that the balladeer had built sixteen years earlier. The tangible memories of Marietta's embrace and kisses stirred Humberto's blood like a third cup of coffee, and he rambled around his home in an attempt to diminish the surfeit of energy.

During his sixth moonlit orbit, the balladeer paused at the wooden swing set that he and his cousins Pablo and Pablito had erected on Anna's third birthday, one year before it became apparent that she would need to use crutches for the remainder of her life. The fifty-four-year-old man sat upon a dangling wooden seat, withdrew his crushed timepiece, rocked forward and watched the reflection of the moon shatter upon the cracked glass.

Unrecognized by the device's dead hands, time passed.

Humberto secreted the crushed pocket watch, stood up and carried his guitarrita into his quiet home. The delicious specter of pernil and roasted chilies greeted him, and he hungrily proceeded across the woven rugs toward the kitchen.

"Papa."

Humberto looked up the long dark hallway that traversed the entire house. The doors leading off of the passage were shut, excepting the final room—the addition where his younger daughter slept.

"Papa." The timbre of Estrellita's solicitation was odd.

Humberto felt an uneasy chill, set his instrument down and walked toward the gun rack to retrieve his rifle. His stomach sank when he saw that the weapon was missing.

Estrellita squealed.

The balladeer yanked his guitarrita from its case, held it by the neck (as if it were an axe) and sped up the hall into the addition.

"Stand still or I'll kill them."

Humberto froze.

A lone candle shone upon the black clothing, gleaming gun barrels, glass eyes and rubber head of the tall narrow man who was seated upon the girl's bed. At the intruder's feet and facedown upon the floor were Patricia, Anna and Estrellita. They were blindfolded, hog-tied and had plums, secured by wire, filling their mouths.

Humberto was horrorstruck.

The tall shade with the rubber head pointed one gun at Estrellita's back and the other at Humberto's left thigh. "Remain calm."

The balladeer's hands tightened upon the neck of his instrument. "I will do whatever you want." A long fingernail cut through an E string, and it twanged.

Patricia, Anna and Estrellita wept through runny noses.

"Set the guitar down."

Humberto placed the instrument upon the floor.

"Come into the room and shut that door behind you."

Instantly, the balladeer complied.

The tall shade pointed the barrel of a pistol toward the far corner. "Sit on that wooden pony."

Hands trembling and guts expanding, Humberto strode toward the oaken quadruped, sat down and faced his captor.

"I have some questions. You will answer them succinctly and honestly. Do you understand?"

"I understand." Humberto stared at the lenses that covered over the intruder's eyes, and in them saw only the glaring white reflections of the candle flame.

"If you lie to me or make me repeat myself, I will put a bullet into one of these women."

Humberto's vision became blurry.

"Do you understand?"

Horrified, the balladeer nodded his head. "I understand." His voice was a weak whisper.

"You had a meeting last night with two of my associates. Do you recall this meeting?"

"Yes."

Prone upon the rug, Patricia turned her head toward her husband. A splinter of cartilage jutted from her smashed nose, and her right eye was purple.

The tall shade asked, "Do any of the women in this room know the identities of my associates?"

"No."

"Have you told any other person the names of my associates?"

"No," admitted Humberto.

"You are lying."

The heel of a black boot landed upon Anna's curved leg. The fourteen-year-old girl screamed into her plum and writhed.

Humberto vomited wine upon the floor. He shut his eyes, clenched his fists and restrained the violent impulses that he knew would get his entire family killed.

"Look at me!"

Humberto opened his eyes, and tears flooded down cheeks.

The tall shade with the rubber head placed the tip of a revolver into Anna's right ear.

"¡No!" The balladeer's heart stopped. ¡"Por favor! ¡Por f—"

"To whom have you given the names of my associates?"

"Nobody! I promise. I swear I have not told anybody."

"Are there any papers in your possession—or in a vault or in the mail—that contain the names of my employers?"

"No."

The tall shade pointed a black circle that was the end of a gun barrel at the balladeer's face.

On the floor, the women wailed into their plums.

At that moment, Humberto knew that he was going to die.

"If I find out that you lied to me," the tall shade warned, "I will execute your wife and give your daughters over to men who fuck little girls and cripples." The wraith set the heel of his left boot upon the back of Estrellita's head. "Did you tell me the truth?"

It took Humberto a ponderous moment to remember how to speak. "I did. I knew better than to involve any innocent people in this."

"I believe you."

The black circle flashed twice.

Humberto flew off of the wooden horse, felt the floor slam into his back and saw gore that was part of his head run down the west wall of Estrellita's room. He said goodbye to his family, who wept and screamed one hundred thousand miles away, and also to Marietta, whom he realized had been sent by the Lord to save his life.

Chapter VI
The Sunken Land

The stagecoach wheels turned across the defile floor, reducing small rocks into pebbles and grinding the latter into grit. Within the vibrating vehicle, Nathaniel Stromler watched crenulate stone walls scroll past the window.

"¡Muchachos," the driver exhorted, "alto!" The whip snapped twice and was a dozen times reiterated by echoes.

Outside Nathaniel's window, the rock wall was swallowed by darkness. Two eyes and a blade gleamed within the shadows, and a cold finger of fear poked the gringo's stomach.

Ubaldo landed in front of the window and said, "Dos Árboles," which meant Two Trees.

A craggy-faced old native, wearing a black poncho and carrying a bayonet rifle, stepped from the hiding nook and into the defile.

Ubaldo raised a covered basket.

With an oddly accented Spanish, Dos Árboles asked if the vessel contained dried plums and almonds.

Ubaldo confirmed that indeed prunes and almonds laid therein.

The old native asked if the basket contained any animal flesh.

"No carne," said Ubaldo, shaking his head.

Dos Árboles took the basket by its handle and carried it into his niche. Nathaniel could not tell how deeply the hiding nook receded from the wall of the defile, but he did glean a cubbyhole that housed several clay jugs, an old book and a statue of a divine being with three heads.

Ubaldo landed his buttocks upon the driver's bench and cracked his whip. The vehicle jerked forward, and the dark niche was replaced by crenulate stone. After Nathaniel had fulfilled his obligations to the Plugfords, he would not attempt to escape along this guarded route.

For ten minutes, the crimson stagecoach rolled along a curved rut that threaded the mountains. The vehicle slowed, and the gringo looked outside. From a dark nook located twelve feet off of the defile floor emerged two dark and knobby hands. Ubaldo gave the bodiless appendages a bundle of comestibles and cracked his whip, and the horses resumed their brisk canter.

The stagecoach emerged from the defile and traveled upon a road that hugged the skirt of a shale mountain, which was adorned with shaggy weeds and pale boulders.

Nathaniel removed his pocket watch, pressed the release, turned the face to the moon and saw that the little hand sat halfway between ten and eleven. It had been more than an hour since they had departed Nueva Vida.

"¡Hombres," the driver called out, "cuidado!"

Inside, the passengers grabbed the dangling straps. The front of the stagecoach tilted down, and Nathaniel and Juan Bonito were pulled forward. Leather tack and wooden poles creaked.

The stagecoach descended.

Gripping his strap tightly, Nathaniel leaned his head outside the window and looked forward. On the western horizon stood three mountains, but between the far-off peaks and the stagecoach laid a vast dry depression.

"Catacumbas is below," stated Juan Bonito.

Nathaniel withdrew his head from the gaping night.

Toward the depression descended the stagecoach, yielding the altitude that it had gained during its initial climb. Presently, the vehicle rolled onto the level plain, and the passengers leaned back in their seats.

A portly fellow who had shouted the Spanish word for triumph whenever he won a hand of cards at Castillo Elegante asked a handsome Mexican what event the party at Catacumbas commemorated.

Shrugging, the gentleman replied that he did not know the precise reason for the celebration.

The triumphant man looked at the other passengers and asked if anyone could explain the revels.

Nobody responded with factual information, although an older man in a striped suit theorized that Gris had decided to have a party so that he could raise the transportation and liaison fees.

The handsome fellow told the triumphant man that Francesca had returned to Catacumbas.

"¡Triunfo!"

For more than twenty minutes, the stagecoach rolled toward the southwestern rim of the drear sunken plain.

"¡Hombres!" Ubaldo called from outside.

The passengers looked up at the driver's unseen buttocks.

"¡La buena diversión comenzará pronto!" The man with the wooden nose cracked his whip to emphasize (and perhaps illustrate) the pleasing diversions that they would soon experience.

Soon, the horses slowed and stopped, and a wave of trailed dust enshrouded the stagecoach. Ubaldo dropped to the plain, leaned over, unfolded a short ladder and drew open the west door.

Nathaniel descended the steps and walked onto hard land. Aches, engendered by the percussive journey, bothered his legs, arms, shoulders, back and buttocks.

"That is Catacumbas." Ubaldo pointed west.

Nathaniel looked in the indicated direction and saw several vast tiers of weathered stones that appeared to be the remains of an ancient step pyramid. He tasted dread in his mouth, but forced a smile to his face.

The Mexican gentlemen filed out of the vehicle, replaced their hats, inserted cigars and struck matches. Each hombre handed the driver one hundred pesos in banknotes, but when the gringo attempted to draw out his wallet, the little mestizo grabbed his wrist with a yellow glove, admonished him and paid his fare.

"Gracias." (Nathaniel could no longer employ the word 'friend' without feeling ashamed.)

Ubaldo placed the bills inside his jacket, scratched an itch beside his wooden nose and motioned with his right arm. The gentlemen followed the driver toward the ancient ruins.

In a corral beside the structure, Nathaniel noted fifty horses and a dozen crimson stagecoaches, and atop the lowermost tier, he saw two riflemen, dangling their legs over the edge of a stone. A thirty-foot drop separated the soles of their moccasins from the ground and conveyed the immense scope of the mostly-absent ziggurat.

"¡Buenas noches!" Ubaldo waved to the armed sentries and announced that he had transported six men of distinction from Nueva Vida to Catacumbas.

One of the riflemen tossed six colored pebbles into a metal bucket.

Ubaldo asked if the bucket was full.

"Si," said the rifleman.

The man with the wooden nose looked at the gentlemen and remarked, "The fiesta is underway."

After a few strides, the triumphant man asked what event the party celebrated.

Ubaldo shrugged.

The gentlemen neared a reddish-orange square that did not match the remainder of the ochre-gray ruins, and presently, Nathaniel saw that the discoloration was comprised of modern bricks and mortar that had been employed to seal up the vast original ziggurat entrance. Standing at the center of the refurbished area was a lone iron door.

Girls, games, spirits and tobacco leaves were discussed by all of the gentleman, excepting the gringo, who was unable to do anything but stare at the metal entrance, which ten more strides revealed was covered with rows of outthrust steel spikes. Nathaniel was assailed by very significant doubts as to whether the Plugfords—even with the aid of their skilled native and ruthless gunfighter—had any chance of rescuing their abducted kin from such a place. The Hopi natives and Spanish War prisoners locked away in Alcatraz seemed as easily accessed as a person locked within Catacumbas.

Immediately beside the spike-adorned iron door, Ubaldo halted.

A blunderbuss emerged from a crenellation in the brick wall and trained its black eye upon the gringo and those with whom he had ridden. Nathaniel stopped breathing. He thought of Kathleen and his ruined hotel and his mother, a widow in Michigan with a candy store that nobody ever visited.

To the gun barrel, Ubaldo said, “Buenos hombres. Todos.”

The blunderbuss withdrew, and Nathaniel relaxed.

Beyond the iron door, a stone cracked, and a gear turned.

The gringo told the mestizo that he looked forward to meeting the gringas.

“I take care of those womens,” Ubaldo remarked, “that is why I learn good English.”

“I would like to see them.”

“I bring you.”

Nathaniel stomped upon his fears and steeled himself—he would locate these women, collect the remainder of his stipend and ride away from this awful drama as fast as his tan mare could carry him.

The spikes withdrew, and the iron door opened.

Chapter VII
Catacumbas

Ubaldo escorted Nathaniel Stromler and the hombres into a large anteroom that was illuminated by ensconced torches. The high walls of the enclosure were made of ancient triangular stones that were stacked in alternating inversions, and a quartet of dangling brass censers yielded aromatic cinnamon-and-vanilla bean smoke that obfuscated the aromas of lichens and centuries.

The assemblage walked along a gigantic tapestry that depicted the ancient ziggurat, whole, surrounded by a high tide of bloody bodies, most of which were short at least one appendage. Atop the step pyramid, warrior priests poured glowing hot coals onto the faces and genitals of captives.

"That is pleasant."

Ubaldo escorted the gentlemen to a stairwell that led into the earth and advised the men to hold onto the banister as they descended.

Resting a white-gloved hand upon the rail, Nathaniel proceeded down the steps, toward the luminous amber portal at the nether end of the declining passage. It would not have surprised him overmuch to see the Devil stride through the opening.

Presently, the gringo emerged from the stairwell and entered a cavernous enclosure, which seemed like it had once been a place of worship or funereal ritual. The far side of the vast room had a dais, and the ceiling was covered with the strange sigils of a lost religion. Occupying the blasphemed temple and warmly illuminated by hundreds of ensconced candles were sixty gentlemen and half as many women.

A beautiful Mexican lady with full hips, long eyelashes and a strong jaw adjusted her rose kimono, approached the newly arrived sextet and greeted several gentlemen by name, including Juan Bonito.

"Buenas noches Pia," replied the hombres.

Without provocation, Ubaldo and the Mexican gentlemen began to remove their shoes.

The madam looked at the tall gringo and said, "Welcome to Catacumbas, Señor. Please remove your shoes."

Nathaniel inquired why he needed to discard his loafers.

"Gris wants to preserve the ancient craftsmanship." Pia pointed to the floor of the funereal temple, and the gringo saw that it was comprised of innumerable clay tiles, every one of which one a perfect nonagon. "It is nice, no?"

Nathaniel complimented the nine-sided tiles and removed his black loafers.

Ubaldo and Pia exchanged a communicative glance.

"I have been informed that you favor the company of gringa women." Radiating warmth and the scent of star anise, the madam advanced. "You do not appreciate the beautiful and passionate mujeres de Mexico?" She slid her hand along the gringo's thigh.

Nathaniel told Pia that his wife was a beautiful woman from Mexico. (Kathleen's family was entirely Irish, excepting a Jewish grandmother who had been an opera singer in Austria.)

"That is why your Spanish is so true," commented the madam.

"And why I would like to spend time with a gringa."

Pia laughed, a rich cachinnation that emanated from her belly, and said that she understood the value of variety.

"Señor Weston," Ubaldo said, "make a seat and I will go speak with the gringas."

"Gracias," responded Nathaniel. "I would like to view them both before I make any decisions."

"One has blonde hairs and the other has red hairs. They are both muy bonita, but…" The man with the wooden nose hesitated. "One has lost her right foot."

The gringo acted as if he were pleased by what he had just heard. "That sounds interesting."

Ubaldo looked directly into Nathaniel's eyes. "You will like these womens." Air whistled through his artificial nostrils.

"Perhaps I will spend time with both of them."

The flat line that was Ubaldo's mouth curved, and his wooden nose tilted. "You are a good hombre." A small dark joy crept into his eyes. "I will return." The pale man strode off, toward one of the eight passageways that radiated from the temple out into the catacombs.

Clay nonagonal tiles pressed into Nathaniel's socks as he walked to the area where divans, fainting couches, bagatelle tables and stools rested upon a luxurious rose rug. He seated himself and was immediately given moccasins by a woman in a golden kimono.

"Gracias Señorita."

Nathaniel donned the soft shoes and surveyed the assemblage. The clients were well-dressed Hispanic men, excepting a group of Orientals who played a game of mahjong in a far corner. The robed women who orbited the area like silken monks were a far more variegated group—Mexicans, South Americans, mulattos, negresses and Orientals offered themselves and kind words to the clientele. Not one of the female employees seemed to be distressed or compelled to perform her role, and Nathaniel doubted that it was because they were all terrific play-actors. It appeared as if many or most of the women who worked at Catacumbas did so by choice.

A striking man of fifty with a thin nose, full lips, ivory white hair and one eye stared down from a glistening oil painting that hung upon the wall. Below the left heel of the seated subject laid a swollen corpse that had a sliced open stomach from which poured a deluge of black oil and scorpions. Nathaniel pivoted so that he no longer faced the cruel tableau.

A rust-colored mongrel with a crooked snout trotted out of the hallway that Ubaldo had entered. Across the tiles, the canine gaily padded, tongue dangling.

"Henry!"

The dog stopped.

Ubaldo emerged from the portal and told the animal to behave like a gentleman.

Henry reared up on its hind legs and walked forward, upright, across the clay tiles.

The Oriental men applauded the nascent biped, and several Mexicans cackled.

Ubaldo patted the vertical dog's head and approached Nathaniel. "Henry was a circus animal. He knows special tricks."

Nathaniel asked after the gringas.

"The womens have friends right now," Ubaldo replied, "but you will see them later."

The canine staggered upon its hind legs in ever-narrowing circles, as if it were insane.

Nathaniel Stromler silently empathized.

Chapter VIII
Swallow Your Spit

A tiny azure star rose from the base of the southwest mountain range, paused, brightened, dropped, trailed blue sparks and disappeared whence it had arisen.

"That's the beacon," Brent Plugford said to the men who waited in the shadow of a huge igneous rock.

"I marked it." Patch Up lowered his spyglass and pointed a mostly invisible finger at the dark mountains. "There's a defile in that area."

"Okay." Brent faced northeast and scanned the grayish black plain that laid in-between his crew and the distant fungal effulgence that was Nueva Vida, but he saw no rider. "Long Clay should be with us."

"He's comin'." John Lawrence Plugford's words were confident, and his brusque tone precluded any further questions.

The cowboy was almost certain that the gunfighter's ancillary mission involved Ojos. When Brent thought of the helpful Mexican being threatened or injured (or worse) he was disturbed, but as he had learned during the robbery, he was not responsible for the actions of Long Clay, nor would he be able to alter them in any way. The ruthless tactician had come on this ride as a favor to his old partner and would not answer to some cowboy foreman or anybody else in existence.

Brent snapped tack at his pointless contemplations. "Let's get on." Underneath him, the brindled mustang surged forward, and summarily the remainder of the crew coaxed their beasts into action. John Lawrence Plugford trailed the palfreys that bore the sidesaddles for the girls, Stevie led the dandy's tan mare (which had been retrieved an hour earlier from Nueva Vida) and Patch Up whipped the rumps of his ragged brace. The group paralleled the edge of the range so that it would be difficult to see them from any vantage points within the mountains.

"You think anybody else noticed that signal he sent up?" asked Stevie. "I wouldn't want to tip our hand with no Fourth of July practice."

"Either he released the arrow where no guards could descry it," Patch Up said, "or he's taken care of the guards."

"Deep Lakes is skilled," added Brent.

"If he's so skilled," Stevie inquired, "then why'd they throw him in the fire?"

"He was a little infant when they done that," Brent said to his brother, "and you shouldn't be talkin' 'bout it neither. Ain't your business." The cowboy looked at his father and saw that the huge man was frowning.

"I was just wonderin'," Stevie continued, "if that Indian's such a marvelous talent, why his kin treat him like a log." The way the young man slurred his words and carried on betrayed the fact that he had been drinking.

"Gimme that goddamn flask you dumb fool," said Brent.

"No. And I only had a little."

John Lawrence Plugford cut his horse and was directly beside Stevie's careering colt. The huge man raised his hand and slapped his son across the face.

"Goddamn!" Stevie wobbled and righted himself. "I barely drunk a—"

The huge palm struck his face a second time.

Unbalanced, the young man grabbed his horn so that he did not fall out of his saddle. His right cheek was halfway between red and purple.

"Give it," ordered John Lawrence Plugford.

Stevie reached into his saddlebag, withdrew the flask and proffered it to his father. The huge man took the metal vessel and put it inside the front pocket of his gray overalls. Beneath the men, horse hooves rumbled.

"I barely drunk—"

The huge hand slapped Stevie's mouth shut. Lines of white moonlight that were spilled tears tracked down the young man's discolored skin. The horses cantered apace, but to Brent the tableau seemed devoid of motion.

"Stop makin' excuses," the cowboy advised his brother.

Stevie remained silent.

John Lawrence Plugford looked at Patch Up. "Grab out a big handful of coffee beans."

"I will."

The patriarch looked at his drunken son. "Chew 'em until I say you can spit 'em out."

"Yessir."

With a baleful glare, John Lawrence Plugford added, "Your sisters need us clear."

Remorse filled Stevie's face. "I'm sorry."

"Take a sip of liquor before we get home, and I'll hold your arm to the fire."

"I won't drink nothin'. I swear."

The huge man hastened his stallion away from the colt that carried his youngest child.

"Stevie," said Patch Up. "Ride over."

The chastened young man wiped his face with his shirt and guided his horse toward the front of the wagon.

Patch Up extended a tin cup, the contents of which rattled. "Take it." A wagon wheel struck a stone, and two coffee beans leapt into the air like roused horseflies.

Stevie took the tin cup, poured its dark contents into his mouth and chewed. His head rumbled like a quarry. Brent recalled chewing coffee beans when he was a kid, after his father had caught him and Dolores drinking from a purloined bottle of wine.

Without warning, John Lawrence Plugford spun around in his saddle and pointed his sawed-off shotgun northeast. Brent withdrew his pistol and over his barrel scanned the area at which his father aimed.

A tiny light flashed thrice and disappeared.

Brent recognized the signal. John Lawrence Plugford holstered his sawed-off shotgun and faced forward.

From the darkness emerged Long Clay, atop his galloping black mare.

"Did you see the arrow?" the cowboy asked the gunfighter.

"What color was it?"

Brent knew that Long Clay had clear eyes, but for some reason did not see colors at this point in his life. This optical degradation was the gunfighter's lone physical deficiency and John Lawrence Plugford had warned his sons not to ever comment upon it.

"It was blue."

Long Clay nodded.

Brent had recently learned about the burning arrows, which were signals that his father and the gunfighter had devised back when they were shaking trains and doing other operations. A lone blue shaft was lodestone, a beacon to be followed.

Stevie crunched beans and spat black ichor into the wind.

"Swallow your spit," ordered John Lawrence Plugford.

"Yessir." The young man gulped down his retched saliva. A few drops of dark drool stained his beige shirt.

A burning arrow flared within the southwestern mountains, disappeared, reappeared at a higher altitude, vanished momentarily, climbed to its apex and paused. For two heartbeats, the eyes of the riders and their horses were a luminous crimson.

The beacon plummeted through the same two open areas and disappeared into the range. Darkness spread across the plain and filled Brent Plugford. The crimson arrow was the signal that the cowboy had hoped he would not witness.

Patch Up stated, "He's killing."

Chapter IX
Entertainments for Entrepreneurs

Nathaniel Stromler watched the circus dog sit, roll over, 'get drunk,' 'talk,' 'play cards' (it raised and observed its paws), 'be a wife' (it whimpered irritating frequencies), 'dip his biscuit in tea' (it performed an inexplicable gesture) and 'walk like an American' (it slid across the rug on its belly like a serpent). Shortly after the canine's weird display ended, Juan Bonito disappeared into a passage holding the hand of a voluptuous Mexican woman who dwarfed him so substantially that the pair looked like mother and son. Four different Mexican women, a mestizo, a mulatto and an Oriental sat beside the gringo and tried to lure him back to their rooms in the catacombs, but he politely denied all of them. Instead, he drank a small amount of scotch and ruminated upon his predicament.

A stunning woman who looked like a confluence of Oriental, Caucasian and native lineages approached Nathaniel. Her eyes were onyx enigmas framed in luxurious lashes, and the sharp tips of her breasts prodded the purpureal silk of her robe each time her forward foot contacted the ground. The gringo looked away from her mesmerizing beauty and toward the wall upon which sat the gruesome oil painting of the one-eyed man.

"What are your opinions of this portrait?" inquired an unaccented male voice.

To his immediate left, Nathaniel saw the subject of the painting rendered in three-dimensional flesh that was clothed in a white linen suit, a rose shirt, matching gloves and Italian loafers. The lid over the man's missing eye was closed, and his white hair was slicked back from his oddly handsome face.

"The subject has been richly rendered," Nathaniel replied, "but the walls of the room and the scorpions look unfinished."

"Your evaluation is correct—the artist has not yet completed the piece." The man with white hair and one eye proffered a rose glove. "My name is Gris."

A tingling chill descended from Nathaniel's nape to his tailbone. "I am Thomas Weston. Buenas noches." The gringo shook the man's covered hand and summarily complimented all that he had seen of Catacumbas and its employees.

"Are you inclined toward conversation while you wait?" asked the proprietor.

Nathaniel knew that he had no choice but to invite Gris to join him, and thus motioned to the rose-colored fainting couch opposite his divan. "Please allow me to buy you a drink."

Gris sat at a comfortable angle upon the satin cushions. "The drinks that we share are my gift to you."

"I insist."

"I would rather not owe a debt of kindness to a man whom I do not yet know."

"Then I shall refuse your gift for the exact same reason," replied Nathaniel.

"That is understandable." Gris fingered a silver eyebrow and fixed his gaze upon Nathaniel. "You are a friend of Juan Bonito." This was stated, rather than asked.

"A recent acquaintance."

"His word has value."

A red kimono that was an adroit barmaid flashed in-between the gentlemen and a tiny glass of port wine, which looked like an inverted dinner bell made out of crystal, materialized in Gris's left hand.

"With which type of American business are you involved?"

"I am a hotelier." Nathaniel hoped that the shrewd man would not inquire after too many details.

"You are successful in this enterprise?"

"I am."

Gris sipped his carmine beverage. "Un sabor delicado." His Spanish accent was that of a European Spaniard, not a Central or South American. "Where was your Mexican wife born?"

The question was asked casually, but Nathaniel felt as if he were suddenly inside of a courtroom. "Mexico City."

"I am pleased to know that a distinguished American entrepreneur appreciates Hispanic women." Gris saluted the gringo with his tiny glass of port wine and took a quiet sip.

Nathaniel wanted to guide the conversation away from potentially difficult terrain. "How long has this establishment been extant?"

"In which year did the USS Maine explode as a result of its incompetent crew?" Gris's face was inscrutable.

The gringo's unease was grown by the Spaniard's blunt and colored reference to the event that was the catalyst for the war between Spain and America. "Eighteen ninety-seven."

"My establishment opened that same year." The proprietor's eye did not blink.

The gringo tried to think of a way to guide the conversation away from the inflammatory topic.

"Do not be concerned," Gris said, "I do not hold you personally responsible for diminishing the Spanish empire."

Nathaniel relaxed. "I appreciate your exoneration. I was managing my mother's candy store at that time and wholly uninvolved with warfare."

"The capital for your hotels came from this candy store?" Gris sipped carmine fluid from the tiny inverted bell.

"My fiancé's uncle loaned us the capital for the first hotel, and its success begat the subsequent structures," replied Nathaniel, aware that good lies did not require this much exposition.

"A sizable loan for a risky venture, a burgeoning business and a lovely Mexican wife." Gris raised his tiny glass and saluted. "You are a very fortunate man."

"I am fulfilled." The lying gringo drank from his glass of scotch.

"I would like for you to know that Catacumbas contains several very secure and well-guarded vaults if ever you seek a place to deposit some of your rapidly growing wealth outside of America."

"I shall keep that in mind." (Nathaniel would be certain to tell the Plugfords that there existed additional guards within the catacombs.)

A shadow slid across the rose rug, directly in-between the two gentlemen.

"Perdón."

Nathaniel looked up and saw Ubaldo.

"The gringa womens are watered and pleased to meet you."

"Gracias."

The proprietor motioned toward the dark catacomb portals. "Please do repair."

"I shall." The gringo rose from the divan.

Gris stood and shook Nathaniel's right hand. "Have a fulfilling evening, Señor Weston." The Spaniard lifted the lid that covered his bad eye, revealing a jagged gray rock, which was gripped by thin red strands that were either muscles or nerves. "Buenas noches."

"Buenas noches."

Gris withdrew his hand and covered over the stone in his face.

Nathaniel turned, followed Ubaldo toward the passageway and for the first time since his journey had begun, felt that Kathleen, his half-erected hotel, Leesville and all of the New Mexico Territory were far too close to Mexico.

Chapter X
I Was

"You talk with Gris," Ubaldo said as he strode toward the southernmost portal on the west wall. "He a good man. His words very valuable."

"Very valuable," Nathaniel Stromler mindlessly echoed.

"He has five sons. No girl childrens—only boys. This is impressive, no?"

"Certainly."

"He do a ceremony in the temple to have only the boy childrens."

"Oh?" Nathaniel did not know what this meant, but was too preoccupied to ask for any further explanation.

The duo entered a descending torch-illumined hallway, where petrified wood and ochre stones withheld the crushing weight of the surrounding soil. A troglodyte with ugly wooden sandals and a dark head that was shaped like a coconut walked from the opposite side of the passage and passed by Nathaniel and Ubaldo. He smelled like fish guts.

The man with the wooden nose glanced at the gringo. "You would like to see first the one with blonde hairs or the one with red hairs and no left foot?"

"It does not matter. I intend to see them both before I make any decision."

"I will take you first to the blonde hairs gringa."

Nathaniel, following Ubaldo, neared an ensconced torch, and cool air blew upon his nape and excited the flames. Puzzled by the chill current, he looked up at the ceiling,

"There are holes of air in some walls," explained the man with the wooden nose.

"I was told that the rooms were completely private," remarked Nathaniel, perturbedly. "I do not want people listening to my assignations."

Ubaldo stopped and turned around. "Of course, Señor Weston. You have the complete privacy. Do not you worry."

The gringo motioned for his escort to proceed.

Presently, the duo arrived at a low entranceway upon the south wall. Nathaniel removed his stovepipe hat and followed Ubaldo onto a descending stairwell, wherein candles, nestled inside of cubbyholes, radiated amber light and the scents of flowers. An ambitious lock of the gringo's lank blonde hair was snagged by a ceiling stone and jerked his head back. He pulled most of the twine free and continued down the steps, silently cursing.

Ubaldo landed upon the torch-illumined lower level and veered to the right. A moment later, Nathaniel exited the stairwell and strode into the middle of a finite passage, where wooden doors, braced by thick iron, sat upon the north and south walls.

"This part was the prison when the natives builted it."

"That is apparent."

Ubaldo walked to the farthest door on the north wall, inserted a key into its lock and twisted his fist. Metal groaned and torches quivered. The bolt clacked, reverberant.

"I show the blonde hairs." The man with the wooden nose opened the door and motioned for the gringo to walk inside.

It seemed as if the moment of identification had finally arrived, and Nathaniel, hopeful that his ordeal might soon end, strode into the darkness. The cloying smells of flowers, cinnamon and vanilla filled his nostrils. Behind him, the door closed, but remained unlocked.

"I will return in ten minutes," Ubaldo said from outside the cell, "and take you to see the other."

"Gracias."

Nathaniel's eyes adjusted to the dim radiance of the candles that were nestled within the far wall. In the bed beside the tiny flames laid a blonde woman. Her lean body was draped by a diaphanous rose negligee, and upon her angular face, within symmetrical gray craters, were two wet black slits that were her eyes.

Deeply unsettled, the gentleman cleared his throat and located his voice. "Hello."

The woman stared.

Nathaniel walked across the stones, toward the piteous being whom he did not yet recognize as either Plugford sister. The woman's face and arms were covered over by powder, and her neck looked as if it were made of cables. Jutting sharply against the fabric of her negligee were two sharp triangles that were her hipbones.

"I am sorry," whispered the gentleman, as if he must apologize for the odious gender to which he belonged. "I am so very sorry." His eyes began to sting.

The woman clasped Nathaniel's hand, tilted her head back and smiled hideously. "If you get me medicine," she said with an enervated voice, "you can do anything you want to me. Beat me. Sodomize me. Strangle me. Anything."

Nathaniel had never believed in a higher power, and now he felt as if he looked at irrefutable proof of His absence. He was horrified, unable to respond.

"Please," the woman pleaded, "I need it." The segmented bones that were her fingers tightened. "It's been two days and I'm dying."

The tall gentleman from Michigan found his voice and knelt beside the bed. "I have something to ask you," he whispered, "but you must answer me quietly so that Ubaldo does not hear."

The emaciated being was silent.

"Are you Yvette Plugford?"

The woman released the gentleman's hand and stared forward, frightened.

"Are you Yvette Plugford?" Nathaniel quietly repeated.

"I…I was."

The gentleman assumed that the woman's 'medicine' had confused her, and so he restated his question. "Is your name Yvette Plugford?"

"It's Yvette Upfield now—I got married back when I was twenty-three."

Nathaniel did not recall Brent ever mentioning that either sister had a husband.

Yvette sat upright. "How do you know who I am?"

"Please speak quietly—I do not want anybody to hear our conversation."

"Okay." The skeletal woman was trembling.

"Your father and brothers hired me," said Nathaniel. "They are going to rescue you."

Yvette's bleary eyes brightened and sparkled. "Thank you Jesus." Tears spilled down her cheeks. "Thank you Lord."

Nathaniel desperately hoped that the Plugford crew could save this poor woman.

"I wonder if…" Yvette looked down at herself and rearranged her negligee. "I wonder if they'll even recognize me now." She covered her emaciated legs with a blanket. "Maybe they won't want me back."

Nathaniel took her cold hands in-between his palms. "They want you."

"How come my husband didn't come with them?"

"I am uncertain why he is absent."

"Samuel C. Upfield IV doesn't want a ruined woman is why." Yvette withdrew her hands.

"Brent, Stevie and your father are coming, and all of them love you dearly."

"They need to get Dolores too," Yvette remarked, "I think she's in here."

"They shall rescue her as well."

"Should you get on top of me so Ubaldo doesn't get suspicious?"

Nathaniel was horrified by the idea.

"I see that you don't want to be with some used up whore." Yvette lowered her gaze.

"You are a very beautiful woman," Nathaniel explained, "but I need to visit your sister and let her know about the rescue."

"I should probably take my clothes off so that Ubaldo can see you had a look."

Although Nathaniel was uneasy with this idea, he recognized that it had some merit. "Go ahead." He rose from beside the bed, turned his back to the woman and heard the soft rustling of fabric. The moment the noises stopped, he became extraordinarily uncomfortable.

"You can peek if you want," said Yvette, employing a girlish voice. "I won't tell Pa or my brothers."

Nathaniel neither responded to the invitation nor turned around. For three long minutes, he stared at the door while his beating heart marked the chill progress of sweat droplets down his scalp, skull, nape and spine.

"You need to get me some medicine," Yvette said, "and we need to get Henry, the circus dog."

A knock sounded upon the door.

"¿Señor Weston?"

"Yes?"

"Would you like to see the other gringa or are you wanting to stay here for some time?"

"I would like to see the other one."

The door withdrew from the wall and revealed Ubaldo, who stood in the hallway, holding a small purple box in his hands. Nathaniel exited the room.

"You like this gringa?"

"I am pondering some possibilities."

The man with the wooden nose locked the door and scratched the stitches that held his false proboscis in place. "We have—what is English word for equipaje?"

"Equipment."

"We have equipment."

Nathaniel did not ask the man to elucidate his statement.

"Come follow." Ubaldo led the gentleman toward the westernmost door on the south wall. "The red hairs is more stronger, but the foot."

It was not easy for Nathaniel to feign licentious enthusiasm.

The man with the wooden nose inserted a bronze key and twisted his fist. Lock tumblers groaned, and a bolt clacked. "I hope you like." He pulled the door wide and inclined his head toward the dark interior.

Nathaniel walked inside a candlelit room. Behind him, the door closed, but remained unlocked.

"Are you American?" asked the figure who laid upon the bed. The candles in the adjacent cubbyholes threw light upon the woman's rose corset, folded hands and round hips, but her face was in shadow and her legs were secreted beneath a blanket.

"I am an American," Nathaniel said as he strode across the stones.

The woman leaned forward. Candlelight divined her high forehead, sleepy eyes, upturned nose and Teutonic jaw from the darkness, and it was immediately clear to Nathaniel that she was Brent's twin sister. The air around her smelled like wine.

"Take it easy on me," the redheaded woman requested, "I've had five others tonight." She shifted her legs beneath the blanket and drew long red curls behind her ears.

Nathaniel put his index finger to his lips. "We need to speak quietly," he whispered, "I am—"

"Why? You gonna rescue me?" The woman's voice was loud and hostile.

"Please speak quietly—"

"No. I played this game before. There was a Englishman who told me he was gonna rescue me, get me outta here, in exchange for certain acts I'm not s'possed to do with clients. And I did them—all of them—but here I am, five months later, lookin' at you." The woman pulled a bottle of wine from the wall and paused. "You ever had your mouth and nostrils filled up with excrement?"

Nathaniel had no reply.

"Keep your stupid games." The embittered woman uncorked the bottle and drank wine that looked like blood. "You can fuck me regular—just don't talk any of that goddamn Mr. Rescuer stuff." She jammed the cork into the neck, tamped the cylinder down and replaced the bottle inside of a cubbyhole.

Nathaniel clapped his hand to the woman's mouth and whispered, "Your name is Dolores Plugford. Brent, Stevie and your father John Lawrence sent me to find you."

Hot air shot from the woman's nostrils, and her bloodshot eyes filled with fear and confusion.

"I am going to release you," the gentleman said, "but please mind your volume."

Into Nathaniel's palm, Dolores mumbled, "Okay. I will."

The gentleman uncovered the woman's mouth and sat beside her upon the bed.

"Maybe you learned them names somehow," Dolores hypothesized, "to trick me like that other."

"For what purpose? I have not asked you to do anything."

The woman ruminated for a moment. "No. You haven't." She drew her knees against her corset and hugged her covered shins.

"I came only to identify you for your family. I can proffer descriptions of them if you would like some assurances that—"

"No." The woman's suspicious face softened. "I believe you." Dolores looked up from her knees and into Nathaniel's eyes. "It ain't easy to trust a strange man at this juncture—but you seem true honest."

"I promise that—"

The lock groaned, and the bolt clacked.

Nathaniel's stomach sank. He looked at the door and inquired, "Does Ubaldo typically employ the bolt when you have a client?"

"Not usually."

Needles climbed up the gentleman's spine like a caterpillar.

"Yvette's here too—they need to get her."

"I already spoke with her," replied Nathaniel, preoccupied by the locked door.

"What'd you tell her?" Dolores's voice was sharp.

"I told her precisely what I told you. That your family is coming to rescue—"

Dolores swatted Nathaniel's shoulder. "You're a fool! Couldn't you see how she was?"

The gentleman did not at all understand the woman's sudden anger. "I saw."

"She's addled—a dependent," explained Dolores. "They get your mind that way and you'd cut your own mama's throat for another shot." Tears filled her eyes. "I bet she already told him everything!"

Nathaniel was nauseated. "Jesus Christ." His terrible blunder might cost him and all of the Plugfords their lives.

"You dumb fool!" Dolores slapped the gentleman's neck and face as if she were attempting to kill a fly. "You goddamn fool!" Tears dripped from her lower eyelashes. "You have any idea what you done? What they're goin' to do my family and you also?"

"I have some ideas."

Nathaniel's stomach began to revolt. He stood, stumbled toward the door and shuddered. A violent paroxysm seized his body, and he expelled a bitter greenish-brown variation of Patch Up's rabbit, grouse, potato, carrot and turnip stew onto the stones. Sweat streamed down his face, burned his eyes, soaked his tarnished mustache and dripped from the dangling twines of his blonde hair into the puddle of excreta. The stooped gentleman's neck and face stung from Dolores's assault, and his right inner ear sang a high pitch.

A bolt clacked, and the lock groaned.

The door opened.

Nathaniel looked up.

Standing in the doorway and twirling a syringe in his right hand was the man with the wooden nose. He pointed the needle at the puddle of vomit upon the floor, looked at the bent gentleman and remarked, "It looks like your belly has room for scorpions."

Chapter XI
Insectile Notions

Yvette Upfield stared at the crimson dot. A beneficent warmth like rich honey spread from the place that the man with the wooden nose had pierced with his syringe, and the world quietened. The circle became a swollen three-dimensional crimson bead that tracked across her powdered skin.

The bed rose up to meet the back of Yvette's head, and the ceiling slid before her glassy eyes. A segmented bug with innumerable legs crawled across a wooden beam, and she recognized the creature as the vessel into which she sent her spirit while her body withdrew semen from weak men as if it were a toxin.

Luxurious warmth spread from the red dot and replaced the hurt cells that comprised her bones, muscles and tissues. The fabric of her body became soft and homogeneous—a dense spongy material that absorbed her agonies.

Yvette tried to recall what she had told the man with the wooden nose, but her mind was a marsh.

"What did I say?" she asked the insect.

The many-legged thing upon the ceiling described an ellipsoidal pattern, halted directly above her face and stared down with multifaceted onyx eyes.

"What're you trying to tell me?"

The watcher remained silent.

A drop of blood aspired to the tip of Yvette's right index finger and dripped to the floor. It was suddenly very clear to her that if she touched the bug's eyes, she would be able to communicate with it. She attempted to employ the muscles in her arms, but could not remember how to operate them. "Maybe later."

A second or ten minutes later, blood tickled Yvette's fingertips. To the vessel into which she often escaped, the gaunt woman said, "I need you to get Samuel. My husband."

Candlelight flickered upon the bug's multifaceted eyes.

The woman with the homogeneous body knew the truth. Yvette Upfield was a spoiled lady whom Samuel C. Upfield IV no longer wanted. Hundreds of men had used her, and she had entertained doubts about Him. Four months ago, a child had burgeoned within her belly, and even though she had cut herself to imitate her monthly bleeding, the man with the wooden nose had seen through her ruse and applied an abortive salve that smelled like berries, sulfur and burnt chicory, and she had lost the innocent to a terrible searing pain. Shortly after that incident, the man with the wooden nose had given her medicine (so that she could stop weeping) and she had been drug-addled ever since. Sins had been committed to her, by her and deep within her.

"I was different," Yvette said to the bug.

Upon the ceiling, the vessel adjusted twelve of its legs.

The woman with the homogeneous body thought of her husband, Samuel C. Upfield IV, the articulate thirty-eight-year-old entrepreneur whose percolating mind contrived elixirs and devices as if he had a telephone cable that connected him directly to the great Creator. Although his ultimate ambition was to invent a very important thing (such as a motor vehicle or a telephone), he spent most of his time selling elixirs and investing small sums in prospecting ventures.

"If I'd been born in the antebellum period," Samuel C. Upfield IV said to Yvette from the oak table that dominated the main room of their cozy apartment in San Francisco, "I would have a great number of important inventions to my credit. Myriad noteworthy contrivances." He looked up from the sketches that filled 'The Upfield Book of Very Important Diagrams' and gazed through the bay window. Turquoise waves thundered harmlessly beneath the pendulous legs of circling seabirds. "But they've invented so much already…"

Doubt assailed the educated, pious and pretty blonde man who was the exact same height as his wife.

"I believe in you." Yvette walked toward the table.

Samuel stood, withdrew a chair for his wife (he always chose the seat closest to his own) and presented it to her buttocks. "Set down the blessed posterior."

Yvette sat into the airy folds of her bright blue dress, and Samuel placed earrings, which were gentle kisses, upon her bare earlobes. He slid the seat underneath her.

"Perfect." The choirmaster laid her sheet music upon the table and looked at her husband. "The Lord has bestowed upon you a great gift so you could make the world a better place. And you are."

Samuel seated himself, gazed wanly at 'The Upfield Book of Very Important Diagrams' and sighed. "I fear that I won't ever realize my greatest potential. I had such grand plans for that traveling lighthouse, but then…"

(Electricity was a word rarely uttered by the Upfields.)

"Your elixirs help people," defended Yvette.

"But are elixirs significant? Will they change the world?" Samuel shook his head twice, answering his two-pronged inquiry. "They will not." He drank from his mug of spiced brandy.

"They already do—they help folks lead happier lives right now. Todd Parks had that bellyache for three years until he drank your restorative."

"You are partial," protested Samuel. "Lovely, but partial."

"And our choir uses your throat tonic when we sing our praise and devotion direct to God each week. Ain't that—isn't that significant?"

"It is." Samuel brightened, set down his brandy, fixed his cravat, stood, took one stride to Yvette and kissed her upon the forehead. "Lower the drapes."

The choirmaster closed her eyes, and as she tilted her head back the floorboards creaked. Samuel's soft lips landed upon her left eyelid and then its sibling. Presently, they kissed.

Yvette opened her eyes.

The bug with innumerable legs watched her from the ceiling of her cell.

"Where are you?" Tears leaked from the corners of her eyes, and a drop of warm blood tracked across her right arm, grew cold and dripped to the floor. She looked down. The tiny crimson hemisphere sank into the ancient stone, and was wholly absorbed.

A person outside the door shouted, "¡Gringo, vas!"

The imprisoned, drug-addled, choirmaster who was born in Shoulderstone, Texas and lived in San Francisco, suddenly recalled whom she had betrayed to get her medicine. Upon the ceiling, the segmented bug moved its myriad legs, entered a hole in the ancient stone and disappeared.

Yvette's soul was lost inside the walls.

"No." The woman thought of her family and the tall blonde gentleman, and how her need for medicine, her sinful weakness, had doomed them all. "No!" shouted Yvette, even though the word did not have any meaning in Catacumbas.

"No!"

Chapter XII
Sharp Embodiments

Rising from the depths of oblivion, Nathaniel Stromler dimly apprehended the tight ropes that bound his wrists and ankles to the limbs of a heavy chair. His senses sharpened and he recognized the smells of wine, seafood and cream. Fork tines clinked upon ceramic plates, startling him.

The bound man shut his gaping jaw and opened his eyes. From the ceiling directly above him depended two gold-plated candelabra, European in style, and upon the surrounding walls of grayish-ochre ziggurat stones, hung tapestries that depicted hunting tableaus and galleon arrivals.

A man with European-accented Spanish remarked that the foreigner was awake.

"Señor," enjoined a deep and familiar voice.

Nathaniel tilted his head forward and saw that he was seated at a long dining table. At the far end of the oaken slab sat Gris, accompanied by two men who wore dark cherry suits. Steam rose from the shrimp, peas, yellow rice and béchamel sauce that filled their plates.

Upon the table directly in front of the captive gringo laid two wooden bowls that were covered with heavy stone lids. Something living rustled within the vessel on the left.

Nathaniel jerked. "No." He twisted in his seat, but his chair was made of stone and did not move even a fraction of an inch. Had he not already emptied the contents of his bladder and stomach, he would have done so upon hearing that insectile noise.

"Diego," said Gris.

A gentleman with a neatly-trimmed black beard stood from his chair, withdrew a glove from his dark cherry slacks, inserted his left hand and waggled his fingers.

Nathaniel's heart pounded.

"I am left-handed," Gris declared, "as are all five of my sons."

The bearded man, who had a thin nose and thick lips like his father, walked toward Nathaniel.

"Do you believe this is a coincidence?" Gris inquired as he speared a pink shrimp with his fork.

"I do not know," responded Nathaniel.

"Scandinavian studies have proven that left-handed people think differently than do the majority and quite often reap the rewards of their atypical thought processes."

Gris pointed his speared shrimp at his bearded progeny. "At a very early age, Diego was instructed to favor his left hand and was punished for contrary behavior."

Nathaniel doubted Gris's sanity.

"Like all of my sons, Diego learned to become left-handed." The one-eyed Spaniard ate the shrimp and summarily thrust his fork into another pink morsel. "That was my will."

Unable to entertain desultory conversation any longer, Nathaniel demanded, "What do you intend—"

"Dolores Plugford is but two months away from fully accepting that she is a whore and my property," stated Gris. "Yvette Upfield has a longer journey—her religious devotion is an obstacle—but she too will grow to accept that she is what she does. That is my will." The white-haired Spaniard looked at Nathaniel with both his good eye and the gray rock that was lodged within his left socket. "Both of these women could have avoided many terrible—and pointless—agonies had they yielded to my will when they sat in the chair that you now occupy."

Diego raised the thick stone lid from the right bowl. Deep within the vessel was a shallow puddle of pure black oil, upon which sat dim stars that were reflections of candelabra flames. Gris's son uncovered the left bowl and revealed a roiling confluence of gray pincers, spindly legs and curved tails. The rustling and clicking of the arachnids sounded like a brush fire.

Nathaniel began to shake.

Gris said, "My son shall show you the embodiment of a lie."

With his protected index finger and thumb, Diego extricated a small gray scorpion from the left bowl, held it above the adjacent vessel and let go. The arachnid plopped into the black mire. The legs of the ichor-covered creature clicked furiously upon the wood. Nathaniel felt a numbing horror spread throughout his chest and head.

"Each lie you utter shall be thus embodied," stated Gris. "You are aware of this creature's ultimate destination?"

Lightheaded, Nathaniel nodded.

The scorpion scrambled in circles, but could not ascend the bowl's slick walls.

Gris inquired, "When does your group plan to raid Catacumbas?"

"Whenever I give them the signal. There was no set time."

"How large is this raiding party?"

"Three men." (Nathaniel had not mentioned Long Clay, Deep Lakes and Patch Up to Yvette.)

"Three men plan to raid Catacumbas?" The one-eyed Spaniard was doubtful.

Diego glanced at his father.

"I was hired by three men—the father and brothers of the women I visited."

"The little husband was not involved?" inquired Gris.

"I was completely unaware of his existence until Yvette mentioned him to me."

Gris inclined his head toward the unnamed silver-haired son and whispered into his ear. The gentleman nodded twice, rose and departed. A heavy door closed.

The one-eyed Spaniard returned his attention to the captive gringo. "What is your name?"

Once Nathaniel revealed his true identity, the path to Kathleen and his mother and sister in Michigan would forever be open to this repellant creature. "Thomas Weston."

"It is unfortunate that you have chosen to disregard my advice."

Strong hands gripped Nathaniel's forehead and jaw, and his mouth was pried open by the unseen restrainer who stood directly behind him. A wooden ruler pressed his tongue flat. Diego reached into the oil and withdrew the dripping scorpion. Its wriggling legs showered black droplets upon the table.

Nathaniel shut his eyes. Needlelike legs tickled his cheeks, and pincers poked his soft palate. Uselessly, he struggled against the restrainer and the stone chair. He gagged, but his empty stomach had no more contents to expel. Spindly appendages pricked his nasal passages and esophagus.

"A bajo."

The ruler was pulled from Nathaniel's mouth. His jaw was slammed shut and his head was jerked back. The oily mass descended his throat like chewed chicken bones. It transgressed his neck, flinched once and entered his chest.

The strong hands released the captive's jaw. Nathaniel tilted his head forward, and his vision began to narrow. Diego reseated himself and contemplated the manifold scorpions within the left bowl.

"What is your name?" repeated Gris.

Nathaniel recalled his monogrammed handkerchief. "Nicholas Samuelson."

Gris contemplated the answer and nodded. "Do you have a wife?"

"I do not."

"The discoloration upon your ring finger intimates a different truth."

Diego reached his glove into the left bowl and withdrew a beige scorpion from its sharp contemporaries. Its legs wriggled continuously as if it were the conductor of an arachnid symphony.

Nathaniel said, "I am engaged to be mar—"

A stinger pierced his stomach, and he shrieked. The dire agony thrust him into a new stratum of existence, and his entire life prior to that extraordinary pain seemed numb and insensate by comparison. As the stinger withdrew from his stomach lining, a terrible coolness flooded his guts.

Death loomed, undeniable.

Nathaniel Stromler knew that his living remainder would be filled with bright red pain. The only thing that he could do was withhold information that might endanger

Kathleen or his mother and sister. Presently, the dining room turned to watercolors and slid down his cheeks.

The silver-haired son returned to the room, sat at the table and put a napkin upon his lap.

Gris appraised Nathaniel momentarily. "Once el escorpión settles, we shall talk more about your fiancé." The one-eyed Spaniard picked up his fork and knife. "I am a great admirer of women." He stuck his tines into a delicate pink shrimp, which was covered with béchamel sauce, and raised it from its embryonic peers.

A burning harpoon that was a stinger lanced Nathaniel's insides. He yelled. His pierced stomach shuddered and tried to jettison its attacker, but the arachnid clutched tissues with its toothpick legs and would not be expelled.

Consciousness leaked like a vapor from Nathaniel's head. Candelabra flames fell like dying stars, and darkness blossomed.

Gris's son complemented the shrimp.

Chapter XIII
Mean Men

Dolores Plugford watched the Oriental secret his damp dark phallus inside his drawers and reach for his opalescent silk shirt. A taste like soap and copper haunted her palate and she reached for the bringer of purgation (and obliteration) that was her wine bottle.

"You are skilled with your mouth." The Oriental slid a manicured hand through a shirtsleeve; silk whistled.

Angry that she was adept at pleasing the different types of mean men who came to her in Catacumbas, Dolores drank. She washed the foul taste from her mouth with a bitter draught as she thought of freedom, her family and the tall dumb dandy who had ruined everything. After eight months of imprisonment, the dwindling star of hope had vanished utterly from the black sky.

The Oriental buttoned his shirt and glanced at her shorn left ankle. "What happened to your foot?"

"I s'pose they threw it out."

"How did you lose it?" the man inquired, as if he were discussing a misshapen cabbage with a grocer.

"A man shot it."

"A doctor should've pulled out the bullet and fixed the hole."

"Nobody thought of that. I sure wish you'd been around to give us advice." (The idiot did not seem to realize that she was making fun of him.)

"I once helped a doctor remove a bullet. It's not so difficult."

"I had six bullets." Dolores's left foot had been an unrecognizable mess the last time she had seen it.

The Oriental poked an ivory cufflink into his left sleeve. "The man who shot your foot must've been very angry."

"You must be a professor."

The Oriental paused. "Are you belittling me?"

"You're little enough."

A dark fist landed in Dolores's stomach, emptied her lungs and doubled her over. Iron fingers grabbed curls of her red hair and yanked her upright. With a long and pointed fingernail, the Oriental tapped the woman's tender stump. "I understand why you lost the foot."

"Go roast."

The man was perplexed by her remark.

"Roast in Hell you stupid mongoloid," clarified Dolores.

Deep within the man, something smoldered. "I am not stupid." The fingers clutching her hair tightened. "I have a good education."

"So does that circus dog." At that moment, Dolores knew that she wanted to die.

The wall impacted her ear, retreated and slammed into her nose.

Soon, the Oriental's dark face expanded. "You are a dumb whore. Very, very dumb." He inhaled wetly.

Spit struck Dolores's left eye and dangled like a mucoidal tear, but she did not bother to wipe it away.

The man released her hair. "I will get the equipment. And I will return." He turned away from the bed and walked toward the exit.

On the far side of the chamber, the door opened.

The Oriental paused.

Ubaldo stumbled into the room and dropped to his knees. His right eye was purple and hugely swollen, and his gaping mouth looked like a crushed tomato. Standing in the open doorway was a huge man who wore a rubber mask over his head, a thick iron tabard atop his gray overalls, four guns and giant work boots.

"Daddy?" said Dolores.

"It's me angel."

The huge patriarch sped at the terrified Oriental.

"Don't hurt me, I—"

The small man was seized by the neck and slammed against the wall.

"Please—"

Thick fingers burrowed into the Oriental's neck and yanked out his throat. Vomit sprayed from the open end of the corrugated tube like a garden hose, and his larynx buzzed a shrill pitch.

Dolores saw another man materialize in the hallway outside her cell. He was five foot nine and wore a rubber mask, an iron tabard, a beige shirt, denim jeans and cowboy boots.

"Brent?"

The man bolted across the room and threw his arms around her. "It's me," her twin brother said through his mask, "It's me, I'm here."

Tears spilled down Dolores's face. "Oh god Brent. I can't believe this ain't a dream."

"We're here for real." Brent pulled off his rubber mask, and his cheeks were wet with tears. "I love you." He kissed her on the forehead. "We love you."

Dolores squeezed her brother so tightly that the iron plate he wore dug into her corset and ripped the fabric.

Ubaldo crawled toward the door. John Lawrence Plugford stomped upon the Mexican's forearm, snapping it. The crawler collapsed.

In the hallway outside appeared a tall narrow man who gripped two ebony pistols and wore a blood-splattered rubber mask, an iron tabard and black clothing. "Hasten."

"Get your mask on," the patriarch said to his son, "and carry her."

"Got her." Brent pulled on his rubber mask, drew a blanket over Dolores and slid his arms beneath her knees and behind her back. "Grab hold."

The woman leaned forward and held her brother's shoulders.

John Lawrence Plugford snatched Ubaldo's collar and raised him to his feet. "Let's get the other."

The cowed Mexican silently endured his injuries and walked from the room, followed by the patriarch.

Brent raised Dolores from the terrible bed and carried her across the chamber, through the door and up the hallway to the tall narrow man, whose revolvers were aimed at the dark ascending stairwell. The stranger's rubber mask swiveled minutely, and behind the glass goggles the woman saw two cold blue eyes, which appraised her face and body and lingered momentarily on her stump. He turned back to the stairwell.

"Are you Pa's old partner?" asked Dolores.

"I am."

The woman had heard her mother refer to Long Clay as 'the fellow who the devil was afraid of.' "Thanks for helpin'."

The gunfighter nodded.

Accompanied by the patriarch, the injured Mexican walked toward the far side of the hallway. The pair brightened as they neared the ensconced torch and darkened shortly thereafter. Presently, they stopped outside the final door.

Ubaldo released his fractured right arm, winced as gravity strained the appendage, reached his left hand into his trousers, withdrew a bronze key and inserted it into the lock. Tumblers groaned, and a bolt clacked. The man with the wooden nose pulled the door wide and said, "The other."

John Lawrence Plugford took a step forward and looked through the portal. He surveyed the room for a ponderous moment. "That ain't—" His voice cut out.

"They made her dependent," Dolores announced from Brent's arms.

Staring into the darkness, John Lawrence Plugford inquired, "Yvette?"

"Is that you Daddy?"

"Yeah." The patriarch's voice was a translucent whisper. "It's me angel."

The huge man stood outside the room, still and silent for an awful moment, and then turned to face Ubaldo. Terror filled he man with the wooden nose.

"Don't kill him yet," cautioned Long Clay.

John Lawrence Plugford shoved Ubaldo against the wall; the Mexican's skull smacked against the stone. The patriarch pressed the meat of his left palm to the man's wooden nose, and the stitches that held the false proboscis in place pulled upon the surrounding skin.

"No," pleaded Ubaldo. Air whistled through his nostrils.

John Lawrence Plugford thrust his hand upward. Wires ripped free, and crimson beads scattered into the air. The Mexican wailed.

"He deserves it," said Dolores.

Ubaldo's wooden nose dangled, anchored to the skin adjoining his corroded nasal cavity by two wires. He cupped his face. John Lawrence Plugford turned away from the dripping man and walked into the room wherein laid his daughter.

"I lost my soul in the walls," declared the unseen woman. "There's a bug that's got it." Her voice was enervated and girlish.

"Don't worry," said the patriarch.

"It took my soul away, and now I can't move."

Heavy footsteps echoed within the room. Presently, John Lawrence Plugford strode from the darkness, carrying an enshrouded corpse that Dolores soon realized was both alive and her sister.

"Oh God," Brent quietly exclaimed within his mask. "Oh God." His hands squeezed his twin sister. "Oh God. Oh God." He shuddered.

"This place is terrible." Dolores looked away from the skeletal thing that her father carried. "This goddamn world is terrible."

Brent cleared his throat and looked at Ubaldo. "You...you got any other women pris'ners in this goddamn place?"

"No," replied the dripping man through the glistening hand that held his face. "You can look—no other cells is locked."

Dolores surveyed the hall and saw that most of the doors were ajar. "Where's that fellow we sent here earlier," Brent asked Ubaldo, "the tall blonde dandy?"

"He's having dinner with the boss."

"You're gonna get him for us," stated Brent.

"Si."

The injured Mexican walked up the hallway. Carrying his piteous daughter, John Lawrence Plugford followed.

Long Clay turned to Ubaldo. "Stop."

The Mexican halted.

"Let me see your face."

Ubaldo lowered his left hand, and his nose twisted on its wires like a cat's toy. Long Clay placed the tip of his long black revolver inside the man's nasal cavity. Steel clicked upon recessed cartilage, and lambent torchlight dripped from the Mexican's eyes.

"Do not cross us."

"I will do what you say." Ubaldo's words buzzed inside the gun barrel. "I swears." His breath caught erratically.

"He's gonna sneeze," warned Brent.

The gunfighter withdrew the tip of his revolver.

The Mexican sprayed gore upon the stone, groaned and stood upright. Long Clay yanked the dangling proboscis loose and discarded it. "Go." The nose smacked against the wall and skipped up the hallway.

Cupping his dripping face with his good hand, Ubaldo entered the stairwell.

Long Clay looked at Brent. "Wait for my signal."

"Okay."

The gunfighter lowered his head and entered the portal. As he climbed the steps, the back of his iron tabard flashed.

Dolores looked at her younger sister, who was collapsed and pale in the arms of her father. It took the redheaded woman a moment to find her voice. "Yvette?"

The emaciated choirmaster brushed away the hair that hung before her dilated eyes. "You still look pretty."

Dolores knew that she would sob hysterically if she attempted to respond, and so she reached for her younger sister's hand, clasped what felt like a raw poultry and squeezed. It took all of her strength not to weep.

"Why didn't my husband come?" asked Yvette. "Why isn't Samuel here?"

Dolores felt Brent's arms stiffen. She looked up at his rubber mask and saw that his eyes were narrowed and filled with hate.

Exasperated, Yvette whined, "Doesn't anybody know?"

John Lawrence Plugford said, "We'll talk about him later." His words were black and irrefutable.

Dolores replaced her sister's hand upon her narrow chest.

The family watched the stairwell.

"I don't have no hands free," Brent said to Dolores. "You think you can shoot a gun?"

"I worked at Jasper's for four years." (Although Jasper's Palace of Good Chances and Dancing Cancan Girls was a reputable establishment, drunken gentlemen who lost large sums to truculent dice or restive ball bearings occasionally tried to reclaim their wages in a felonious manner. Resultantly, all employees were schooled in what the owner called 'firearm preparedness.') Dolores drew a nickel-plated pistol from Brent's hip.

"Shoot every single one that touched you," said John Lawrence Plugford. "Or point them out to me."

"I know."

The patriarch patted his daughter's shoulder.

"Don't murder nobody," Yvette protested, "they're weak is all."

Nobody responded to the choirmaster's advice.

Dolores looked at the front of the six-shot revolver, spun the barrel, saw two black holes, turned the weapon over, cracked it in half, discarded the spent shells, located the cartridge sash beneath Brent's iron tabard, plucked out two bullets, loaded them into the empty grooves and snapped the gun shut.

"Did Stevie come?"

"He's actin' sentry upstairs."

Dolores drew six more bullets from the sash and tucked them in-between her left breast and corset cup. "I'm s'prised he made the effort."

"He's sour," Brent replied, "but he cares 'bout you girls."

"I need some medicine," demanded Yvette.

"We'll find you something once we're out clear," said Brent.

"And we've gotta get Henry," Yvette added, "the circus dog. They're mean to him and we've gotta get him out of here."

"We'll grab him if we can."

"We have to save him." The choirmaster sounded desperate.

Near the top of the stairwell, a tiny pinprick of light flashed thrice.

Brent said, "It's clear," and hastened forward. His left boot landed upon the bottom step, and his other foot aspired three levels higher. Dolores pointed the pistol up and out. Grayish-ochre stones and nestled candles sped past. Forty feet behind the twins, the patriarch, holding Yvette in the crook of his left arm and his sawed-off shotgun in his right fist, thundered up the steps.

Dolores was carried from the nether stairwell into a torch-illumined passageway and to the left. The floor wavered nauseatingly and she instantly regretted the quantity of sour wine that she had imbibed after her assignation with the Oriental.

Presently, the siblings passed an ensconced torch, and the flames reached after them like a clutching hand. The floor undulated. Sweat beaded upon Dolores's brow.

"Hold that gun with both hands," Brent advised as he bounded up the hall.

"Okay."

Dolores clapped her left hand upon her right, and the gun steadied. She looked forward. At the far end of the passageway stood a rectangle of amber light. It had been five months since she had last been inside the parlor that laid beyond.

Brent bounded. Sprawled across the floor beneath an ensconced torch was an inert man in a bright yellow suit who was headless. A tarry stain comprised of roasted brain matter, blood, skull shards and hair sat upon the wall beside the flames.

"Pa got that canary," said Brent.

"Good."

The smell of baked gore was noxious, and Dolores held her breath as her brother circumnavigated the corpse.

Yvette yelled.

Dolores looked back at her sister. "Shut your eyes girl."

The sepulchral woman, cradled in John Lawrence Plugford's left arm, stared at the headless canary and was appalled. "You all can't do any more killing."

"Hush now angel," the patriarch said as he bounded up the hallway.

"You can't! I'd rather go back than have all these lives taken."

John Lawrence Plugford poked the barrels of his sawed-off shotgun into a corner of the blanket that draped Yvette and drew the fabric over her face. "Don't you worry about nothin'." The patriarch hugged his daughter close to his chest. "Your daddy's got you now."

With a skeletal hand, Yvette gripped the blanket and pulled it from her eyes. John Lawrence Plugford concealed her face once more.

"Leave it alone," advised Dolores. "You don't wanna see none of this."

"Make us a prayer," suggested Brent.

John Lawrence Plugford carried his enshrouded daughter past the headless corpse.

Dolores faced forward. In the adjacent room stood the black scarecrow silhouette of Long Clay, who had one revolver extended and the tip of its sibling lodged within Ubaldo's nasal cavity. (The Mexican's good and broken arms were bound by a cord.)

"Wait in the hall." The gunfighter shifted his rubber head so that he could see the Plugfords through his left goggle. "They're fetching the dandy."

Brent carried Dolores to the edge of the passage, and there she surveyed the vast subterranean parlor, which was illuminated by hundreds of nook-embedded candles. Upon the nonagonal clay tiles laid eleven corpses, a morass of charcoal faces, iridescent entrails, cracked white ribcages, exposed lungs and severed limbs. The redheaded woman recognized that the deceased men were Catacumbas guards, most of whom had visited her chamber.

"We brung grenades," said Brent.

"Good." The invasive smells of blood, gunpowder, iron and scorched fat filled Dolores's nostrils. "They deserve it." Two baby turtles crawled across a broiled liver.

Dolores raised her gaze from the carnage and looked toward the dais, which was thirty yards distant. Facedown upon the stone floor laid twenty-nine formally-dressed gentlemen and forty whores who wore variegated silk kimonos. Pointing the barrel of a pump-action shotgun at the exposed backs of the prostrated individuals was Stevie, clad in a rubber mask, tattered clothes and an iron tabard. He nodded his orange head at his sister, and she waved in return.

John Lawrence Plugford reached the twins and paused. Beneath her blanket, Yvette quietly prayed.

On the far side of the parlor and next to the stairwell stood the third corner of the sentry triangle, a small pudgy fellow who held a repeater rifle and wore an iron tabard, a maroon suit, a rubber mask and white gloves. He waved a hand at Dolores and summarily gripped his weapon.

The redheaded woman suddenly realized at whom she was looking. "Lord," she muttered to her brother, "that's…"

"Yeah," said Brent. "That's him."

Dolores waved her hand at Patch Up. "I can't believe he'd get involved in this ugliness."

"He's family," stated John Lawrence Plugford.

Stevie called out from the dais, "You girls see any men you want me to execute?"

Yvette prayed louder.

Dolores could not see most of the prone captives, but a rotund man who had squeezed his bulk through her chamber door on several occasions was very visible. "Let me see that one in the second row—the fat one in the purple suit."

Stevie walked over to the indicated man and kicked his head sideways. "Stand up."

The fat fellow from Portugal rose to his knees, wiped dust from his iridescent cuffs and stood upright. His back was to Dolores.

Stevie prodded the captive with his shotgun barrel. "Walk to the front of the stage so she can see you good."

The fat man wended his prostrated peers and strode to the edge of the dais, where he paused, buttoned his double-breasted lavender jacket and aligned his hair, as if he were preparing for an opera recital.

Anger coursed through Dolores's breast. This was the odious creature who had stuffed dirty socks into her mouth and sodomized her.

"There are many important men in this establishment," the Portuguese gentleman proclaimed, "and there will be retribution for what—"

The gunstock impacted his right cheek.

"Don't share your stupid wisdom," advised Stevie.

John Lawrence Plugford leaned close to Dolores. "Did he touch you?"

"Yes."

John Lawrence Plugford stopped breathing.

Brent's hands tightened upon Dolores's shoulders and legs.

Stevie swung his gunstock into the fat man's jaw, and the bone snapped. The rapist from Portugal cried out, exactly as he did whenever he sprayed semen, and he clasped his asymmetrical chin. Near him, the prone captives shuddered, but did not say anything.

"Apologize to her!" boomed John Lawrence Plugford.

"Do it!" yelled Stevie. "Apologize!"

Blood trickled from the fat man's lopsided mouth, down his bulbous neck and onto his white shirt. He looked at Dolores and said, "I am so—"

"Get on your goddamn knees and put your fat hands together!" shouted Stevie. "That's how you apologize!"

The fat man from Portugal dropped to his knees.

"Why you done it!?!" yelled Stevie. "Why you do that to her!?! She's a good woman." His voice warbled unevenly, and Dolores knew that he was crying beneath his rubber mask. "Goddamn you!" The gunstock crushed the man's nose.

"Let him apologize," John Lawrence Plugford said to his youngest child.

The fat man looked at Dolores and opened his mouth. Blood flowed from the carmine hole and down his chin.

"Hands together!" admonished Stevie.

The fat man pressed the palms of his hands together and said with a slurred voice, "I am s-s-sorry that I mis-s-s-streated you."

"Say it true! What you did!" Stevie pressed the tip of his shotgun to the fat man's hands. "Say it true!"

"I am sorry that I raped you."

Barrels thundered. The fat man's hands were obliterated by buckshot, and his face was seared by a brilliant flash of gunpowder.

Dolores felt immediate gratification, as if one of the many painful cysts in her guts had been removed.

The fat man wobbled upon his knees and fell sideways. Blood poured from his truncated arms.

Stevie raised a boot over the charred rapist's face.

"No!" boomed John Lawrence Plugford. "He dies slow."

Beneath her blanket, Yvette wept.

The fat man from Portugal tried to scream, but was unable to pull his seared lips apart.

Chapter XIV
In Adjacent Rooms

London was a large, gray and spectral city filled with ancient mysteries that tantalized Nathaniel Stromler's burgeoning mind. Although he was only thirteen years old, he was capable, mature and tall enough to pass for a man of nineteen (the age that was the intersection of flip adolescence and ambitious adulthood), and naturally he wanted to explore the enigmatic environs unaccompanied. Unfortunately, for him the Itinerary was filled and allowed the youth no time for solitary rambles.

Out of necessity, the thirteen-year-old-fabricated.

On the eleventh morning of the family sojourn, a Thursday, the youngest Stromler announced that he felt ill and would be unable to endeavor the campaign that was described in the Itinerary. The delivered news was reinforced by a quartet of sneezes, which were coerced by pepper that he had ground the previous evening and installed inside his handkerchief. Although his older sister Isabella harbored suspicions regarding the veracity of his illness, the declarations and physical proofs he proffered wrought looks of consternation from his parents.

"Perhaps I should remain with you," Mother said, "should your condition worsen."

"The housekeeper is a dependable person," the boy responded from his bed, "and shall be summoned should my mild illness become notable." Nathaniel applied pepper grinds to his nostrils with the handkerchief. "I am quite confident—" He sneezed. "I am quite confident that a one day abstention from the Itinerary is all that I shall require." The youth improvised a lusty cough.

Nathaniel's parents squabbled over whether or not they could leave their innocent son alone in an English hotel apartment, and after each combatant had twice attacked and defended each position, they gave their assent.

"Do not leave the room under any circumstances."

"Disregard your mother's statement should there be a fire."

"Naturally," the woman replied, "Nathaniel would not remain in the room should it become enveloped by flames."

"I only sought to clarify your advice."

"It is a mother's duty to offer her son guidance, especially when his father is only too happy to abandon him in favor of sculptures and paintings and sherry and glances (which he believes are surreptitious) at buxom English ladies."

The squabble continued for five more minutes. Isabella complained that she was hungry, and presently, the trio departed.

Nathaniel walked toward the window, cloaked himself in striped curtains and looked through the glass. Father hailed an open carriage, Mother summoned its replacement and Isabella pointed out an omnibus toward which they all hastened.

The young man began his toilet and envisioned his private ramble throughout the great gray metropolis of fog. Upon his solitary walk, he would observe English architecture and the people who lived within it, and he would purchase some written works and perhaps a pastry. If he encountered the housekeeper before he departed, he would pay her some farthings to corroborate his whereabouts, but his intention was to stealthily escape the hotel and trust that his absence would not ever be discovered.

After he had completed his toilet, Nathaniel dressed himself in a brown three-piece suit and exited the apartment.

The lank youth entered the hallway and strode upon the pine green carpet that covered the major part of the floor. At the end of the hall, he heard a strange noise and paused. From behind a closed door emanated a loud crackling that he at first believed to be the theoretical fire predicted by his parents.

Concerned for the safety of any tenants therein, Nathaniel approached the portal.

A loud piano note rang and was succeeded by two different pitches. The young man recognized the crackling emanation as that of a wax cylinder amplified in the flower of a phonograph.

Suddenly, the music stopped.

"This is the penultimate piece I'm to sing at the recital," said an Englishwoman located within the room.

"I very much look forward to hearing it," replied a man who possessed a strange accent.

The crackling union of metal needle and spinning wax resumed, and the composition began anew. Nathaniel heard the familiar melody, and when the recorded pianist augmented the single note phrase with thick bass chords, the Englishwoman began to sing.

It was immediately apparent to the young eavesdropper that the lady within the apartment was a professional performer—she rang the pitches clearly and precisely. Although she strained for several high notes, her voice had a plaintive quality that turned this limitation into a virtue, a humble acknowledge of human fallibility. The song modulated to a lower register, and the singer's voice blossomed like a lush lily garden causing the youth's heart to pound within his chest. For the first time in his life, he yearned.

The notes climbed, and the woman followed desperately.

In the third floor hallway of The Hotel Gregory of London, Nathaniel Stromler savored a transformative invisible beauty.

The voice vanished, and the recorded pianist reached his concluding cadence. The phonograph crackled rhythmically for five heartbeats and was gone.

"You have a remarkable gift," said the man with the strange accent. "Herrlich."

"Danke, mein herr. I think of you whenever I perform this particular aria." Buried within the Englishwoman's speaking voice were the myriad hues that her singing had revealed.

For the duration of several heartbeats, Nathaniel heard nothing beyond the door.

"I would like for us to make love," announced the Englishwoman.

The instinct to flee did not overpower Nathaniel's curiosity.

"Ja."

Footsteps resounded within the room, and a shadow darkened the narrow space between the carpet and the bottom of the burnished door.

"A boy is outside," said the German man.

Nathaniel departed from the portal and pressed his back to the hallway wall. Adjacent to the doorframe, the youth lurked.

"Please help me remove my dress," requested the singer.

Tumblers whined, and the lock clicked. Nathaniel's fear of being apprehended abated. The shadow beneath the door changed into the sound of footsteps.

With his back flush against the wall, the lank youth listened. Silken fabrics rustled, buttons clicked, clothing crumpled and fell, fingers slid across skin, the man said, "Alyssa," bedclothes crinkled, wood whined, the woman groaned, the man moaned, the woman said, "There," wood whined, bedclothes rustled, the woman said, "Kurt, Kurt," the man said "I love you," a soft pulse grew louder and louder and louder, the wall throbbed, the man groaned, the woman cried out and together they said, "I love you."

A burning harpoon lanced Nathaniel Stromler's stomach and roused him from his dream.

The twenty-six-year-old gentleman from Michigan opened his eyes. Two scorpions that were covered with black oil scrambled around their wooden prison. In the adjacent bowl, fifty gray arachnids crackled like a spinning phonograph cylinder that had run out of music.

Gris, sitting at the far end of the dining room table, informed his progeny that he would remit the foreigner.

Diego clenched his gloved left hand and said, "Padre. Por favor. Nosotros—"

"Silencio." Gris turned his eye upon the captive. "Your associates have killed many men, taken seventy hostages and demanded your immediate release."

Nathaniel was fairly certain that this was a dream or a ruse (or perhaps the latter embedded within the earlier) and did not proffer any reply.

"Salvation does not seem to lift your spirits," remarked the white-haired Spaniard.

"I am not entirely convinced that—" A new sharp agony seized Nathaniel, and he vomited a small amount of blood and black oil. The inhabitant within him—the third arachnid that had been presented to his digestive tract—harried his stomach lining with pincers that felt disproportionately huge.

"My sons would like to use you as a hostage," Gris remarked, "but my opinion is that you are not very valuable."

"You are correct," replied Nathaniel.

Gris looked sternly at his sons. "We shall deliver the gringo to his associates." In Spanish, he added that he did not want one more innocent person killed because of two foreign whores. "We shall conclude this business immediately."

Diego and his silver-haired sibling nodded.

The white-haired Spaniard looked at whomever stood behind the captive. "Xzavier."

Bright metal slid across the ropes that held Nathaniel's left and right wrists to the arms of the stone chair, and the bindings sloughed. Unbound, the gringo raised a tremulous hand to his mouth and wiped away blood, bile and black oil. Although he still doubted his purported release, a small hope glimmered.

The flashing knife sliced through the fetters that bound his ankles, and dammed arterial blood surged toward his numb feet. For the first time since the painful dinner had begun, Nathaniel saw the person who had braced his head and inserted the wooden ruler. Xzavier was a muscular Mexican with curly black hair, a nose like wet clay and a large 'X' branded upon his neck.

Diego covered the wooden bowls, removed his canvas glove, rose to his feet and announced that he would escort the foreigner to the parlor.

Gris told his son to comply with the intruders.

"Si."

Diego and Xzavier placed their hands beneath Nathaniel's armpits and hoisted him from the stone chair. Hard things that felt like hot coals, needles and broken glass shifted within his belly.

From their seats at far end of the oaken dining table, Gris and his silver-haired son appraised the risen captive. Presently, they returned their attentions to quivering flan.

"Walk," ordered Diego.

Xzavier slapped a palm in-between Nathaniel's shoulder blades, and the gringo stumbled forward, holding his stomach.

The trio strode past tapestries of Spanish galleons, underneath two elaborate candelabra and to the double door on the far side of the room. Diego twisted the silver doorknob, pushed and motioned for the captive to precede him through the open portal. Compelled by Xzavier's hand, Nathaniel walked into a torch-illumined hallway.

Diego exited and shut the door. "Continue."

The three men traversed a long hallway of grayish-ochre stone; Nathaniel's stomach alternately burned and grew cold, and his bruised right eye throbbed.

Presently, they entered a broader passageway, upon the far side of which waited a petite Mexican woman, clothed in a modest brown and green dress. She held an unborn child in her swollen stomach and a small revolver in her right hand. Nathaniel wondered if he was about to be executed by a pregnant woman.

"Halt," Diego ordered.

The men stopped. Xzavier grabbed Nathaniel's collar and screwed his fist clockwise; the fabric tightened around the gringo's throat, and he wheezed.

"Vengo, Rosalinda." Diego walked to the petite woman and from her received the small firearm. He kissed her upon the mouth, and they embraced.

Nathaniel saw that the couple wore matching gold bands upon their ring fingers.

"Gracias, mi amor," said Diego. "Gracias."

Rosalinda said that Gris never should have kidnapped the white women.

Diego stated that his father had fairly acquired the gringas.

The pregnant woman told her husband to be careful.

"Si." Diego kissed the palm of his hand, pressed it to Rosalinda's swollen stomach and said that he would be very cautious.

The woman asked her husband what he intended to do with the pistol.

Gris's son said that he would not employ the firearm unless the intruders fired upon him.

"Si." Nodding, the woman wiped fearful tears from her eyes. "Cuidado."

Presently, Diego kissed his wife, slid the revolver into his left jacket pocket and looked at Xzavier. "Continue."

The Mexican released Nathaniel's collar and prodded him forward. Presently, the captive walked, followed by his captors; Rosalinda remained behind.

The trio entered a wide hall and turned to the left. At the far end of the passageway, Nathaniel saw a rectangle of amber light—the entrance to the parlor.

A shotgun blast resounded.

The trio paused, and Diego withdrew his revolver. Nathaniel's heart raced.

"No!" boomed a stentorian voice. "He dies slow." Nathaniel recognized the speaker as John Lawrence Plugford.

A piteous mewling sound emanated from the adjacent room.

"Where's our damn associate!?!" shouted a man who was either Stevie or Brent Plugford.

"We are bringing him to you!" Diego yelled up the hall.

"You have one minute," said a cold and certain voice that Nathaniel knew belonged to the tall gunfighter, Long Clay. "Each additional minute will result in another execution."

Muttering an imprecation, Diego secreted his weapon. "We are coming now!" He gripped the captive's left shoulder and pulled. "¡Rapidamente, rapidamente!"

Nathaniel clutched his burning stomach and hobbled forward. Xzavier hastened his strides with indelicate shoves. In front of the advancing men, the amber portal grew.

Nathaniel, Diego and Xzavier reached the end of the hallway and entered the vast funereal parlor. Opposite them stood Long Clay, wearing an iron tabard and a weird rubber mask atop his usual black clothing.

Xzavier stood Nathaniel upright.

Diego said, "We have done exactly as you—"

Long Clay's guns flashed.

Chapter XV
Your Whole Goddamn Life is Over

Two muzzles glared upon the clear disks that were Brent Plugford's goggles. Across the parlor, the left hand of the bearded Spaniard exploded, as the head of the Mexican with the branded neck jerked back. The perfectly concurrent shots resounded as one loud report within the parlor.

Presently, the cowboy adjusted his grip upon his sister, whom he shielded from the tableau.

Long Clay's gleaming barrels blazed a second time. The eyes of the bearded man turned black, and gore erupted from the rear of his twice-pierced head.

Gurgling, the Hispanic men fell to the nonagonal clay tiles.

The dandy, covered with dark fluids, stumbled forward, saw the blasted guards and was stunned.

Brent shouted at Nathaniel, "Get to the exit!"

"Over here!" yelled Patch Up from his position beside the stairwell.

Overwhelmed by the tableau, the dandy stared blankly at the negro.

"Go to him!" shouted Brent. "Now!"

"Get!" prompted Stevie.

A loud wail resounded in the hallway behind the dandy, and he turned around.

"Clear out!" yelled Brent.

A woman raced up the passage, toward the bearded man. "¡Diego!" she yelled. "¡Diego, mi Diego!"

The stunned dandy backed away, and the woman, who was pregnant, fell upon the body. Brent felt ill—he knew that the gunfighter had just killed the husband of the expecting mother.

"¡Diego, mi Diego!"

"Get away from her," Brent shouted at the bewildered dandy, "and go!"

The widow reached into her husband's jacket.

Long Clay pointed his guns at her face and heart.

"Don't let her draw!" yelled Brent.

The dandy lunged at the pregnant woman.

Nathaniel's back obscured the struggle for whatever weapon laid within the dead man's pocket.

"I kill, I kill!" the Mexican woman yelled, "¡Diablos—estan diablos!"

Long Clay pointed his revolvers at whatever parts of the pregnant widow were visible to him.

Ubaldo looked at gunfighter. "You no can kill the pregnant woman."

The dandy yelled at his bereaved adversary in Spanish.

Long Clay aimed at the woman's forehead and shoulder.

Stevie walked to the edge of the dais and pointed his shotgun at the entangled duo.

"Hold," John Lawrence Plugford commanded his youngest child.

The dandy won a small revolver from the woman's grasp, stumbled backwards and fell onto his buttocks.

Brent relaxed, as did Dolores.

"¡Vas al Infierno!" The widow threw a hard fist into the dandy's stomach.

Shrieking, the tall gentleman dropped the gun. The firearm clattered against the tiles.

The widow lunged for the weapon.

"No!" yelled Brent.

"Jesus!" exclaimed Patch Up.

Dolores hid behind her brother's iron tabard.

The widow grabbed the revolver.

Long Clay fired.

The pregnant woman shrieked.

Brent's stomach twisted, and Dolores gasped.

The revolver and two curled fingers struck the tiles.

"Get the gun," Long Clay said to the dandy. "Quickly."

Nathaniel clasped the weapon and collapsed onto his stomach. Beside him, the widow clutched her bleeding hand and wailed.

"Don't let her get it again." Long Clay switched out his guns for two fully-loaded replacements.

The prone dandy, pale and convulsive, grunted a reply, and Brent surmised that he had been tortured during his captivity.

"Let's make our departure," announced John Lawrence Plugford.

Upon the dais, Stevie faced the prostrated captives. "Stay flat on the ground 'til we're gone. ¿You Comprende?"

"Si," said the whores and gentlemen.

The young man leapt from the dais and walked toward the dandy. Long Clay monitored the dark catacomb portals with oscillating guns.

Patch Up shouted across the hall, "Once I've made a survey, I'll signal." The negro turned to the stairwell, pointed his repeater rifle into the darkness and ascended.

"Get that gun ready," Brent said to Dolores.

The redheaded woman clasped the nickel-plated revolver with both hands and pointed it forward. "Okay."

Then, the cowboy carried his sister past the blasted guards, toward the exit. The vast subterranean parlor was quiet, but for the sounds of footsteps and sobs. Brent tried not to think about the widow.

After ten strides, the twins reached the gunfighter and his captive.

"Look at me!" yelled Dolores.

Ubaldo turned around and looked at the redheaded woman.

"You hurt me for eight months," Dolores said, "but I'm leavin' this place, and you're whole goddamn life is over!" She aimed the revolver at the man's lower abdomen and squeezed the trigger. Gunpowder exploded flashing white.

A jet of urine sprayed from Ubaldo's pierced bladder, and he dropped to his knees, whimpering like a puppy. He shut his shiny eyes, and pink tears dripped from his open nasal cavity. His face slammed against the clay tiles.

Dolores aimed at the prostrated man's back and fired.

Ubaldo's vertebrae cracked. He choked and twitched, facedown in the puddle of blood and urine that his punctured body grew.

Brent saw that Dolores's hands were shaking.

"Get going," ordered Long Clay.

As the cowboy carried his sister toward the stairwell, which was less than fifteen yards away she cracked her gun in half, replaced the spent cartridges and sealed the weapon.

A dog barked.

"Get off of him!" shouted Stevie.

Brent looked over his shoulder and saw that the widow had fastened her bloody hands to the dandy's neck.

"I'll get her." Stevie set the heel of his right boot against the woman's neck and shoved her backwards. He pointed his shotgun at her inhabited belly.

"Don't!" yelled Brent and Dolores.

"You wanna have that little amigo?" asked Stevie.

The pale and bleeding woman seemed to understand that the young man's threat was real, and she remained still, clasping three red fingers with five others. Behind her in the hallway, a rust-colored mongrel growled.

Stevie hooked a hand beneath the dandy's armpit and helped him to his feet. "Can you walk?"

The saturated gentleman clutched his stomach as if it might drop out of his abdomen and strode toward the exit.

"Grab that dog!" John Lawrence Plugford said to Stevie.

"Okay."

Brent carried Dolores through the portal and into the dark stairwell.

"Come on up," Patch Up shouted from above, "it's clear!"

"Okay!" The cowboy looked down at his sister. "We're nearly out."

Dolores pointed the shaking gun forward.

Brent was a strong man (he did not abstain from digging latrines or breaking broncos or running fences or working tack as did most cowboy foremen), but his additional encumbrances—especially his sister and the iron tabard—made his climb up the steps an arduous journey. A minute of strained exertion brought him to the middle of the stairwell, where he paused, panted and rested his burning muscles.

"Still clear?" the cowboy shouted up the steps.

"Still clear!" confirmed the negro.

Brent resumed his ascent and heard his father enter the nether end of the stairwell.

"I can't believe it," muttered Dolores.

Above the siblings, the dark portal grew.

Brent transcended the final step and entered the anteroom, wherein hung the tapestry of the ancient ziggurat. Only one brass censer remained alight, and the cinnamon-and-vanilla smoke it yielded did not conceal the ripe smells of lichens and blood.

"I can't believe it's happening."

The cowboy carried his sister toward the vertical blue line that shone upon the far side of the anteroom. Prone beneath the glowing slit was a dead man who clutched a blunderbuss. The colorful feathers of a sunken arrow sprouted from his left nostril like a rectilinear flower.

Dolores pointed toward the deep blue light. "That's outside?"

"Yeah."

Tears poured down the woman's face.

"All clear?" inquired Brent.

"All clear!" Patch Up confirmed from outside.

"I can't believe it's really happening."

Brent carried his sister past the last censer, kicked open the iron door and walked through the portal. The twins entered an azure world.

"Oh my God," said Dolores. There was joy in her voice.

A dark blue Patch Up stood beside his dark blue wagon, pointing the bright blue barrel of his repeater rifle across the deep blue plain, toward mountains comprised of variegated blue hues. He waved a light blue palm at the siblings.

"How'd it get to be mornin'?" asked Dolores.

"I don't know," Patch Up said, "I thought it was still hours away."

Brent surveyed the horizons, all of which were clear, and counted his crew's horses, all of which were present. Sprawled nearby were seven men with arrows in their heads and hearts.

"That Deep Lakes came with you," stated Dolores.

"He did."

The woman pointed a blue finger at the pale palfrey. "You brung out Elizabeth."

"Think you can ride her?"

"I can, but Yvette can't sit hers."

"I know it."

Brent heard someone directly behind him, glanced over his shoulder and saw his father bear Yvette, who was enshrouded, into the azure world.

"Any adversaries?" inquired John Lawrence Plugford.

"None standing, approaching or throwing bullets," replied Patch Up.

Brent brought Dolores to her horse, and she returned the nickel-plated revolver to his holster. He set her posterior upon the embroidered sidesaddle, and she righted herself.

"Gimme back the gun."

The cowboy gave the gun to his sister. "You want a holster?"

"I'll hold it."

"Tie somethin' to the handle, so if you drop it, it ain't lost."

"I may be a cancan girl with one foot, but I still got brains."

Brent kissed Dolores's hand and approached his brindled mustang.

John Lawrence Plugford carried his covered daughter toward the white stallion.

"J.L." Patch Up patted the wagon bench. "Put Yvette up here with me."

"I'll hold her."

"Laid out on the bench is better—she shouldn't get tussled."

"I'll hold her so she don't get tussled." The patriarch would not relinquish his girl.

The dandy emerged from Catacumbas, gripping his stomach and wearing a beard of blue-black ichor.

"Can you ride your horse?" asked Brent.

The dandy glared at the cowboy and walked like a weary crone toward his deep blue mare. Four hundred and fifty dollars seemed like incredibly poor wages for whatever tortures he had endured, and Brent did not in any way begrudge the gentleman's anger. Nobody had expected this rescue to become so dangerous or so complicated.

Stevie emerged from Catacumbas, cradling the fifty-pound mongrel in his arms. "I got the dog."

"Put it in the wagon," Brent said, "and get on your horse."

Patch Up received the dog from Stevie and set it within the canopy, where it barked thrice. Brent mounted his brindled mustang. John Lawrence Plugford, holding Yvette to his chest, climbed onto his sturdy white stallion. Stevie mounted his spotted colt.

An explosion thundered within Catacumbas. The ground shook, and Brent felt tremors deep inside his chest.

"What's happenin'?" asked Dolores.

"Long Clay's sealin' up the stairs, so we can get us a good lead."

A second explosion shook the ziggurat ruins. The doorway exhaled a column of azure smoke, and Long Clay materialized, walking.

"Bust up their wagons," John Lawrence Plugford boomed, "and slaughter their horses."

Long Clay reached underneath his tabard, withdrew an oblong grenade, attached a rear taper and hurled the device into the air, toward the horses and stagecoaches that were situated on the east side of the edifice. A mare's neck depressed the plunger, and the device exploded. The horse, nine of its neighbors and four stagecoaches were consumed by the white burst. Against the azure sky, blue limbs spun, blue gore rained and blue entrails twisted.

The remaining animals jerked upon their tethers, but were unable to break loose.

Brent pointed his pistol at the right foreleg of a colt and squeezed the trigger. The beast shrieked and collapsed to the plain. He aimed his gun at the limb of another creature and fired. The animal pitched forward and broke its neck. "Hell."

Stevie fired his shotgun. Buckshot peppered the chests of several horses. They shrieked and bucked, but did not fall.

"Them pellets won't put any down from this distance," chastened Brent. "Use a rifle or a revolver." The cowboy aimed at an animal leg and fired. A dark blue horse collapsed, rolled onto its back and kicked three hooves at the sky.

Stevie sheathed his shotgun, drew his revolver, aimed and shot a horse through the foreleg. It screeched and tumbled to the plain.

Dolores turned her horse away from the massacre.

Long Clay hurled a grenade into the air.

Brent cracked his gun in half, dumped spent rounds to the plain, filled the empty chambers with new bullets and shut his revolver, which clicked.

The plunger struck the roof of a stagecoach, and the grenade detonated. A bright explosion wiped the heads off of seven nearby horses and tore open the sides of five others. Eviscerated and decapitated animals staggered, and a mare with a dangling head trampled the neck of a fallen palfrey that shrieked like a human child.

Dolores pressed her palms to her ears.

Beneath her blanket, Yvette wept.

The dandy stared at the ground.

Brent surveyed the fog of blue dust that obscured the dead and dying animals. Beside an upended black stagecoach were two terrified horses, straining against and nibbling their lines. "Over there." He pointed his revolver.

"I see 'em," said Stevie.

The brothers fired their guns, and the animals collapsed to the plain. Brent heard (or imagined) human shrieks amidst the bestial cacophony, and he wondered if nightmares of this gruesome scene would haunt his sleeping mind for the remainder of his life.

Long Clay mounted his black mare.

John Lawrence Plugford pointed north. "Go!"

Patch Up cracked his whip at the braced quartet, and wagon wheels turned. Brent, Stevie, Dolores and the dandy urged their steeds into a quick canter. John Lawrence Plugford, cradling Yvette and trailing her spotted palfrey, coaxed his mustang into action. Long Clay shadowed.

The Plugford crew departed Catacumbas.

As they did so, the hard stone that had been stuck in Brent's guts for eight months shrank. Although his sisters were not yet safe, they were free and alive, breathing the open air of the great landscape.

Hooves rumbled, and the ruins shrank.

The crew rode north across the blue plain.

Dolores and the dandy rode in-between the flanking brothers, directly behind Patch Up's rumbling wagon. John Lawrence Plugford and Long Clay followed from a distance of forty yards.

"Can we take off these goddamn masks?' Stevie asked from the saddle of his spotted colt. "Mine's drippin' with sweat."

"Not just yet," replied Brent. (Long Clay had told them to wear their masks until they were well beyond the mountain range.)

"They must've figured out who we are anyway."

"That ain't the same as knowin' what we look like."

"I s'pose."

All of Brent's limbs burned, and his throat was raw from yelling. He sat up straight and felt a tight pain in his lower back—a strained or torn muscle. "Hell." Wondering at the greater agonies that his twin sister endured, the cowboy looked east.

Dolores rode the pale palfrey, staring forward and clutching the nickel-plated revolver. Her right leg was nestled in the fixed horn of the sidesaddle, but her shorn leg, although pressed to the leaping horn, did not reach the stirrup and bounced freely against the horse's side.

"Dolores."

The woman glanced at her brother.

"You feel steady?"

"Enough to hold on. Where we goin' to?"

Brent pointed at the distant mountains. "Deep Lakes descried a pass in the north part of the range."

"Let's get there."

"We will."

In front of the Plugfords, blue mountains of one hundred shades expanded.

Yvette's dog clambered to the back of the wagon and barked. A mildewed shirt that was an ersatz patch came loose from the canopy and flew into the air. The specter flitted in-between the twins and twisted weirdly in the wind.

Brent heard something whistle past him. Upon the back of the wagon, a panel cracked and turned into splinters. The dog howled.

"Somebody's shootin' at—" Brent's head jerked forward on his neck. His right goggle eye turned red. Warm fluid ran down the right side of his face and soaked his ear.

The cowboy gripped the neck of his rubber mask, tore it from his head and flung it to the ground. He pressed the heel of his right hand to the side of his head and felt sharp splinters that he knew were bits of his skull.

"Get low in the saddle!" yelled Brent.

Dolores looked at her brother and screamed.

"Get down low!" repeated the cowboy. "Right now!" He hunched forward.

Dolores leaned forward so that she was hidden behind her large saddlebag. "Brent," she yelled, "your head!"

Stevie looked over and was stunned.

"Low in the saddle!" yelled the cowboy.

Stevie and the dandy pressed themselves flush against the backs of their horses. A bullet clanged upon the youngest Plugford's angled tabard and whistled into the sky.

The cowboy clutched his grazed head and felt blood, skull bits, hair and loose skin. "Hell." A bullet whistled past his shoulder and lanced the wagon canopy.

Brent swiveled in his saddle. Forty yards behind him, John Lawrence Plugford, astride his galloping white mustang, huddled protectively over his daughter. Twenty yards south of the patriarch, Long Clay withdrew a telescopic rifle from the vertical wooden case that was fastened to his black mare's haunches.

A distant gunshot cracked. The bullet clanged upon John Lawrence Plugford's tabard and caromed across the plain.

"Goddamn, goddamn!" exclaimed Stevie.

Brent glanced forward and saw that Patch Up had joined Yvette's dog at the rear of the wagon, which was now driverless.

Huddled behind a crate of gear, the negro looked through his brass and ivory spyglass. "There's an automobile!" he yelled. "They've got an automobile!"

Brent glanced past his horse's flashing tail at the southern horizon, but could not discern the vehicle.

"Shoot it to hell, Long Clay!" Stevie advised from his spotted colt. "Bust it to pieces!"

A distant gunshot cracked. The dandy's tan mare shrieked, leaped (as if hurdling a hedge) and impacted the plain. Jarred, the blonde man spewed darkness.

Long Clay prostrated himself across his black mare's spine and aimed his telescopic rifle over the beast's tail. He fired. The gunshot resounded within the vast bowl of mountains and became a tattoo of asynchronous echoes.

"You got someone!" Patch Up shouted from the rear of the driverless wagon.

Long Clay discharged the spent shell. Upon the southern horizon, a tiny black rectangle trailed dust and vibrated.

"Brent," Dolores shouted, "you gotta do something 'bout your head right now!"

The bleeding cowboy recalled his friend Isaac Isaacs, who had been swatted by a bear in South Carolina and afterwards staunched the severest lacerations with breadcrumbs. "Hell." Brent plunged his left hand into his saddlebag, searched for the victuals sack, located it, opened its drawstrings, reached inside, made a fist and withdrew dry oats. Gritting his teeth, he uncovered the wound on his head and filled it with grain.

The world turned black.

Dolores screamed.

Brent regained consciousness and found that he was hugging the neck of his horse. A bullet clanged upon his tabard and caromed into the air.

"You okay?" asked Dolores.

"Yeah." The cowboy turned his head and saw Long Clay, who was backwards and prone upon his horse, aiming his telescopic rifle at the distant pursuer. Presently, he fired.

"You got the driver in the shoulder!" shouted Patch Up. The dog barked jubilantly.

Suddenly, the vibrating black rectangle slid to the west and disappeared inside its own blue wake.

"We killed your dumb automob'le!" jeered Stevie. "Time to roast it up and put it in your uncle's burrito!"

Through the telescopic sight, Long Clay monitored the veil of blue dust that obscured the vehicle, Catacumbas and the southern mountains.

"Keep apace!" ordered John Lawrence Plugford.

The blue plain scrolled underneath blurry blue hooves.

"Brent!" shouted Stevie.

"Yeah?"

"You got oats on your head!"

"I know."

"You gonna be okay?"

"I'll find out when we stop." The cowboy's extremities felt cold.

"They're still coming," warned Patch Up. "Unhappily!"

Brent looked south. Once again, the vibrating black rectangle sat at the vanguard of a large blue wake.

"Go for the tires," said John Lawrence Plugford.

Long Clay fired.

"Got their fender!" shouted Patch Up.

A distant gunshot cracked. John Lawrence Plugford's white stallion reared up and shrieked. The patriarch grabbed his saddle horn and hunched over his daughter. Upon its hind legs, the beast twisted and bucked.

Brent saw that the pursuers had a clear shot at his father. "Pa! Watch it they—"

A distant gunshot cracked. John Lawrence Plugford's goggles turned red.

"No!" shouted Brent.

"Daddy!" cried Dolores.

"J.L.!" yelled Patch Up.

The agitated white horse returned its forelegs to the plain. John Lawrence Plugford collapsed onto his daughter, but remained in the saddle, gripping the horn.

Stevie shouted, "Goddamn, goddamn, goddamn!"

Brent felt empty.

"Keep riding north!" shouted Long Clay. "I'll get them." He turned himself forward.

Stevie pulled tack and said, "I'll help—"

"Keep ridin'!" Brent yelled at his brother. "You can't get shot too!" The cowboy felt as if he were witnessing the awful scene from a great distance, over the shoulder of an uninterested God. "We gotta make all this worth somethin'."

Stevie yanked off his mask and threw it down. "Goddamn!" The colt's left foreleg flung the empty rubber head into the air. "I'm goin' to kill all them fellas that did this! All of them!"

"I hate this!" shouted Dolores. "I hate this!" She clasped the mane of her galloping palfrey and yelled, "Goddamn this mis'rable world! I hate all of it—every bit!"

"Keep low in the saddle!" the cowboy yelled at his siblings.

Dolores and Stevie lowered themselves, and Brent looked back.

Long Clay reached the white stallion and dismounted.

A distant gunshot cracked, and the bullet whistled overhead.

"Rotten bastards!" yelled Stevie. "Dumb Mex'cans!"

With his sharp black boots planted on solid ground, the gunfighter aimed his telescopic rifle at the vibrating black rectangle, squeezed the trigger, slid the bolt and fired a second shot.

"Got the driver in the neck!" shouted Patch Up.

The small black rectangle swerved and disappeared into a blue plume.

Long Clay slung his telescopic rifle onto his left shoulder and took Yvette from beneath the huddled body of John Lawrence Plugford. Skeletal fingers emerged from the blanket, clasped the patriarch's huge right hand and let go.

The gunfighter set Yvette upon the ground, laid John Lawrence Plugford across the saddle, secured the body, took a line from the animal's bridal, scooped up the woman, mounted his black steed and hastened forward.

Brent looked north. Sitting upon a crate at the rear of the rumbling wagon was Patch Up. The cowboy could not look at the negro's face.

In front of the fleeing Plugford crew expanded the north range of Gran Manos. The eastern faces of the mountains were ablaze with sunlight and sharply contrasted the major part of the blue vista, as if the whole tableau were an enormous stencil, backlighted by a white fire that would sear the eyes of any man stupid enough to look up.

Brent Plugford felt small, inconsequential and weak.

Part IIII

The Blood Hierarchy

Chapter I
Elixirs Denied and Given

Yvette Upfield looked at the tall narrow man who held her bundled body. A rubber mask concealed most of his face, excepting his blue eyes, which were visible through his blood-spattered goggles. An uneasy feeling burgeoned within the choirmaster's heart, and she turned away from the dark man.

A luminous white stallion appeared.

Tied across the saddle of the animal was a huge arch of flesh that was John Lawrence Plugford. The man's hands and feet reached toward the ground, swaying like the frills at the bottom of a dress. Tethered to the funereal animal and wearing a sidesaddle was a brown palfrey that Yvette had not ridden since her wedding day.

"My father's dead, isn't he?"

"He is."

Yvette felt cold. "They shot him."

"They did."

With a hard skeletal hand, Yvette wiped tears from her eyes. "I'll say a prayer for him." Although John Lawrence Plugford was a good and loving father, he was an unbeliever who had committed many terrible sins, and the choirmaster doubted the efficacy of any prayer that she might say on his behalf.

"Do that," said the tall narrow man.

Yvette closed her eyes and attempted to recall the words Minister Johnstone had uttered at Roger Field's funeral service, but her dependent body cried out like a starving mendicant. The world wrought by God—the sphere of clouds, mountains, trees, churches, families, horses, dogs, bugs, diseases, rape and murder—shrank until it became one sharp scintillating point from which dripped the elixir of salvation.

The woman who had forgotten her name opened her eyes and looked up at the stranger. "I need medicine."

"How long since your last shot?"

"All I had in the last four days was a tiny bit last night. It wasn't—"

"You went through withdrawal?"

"I did, but—"

"You're through the worst of it."

"I need some now."

"I don't argue."

"But you have to find something." Yvette began to tremble. "I can feel my insides." A paroxysm seized her body and she kicked her left leg.

Coolly, the tall narrow man looked away.

The woman who had forgotten her name rested her heavy head, shut her eyes and tried to send forth her soul.

A hoof shattered a rock and awakened Yvette. Ahead of her, mounted insects, which were her siblings and the tall blonde gentleman who had refused to look at her naked body, ascended the steep terrain, preceded by the family wagon. Sand and stones dripped from the hooves of the straining beasts and rattled down the incline.

Yvette adjusted her cold and wet blanket. "Did it rain?"

"You have a fever," stated the tall narrow stranger.

"I need my medicine is why. I'm gonna die—you don't understand." The woman convulsed twice, and felt as if she were about to vomit. "I need it!" Clear fluid dripped from her nose.

The mounted insects that were her siblings looked back.

"Is Yvette okay?" asked Brent.

"She's fine," answered the tall narrow man.

To her brother, Yvette yelled, "I'm gonna die!"

The stranger looked down at her and said, "You must rest."

"You're the devil! I know it!" Yvette's skin was burning and she smelled sulfur. "You're the devil in the flesh!"

The tall narrow man stroked her forehead.

"Where's my Samuel? Do you know what happened to him? Why he ain't—why he isn't here?"

"You must rest."

"I'm gonna die!"

The black horse crested a ridge. Yvette watched her father, borne by the white stallion, rise from the dirt. The emaciated woman trembled, shut her eyes, curled herself into a ball within the devil's arms and heard something hiss.

The darkness expanded.

Twenty-two years old and wearing a modest tan dress, Yvette Plugford marched through the swinging doors of Bess Hack's Saloon of San Francisco. Heads emerged from slumped shoulders, turned toward the new arrival and flashed watery eyes that were simultaneously defeated and stimulated. The blonde woman surveyed the champions who intended to conquer their sobriety two hours before noon on a Wednesday. Atop a wooden barstool and melting like a candle was Gunther Linderson, the sixty-two-year-old organ player.

Yvette approached the negligent musician. “Mr. Linderson.”

The Swedish organist lifted his flat face from his hands and swiveled. “Miss Plugford.” His eyes were red and his overalls smelled like August.

“I’m not goin’ to lecture you.”

“This is how the lectures begin.”

“We don’t got—we don’t have any time. You were supposed to be at the church thirty minutes ago. Lots of folks depend on you.”

“I’m independent.”

“You’re drunk is what you are. Let’s go.” The choirmaster grabbed the Swedish man’s right elbow and tugged.

Mr. Linderson did not rise from his seat.

Yvette looked at the stout and dour barmaid, Bess Hack, who was her eternal adversary. “I asked you to mind what he drank on Wednesdays.”

“I heard your request.”

The choirmaster knew that she did not have time to scold the woman properly, and thus focused her energies upon the organist’s arm. “Don’t make this difficult.”

A diminutive and dapper blonde man, wearing an olive three-piece suit and matching bowler cap, strode toward the bar. To Yvette, he said, “Allow me to offer my assistance.”

“Get his legs.”

The pretty gentleman grinned and said, “I have a bottle that will help restore him—a healthful elixir that provides energy and combats the affects of alcohol.”

Mr. Linderson was aghast. “Why do you have such a terrible thing?”

“I only wish to help you fulfill your obligations.”

“We ain’t—we aren’t buying any cure-alls,” said Yvette.

“What I proffer is not a cure-all, but rather a highly effective restorative.” The dapper salesman pointed a scintillating index fingernail at the organist. “I shall administer to this dilapidated fellow—”

“What are you calling me?”

“I shall administer to this dilapidated fellow one free dosage of my elixir and, in so doing, prove its highly potent efficacy.” The dapper salesman revealed the whitest teeth that Yvette had ever seen.

“Okay.” The choirmaster looked at her frowning adversary behind the bar. “Please give Mr. Linderson a cup.”

“We don’t have ‘cups’ in this saloon.” Bess Hack slammed a small glass upon the table. “We have tumblers.”

Yvette held her tongue.

The dapper salesman reached inside his olive jacket and withdrew a dark flat bottle that bore a caricature of himself, smiling and winking, and the words, *Upfield’s*

Restorative Elixir. His finely-manicured fingers rotated the bottle one hundred and eighty degrees so that Yvette and the barmaid could see the declaration, *'It certainly works!'*

"The size of the dosage," the dapper salesman informed the women, "is mathematically proportional to the patient's body mass." He appraised the organist, nodded, removed the cork and poured out a thick, tarry concoction.

"I know what death looks like," remarked Mr. Linderson.

"Drink it down," said Yvette.

The drunken organist raised the tumbler to his lips, shut his eyes, opened his mouth, tossed the ichor inside and swallowed.

Expectantly, the salesman folded his hands.

Yvette and Bess Hack waited.

Mr. Linderson opened his eyes. "This tastes like coffee."

"That is one of the elixir's numerous ingredients."

The organist savored the flavor a moment longer. "Bad coffee with some prune juice and black pepper." He smacked his lips. "Maybe cinnamon."

"Do you feel restored?" asked Yvette.

"I feel—" The fellow clutched his stomach and rose to his feet. "I need a latrine."

"Behold the self-motivated man!" The dapper salesman threw his hands to Heaven for emphasis.

Mr. Linderson ambled toward the swinging doors, and Bess Hack walked toward wanting inebriates at the far end of the bar.

Yvette looked at the dapper salesman. "Thanks for helpin',"

"You are quite welcome. And please call upon me, Samuel C. Upfield IV, at Hotel Adams, should you wish to purchase a supply of the elixir."

"Okay." The choirmaster walked after the organist, paused and looked back at the ebullient, articulate and pretty little dandy. "You should come on over to church if you want to connect with some good folks and God. I know that the life of a traveling salesman can be lonesome."

"Thank you for your invitation." Samuel C. Upfield IV replaced his elixir bottle within his jacket and ruminated momentarily. "I have not been to church in several months, and I feel an absence."

"I'll be there too," stated Yvette.

"Then I have absolutely no choice, but to attend." Samuel C. Upfield IV looked directly into Yvette's eyes and smiled brilliantly.

The woman's pulse quickened.

Darkness receded.

Wind blew upon Yvette Upfield's forehead and snapped the fabric of her damp blanket. Beneath her spine, heavy hooves rumbled like boiling water. The emaciated woman opened her eyes and saw the triangular bronze face of the man who carried her. Cold blue gems glinted beneath his iron eyebrows, and a slender silver mustache sat atop the slit that denied her requests for medicine. The sun glared, tiny and hostile, upon his right shoulder.

Shielding her eyes from the burning orb, the woman looked south and saw, upon the white stallion, her dead father, far larger than the mountain range that laid behind him.

"How long've I been out?" Yvette's mouth was dry and pasty, and the air was hot.

"Two hours. How do you feel?"

"My head hurts bad."

"Are you hungry?"

Yvette tasted the sour chicken soup upon which she had subsisted for the last eight months and shuddered. "No."

"Drink slowly."

A canteen appeared. Yvette took the vessel, removed its stopper and poured cool water into her dry, empty body.

"You must rest." Gloved hands reclaimed the canteen.

"I'm not tired."

The tall narrow man pulled the blanket over the world. "Rest."

"I'm not tired." Yvette's eyelids drooped. "I'm not tired." Hooves boiled, darkness expanded, and in a dream that was reality, the wagon bench pressed against her back.

Chapter II
A Brief Respite for the Troglodytes

Pincers pricked Nathaniel Stromler's soft palate, and spindly legs poked his cheeks. For the fifth time in thirty seconds, the tall gentleman from Michigan coughed as hard as he could.

"I think the dandy's chokin' to death," Stevie remarked from atop his cantering colt.

Nathaniel reached his left index finger and thumb into his mouth, pinched the prickly scorpion corpse and pulled. The tail slid up his throat and its folded legs blossomed like a hideous flower.

Dolores yelled.

"Goddamn!"

"Does he need help?" Patch Up asked from the front of the rumbling wagon.

The gentleman flung the scorpion to the brown dirt, attempted to speak, felt a sharp pain in his throat, coughed up an insectile leg, spat it out and shook his head.

"He don't," replied Stevie.

Nathaniel had dislodged two of the ingested scorpions, but the third was no longer a presence within his throat or stomach and had descended into his intestines. The journey and ultimate emergence of the dead arachnid was not a pleasant thing to ponder.

On the northern horizon, creosote bushes, yucca trees and black grama expanded like spilled paint. The stand of vegetation was far taller and broader than anything Nathaniel recalled seeing on the journey down and engendered a new concern.

He spat bile and oil and hastened his horse forward, toward the wagon. The tan mare, exhausted and carrying a bullet in its hindquarters, strained to close the distance.

"Your horse ain't doin' much better than you," remarked Stevie.

(The young man was not Nathaniel's favorite Plugford.)

Presently, the tan mare overtook the wagon until the gentleman and the negro rode abreast. Upon the bench beside Patch Up was the unconscious body of Yvette, whom Long Clay had deposited an hour earlier.

The negro said, "It's the dandy," and smiled sadly. Underneath the canopy, the circus dog barked.

"This is not the way we came," observed Nathaniel.

"You're correct."

"Why are we not riding directly for Leesville?"

"Do you want to lead whoever's following us into a town filled with innocent folks? To your fiancé?"

Nathaniel became uneasy. "Is it a certainty that we have pursuers?"

"You're much smarter than that question, Mr. Stromler."

Creosote leaves slapped the legs of the horses, and stalks of dry black grama crackled underneath the wagon's wheels. The tan mare bucked, unhappy with the flagellant flora, and Nathaniel gripped the horn to steady himself. Upon the bench, the bundled body of Yvette stirred.

"Goddamn," Stevie cried, "lookit Brent!"

Patch Up rose from the bench and gazed over the canopy; Nathaniel faced south. The cowboy was slumped forward in his saddle, unconscious.

"We gotta get him before he falls!" Dolores reined her palfrey toward her brother and her red hair flashed south.

Brent wobbled in the saddle of the cantering mustang.

"Wake up!" Stevie drove spurs into his spotted colt and rode hard. "Get the hell awake!" His horse thundered.

Creosote leaves slapped Brent's dangling right arm.

"Wake up!" yelled Dolores. "Brent!" Her palfrey galloped.

A bramble snatched a glove from the unconscious rider's dangling hand.

"Wake up!" Stevie, twenty yards distant, fired his shotgun into the air.

Brent slid from the saddle.

A shadow grabbed the cowboy's collar and resettled him. "Everyone hold here!" Long Clay snatched the brindled mustang's loose reins.

Nathaniel slowed his horse; Patch Up pulled tack; Dolores and Stevie rode beside the gunfighter. Hooves and wagon wheels crushed irritating flora and stopped.

The negro stood from his bench and turned around. "Is he bleeding?"

"Not currently," replied Long Clay.

"Bring him here—I'll fetch my needles and snippers."

The gunfighter, trailing the white stallion, the brown palfrey and the brindled mustang, approached the wagon, followed by Stevie and Dolores. Ambitious black grama blades harassed the pendulous limbs of John Lawrence Plugford and his wounded son.

Long Clay dropped from his horse, lifted Brent from the brindled mustang and set him inside the canopy, beside the pile of iron tabards.

"All of you are troglodytes!" Patch Up proclaimed from deep within the wagon. "Imbecilic troglodytes!" The circus dog barked a confirmation of the more descriptive rejoinder.

Long Clay, Dolores and Nathaniel silently accepted the insult.

After a moment, Stevie said, "He told us he could ride."

Patch Up spun around, and his face filled with anger. “Does he look savvy?” The negro pointed a pair of bright medical scissors at Brent’s wound. “Is that what head trauma usually yields? Clear-thinking?”

“I didn’t think it—”

“And which one of you shoved oats into the wound?”

“He did that himself!” tattled Stevie.

“Heat up some water,” Patch Up said to the youngest Plugford. “I need to flush this clean before I can mend it.”

Stevie jumped out of his saddle, bounded three strides, clambered into the wagon and opened a crate.

“Keep the fire small,” Long Clay ordered, “and disperse the smoke.”

“I will help.” Nathaniel held his stomach and climbed from his mare.

Stevie raised a tin kettle of boiling water from the three-tongue fire and carried it toward the wagon. Nathaniel dispersed smoke with a mildewed shirt that smelled far better than did he.

Underneath the canopy, Patch Up received the steaming vessel and set it beside his patient. “You stay in the vicinity in case we need to brace him.”

“I will.” Stevie stared at his brother, concerned.

Patch Up dropped a white cloth into the pot, wrung out the excess water and pressed the hot fabric to the hairy raspberry cobbler that was the side of Brent’s head. The cowboy flinched, but did not awaken. “Oats,” lamented the negro. The circus dog yawned derisively.

Nathaniel saw a white splinter that he recognized as a skull shard and turned away from the grim ministrations.

Sitting atop a flat stone on the opposite side of the three-tongue fire was Dolores. Her legs were concealed beneath the hem of the lavender dress into which she had just changed, and in her lap was a water canteen.

“How are you feeling?” inquired the gentleman.

“Weak, but okay…considerin’.” Dolores looked at the fire. “I want to apologize for hittin’ you—back in Catacumbas. And yellin’ at you.”

“I had completely forgotten about that.”

“I was real drunk, but it was wrong and I’m sorry I did it.”

“You are forgiven.” Nathaniel dispersed smoke with the mildewed shirt. “Your assault was quite mild compared to the violence I have seen and experienced these last two days.”

“I’m glad you ain’t holdin’ no grudge.” Dolores drank from a canteen and handed it over to him.

"Thank you."

"You got yourself a woman?"

"I do." Nathaniel drank from the canteen.

Dolores adjusted the hem that covered her mismatched legs. "Is she pretty?"

"She is pretty."

"I bet she's got culture, too. Speaks good English and knows all about which forks to use at dinner and Europe and things like that, don't she?"

Nathaniel felt that it would be unkind to articulate Kathleen O'Corley's many virtues to Dolores. "She is a good woman."

"You married her?'

"We are engaged to be married."

"That must be real nice," Dolores said, "to have all that to look forward to."

The woman's statement contained a note of defeat, and the gentleman was unable to do anything but nod an affirmation as if he were mute.

A man yelled.

"Hold him!"

Nathaniel and Dolores looked over at the wagon.

Stevie braced Brent's shifting shoulders as Patch Up guided the needle through skin and air.

"Do you fellows need any assistance?" inquired the gentleman.

"We got him," said Stevie.

Nathaniel turned back to the three-tongue fire, raised the mildewed shirt, and saw a dusty figure emerge from the yuccas.

"What's wrong?" asked Dolores.

Presently, the gentleman recognized the new arrival. "Deep Lakes has materialized."

"Greetings," hailed the native, as he approached.

"Greetings," replied Nathaniel and Dolores.

Two bird carcasses hung from Deep Lakes's denim vest, and his right hand gripped the strange bow, which had seven holes arranged in cruciform upon its belly and three strings. Dark brown poultices sat like huge leeches atop injuries on his left ear and shoulder.

Dolores pivoted upon her stone and looked up at Deep Lakes. "Thanks for helpin'."

"I'm sorry about what happened to your father."

The woman shut her eyes and nodded.

"We leave in five minutes," Long Clay announced from beside his black horse. "Brent will stay in the wagon." The gunfighter pointed at the gentleman. "Ride his mustang instead of your mare."

"What is our destination?"

"An outlying part of the New Mexico Territory."

"And what exactly shall we do there?" pressed Nathaniel.

"I can't accurately answer that question until I've gauged our opposition." Long Clay turned away from the gentleman.

"Do you intend to treat them as kindly as you did those horses and that pregnant woman?"

Upon sharp black boots, the gunfighter strode directly toward his critic. "Would you like to proffer some advice on how I should run things?" The viperous visage loomed, radiating the smells of iron, blood and cinders. "Please opine, Mr. Stromler."

Nathaniel would not be bullied. "Do not try to intimidate me. I deserve truthful and clear responses. After what I have suffered, I demand them."

"Let me clarify the hierarchy." Long Clay unbuckled his gun belt.

"Don't," said Dolores.

The revolvers landed upon the dirt.

Nathaniel positioned his feet as he had during his college fencing tournaments, but he raised fists instead of a rapier. Although he was certain that he would lose, he would do his best to land a few satisfying blows.

"Clay!" Patch Up shouted from deep within the wagon. "If you punch the dandy, you'll lose your cook and your doctor."

Long Clay paused.

"And if you get yourself shot," the negro elaborated, "you'll hear some heartless nigger whistling gay tunes while you bleed to death. That'll be me."

Long Clay snorted.

"You know I don't bluff."

The gunfighter picked up his weapons. "I am aware."

Relieved, Nathaniel lowered his fists.

"The dandy deserves to have his questions answered," stated Patch Up. "Tell him the plan."

The gunfighter refastened his belt and looked at the gentleman. "Our pursuers are invested in us, and they'll give chase until there's a violent confrontation. We need to kill all of them or diminish their number until they are cowed."

Nathaniel's stomach sank. "The well-considered plan is to have a shootout with however many men are following us and…and…hope that we are victorious?"

Long Clay's mouth became a thin line. "J.L. and I located a fort that will give us a big tactical advantage. That's where we're going. If you don't approve of this plan, I suggest that you ride off and see what follows you home." The gunfighter strode away.

Nathaniel felt helpless, as if he were stuck in the middle of a war between two foreign countries. "I am not going to kill anybody."

Seated upon the back of the wagon, Stevie inquired, "What're you gonna do while we're throwin' bullets into Mex'cans? Play chess with the dog?"

"Be quiet you ingrate," hissed Patch Up. "Respect that this man's already suffered overmuch for a bunch of damn strangers."

"You should take one of Pa's guns," suggested Dolores.

"No."

"Why not?"

Nathaniel walked away from the three-tongue fire. He approached the assigned mustang and recalled the day, twelve years ago, when his father had summoned the entire family to the library.

Mother, Grandmother, Isabella and Nathaniel seated themselves upon the sofa, and the silver-haired patriarch dropped his English wool jacket directly onto the floor, which was a unique occurrence in the history of the Stromler household. The perspicacious youth knew that something was terribly amiss.

"There was an incident at the bank," announced Howard Stromler. "A…dreadful incident."

"Were sums taken?" asked Nathaniel.

"What has occurred?" Mother's voice trembled.

Howard Stromler wiped his gleaming forehead with a French cuff. "I was in the vault, alone and with the door open, when I first heard the disturbance. It emanated from the lobby. The clamor grew louder, and I heard someone scream.

"I took the emergency rifle from the wall, and an angry man yelled, 'Everybody get on the ground!' and there was a gunshot, and I heard a man cry out in pain.

"I drew a cartridge into the chamber of the rifle and slid the bolt forward, slowly and quietly, so that I would not be discovered. The mechanism clicked, and the bullet was in place.

"A woman got hysterical, and the angry man said, 'Shut her up or I will!' and I heard people try to quieten her, and I heard the angry man yell, 'Take me to the vault!' and I pointed the gun toward the hall, and I heard footsteps on the floor, and I saw a shadow rise up on the open door, and I saw the angry man walk into the vault, and…

"And…

"I squeezed the trigger. The bullet went over his arm, hit the metal door and ricocheted.

"And I heard the teller scream."

Nathaniel was stunned.

"Two people shot the angry man in the back, and the other robber was overpowered, but I could not move. I just held the rifle and stared at the smoke that rose from its muzzle until it was invisible.

"I heard someone yell, Candace Carter is dead!' and I knew that it was my bullet that had killed her. I killed her. I took a human life."

"It was an accident," protested Nathaniel.

"I killed an innocent woman."

Nathaniel's father never again returned to work. He became tacit and replaced his daily meals with increasing amounts of whisky. At night, he wandered through the snow-covered woodlands and became violent if anybody tried to stop him. On one occasion, the forty-six-year-old man had disappeared for a period of three days, and when his family finally recovered him in a neighboring town, he failed to recognize them.

Five months after the incident, Howard Stromler was discovered in the bank vault. The barrel of the security rifle was in his mouth, and the steel walls were splashed with his red guilt. Soon thereafter, the remaining Stromlers moved to a different town in Michigan and took no more trips to Europe.

"He's mended."

Nathaniel looked into the wagon. Patch Up rested Brent's bandaged head upon a rolled-up towel, and Stevie buttoned his brother's shirt.

"Get to your horses," ordered Long Clay.

"Mr. Stromler."

Nathaniel looked over at Dolores.

"Will you help me onto mine?"

Long Clay said, "Stevie will assist you."

"I'll get her." Bearing red keepsakes from his brother upon his sleeves, Stevie hastened from the rear of the wagon, toward Dolores.

Nathaniel knew that the interference had been deliberate (Long Clay clearly did not want the gentleman to have any more allies in the crew), but he would not remark upon such a triviality. He walked toward the brindled mustang previously ridden (and stained) by the cowboy.

"Deep Lakes."

The native looked at the gunfighter.

"Poison the site."

"I shall."

Stevie inquired, "What're you leavin' behind?"

Deep Lakes extricated a crackling sack from a burlap bag. "Datura and caladium leaves soaked in lard."

"I hope them Mex'can horses are hungry."

Nathaniel grabbed the saddle horn and pulled himself atop Brent's brindled mustang. A pain shot across his stomach, but he remained silent.

Stevie scooped Dolores from the ground and carried her to the pale palfrey.

"Poison some potatoes and a rasher of bacon," Long Clay added, "and leave it in a victual sack by the fire, like we forgot it. We might get more than just horses."

Nathaniel turned the mustang north so that he did not have to look at the loathsome gunfighter.

Chapter III
Defining the New Mr. Plugford

Lying upon the rattling wagon bed, Brent Plugford awakened, turned his head to the left and looked at the huge man who laid directly beside him. A wheel struck a stone, and blood sluiced across the goggles that covered the eyes of John Lawrence Plugford.

The cowboy turned away from his deceased father, lifted his stitched head, looked past the brass tips of his brown boots and saw grass that was colored gold by the twilight sun. Atop the metallic flora cantered the horses that bore Dolores, Stevie, the dandy and Long Clay.

A groan emerged from the black trunk.

Brent slapped the portable prison. "Quiet." He had completely forgotten about the captive. "We didn't forget about you."

The man gurgled.

"Patch Up," said the cowboy.

"Yes, Mr. Plugford?"

"Why'd you call me that? I ain't no Mr. Plugford. I'm Brent."

"You're the man of the family now."

"Long Clay is in charge."

"He's running the tactics, but you're heading up the family."

"Same thing."

"There's a difference." Patch Up whipped a sluggish rump. "Long Clay was your father's partner for a long while, but he isn't family."

"That's certain true. But you're family—Pa always said so."

There was a long pause. "I know that he did."

Brent looked at the recumbent patriarch and remembered his forgotten question. "How come Pa's still got his mask on? It's full up with gore."

"Once we've settled at the fort, I'll clean him properly. He deserves—" Patch Up stopped speaking.

Brent twisted around and looked toward the front of the wagon.

Patch Up turned away.

"You okay?" asked Brent.

The negro nodded, but did not finish his statement.

Useless tears began to fill the cowboy's eyes, and he became angry. "Don't blubber!" he said, reprimanding both Patch Up and himself. "Ain't no use in it."

"You're right."

Patch Up set the bulb of the whip in its socket and turned to Yvette, who was curled up on the bench beside him like a kitten. Kindly, he caressed her forehead.

A sharp concern twisted Brent's guts. "Does she know…who we got in here? In the trunk?"

"No. She hasn't been awake more than a few minutes, and he's been quiet." Patch Up wiped his nose. "What do you intend to do with him?"

"Don't know." Brent considered Yvette's religious views and her absurd capacity for forgiveness. "Maybe we should just execute him be—"

An appendage thudded within the trunk.

"You keep quiet," the cowboy hissed, "or I'll do what I did in Colorado."

The man was silent.

Brent returned his gaze to Patch Up. "Maybe we should execute him before Yvette gets lucid. We're long past using him for barter with Gris, and it's certain definite that Dolores—when she learns what he done—will want him dead and would kill him herself, and Stevie and I want him dead, and Pa would've tore out his throat in six different states if me an Stevie hadn't've stopped him every time."

"That's all true," said Patch Up.

"But…" A consideration troubled Brent. "Yvette ain't hardly herself right now—she's like a ghost. And she might want him alive. Even with all that he did, she might still want him."

"That's true."

Brent glared at Patch Up. "What in the hell kind of counsel is that?"

"I'm not counseling you Mr. Plugford, I'm—"

"Don't call me that. I'm Brent."

"No. You're Mr. Plugford."

"Hell." The cowboy snorted. "He should be killed a hundred times for what he did. For what happened to my sisters and my Pa and them horses too. But—" He shook his head. "But I can't give Yvette another grievance. I can't hurt her in any way, even if it's doin' right by Dolores and Pa and all the rest of us. I just can't hurt her no matter what."

"That is a thoughtful and kind decision, Mr. Plugford." Patch Up stroked Yvette's forehead.

"Dolores and Stevie ain't gonna swallow it easy."

"They aren't."

The cowboy looked at the black trunk. "Your wife is gonna have the decision on what happens to you."

From behind the wood, Samuel C. Upfield IV gurgled two muffled wet words that might have been 'thank you.'

"If she don't forgive you, we're gonna throw rocks at you 'til you're dead. The whole family is."

Chapter IV
The Family Agenda

Sitting on the wagon bench, Brent Plugford caressed Yvette's chill forehead. The falling sun was a brilliant gold scalp above the northwestern hills, and in the oblique light, the gaunt woman's face looked like a skull covered with wax.

Resolved, the cowboy turned around and looked at his trailing siblings. "Ride up here 'longside me."

"Okay," responded Dolores.

"Comin'," said Stevie.

Brent carried Yvette inside the canopy and felt as if it were a small sick calf that he bore instead of an adult human being. He knelt upon the wagon bed, laid his sister beside the patriarch, put cotton into her ears, kissed her forehead, slid the black trunk to the opposite end of the wagon and walked forward.

Dolores and Stevie were riding beside the driver's bench when Brent returned.

"How're you doin?" The youngest Plugford pointed to the cowboy's bandaged head.

"Fine."

Dolores inquired, "How's she doin'?"

"Seems better—hasn't kicked in a while. And she ate some stew a little while back and kept most of it."

"Good."

A chubby hand that belonged to Patch Up squeezed Brent's shoulder.

The nascent Mr. Plugford said to his siblings, "I got somethin' to say to you both, but I want you to hear me out full before you get hot at me. I made a decision neither of you is gonna like, but it's the right one."

Dolores, perplexed by the preamble, stared.

"If this is about the goddamn captive," Stevie grumbled, "you can roast." The young man's reaction was not unexpected.

Brent looked over at Patch Up. Nodding, the negro put the bulb of his whip into the socket, grabbed his rifle and disappeared into the wagon bed. The cowboy informed his brother and sister, "He's guardin' the trunk until there's some unity with us."

"What the hell're you boys talkin' 'bout?" asked Dolores.

Brent looked at his sister. "You girls got took because of Yvette's husband. We know it certain true."

Dolores was shocked. "How? Why?"

"We'll get to the details later," the cowboy said, "but it's his fault, all of what happened. And he don't deny it either."

Dolores's eyes filled with fury.

Brent continued, "We brung him with us to use for a barter, or in case he remembered somethin' important, but he was double useless."

Dolores's eyes widened. "Samuel's here?"

"He's here. And I want him dead. Stevie sure does and Pa tried to kill him six times, but we stopped him. Killin' Samuel C. Upfield IV's the right thing to do and nobody knows that more than you. But you've seen how Yvette is."

Dolores hissed, "This ain't up to her!" Her wrath was a physical force inherited directly from her father.

"I say it is," stated Brent.

Stevie growled, "Roast in Hell you dumb sodomite."

The sky, grass and trees disappeared from Brent's view, and his skin tingled. "I already whipped you once this trip for that sort of talk."

"It's true goddamnit! That's why you couldn't be no husband to that Janie Dill. I'd wager you never even put your pecker in a—"

Dolores slapped Stevie. "Shut your dumb mouth! That ain't what we're talkin' about here."

Brent doubted that he was a sodomite, but he had not fornicated with a woman since he was a teenager (and he had been drunk during those endeavors), and he knew that he was atypical. He did not desire sexual relations with women or men, and he wondered why such shuddering assignations so thoroughly preoccupied the cowboys with whom he rode—men who chose to live in the saddle and explore the great landscape, free from the constraints of little wives and tiny towns.

"You can't hit me," complained Stevie, as if he were a petulant child.

"Talk 'bout Brent like that and I will," threatened Dolores. "I promise you."

"Goddamn." Stevie rubbed the scarlet handprint emblazoned upon his face. "You hit hard." He shook his head. "Like everybody in this family."

"Let's finish the discussion," said Brent

Dolores and Stevie looked up.

"Whenever Yvette's awake," the cowboy resumed, "she asks for him. Again and again. 'Why isn't Samuel here?' and 'Where is my husband?' kind of stuff."

"Then we should sink him in a pond and not tell her what happened," suggested Stevie.

"No." Brent shook his head. "Yvette had a whole other life with Samuel out there in San Francisco—away from the Plugfords—and it's clear visible that him and God are what matter to her the most. That's a certain fact. And I wouldn't want us to kill one of the two things she cares 'bout." He watched his siblings for a moment and added, "You all know what can happen when a hurt person ain't got nothin' left in the world."

"I know." Dolores contained her fury.

Stevie slapped his pommel. "That bastard should be killed slow with rocks like we said we would do."

"I want him dead and you want him dead," Brent responded, "but I'm askin' you to think beyond yourself."

"Go roast."

"What I'm talkin' 'bout," Brent continued, "ain't justice or what we want, but allowin' Yvette to keep her husband if she wants him. She's dwindled, and we can't take anything away from her."

Dolores lowered her face. "So you just wanna let Samuel go free?" Her voice was a distant whisper.

"No. He wrote out a letter sayin' how it all happened—in case we killed him or traded him over—and he wrote it true correct. I'm gonna give that to Yvette and tell her to read it and know what he done, because that has to be clear—this ain't somethin' to put under the bed. And after she knows what occurred, I'll tell her she can decide what happens to him."

"I want to read that letter myself." Dolores squeezed the horn of her sidesaddle as if she wanted to strangle it. "And I want to tell her exactly what I think should happen to him."

"That's fair," opined Brent.

"I was raped the same as her. And our daddy is dead." Dolores pulled upon her reins, and her palfrey cantered away from the men.

Brent looked at his kid brother. "You accept it goin' this way?"

Stevie spat. "I don't."

Patch Up emerged from the canopy, holding a repeater rifle. "Stevie."

"What?"

"Listen to your brother." Patch Up tapped the stock of his gun upon Brent's shoulder. "He's the man of the family and knows how to run things."

"I ain't listenin' to him or to you. Samuel's gettin' executed like he deserves."

Patch Up flung his trigger-guard forward, and a cartridge clicked into the chamber.

"You ain't shootin' me," said Stevie.

"I will if you go against your whole family." Patch Up's voice was flat and grave. "I'll go for a leg."

"I got guns too."

Stevie snapped reins and applied spurs.

"Stevie!" shouted Brent. "Don't you—"

Furious, the young man cut in front of the wagon, rode up a green hill that was thirty yards to the west and pulled his pump-action shotgun from its sheath. The scalp of the sun sat beneath the hooves of his silhouetted colt like an infernal emergence.

"He can't be this stupid," Brent said to Patch Up.

"He's been on his way for a while."

"I hope there's no liquor in him."

"Listen!" Stevie pumped his shotgun, and a spent shell flew into the air, buzzing like an insect. "Give over Samuel or I'll come get him!"

Brent did not know whether or not his brother was bluffing.

Yvette's dog began to bark.

A black shadow interposed itself between Stevie and the wagon. "Don't interfere with—"

Long Clay jerked the shotgun from Stevie's hands and flung it to the ground.

"I was just tryin' to get Samuel," defended the young man.

"You were going to charge your family with a scattergun," stated the gunfighter.

"We need to execute him. He's the reason it all happened."

"The only thing we need to do," Long Clay coolly replied, "is prepare for the next engagement."

"You don't want no revenge?"

"Revenge is a fool's obsession." The gunfighter tugged the reins of his black mare and turned away.

Embarrassed and angry, Stevie remarked, "Seems like you don't care what happened to Pa none at all. I thought you were partners."

Long Clay pistol-whipped Stevie. The young man yelled, dipped in his saddle and clutched his broken nose.

"I'm done coddling you," said the gunfighter. "You've got a tally with one mark."

"No." Stevie's eyes widened with apprehension. "No!"

Brent was stunned by the declaration. The tally was how Long Clay and John Lawrence Plugford had disciplined unruly posse members long ago—each and every mark guaranteed a broken limb once the job came to its conclusion. Grimacing, the cowboy recalled the story of a fellow who had garnered eight marks and had each leg and arm broken twice to cover the deficit.

"You can't do that to me!" cried Stevie. "You don't got the authority!"

"Now you have two marks."

"Close your stupid mouth!" yelled Brent.

The young man lowered his gaze, wiped blood from beneath his broken nose and spat pink. A moment later, Long Clay rode back to the horses that he had abandoned prior to his intercession.

Stevie clambered from his saddle, reclaimed his pump-action shotgun, and looked at the spotted colt. "He gave me a goddamn tally." The beast flashed a tail, dismissively. "Two goddamn marks."

A dark blue blanket covered over the magenta vault. The motley horses that pulled the wagon were weary and had grown immune to the negro's administrative efforts with the whip, but still they plodded onward, through the grasslands, up the inclined terrain, toward the sere land atop which stood a vast mountain wall.

"I've descried it," announced Patch Up, who had one eye to his brass and ivory spyglass.

"Any tenants we gotta evict?" asked Brent.

"None that I can see." The negro handed the spyglass over to the cowboy. "Peruse the site."

Brent raised the telescope to his right eye, peered through and saw the sheer and crenulate face of the beige mountain wall.

"Look west," Patch Up advised, "near the split."

The cowboy panned the lens to the left, located the defile, and soon discerned a rectangular edifice made out of white stones. "I see it." Narrow vertical lines that were crenellations for weapons sat upon the fort's façade, and upon the slanted roof were two small iron chimneys. Adjoining the eastern side of the structure was a cylinder that looked like a well, and to the west were arrayed the mismatched rocks and wooden crosses of a small cemetery.

"This is where it'll happen," announced Brent.

"This is it."

Chapter IV
Family Allowances

Dolores Plugford was carried by her purple-nosed younger brother to the stone bench that stood outside the eastern face of the fort and set down. The sole of her riding boot pressed into the grit, and her shortened left leg dangled. Blood tingled like electricity within the stump.

"Thanks."

"Mmh." Stevie departed.

Dolores leaned against the fort and looked up. After eight months of confinement, the open night sky seemed vast and alien—a thing from another person's childhood. She looked away from the daunting vault and adjusted the folds of her lavender dress. Nearby, dark shapes that were men brought horses into the sunken stable that was located behind the fort.

"Can I help?" inquired the redheaded woman.

"Not just yet."

Brent carried Yvette and a bedroll into the fort. Patch Up followed, illuminated by an oil lantern that he shielded from the horizon. The amber flame disappeared into the darkness.

Mr. Stromler carried five empty canteens to the well, set them upon the ground and cranked the handle. A thick old rope twined around the turning bar, emitting creaks and dust. Beyond the gentleman, Long Clay walked into the wagon and returned, shouldering a heavy iron box that clanged with each stride.

The moment that Brent emerged from the fort, Dolores seized his right wrist. "Give me the goddamn letter."

Her brother reached his free hand into the rear pocket of his denim pants and withdrew a folded envelope. "Don't tear it up, Yvette needs—"

"Quit speechifyin'."

Brent paused for a moment. "She needs to be able to read it."

Dolores snatched the missive from the man's left hand. "You ain't Pa." Although she was aware that her anger was misdirected, she was unable to control it.

Her brother squeezed her shoulder affectionately. "Talk to me when you're done. Please."

"Okay."

Brent strode toward the wagon.

"There's a lantern inside," remarked Patch Up, as he emerged from the fort. "Let me take you in so that you have some light."

"I want to read it out here."

Patch Up looked at his palms. "I can barely see the side that gets to vote."

"I got used to the dark."

Saddened by the remark, the negro nodded. "Do you need anything?"

"I'd like a crutch so I can get 'round on my own and help out."

"I'll make you something you can use." Patch Up kissed her forehead and walked toward the wagon.

Dolores looked down at the missive. One word was written in the exact center of the rectangle.

Yvette

The redheaded woman turned the envelope over, lifted its flap, reached her fingers inside and withdrew a thick letter that was stained brown with old blood.

"Good."

Dolores unfolded the papers and saw that they were filled with an elaborate and uncommonly beautiful calligraphy. "Pompous fool." She surveyed the top of the first page.

The Coerced but True Confessions of the Man who was Samuel C. Upfield IV

Ninth Draft

Thirty minutes later, Dolores dropped the last page of the letter to the ground. Her guts boiled with a dire, poisonous hatred for Samuel C. Upfield IV.

"Brent!"

The cowboy hastened from the fort, knelt beside the bench and took his sister's hands.

Trembling with fury, Dolores said, "We can't let Yvette forgive him after what he did. We can't. He's the reason for it all—one hundred percent."

Brent squeezed his sister's hands. "I know."

"I got raped—I was fucked by hundreds of men and had my foot blasted off and Pa got killed and Yvette's ruined 'cause of that dumb weakling!" Dolores shoved her brother away and shouted, "We gotta kill him! You're my brother, my twin brother, and my closest in the whole world—how can you let him be? How can you allow him after this? How can you!?!"

Brent's eyes filled with tears. "Dolores…Please…" Stars dripped down his cheeks. "We gotta think 'bout Yvette too."

Dolores hammered her fists against her brother's chest, and he did not resist her assault. After ten blows, she stopped.

"Go ahead and hit more if you want to," Brent said, "I can take it." He wiped his eyes and proffered his chest.

"I've gotta throw rocks at Samuel before Yvette reads the letter and forgives him. I've got to."

"You can't kill him."

Dolores wiped her eyes and nodded. "Deal."

Chapter V
Crucibles and Defeat

Wearing his yellow riding clothes and carrying three filled canteens, Nathaniel Stromler ducked his head and entered the fort, which had been built for the Mexican-American War or the Civil War or some less renowned conflict that Mexicans or Americans had with natives. (Nobody knew the history of the edifice, and the graves were unmarked.) He passed the latrine and strode into the common area, where a lantern shone upon three tables, two cast-iron potbelly stoves (a rusted unit, and its warped mate) and thirty deteriorating wooden bunks. The enclosure smelled like dust and lamp oil.

"Please put them in the corner," Patch Up said from his stool beside the bunk within which laid John Lawrence Plugford.

Nathaniel leaned over, felt a dagger stab his bowels, dropped the canteens, stumbled to one of the tables and regained his balance.

"Are you okay?"

"It will pass in a few minutes." The pains were infrequent, but sharp and lingering whenever they occurred.

"Let me know if I can do something for you." Patch Up wiped blood from the dead man's face.

"Thank you." Nathaniel sat atop a table and massaged his lower abdomen. "How long did you know him?"

"My whole life." Patch Up rinsed the white washcloth. "Before I was born, J.L.'s father, Lawrence Gregory, bought my father and freed him, and like every negro that man freed, my father stayed on at the Plugford plantation and was treated fairly, like an equal." The negro scoured the patriarch's rubbery ears. "That's where my father met my mother and had me. This was over in Florida—long before the war." He wrung the pink cloth.

"I was raised there, alongside J.L., like kin. He told his father that I was clever and a quick study, and so I assisted the plantation doctor and the accountant, instead of doing menial labor." Patch Up wiped the crust of blood and dust from the dead man's lips. "That's probably why I've always had this belly."

Nathaniel's pain subsided and he inquired, "Would you like some water?"

"Thank you, I would."

The gentleman walked to a canteen that depended by its strap from a nail in the wall, removed the stopper and carried it over.

Patch Up set the washcloth across John Lawrence Plugford's wrinkled eyes. "The lids won't stay down." The negro accepted the canteen, drank and returned the vessel to Nathaniel, who wiped the nozzle and swallowed a full draught.

"One dry hot summer night, the plantation caught fire, and the blaze roared across the whole property." Patch Up reclaimed the washcloth and wiped the edges of the flower-shaped cavity that sat above John Lawrence Plugford's left eyebrow. "J.L. and I were teenagers then, and we pulled children and oldsters from the servants' houses, and we threw buckets of water, but the water turned to steam before it ever even touched the flames and didn't affect anything. It was like we'd crashed into Hell.

"Lawrence Gregory and Darren, J.L.'s younger brother, tried to get J.L.'s mother out of the main house—she was trapped inside—and all three of them were burned to death. While all of this was happening, Teddy Tinkers, one of the slaves J.L.'s father had freed, took the safe that contained all of the family's wealth—Lawrence Gregory did not believe in banks—and ran off with it." Patch Up shook his head and frowned. "I still hate that nigger right now.

"J.L. lost almost everything that mattered in that fire. All he had left was a scorched plantation and me." Patch Up wiped dirt and blood from the dead man's huge hands.

"The workers stayed on for a week—for free—to help us salvage what we could, and shortly after the last rice and tobacco had been harvested, J.L. sold the property for half a pittance."

"I learned, through some loose-lipped negroes at another plantation, that the fire had been started by a muleskinner named Jake Porter, and that he had been hired by two competing plantation owners who had been undersold by the Plugfords for many years.

"I told J.L.

"That was the first time he ever went dark. I was angry about what happened, and I helped.

"Not so long after that, while he was still filled with despair and anger, he met Long Clay, who was no different then than he is now.

"J.L. became an outlaw, and he and I were out of touch for a handful of years." Employing a toothpick, Patch Up scraped grit from beneath the corpse's fingernails.

"When J.L. met his willful little wife, he softened. He quit robbing banks and trains, and his great anger was gone—drained right out of him. He became a fulltime rancher, husband and father.

"J.L. asked me to come out to Texas and help him run things, and I accepted his offer." Patch Up crossed John Lawrence Plugford's arms together. "He was the same J.L. who I remembered from before the fire, and he stayed that way until the day that his daughters were taken from him."

"It was clear how much he loved his girls," remarked Nathaniel.

"They were his absolution."

"Patch Up!" called Stevie from outside.

"Yeah?"

Nathaniel faced the south wall.

A silhouette approached the center slit and became a swath of Stevie's face that contained one eye and six teeth. "I looked all the hell over. Where're the shovels and pick axes?"

"Tied to the underside of the wagon."

"Why're they under there?

"So armadillos can admire them."

"Ain't you the wittiest nigger in the N.M. Territory? Don't go hidin' things for no reason."

"I did it to make room for your father and Yvette."

"Oh." The halved face eyed the recumbent corpse. "We gonna bury him here?"

"Only if we have to."

Stevie's eye swiveled to Nathaniel and Patch Up and vacillated back and forth. "We need you two to come out and help us make holes for all these land torpedoes Long Clay brung 'long."

Nathaniel grimaced, but did not offer a verbal response.

"I'll be there," said Patch Up.

Stevie disappeared from the narrow opening and was replaced by a strip of blue-black night sky that contained seven dull stars.

Patch Up looked at the gentleman. "I suppose that you don't intend to help us bury land torpedoes?"

"I do not."

The negro nodded, put a cloth over John Lawrence Plugford's wrinkled eyes, rose from his stool and stretched. "I'm going outside." He reached his interlaced fingers toward the lantern and his vertebrae cracked. "If Yvette awakens, please give her some water. And try to get her to eat some more stew."

"Certainly," replied Nathaniel.

"Thank you." Patch Up drank from the canteen and wiped his mouth. "I'm not going to pry and ask why you refuse to carry a firearm—it's not my business and I certainly admire your decision not to wield an instrument of murder. But you should know that the odds of us winning the coming engagement are poor."

The skin upon Nathaniel's nape tightened.

"We are a small crew and every person counts," stated Patch Up. "I'm very sorry that you've suffered and that you're here with us now…but you can make a difference. You know who our enemies are, and what they're capable of doing."

Nathaniel nodded.

The negro claimed his repeater rifle from the bunk above the corpse and slung it over his shoulder. "I won't badger you—I only ask for you to consider what I've said. You're a very determined and intelligent man, and I believe that you can retain your integrity—and maybe even some of your youthful idealism—if a terrible situation forces you to waver once from your most firmly held belief."

"I will think about all that you have said," replied Nathaniel. "And I thank you for speaking to me in this manner."

"I hate squabbles," Patch Up remarked as he walked out into the night.

Nathaniel looked at the corpse of John Lawrence Plugford and the bundled body of Yvette, who slept upon the adjacent bunk. Although the gentleman knew that he would be changed irrevocably by the act of killing another man, he admitted to himself that he was already different—aware of his mortality in a physical way and cognizant that his most cherished viewpoints did not in any way alter the world that happened violently around him. The scorpions had shown him that he was not immune to death.

It became apparent to Nathaniel that fear, denial and stubbornness were the reasons that he still refused to arm himself in this desperate situation. At that moment, he knew that survival meant more to him than did his ideals.

At the age of twenty-six, Nathaniel Stromler relinquished a core and formative belief to the senseless world, balled his empty hands into tight fists and was defeated.

He exited the fort, felt night settle upon him like a cloak and surveyed dark horizons for the men alongside whom he would fight. Four upright figures, each darker than the dirt, stabbed shovels into the earth and opened black holes.

"Do you have another shovel?"

"I'll fetch you the gilded deluxe," responded Patch Up.

Long Clay led Nathaniel to the edge of the trench that encircled the fort, put the tip of the shovel into the dirt, gripped the handle, walked west for twenty paces and stopped. "Dig ten holes along this line—one yard deep and one yard wide. Cover the mark when you're through." The gunfighter returned the tool to the gentleman and strode away.

Nathaniel stabbed the shovel into the dirt, slammed the heel of his riding boot upon the metal, pulled the handle toward his chest and scooped up earth.

Somebody screamed.

The gentleman looked northwest, toward the fort, but did not see the exclaimer.

"Don't worry 'bout that," advised Stevie, who was knee-deep in a hole. "It's just some family business."

Nathaniel noticed that Brent was missing.

Again, the man screamed. The cry echoed in the gorge immediately east of the fort.

"Who is that?" asked Nathaniel.

"The reason all this happened." Stevie flung dirt at the stars.

The circus dog barked.

"You'll rot in Hell for what you did!" yelled a woman Nathaniel recognized as Dolores.

The man screamed.

Stevie sullenly stabbed his shovel into the ground. "I wish I could watch."

"We've got work," said Long Clay, who was submerged up to his waist in a southern hole.

The anonymous man screamed.

Nathaniel ripped open the earth and sank into the ground.

Chapter VI
The Goddamn Letter

Yvette Upfield felt a coarse slug slide across the back of her right hand and knew for certain that when she opened her eyes, she would be in Catacumbas, beside the dead baby turtle. The moment that she engaged reality, she would see that her rescue was imagined and that she was still a whore.

"I shouldn't've let you get that far—his whole jaw is broke." Yvette recognized the speaker as Brent.

"Gimme that crutch," said a woman who was Dolores.

Grit crackled beneath a lopsided gait.

The coarse slug slid across Yvette's right wrist and radiated hot moist air. Presently, the choirmaster opened her eyes and saw the circus dog, sitting on its rump, staring at her as if it were a doctor with a dangling pink tongue for a stethoscope. Lying upon the sweat-dampened wood, Yvette surveyed the strange enclosure in which she found herself and saw numerous bunks, several crenellations, some dismal furnishings and the soles of her dead father's work boots.

"Mano."

The circus dog raised its right paw into the air.

Yvette reached out and shook the proffered appendage.

Dolores ambled into the room, employing a crutch that was a conjoined broomstick and gunstock. She looked at her sister and paused. "You're awake."

Yvette nodded, and the world wobbled.

"How do you feel?" At the bottom of her lavender dress, Dolores's truncated left leg swung like a pendulum.

"Better than before...but I don't know where we are."

"At a fort in the New Mexico Territory—gettin' ready for a stand-off with Gris and his crew."

Yvette knew that there would be more killing, and also that she was powerless to stop it. She loved her family, but they were deaf to His exhortations and wisdom.

"You've got your wits?" asked Dolores. "Can think lucid?"

"I think so." Yvette's desire for medicine had definitely diminished. "Do you know why Samuel ain't—why Samuel isn't here?"

Dolores turned away from her sister, ambled to the south wall and through an opening yelled, "Brent!"

"What?"

"She's awake and clear. Give her the goddamn letter."

Hope fluttered within Yvette's breast. "Is it from Samuel?"

"It's from him."

Something about the way Dolores spoke gave Yvette a chill.

Half of Brent's face appeared in a slit, and his bisected mouth inquired, "How are you feelin'?"

"Better," replied Yvette. "Please give me my letter."

Brent's eye stared at her for a moment. "You ain't gonna like what he wrote."

"You went and read it?" The gaunt woman began to shake. "He's my husband and what he wrote to me ain't—isn't your business." She sat up and said, "Give it over now—those words are private."

A yellow rectangle slid through the narrow opening, two feet below Brent's isolated eye. "Dolores. Take it over to her."

"I'll get it myself." Yvette discarded her yellow blanket, stood up, felt the room melt, steadied herself, saw the room solidify, staggered toward her brother, grabbed the missive, hobbled back to her bunk and collapsed, exhausted and panting.

"I didn't think you could walk," remarked the cowboy.

"I had a reason."

Brent looked meaningfully at Dolores.

Yvette's heart was pounding from her exertions, and bright lights coruscated in her peripheral views. Her lungs, wet and weak, pulled at the chill night air and shuddered.

Dolores looked at Brent and said, "I'll stay with her."

"And hold her."

Yvette surveyed at the envelope. "How come it don't—doesn't say Upfield? It just says Yvette. No last name."

Neither of her siblings answered the question.

Dolores sat down and put her right arm around her sister's shoulders.

Brent walked away from the crenellation.

"It's his calligraphy for certain," remarked Yvette.

"He wrote it."

The choirmaster turned the missive over, reached inside and withdrew papers that were spattered with brown droplets. "Somebody got something on it." She laid the envelope down, so that her name was facing up. "Brent probably dripped some coffee or tobacco juice—Samuel is fastidious."

Dolores said nothing.

Yvette unfolded the papers and saw that they were numerous and filled with her husband's pretty calligraphy. Her eyes went to the top of the first page.

The Coerced but True Confessions of the Man who was Samuel C. Upfield IV

Ninth Draft

"Oh Lord Jesus," Yvette exclaimed, "he found himself a new wife while I was gone." Tears filled her eyes. "That's what this is—a goodbye letter. That's why nobody's saying anything about him."

Dolores said nothing.

The choirmaster wiped tears from her eyes and read.

A Brief Foreword

Undoubtedly you, my spouse, are intrigued—if not befuddled—by the number of drafts that precede the finished document that you currently hold in your hands.

I shall explain this to you.

I was asked to pen a letter that would detail my mistakes, my betrayal, your capture and my subsequent actions. In previous versions of my confessional essay—the first five drafts—certain passages, reminiscences and solitary adjectives were determined by the Editors of the document to be overly piteous pleas for your forgiveness. The Editors did not feel that I should in any way attempt to engage your sympathies, and I agreed with them, although perhaps the manner in which they communicated their critiques to me, the author, was not the preferred. The sixth, seventh and eighth drafts saw a new creative direction for the confessional essay, a turn for the literary, especially as it became apparent to me that this work would likely become my last communication to you and, in fact, the world.

Yvette's eyes widened in horror. "What's happened to him?" Her thin body shook with a desperate panic. "What's happened to my husband?"

"Brent and I will tell you after you've finished readin'," stated Dolores.

Sickened and fearful, Yvette returned her gaze to the tremulous letter.

The Editors felt that these later drafts contained far too many apologies, and so suggested that I replace all apologetic remarks with an asterisk (*) to convey this sentiment, and this current version adheres to this stipulation. Additionally, there are some subjects that I did not fully explore during my allotted time at the desk, and so

I have written notes to myself (enclosed in parenthesis) suggesting possible future elaborations should I live to author a Tenth Draft. I should also point out that the Editors will draw lines through any text that they deem objectionable or irrelevant, and you are advised by them to skip over all words and phrases thus marked.

The following confessional essay contains nary an untrue word.
*You deserve to know exactly what occurred.**

Dear Yvette,

In early December 1901, I received a pair of telegrams that contained news about the prospecting ventures into which I had very heavily invested our life savings.

The first telegram informed me that a ruinous collapse had befallen our Arizona copper mine, and also how the terrible event had trapped and killed two unfortunate men. Immediately after the incident, the boss was seized and violently thrashed by a mob of angry workers, who had apparently warned him of the danger weeks earlier. The outraged legion claimed the cashbox, which was filled with payouts for the last three months of sales, and absconded with it. I never learned why the boss had not deposited these earnings into the Bank of Phoenix as he had been directed, but the money was gone, and he was crippled, and half of our life savings were naught but still wind.

The second telegram, which I received only two days after the first, informed me that the eighteen hundred beeves I had purchased from Jeffrey O'Mallory had become ill halfway in-between Montana and Colorado and had to be slaughtered, without exception. Not only did we lose all of the money invested in the cattle, but the cowboys, whose wages were supposed to come directly from the sum that the animals earned, were still owed payment for their work.

The two sturdy ventures into which I had invested the major part of our savings had fallen into ruin during the same week, and all of the money that remained—six hundred dollars legal tender in the Trusted Bank of San Francisco—could not even cover the debt owed to the cowboys. We were destitute.

~~(Elaboration: The inherent risks of investing in business ventures one cannot personally oversee or directly affect.)~~

Two days after I received the second telegram, your sister Dolores arrived at our apartment, where she was to stay and with us celebrate both Christmas and the New Year. I decided not to apprise you of our unfortunate circumstances, because of her presence and the coming celebration of His birthday. Additionally, it was my hope to achieve a modicum of amelioration before I involved you directly.

My anxieties were further aggravated by a telegram that I received from the cowboy boss—a communication in which he promised to visit San Francisco and collect the money that was owed to him and his riders if I did not presently remit. We possessed but a fraction of the deficit, and thus I decided not to respond at all to the aggrieved leader's request.

Throughout the week that followed, while we were entertaining your sister and showing her the city of San Francisco, I pondered my options. You will very likely recall your comments about my detached manner, and now you know the cause of my worrisome preoccupations.

Four days before His birthday, I received a telegram from the cowboy boss notifying me that he and six of his riders were on "(their) way to San Francisco, to get (their) wages, and also to deliver out a rough whipping for all the hassle. Merry Christmas."

I feared that our bank might be contacted directly by the cowboys or some legal official, and so I withdrew all of our money.

Undoubtedly, you now understand why I burst into tears when you informed me that you had prepared my favorite meal.* It was not easy to enjoy roasted goose with chestnut-bacon stuffing when monetary, physical and matrimonial ruinations loom. Nor was it possible for me to offer you my physical affections as I had throughout our courtship and marriage.*

You will recall that our friend David joined us for that meal and afterwards, for sherry in our little parlor, where he showed a clear interest in your sister that was rebuffed. His spirits sank after Dolores's denial, and I volunteered to escort him home and leave you and your sibling to discussion and perhaps retirement, if you were seized by drowsiness. You helped me into my coat, located my bowler hat and kissed me upon the lips. I looked into your soft blue eyes, and nearly confessed our predicament. ~~I desperately yearned to share with you the burden that had grown more ponderous with every waking moment.~~

As you will recall, I said nothing.*

I left the apartment with David, descended three flights of stairs, passed through the front door, and was struck by the icy winter winds of our seaboard city. With my head tilted down, I perambulated the cold avenues with my friend, endeavoring desultory conversation that is now difficult to recall because of my overindulgence in sherry earlier that evening. I know that twice I contemplated confiding in David, but did not because I feared that I would become hysterical in public. The gas lanterns along the avenues hissed, and the shadows cast by their unnaturally bright fires were opaque.

I watched David enter his apartment, and the very instant that I was alone, I began to weep. I had ruinously invested our life savings and was about be violently thrashed.

I thought it quite likely that you would have to return to your family in Texas—a place where I was obviously unwelcome—and at that moment, I felt an utter desperation.

"You should've told me," Yvette said aloud.

I thrust my cold hands into my pockets and clutched our savings, which were the only barrier between us and abject poverty, and I went toward the central square.

"No." The choirmaster knew where her husband had gone. "No."

The church has many adversaries in the modern world. Saloons and brothels are tawdry places wherein obvious transgressions nightly occur, and yet I am convinced that the casino is the establishment that conjures the most fabulous and dangerous hopes. The gambling den is the place where a man can change his entire life—through determination, skill and a mote of luck—and achieve his proper station in the world. At the betting table is where the fallen individual, prostrated by misfortunes, can raise himself up again. Agreeable ivory or beneficent cards are all that he requires to pay off his debt to the cowboys and treat them to a fine seafood dinner so that they might amicably conclude their business. ~~*With his amassed winnings, the resurrected man will be able to purchase a large apartment, wherein he and his wife shall live in great comfort and raise a beautiful and pious family.*~~

These are the delusions—aided by alcohol and despair—that turn a reluctant gambler, such as I, into a man who is willing to risk money that is not even his own.

The Editors have asked me to state that conditions of depression, inebriation and desperation neither excuse nor diminish my deplorable behavior.

I entered the casino and went immediately to a table whereupon people played blackjack, a game with which I was well-acquainted and possessed some small degree of mastery. ~~*As I gambled, my face reddened, and often I felt as if I had no control over my actions, as if my body were an automaton that I witnessed from a great distance.*~~ *In thirty minutes time, I had reduced our remainder by half and had no more than three hundred and ten dollars.*

Presently, I seated myself at a poker table, where I saw a man I knew from church, as well as two strangers. I played for a period of an hour, and I lost and won equal amounts. Eventually, I was joined by a striking, finely-dressed gentleman who possessed only one eye and was younger than his white hair intimated.

Yvette's stomach twisted.

The distinct individual introduced himself as Gris, which I believe is the Spanish word for 'gray,' but he did not proffer a full name. He proclaimed that he was from Spain, although his delivery of our language was perfect and did not in any way betray his country of origin. A man at the table, a plump codger who wore cracked glasses, stood up from his chair and departed—apparently he was still upset about that little argument America had with Spain a few years earlier.

We proceeded to play several more rounds of poker, wherein I lost one hundred dollars to the house, and Gris won from them twice that amount. He saw that I was anxious, purchased for me a drink, and recommended that I leave the table before I lost any more money. I thanked him for his generosity and advice, drank my bourbon, and proceeded to winnow our entire life savings down to sixty dollars, which was less than one-tenth the sum I had brought into the casino only two hours earlier. ~~I was filled with despair.~~

Gris collected his winnings, which were quite substantial, and invited me to join him in the lounge, where an old man played piano while a negress performed buck dance with wooden shoes. I accepted his invitation.

The Spaniard purchased for me another bourbon, which I refused and summarily drank. After I had finished, the man asked after my troubles. I told him everything that had happened throughout the previous month. I found it easy to confess my woes and unburden myself to this stranger, a person who was not a part of my daily life, and thus far had been extraordinarily kind.

Shortly after I had finished detailing my misfortunes, Gris enquired, "Do you possess a photograph of your wife?" His eye did not leave the furious, percussive feet of the negress buck dancer when he asked this question.

I claimed the wallet from my vest and from it withdrew the photograph taken at our wedding, ~~the single happiest day in my entire life~~. I delivered the image of us to him, and he looked at it for the time it took the negress to punctuate eight measures of music with her hard shoes.

Gris returned the photograph to me and remarked, "She is very beautiful."

~~"There is no more beautiful woman in the world," said I.~~

"Shall we return to the poker table?" he enquired.

The difference between sixty dollars and bankruptcy is nigh negligible, and I agreed to join him. I made several silent promises to our Lord as I walked toward the table, and I hoped for divine aid.

In a very short while, I was penniless. I sat and stared forward like a dumb imbecile.

Gris erected a two hundred dollar pillar of blue poker chips and slid it across the table, until it stood directly in front of me. He said, "Buena suerte," which means 'good luck.'

I thanked him for his generous endowment, and in an impressive amount of time, lost this sum as well.

Resolved that I should return home and finally disclose everything to you, I rose from my chair, claimed my jacket and turned away from the poker table.

"Mr. Upfield."

I faced my benefactor.

"Please await me at the location of our earlier repair. I shall join you presently."

I had no choice but to agree, and so went to the indicated table and sat, envisioning the terrible look upon your face when I informed you of our financial ruin and my deplorable behavior. While I awaited Gris, another bourbon arrived, but I abstained from drinking any of it. I was through with pointless diversions and wanted to return home.

Presently, my benefactor arrived. "Mr. Upfield." Gris sat in the chair opposite me and luxuriously reclined. "You face great difficulties."

I did not disagree with him.

"How do you intend to repay my loan?"

I was surprised by his choice of words. "I was unaware that the money earlier proffered had been a loan," said I.

"Do you commonly receive gifts of two hundred dollars from strangers?"

I had no ready answer.

"I leave San Francisco tomorrow morning," Gris informed me, "and I must be repaid prior to my departure." Shortly after he said this, a man with a rotten nose joined us at the table, as did a third individual who wore a beard and a dark cherry suit. Nobody was smiling.

From the inner pocket of his white linen jacket, Gris withdrew a deck of cards. "Would you care to win back your debt?" he enquired.

I shook my head—I did not think that I could win any amount of money from him.

"If you are not inclined toward more games," Gris responded, "six men who work for me will follow you to your home and seize items of an equivalent or greater value."

I agreed to play cards with him.

After twenty minutes of gaming, I owed Gris two thousand dollars. I wanted to die. The buck dancer returned, and I felt the tattoo of her wooden shoes upon my spine.

Gris remarked, "I fear that you cannot resolve your debt."

"You are correct," said I.

The buck dancer's shoes impacted the floor like musical gunshots.

"I own an entertainment parlor for gentlemen," Gris stated, "wherein each female employee earns approximately two thousand dollars per year." Gris fixed his eye upon me. "Your wife shall render services and pay off your debt."

My stomach lurched. I careered to the water closet and expelled goose and everything else that I had eaten. Presently, the man with the rotten nose escorted me back to the table and I sat. My suit, saturate with perspiration, squeaked upon the chair.

"I cannot allow my wife to work in such an establishment," said I to Gris.

"You owe me two thousand dollars that you do not have. You are not empowered to allow or disallow anything." Gris opened his ruined eye, and I saw that a gray rock was lodged deep within the socket. "Mrs. Upfield shall be taken to my establishment, treated fairly and returned to you whenever she has cancelled the family deficit. If you raise an alarm or in any way attempt to thwart me, you shall be murdered, and she shall be taken to the exact same place for the remainder of her life."

I began to weep. I swallowed the glass of bourbon that I had previously neglected and pleaded, "Might I have one last chance to win back my debt?"

"With what collateral?"

"My wife's sister is in town for the holidays."

Horrified, Yvette turned to Dolores. "I—I…I can't believe he…that he…I'm…I'm so, so sorry."

"You have nothin' to apologize for."

"But my husband—"

"Finish the goddamn letter."

*"My wife's sister is in town for the holidays. She is at our apartment."**

"You are proposing a double or nothing wager?"

I nodded, but was unable to speak.

"If you lose," Gris clarified, "both sisters shall work for me until they have earned a sum of four thousand dollars."

I nodded.

"Is the sibling comparably attractive?"

I nodded and eventually found my voice. "She is a redheaded cancan dancer."

"I accept," replied Gris. "Which game would you like to play?"

I knew that the Spaniard's gaming skills were superior to my own, and so I wanted to keep things simple and place the outcome directly into His hands. "I would like for us to draw cards."

"Agreed."

I selected a nine of clubs.

Gris withdrew a queen of diamonds.

I fainted.

Outdoors, I was roused by a slap across the face. Gloved hands pressed me against a wall of coarse brick. Six unfamiliar men, all dressed in dark overcoats, stood close around me, and cold wind whistled up the empty avenues, past their shoulders and pale ears. In the fists of five of these wraiths were clutched the handles of revolvers and knives.

The sixth man, a fellow with silver hair, withdrew his left hand from his coat pocket and displayed to me a small vial. "This is a sleeping draught," said he.

I took the vial from the man and asked how I was to administer the sedative.

"If they are asleep, put a small amount directly into their mouths."

I asked if a milligram would be a sufficient dosage.

"Yes. And if they are awake, install twice that amount into whatever fluids they are drinking."

As I trod upon the drear gray avenue, ~~assaulted by harsh winds and the hissing flames of gas lanterns,~~ I contemplated engaging my adversaries as would a gunfighter, but these hideous men were all armed murderers, and I was an unarmed elixir salesman. My body fearfully continued along the familiar route toward our home, ~~and I loathed myself.~~

~~I neared Deever's Butcher Shoppe, which was closed like every other establishment at that late hour, and I smelled a powerfully pungent odor that I am unable to accurately describe. Suddenly and violently, I collapsed upon the avenue and became convulsive. The wraiths monitored my paroxysms from an alleyway and smoked cigars that smelled of anise.~~

~~Presently, I regained myself, continued my journey and unhappily arrived at the building on the corner of Clarkes and Hughley in which we lived. My prayer for it to be removed and shuttled to some safe place had gone unanswered.~~

I climbed the familiar stairwell, ~~and it seemed to me as if an entire year had passed since I had descended the steps with David.~~ I arrived at our apartment, shadowed by two of the six wraiths. "Do not lock the door," one of them whispered, and his accomplice displayed his weapon to me in a threatening manner. I walked through the threshold, and the hideous pair remained in the hallway, while their peers monitored both the front and the rear of the building from outside.

You and Dolores were asleep.

Perhaps you will recall that the damp San Francisco winter had given your sister a modicum of nasal congestion, and that these clogged sinuses had caused her to sleep with her mouth agape, displaying her tonsils to the unfinished ceiling of the guest room.

*I sneaked beside Dolores and drizzled a gram of the draught into her exposed throat.**

Unable to see through her tears, Yvette set down the letter, flung the segmented sticks that were her arms around Dolores and squeezed. "I…I can't read anymore of this. I just can't."

"You need to finish it."

Shaking her head, Yvette said, "It's horrible."

Dolores raised the remaining six pages and said, "I can read it out loud if you want."

Yvette wiped tears from her eyes and reclaimed the odious confessional essay.

I crept into our room and saw you, asleep beneath the maroon wool blanket that your father's house negro had given us, and I was forced to look away. Upon the nightstand beside you laid sheet music for choir hymns, marked by your late night marginalia, and I was compelled to turn the papers facedown. My rustling roused you.

"Samuel...?"

"Yes, my most beloved treasure?" said I, replacing the vial within my shirt pocket.

"Why were you gone for such a long time?" you enquired, as you may recall.

I had not planned to converse with you and was unable to extemporize anything particularly imaginative. "David is troubled," said I.

"What happened to him?" you enquired.

"The poor fellow invested all of his savings in a prospecting venture that collapsed, suddenly and utterly. He is ruined and filled with despair."

You sat up and drew the front of your nightgown close to your bosom. "Why didn't he talk about this at dinner? We're his closest friends in all of San Francisco."

"I do not know why he remained silent," said I.

"Why're you crying?" you asked.

You may recall that I was unable to answer your enquiry.

"Should I go warm up some milk?" you offered.

"I shall do it," said the vermin to whom you were married.

*I retreated to the kitchen, put a saucer atop the stove and heated a small quantity of milk for the two of us. I returned to our room and gave you the glass into which I had poured the prescribed dosage of the sleeping draught.**

You drank the tarnished milk, and afterwards, yawned ponderously.

I said, "Lower the drapes."

You shut your eyes and I kissed your splendid eyelids. You fell into a deep sleep.

*The wraiths came inside our apartment and claimed both you and your sister.**

I collapsed and was unconscious for many hours. At dusk the following day, I awakened and drank the remainder of the sleeping draught, but I disgorged the serum, violently, and my suicidal endeavor proved to be no more successful than my business ventures and marriage.

The morning after my failed suicide attempt—this was two days before His birthday—an unexpected visitor knocked upon the door of our apartment. I ignored the individual's solicitations, and he departed after a short while. I drank the champagne that you and I were to share with your sister when we celebrated the New Year, but was unable to do anything with the food in the icebox but watch it decompose.

At ten o'clock that same evening, the visitor returned and vigorously applied his fist to our front door. The Lauders were disturbed by the caller's inexorable rapping, and emerged from their apartment to comment upon his clamor. He announced himself as Brent Plugford, the brother of the woman who dwelled within 3B, and our neighbors recalled him from his visit the previous winter.

"The Upfields have entrusted us with a spare key," said Jill Lauder. "Allow me to fetch it."

"Thank you very much ma'am," said Brent.

At this point, I knew that I could either admit your brother into our apartment or defenestrate myself to the pavement below. I pulled a plaid robe over my disheveled garments and walked toward the front door, concocting lies that could explain your absence, your sister's absence, my sorry condition and the dismal state of disrepair that had befallen our home.

I pulled the door wide. "Good evening, Mr. Plugford," said I.

"It's Brent." Your brother surveyed me for a moment and enquired, "How come you didn't answer?"

"I was asleep."

Jill Lauder emerged from her apartment with our spare key, and I dismissed her.

"Please come in," said I to Brent. Then I affected a terrible cough that did not seem to concern him whatsoever.

Brent entered our apartment and looked at the liquor bottles upon the floor, the stains upon the Oriental rug, and the sodden bedclothes that I had dragged to the couch because I was unable to sleep in our room. "What's goin' on here?" he asked. "And where're the girls?"

"I contracted a dread malady, and so your sisters retreated to my Great Uncle's home in the country, where—"

"When did you get sick?" Your brother did not say this as if he believed I was actually suffering from any illness.

"Insalubrious conditions began four days ago."

"Why didn't I hear 'bout that in the telegram?"

"Of what telegram do you speak?" I anxiously enquired.

"The one Yvette sent me in Portland—three days ago—askin' if I'd come down for the holidays."

"Perhaps she had hoped that I would make a hasty recovery? She is an optimist."

It was clear that Brent did not believe any of what I told him, and he marched directly into the guest room—where he had stayed during his previous visits—and presently returned with the lavender valise that belonged to Dolores. I stared at the luggage in his right hand for a long time.

"What's the explanation for this bein' here?" enquired Brent.

"Dolores forgot it."

The hurled valise struck my face and knocked me over. I concussed the apartment floor so loudly that our downstairs neighbor thumped an angry complaint upon her ceiling with the handle of her broom.

More violence occurred.

*I was too ashamed to confess aloud my vile deeds, and in my delirious state, I proffered weak and inconsistent tales of burglars and missionary work and European sojourns, and all of these preposterous fabrications earned me more beatings. I will not detail my agonies, because they are deserved and compared to whatever ordeals you have suffered, insignificant.**

Thereafter, I was enjoined by your brother to take up residence within the pantry.

I was removed at some later time—the day after Christmas, I believe—to greet the unpaid cowboys who had arrived from Montana to collect their due and dispatch hard fists. As a matter of coincidence, your brother knew two of them from previous cattle work, and dealt with them agreeably.

More violence occurred.

The cowboys left, taking several of my teeth and every item of value from our home, excepting the phonograph given to us by your father on our wedding day.

Shortly after the New Year had been celebrated by revelers above and below the pantry, your father arrived, accompanied by your younger brother and the house negro. Without delay, Brent sat me opposite them ~~at the table where I devised my petty elixir recipes and worthless inventions.~~

"Samuel C. Upfield IV," your father said, "I gave you my permission, before God, when you asked for Yvette's hand. I walked her down the aisle and gave her over to you. Honor that trust and tell me what happened to her and Dolores, so we can find them quick."

I confessed.

John Lawrence Plugford seized my neck, pulled me across the table and would have ripped my head from my shoulders had not Brent, Stevie and the negro interceded. They hastily returned me to the pantry, where I was hidden from your father, who had wholly transformed into an unrecognizable angel of wrath.

Later that night, or perhaps some other evening—it is not easy to mark time in the pantry—I awakened and heard your father, your brothers and the negro in conversation. Your father said, "Send a wire to Long Clay, and tell him to get Deep Lakes and meet us back in Shoulderstone. Let him know this is goin' all the way dark."

I was relocated to smaller accommodations and taken to Texas.

The terrifying individual named Long Clay informed your family that I might possess some value in a barter situation, and thus I have been kept alive as a corporeal bargaining chip. The hope that I might somehow assist or facilitate your rescue is why I have not again attempted suicide.

Your family searches the country for you and your sister, tirelessly, inexorably, with a loving devotion that shames me greatly.

~~*Several times during the period of my captivity, I have had an unsettling dream that I believe to be a religious vision, and I wanted to share it with you, even though the Editors will likely draw a line through its description.*~~

~~*Upon my bent back and across a vast riven plain, I bear a large black trunk. Beneath a red sky that continuously rains ashes, I carry this heavy burden and inhale mephitic vapors. I wander for years and years, until I chance upon a tall and narrow man, dressed in a black robe, who has rocks instead of eyes. I ask him if he has seen Yvette Upfield, and he nods his head in affirmation. He withdraws the stones from his sockets and thrusts them deeply and violently into my face, bursting my eyeballs, and for a moment I am blind.*~~

~~*The stones grow warm and gradually I regain the power of sight. I find that I am on the cold gray avenue that is immediately outside our apartment in San Francisco.*~~

~~*I carry the trunk up the stairs and through the threshold and find you asleep in bed. The sheet music with your late night marginalia is facedown upon the nightstand, and when I reach out to turn it over, I see that I am a shadow, a wraith, and not of living flesh.*~~

~~*I drop my burden, and its concussion rouses you from your slumber. You descry the black trunk, raise its lid and see the man who lies within it. "Who are you?" you ask the battered body of Samuel C. Upfield IV. "Who are you?"*~~

~~*You do not recognize me, and I am thankful.*~~

Undeserving of salvation or forgiveness,
The Man who was Samuel C. Upfield IV

Chapter VII
God Ain't Here

Yvette Upfield set the letter down and raised her gaze. Standing before her were two solemn and silent men—Brent and Patch Up. She did not need to ask if they were the Editors of the essay.

An enormous unanswered question sucked the air from Yvette's lungs and made her lightheaded. The walls of the fort throbbed, and the tubes within her ears popped, as if from a rapid change in atmospheric pressure.

"Is he alive?" The choirmaster was painfully aware that neither answer would bring her heart any joy.

Her brother nodded. "He's alive."

Nauseated, Yvette turned away from Brent, Patch Up and Dolores and crawled toward the far corner of her wooden bunk.

"Do you want to see him again?" the cowboy inquired.

Yvette did not know the answer to that question. The pious and pretty blonde prince, whom she had married before God and loved, had evaporated when faced with financial misfortune and become a drowning rat, desperate, shameless and immoral. Stunned, the choirmaster leaned her forehead to the chill stone bricks.

"Do you want to see him again?" repeated Brent.

Yvette wished that she could slip into the cracks and disappear.

From the edge of the bunk, Dolores said, "That man sold us to be fucked—and we were—and you're a awful skeleton, and I'm a cripple, and our daddy is dead and we still ain't home yet. Goddamn!" She slapped the palm of her hand against the wood. "Don't you hate him?"

Yvette nodded her head and felt the stone rub against her skin. "Of course I do. And I pity him."

"Ain't nothin' to pity."

The choirmaster did not want to argue with her sister. "Please leave me alone."

"I know you're a forgivin' Christian," Dolores said, "but this ain't the time for that."

"Faith is what I have left," replied Yvette.

"Well God ain't here. And your husband is a thousand miles and a hundred years beyond forgivin'."

Dolores's condemnation and hypocrisy redirected Yvette's thoughts. The choirmaster turned from the wall, sat up and faced her sister. "And how about Daddy?"

Brent and Patch Up were still.

"What's he got to do with this?" asked Dolores.

Yvette looked at her sister's confused face. "You love him don't you?"

"Of course." Dolores's eyes flickered to the patriarch's body.

"Even though he was an outlaw?"

"Yvette," cautioned Brent.

"That ain't got no connection to your Samuel C. Upfield the Fourth!" spat Dolores. "Daddy raised us proper, and he loved us. He was a good man."

"How many innocent people do you think he hurt or killed when he was an outlaw with Long Clay?"

Dolores lunged across the bunk toward Yvette, but Brent restrained her. The circus dog barked at the redheaded woman and growled.

"Calm down," Brent said to Dolores. "You can't hurt her."

"She's comparin' our daddy to that goddamn rat she married!"

"Daddy never betrayed us like Samuel did," Yvette said, "but he killed plenty of strangers for money, which is just as bad."

Dolores shouted something that was not a word and struggled to free herself from her brother's arms.

"You can't hit her no matter what she says," stated Brent. "It's only words and she's weak."

Dolores gazed balefully at Yvette. "You think you're so goddamn superior to all of us, huh? Well go ahead and be a Upfield—the Plugfords don't want you no more. Go back to San Francisco with that coward you married and stay there fixed permanent—until he goes and bets you for a cigar butt!" She shoved away her twin brother, reached for her wooden crutch, rose from the bunk and ambled toward the exit.

"Quieten the women," Long Clay ordered from the darkness outside, "and get back to work,"

"Okay," said Brent.

Dolores paused before the open door and looked over her shoulder. "Your important Jesus Christ didn't do nothin' while we was gettin' raped for eight months. It was Daddy, the terrible sinner, who came down to Hell to save us." She leaned upon the gunstock that was the top of her crutch and ambled into the night.

Without a word, Patch Up walked across the fort and departed.

Brent handed Yvette a canteen. "Drink some."

The choirmaster drank, and the water soothed her raw throat. Around her head, walls wavered.

"You want to see Samuel?"

"No." Yvette knew that she could not bear to look upon the quivering epilogue of her marriage.

"Ever?" Brent attempted to appear impartial, but it was obvious that he wanted to rid the world of Samuel C. Upfield IV.

"I…I don't know."

"I'll leave him alone 'til you decide. And you should lie back down—you're pale and shakin'."

Yvette lowered herself to the wood.

Brent pulled the yellow blanket over his sister's bones. "Me and Patch Up and Stevie got a surprise for you—a good one—for when you're feelin' a little better."

It was difficult for Yvette to feign any interest. "Thank you."

"Get some sleep." Brent kissed his sister's forehead and walked through the black portal.

Yvette imagined the betrayer, Samuel C. Upfield IV, whispering the words, "Lower the drapes." She shut her eyes, pressed her face into the cold coarse stone and asked, "How could you?"

Chapter VIII
Eyes of the Unguarded Interior

Brent Plugford walked into the dark outdoors, where the halved moon was shielded by a swath of pregnant gray cotton that would carry rain to some other part of the world. He surveyed the open terrain and saw Long Clay, Patch Up, Stevie and the dandy arrayed along the close side of the trench, digging holes for land torpedoes. The skin of every man was glazed with moonlight.

"Where's Deep Lakes at?" asked Brent.

"On the perimeter," answered Long Clay as he shoveled.

"Any burnin' arrows from him?"

"No."

The cowboy reclaimed his shovel, strode to the eastern side of the trench and applied himself vigorously. For twenty minutes, he plunged, jerked and heaved the iron head of his shovel; grit climbed to the stars and fell back to the earth.

"Stevie," said Long Clay.

"Yessir."

"Get the land torpedoes."

"Yessir."

Stevie stabbed his shovel into the ground, climbed from the earth and walked toward the rear of the fort, where the wagon had been parked inside the sunken stable.

"Brent."

The cowboy looked across the dirt at the gunfighter's torso. "Yeah?"

"Drive iron stakes into the façade."

A chill descended Brent's spine. He knew how these metal extrusions would be employed.

"Set them high," Long Clay specified, "in-between the crenellations."

"There's a stepladder under the wagon," added Patch Up.

After climbing out of his hole, the cowboy stabbed his shovel into the dirt and walked toward the rear of the fort. The dandy watched him go, but did not say anything.

Brent ascended the stepladder, put his index finger between two stone bricks, ran the digit east, found a tiny niche in the mortar, inserted the tip of a two-foot long iron stake, covered the blurred half-moon with his hammer and brought the heavy head down. Metals clanked, and three sparks shot west. The point pierced the wall. Down the wall, grit sizzled.

He covered the lunar segment and swung again. Metals clanked, and the iron stake penetrated deeper.

"You gotta eat," said Dolores. "Please."

Brent looked into the fort, through the nearest crenellation.

Dolores was seated at the edge of Yvette's bunk, dipping bread into a bowl of stew. "Just take a little."

The gaunt woman did not turn around from the stone wall.

"I'm sorry for what I said 'bout Jesus."

"You don't need to apologize. You've got every right to feel how you do and say what you did. It was wrong for me to lecture you."

Dolores placed her free hand upon her sister's right shoulder and pulled her away from the wall. The skin upon Yvette's face was red with scratches, abraded by the coarse stone against which she had pressed herself.

"Girl...please....take care of yourself," said Dolores. "Eat some." She placed a piece of the stew-soaked bread into her sister's mouth. "Chew it. Please."

Yvette's jaw moved.

"Good."

Brent knew that all of the Plugfords might perish in the very near future, and he swung his hammer at his fears. He pounded the iron stake ten inches deep, descended the stepladder, carried it in-between the two adjacent crenellations, climbed to the top, ran his finger along the mortar, found a crack and set the tip. Metals clanked, and sparks shot west. Iron pierced stone. Grit sizzled.

A distant hooting garnered the cowboy's attention, and when he turned around he saw, silhouetted against effulgent clouds, a tiny speck that was an owl. Without warning, the creature plummeted from the sky.

Near the trench that laid one hundred and ten yards south of the fort, Stevie clapped. "I hope that owl had on his favorite sombrero!"

"We're in the Territory," Patch Up stated, "and that bird was an American."

"According to what I've seen, this New Mex'co ain't no better than the old one."

Brent drove a seventh iron stake into the mortar, descended the ladder and positioned himself beside the last of the eight crenellations that were located upon the south façade.

"I need two hours," said Deep Lakes.

"Fine," said Long Clay.

Brent turned from the wall. The Indian, who was covered with dark dirt, approached the fort, clutching the talons of an upside-down great horned owl, which possessed giant yellow eyes.

Patch Up said, "I'll get the perimeter," and shouldered his repeater rifle.

"When you return," Long Clay cautioned, "give this entire area a wide berth." He gestured at the dark holes into which he had just deposited the land torpedoes. "Ride straight for the mountain wall and cut east through the cemetery."

"I'll do that."

The youngest Plugford japed, "Wouldn't want you gettin' blowed up."

Patch Up walked toward the stable. "If only one of us lives through this, I sure hope it's Stevie."

"Wear a tabard," Long Clay called out, "and ride my mare—she'll outrun any other."

"Thanks."

Ten yards from Brent, Deep Lakes entered the cemetery, pressed the heel of his left boot to a gravestone, shoved the marker over and set the owl upon the smooth rock, where the creature attempted to flap its broken wings to no avail. From his denim vest, the Indian withdrew two wooden blocks, each two inches tall, and set them upon either side of the bird's head. A milky film diffused the creature's big yellow eyes, as if it had contracted a sudden (and very visible) case of glaucoma.

Deep Lakes slammed a flat stone against the wooden blocks, the owl's skull cracked like a walnut shell. The bird grasped at the air with its dying claws.

Astride the black mare and wearing an iron tabard, Patch Up rode out of the stable and waved at Brent. "Mr. Plugford."

"You be careful," cautioned the cowboy.

"I got the negro advantage—and a matching horse." Patch Up dusted his gray hair and rode downhill, toward the dark woodlands that laid five miles south of the fort.

Brent waved, turned back to the façade, pounded his stake ten inches deep and descended the stepladder. Nearby, Deep Lakes scooped a pale morsel from the owl's cracked head and placed it in his mouth.

"Do you feel it inside you?" asked the cowboy. "Its spirit?"

"There's no immediate affect."

Brent moved the stepladder, ascended its five rungs and placed the tip of an iron stake to the façade. "It takes a while? A hour?"

"I must be asleep to absorb an animal's essence."

The cowboy pounded the stake. "Why's that?"

"The sleeping mind is unguarded and can receive a foreign presence." The Indian swallowed another pale clump. "The waking mind is closed."

"Do you dream you're flying when you absorb a bird?" Brent hammered, and sparks flew. "Seein' through its eyes way up?"

"The essence is not manifested that obviously."

"I had some dreams like that—flying ones—after I broke off my engagement. Lots of them."

The Indian ate another pale morsel.

"Does everyone in your tribe eat this way?" Brent regretted the question the moment it left his lips.

"My tribe cast me into the fire when I was a child—because I was a small and unhealthy." Deep Lakes cracked open the owl's head like a clamshell. "This ritual is my own and unrelated to any group." The Indian's face was inscrutable.

"I didn't mean to give offense."

"You didn't give offense." Deep Lakes prised loose a yellow eye, and its obsidian iris dilated.

"Brent."

The cowboy looked over at Long Clay.

"Drive in one more and go rest."

"I can still work some," protested the cowboy.

"I need you hale for the engagement," said Long Clay. "And that suture needs to mend."

"Okay."

Brent swung his hammer and pierced mortar.

Deep Lakes ate the owl's eyes.

Brent walked past the latrine, the iron tabards that leaned against the molten stove, the sleeping women and the array of rifles and loaded magazines that covered the tables, toward the huge recumbent corpse. Although John Lawrence Plugford's face had been cleaned and repaired (the gunshot wound atop his left eye was currently filled with clay), he looked thoroughly uncomfortable. The cowboy affectionately patted the dead man's stacked hands, which were as chill as the room.

"We'll fight hard to the end. I promise."

"Mr. Stromler."

Dripping with sweat, the dandy looked up from his hole in the ground.

Brent opened the wallet that he had just retrieved from the pocket of his father's overalls and withdrew the monetary remainder. "Your due." He proffered the legal tender.

Nathaniel looked at the bills as if they were hieroglyphics.

"I know that this pay is pitiful considerin' all that's gone on," Brent admitted, "but I ain't got nothin' more to give, and you helped save my sisters and are owed this stipend."

The dandy accepted the bills, folded them in half and slid them into the left pocket of his yellow riding pants.

"And I want to 'pologize for all that's happened," added the cowboy. "I know that a apology is just words, but I felt I should say I'm sorry to you."

"I heard you." Nathaniel stabbed his shovel into the dirt and jerked.

Brent knew better than to endeavor any further conversation, and he turned away from the tall, embittered man and walked toward the fort.

"What did you think was going to happen," the dandy inquired, "when you first hired me?"

The cowboy turned around. "Nothin' like this. I thought we'd find a whorehouse—a nice one since we had to hire us a dandy—and get my sisters out and put down that Gris and maybe some others with him. Simple rescue with some justice."

The dandy hefted his shovel. "I am digging a hole for a land torpedo."

"I didn't think we were gonna use all this crazy stuff Long Clay brung 'long. Nobody did—includin' him."

The dandy flung dirt into the sky. "It is fortunate for all of us that he is such a conscientious man."

"He's prepared. Ain't no way you can be no crim'nal for forty years without havin' hard tactics." In a quieter voice, Brent added, "But that don't mean I like him none."

The dandy stabbed his shovel into the earth. "How are your sisters doing?"

"They settled down and got to sleep."

"I admire Yvette's resolve. It is not easy to adhere to one's beliefs...during a situation like this." Nathaniel's voice sounded very, very small.

"She's steadfast," remarked Brent.

The dandy heaved dirt at the stars.

Brent entered the fort, walked past his sleeping sisters and decided, for reasons that he could not fully explain, to sleep in the bunk directly above his father's still body.

Long Clay's distant and dry voice came through the openings. "Ladle the dirt slowly and mind the plungers."

"I'll be careful," replied Stevie. "You don't have to back away from me."

"Don't rush."

Brent wondered if he would be awakened by the sound of his brother's obliteration, and also if an instantaneous death was preferable to whatever awaited the other Plugfords. He dismissed these morbid images from his mind, rolled up his jacket and gently lowered the back of his skull to the ersatz pillow. The wound upon the side of his head throbbed, pulling at its stitches, but did not feel any worse after four hours of manual labor, which was a testament to the hardheadedness of every Plugford and also Patch Up's prowess with a needle. Exhausted, the cowboy shut his eyes and heard the sounds of his sisters' respirations.

Darkness expanded.

Water splashed.

"This pond's cold as hell!"

"My nuts feel like acorns."

"Mine feel like roulette balls—the metal kind."

"I just killed some mighty handsome sperm."

Sitting upon a twilit green hillock, Brent Plugford lowered the letter that he held in his hands and surveyed his cowboy outfit. Fat Jim (who was no longer heavy), Isaac Isaacs, Kenneth Wyler, Paul Caselli, Gramps Johnson, Otis Brown, Dummy II, Chester Bradington, Gregory Tappert, Derrick Selva and Dummy III stood within the shallows of a gully pond—a congregation of pale chests and tan appendages. The shivering men walked upon and sank into their own bright reflections.

Brent looked up at the grass plain that surrounded the dell and saw that the herded beeves were calmly grazing. Riding perimeter around the twelve hundred cattle were tiny dots that the foreman recognized as Apache, the Hall brothers, Orton Walderman, Little Brent, Leonard Cane and Kerry O'Boyle.

"Boss!" yelled Fat Jim.

Brent looked down at the pond. "Yeah?"

Fat Jim's freckled head swiveled upon its mirror image, and his two mouths asked, "You gonna come in?"

"How's the water?"

"Damp."

"I was inquirin' after the temperature," said Brent. "The discussion seemed to indicate it was cold."

Fat Jim's mouths said, "You'll shiver ten times and get used to it."

"That sounds cold."

"Better than twenty shivers."

Isaac Isaacs declared, "It's pleasant." He rose from the water and the diagonal scars that the bear had given him last winter glowed red upon his chest. "Fat Jim thinks everything's cold since he lost his blubber. Come on in."

"I'll join you after I'm done perusin' my letter," stated Brent. "I've gotta post it tomorrow in Kansas, and it's gotta be written out proper correct."

"Get a new author."

Three cowboys splashed Isaac Isaacs.

"Who's that letter to?" inquired Fat Jim.

"My sister."

"The pretty cancan dancer who won't go with no cowboys?"

"The other one," responded Brent. "She went and got herself engaged."

"Well tell her James M. Lyle said congratulations." Embarrassed, Fat Jim covered up his bare nether region. "Don't tell her I said it naked."

"Put that in the appendix."

Five cowboys splashed Isaac Isaacs.

"Leave me alone for a bit," the foreman said, "the light's startin' to dwindle and I need to peruse."

The wet men returned to their bathing and horseplay.

Brent scooted his buttocks across the hillock and stopped the moment that a beam of golden twilight illuminated the letter. His pupils narrowed, and he read.

Deer Yvette,

I hope youre happy out there in San Fransisco.

I was back home in Shoulderstone and got the news from Pa and Stevie and Patch Up that youre engaged to marry ~~that~~ Samuel C. Upfeeld the forth. I want to ~~say~~ write to you and give you and him my congrachulations. While me and him did not get along so good that one time I visted its clear to me that he treats you nice and loves you and is relijus which is important to you and speaks reel good English which is also important to you. It was good and proper that he asked Pa if he could propose to you and I think Pa ~~does not hate him anymore~~ likes him better now.

I offen think about us Plugfords and how we aynt like most familees. I aynt sure why this is so, but maybe if ma had lived after she birthed Stevie, we would all be married and have us big families by now. Or maybe its konnected to what Pa did long ago before he was a family man. But this is who we are. I like riding all over the grate lanscape free and unkonnected and Dolores says no to every man that likes her ever since her feeansay left her and Stevie is wayword and I hope is gonna get fixed better tho I don't know. I think its very good that you found a man who loves you and that you wanna have a familee with because I don't know who else is gonna do it.

I hope that I can ride down and vist with you two before the wedding and I can bring you a good heifer if you need one. I promiss that I will make every effert to get along better with Samuel C. Upfeeld the forth since he will be familee and the father of my nefews and neeses before long. I hope he can forgive the stuff I said about him being like a girl and I won't hold it against him that he called me ~~unejucated~~ uneducated. Him and me are diffrent types, but we both care a lot about you and need to get along so that you can be all the way happy, one hundred persent.

I look foward to youre wedding.

Sinseerly,
Youre brother Brent Lawrence Plugford

P.S. The part about the heifer was a joke. I know you aynt got room for no cow in youre apartment.

Brent folded the paper, placed it within an envelope that Patch Up had addressed to Yvette and slid the missive inside his saddlebag.

"C'mon in!" coaxed Fat Jim.

Although Brent hated cold water, he knew that he needed to wash off his sour accumulations before he rode into Kansas City to drop off the letter. "I'm comin' down." He grabbed the heel of his left boot and pulled.

Darkness expanded.

The face of John Lawrence Plugford wailed and coughed up blood.

Darkness receded.

"Wake up!"

A hand shook Brent's right shoulder.

The recumbent cowboy opened his eyes, but could not see anything. "What's occurred?" The wound upon the right side of his head throbbed audibly.

Stevie gulped a breath of air. "It's started!"

Part IV

The Tacticians

Chapter I
Alongside Corpses

Brent Plugford leaned forward and surveyed the enclosure. Diffuse moonlight crept through the vertical openings and shone upon the extinguished lantern, the weaponry, Stevie and the sleeping women.

Sitting upon the edge of his bunk, the cowboy asked, "Where're the others?"

"Coverin' over…the last…torpedoes," Stevie replied in-between gasps.

"Is Patch Up back?"

"Not yet." Stevie sounded worried. "We heard shots. Distant."

Brent landed upon his feet, felt the impact pull at his stitches and walked toward his sisters. "Dolores."

Beneath the yellow blanket, the redheaded woman stirred.

"You hear me?" inquired Brent.

"Yeah."

"Sit up. I've gotta get at Yvette."

"Okay." Dolores sat forward and revealed the narrow blue line that was her younger sister.

Brent leaned over and banged his head upon the upper bunk. Fiery pain exploded across his skull, and he clenched his jaw to keep from crying out.

"You okay?" asked Dolores.

Brent grunted, bent his knees, leaned over, adjusted the blanket, scooped up the collection of interconnected bones that was Yvette and looked at Stevie. "Open up the pris'ners' cell."

Instantly, the young man hastened to the west side of the north wall and pulled open a thick door. The cowboy carried his sister through the portal into a windowless chamber and set her upon a stone bench, which was directly beside four whistling air holes.

Outside, a distant gunshot cracked. Yvette's eyelashes fluttered like the wings of tired butterflies.

"I put some chow in the cubby for if you get hungry," said Brent.

"Lower the drapes," mumbled Yvette.

Brent reached into his pocket, withdrew two pieces of cotton, plugged up Yvette's ear canals and withdrew from the prisoners' cell. The circus dog ran into the room, and the cowboy shut the door.

Two tall shadows hastened into the fort.

"Grab a repeater rifle and get beside your crenellation," ordered Long Clay.

"Somebody's gotta bring me mine," Dolores said as she hobbled toward the eastern opening, through which half of the stone well was visible.

"I got yours," replied Stevie.

"And some spare magazines." The redheaded woman sat upon Patch Up's three-legged cooking stool.

"I got 'em." Stevie claimed two repeater rifles and twelve cylinders from the table and hastened toward Dolores.

A distant gunshot popped and was succeeded by two sharp reports.

Brent and Nathaniel reached the table upon which laid the firearms.

"You know how to shoot?" inquired the cowboy, feeling stupid that he had not earlier asked this question.

"I went hunting with my father when I was a child."

"Good. This gun's like a huntin' rifle, but quicker to reload—just fling the trigger guard to throw a new bullet into the chamber, and after you send eight shots, change magazines." Brent pointed to the pile of loaded cylinders that were resting within the munitions box. "Get some extra."

Nathaniel claimed a repeater rifle and one additional magazine.

"Take more than that,"

The dandy acquired three additional magazines and walked toward the western slit, through which a sliver of the moonlit cemetery was apparent.

Stevie strode to the easternmost slit in the south face. Against the middle of the same wall, Long Clay leaned two weapons—a telescopic rifle and a repeater. Holding firearms, additional ammunition and a wooden spyglass, Brent walked to the other side of the gunfighter.

"Don't fire until I give the word," announced Long Clay.

"Yessir," said Steve.

"There any chance a stray bullet can set off a land torpedo?" asked Brent.

"Almost none. The plungers must be pressed directly down, and gunshots fly horizontally, diagonally and in long arcs."

"Okay."

Brent raised his spyglass and peered through his opening, over dirt that was pregnant with land torpedoes, beyond the perimeter trench and down at the woodlands that laid five miles south of the fort. The vast forested region was opaque.

Two distant gunshots echoed and were succeeded by five reports. The sounds were tiny and distant, like rocks falling on the far side of a mountain.

"Can you discern anything?" Brent asked Long Clay. "Pa said you could identify guns by their sounds."

"The first two shots were from Patch Up's rifle, and the other five shots were from three different revolvers."

"They won't get him," proclaimed Stevie. "He's smarter than any of them Mex'cans and is skilled."

"We'll know if we hear him fire again," stated Long Clay.

The silence that followed the gunfighter's remark was long and heavy.

Brent felt a drop of blood trickle from his suture, past a torn stitch, beyond the edge of his bandage and down his cheek. The lateral wound burned as if it had been treated with hot coals.

"Goddamn!" exclaimed Stevie. "What's that nigger doin'?"

"I've told you not to call him that," complained Dolores. "It ain't nice."

"I'm just…I'm just worried is all."

"Still."

Brent surveyed the opaque woodlands with his spyglass. A volley of gunshots flashed amongst the black trees—a halo of white fire.

The Plugfords and the dandy looked at Long Clay.

"Patch Up fired the first, eleventh and twelfth shots. The others were revolvers and a shotgun."

Stevie asked, "Why don't he ride back?"

"He's probably pinned."

Brent monitored the woodlands with his spyglass, and saw five white bursts of gunfire along the northern edge. "The fray's comin' towards us."

"None of those were from Patch Up," stated Long Clay. "He's on the run or they put him down."

"No," said Dolores.

"He'll make it," proclaimed Stevie. "He'll make it."

Brent's heart pounded as he scanned the northern edge of the woodlands, hoping that he would witness Patch Up emerge atop the fast black mare, but the perimeter remained still and quiet.

The silence was suffocating.

Upon the side of Brent's head, the laceration throbbed audibly. "Where's Deep Lakes?"

"Getting into position."

The cowboy scanned the terrain for the Indian, but did not see him. At the northern edge of the woods, seven gunshots flashed.

"Three revolvers and a pump action shotgun. Patch Up did not fire."

"Well they're still shootin' at him," Brent said, "so he's still alive."

Gunshots flashed across the woodland perimeter like a line of firecrackers.

"Two shotguns, seven revolvers and two rifles. Patch Up did not fire."

Brent saw a lone black fleck emerge from the northern edge of the forest and careen directly toward the fort. Hope fluttered like a bird's soft wings within his chest. "I think I see Patch Up."

"That's him," confirmed the gunfighter, who observed the tableau through the telescopic sight of his long-range rifle.

At the edge of the woodlands, white fire crackled.

"Is he out of range?" asked Brent. It looked like the major part of a mile separated the negro and his western pursuers.

"He's beyond accurate revolver rounds and buckshot."

The dot that was Patch Up astride the black mare sped north on the grasslands, toward the fort.

"Is anybody giving chase?" asked the dandy.

Brent observed the area where he had last seen gunfire. "I can't descry nobody."

Patch Up neared the weedy terrain that laid in-between the grasslands and the sere rise upon which sat the fort. A constellation of gunfire sparkled at the edge of the woods.

Brent panned his spyglass to the illuminated area and watched tiny black dots drip onto the grass. "Hell. He's got a train."

"How many pursuers?" asked the dandy.

The cowboy studied the fleas. "Looks like…nine."

"Goddamn!" exclaimed Stevie.

"Now eleven."

"Even worse!"

Dolores swatted her younger brother's back. "That ain't helpin'."

"Neither is hittin' me."

Brent divined Patch Up from the weedy terrain, exactly halfway in-between the forest and the fort. The pudgy negro clung to the black mare's neck, and bouncing pell-mell at his side was his rifle. "I can't tell if he's been hit. Can you?"

"I can't," said Long Clay.

A crackling constellation glimmered southwest of Patch Up, and a star glimmered upon his tabard. The black mare shook its head and flashed its tail, but did not slacken its pace.

"Where's that goddamn Indian?" complained Stevie. "How come he ain't goin' red savage out there?"

The black mare galloped toward the edge of the weedy terrain.

"He's more than halfway here," announced Brent. "And his train's falling behind." During the prolonged beeline, the incredible speed of the black mare transpired.

"He's gonna make it," stated Stevie. "I told you all. I told you."

Presently, the cleft moon emerged from the clouds and washed over the landscape, and Brent saw that Patch Up's gray hair was dark with blood. The cowboy felt punched in the stomach. "He's…he's been hit."

"No," said Dolores. "Not him too."

"Goddamn them Mex'cans. Goddamn I hate 'em!"

"How serious is the injury?" inquired the dandy.

"I can't tell. He's got blood on his head, but he's holdin' his horse like he's conscious." The distance between Patch Up and his eleven pursuers continued to widen. "And he's only 'bout four minutes out from the fort."

Two miles south of the bleeding man, eleven riders poked twice as many bright white holes into the night. Shortly after the reports faded, the negro looked up from the mare's neck and waved a gory hand at the inhabitants of the fort. There was no blood upon Patch Up's head other than in his hair.

Brent's dread abated. "Looks like they shot his hand. Maybe he got some blood in his hair on accident—scratching himself—but I don't think they got his head."

"Thank God," said Dolores.

"I told you he's comin out alive!" enthused Stevie.

Brent panned his spyglass east and observed the crew that pursued Patch Up. Mounted upon hale horses and wearing dark clothing were eleven armed men. "They're never gonna catch up with—"

The foremost rider jerked back and spilled out of his saddle. Two men in brown suits guided their galloping mounts around the fallen individual, grabbed their necks, fell and slammed into the bucking heads of the two mustangs that were directly behind them. Concussed and overbalanced, the beasts tumbled forward and catapulted their riders into the air. The heads of three other men jerked back upon their necks, and moonlight glinted for half of a second upon the arrow shafts lodged in their nostrils.

Those who remained fired into the open terrain, reined their steeds in a tight circuit and rode back toward the woodlands. After emptying a revolver in all directions, the southernmost rider arched his back, fell from his saddle and rolled across the weeds. Arrows found the spines of the last two mounted men and knocked them down.

"Deep Lakes got 'em," announced Brent.

"Thank God."

"I always liked the goddamn Indians."

Hunching low in his saddle, Patch Up guided the black mare west, around the trench and toward the mountain wall.

Brent trained his spyglass upon the area in which the pursuers had fallen. One of the thrown riders, a pale fat man with a thick handlebar mustache and a dark green suit, stood up and reached for a gun no longer in his holster. Arrows pierced his right hand, left wrist and right kneecap. He shrieked and collapsed to the ground.

Fifty yards north of the injured and dead riders, Deep Lakes rose from a sinkhole and notched shafts.

"He's gettin' us a captive?" Brent asked Long Clay.

"Several."

Beside the cowboy, the dandy shifted uncomfortably, but said nothing.

Patch Up hastened the black mare northwest, toward the mountain wall, and presently escaped Brent's field of view.

"He rounded the edge of the trench," the dandy announced, "and is now riding directly toward us." The tattoo of the galloping hooves grew louder. "He is bleeding… rather significantly."

"I'll get him." Brent pulled the strap of his gun over his shoulder, hastened to the western door, opened it wide and looked outside. The black mare cantered through the graveyard, toward the fort. Collapsed upon the beast's back was Patch Up.

"No."

Dolores asked, "Is he okay?"

"Patch Up!" Brent ran toward the black mare. "I'm comin'!" His vision blurred. "Hold on, hold on!"

"How is he?" Stevie shouted from within the fort.

As the cowboy reached the cantering horse, he felt an electric horror. The right side of the negro's abdomen was covered with blood. For a moment, the world was still.

"Patch Up." Brent gripped the injured man's right shoulder. "I'm here. Wake up."

"Get out of the open!" ordered Long Clay. "Now!"

Brent pulled the mare and its bleeding burden toward the sunken stable that was situated between the fort and the mountain wall.

Without raising his head from the neck of the black horse, the pudgy negro said, "There are at least sixty more…than what followed me out."

"Okay." Brent was unconcerned with the enemy right now. "How bad are y—"

"Put me alongside your father." Patch Up wheezed.

"We'll get you fixed."

"You won't. They shot me from the side…through the liver…and a kidney." Patch Up gasped for air. "Put me…with your father. I want to be wherever he winds up."

Brent cleared his throat. "We'll put you two together." It was hard to speak with a solid voice, but he knew that he could not break in front of the dying man. "I promise we will."

"Thanks." Patch Up grabbed Brent's hand and squeezed it affectionately. "And tell Stevie that I intend to haunt him."

"Okay."

"Forever."

"Okay."

Presently, the cowboy pulled the mare down the log ramp that led into the stable. The beast's hooves clopped loudly upon the wood, and the tattoo echoed up and down the mountain wall.

Brent asked, "Do you want me to put Plugford for your last name? On the tombstone?"

"I do." Patch Up's voice was almost inaudible. "Thanks."

Brent tied the black horse beside the dandy's tan mare, turned around and caught the falling man.

Patch Up was no longer breathing.

"Is he gonna make it?" Stevie asked from the fort. "He okay?"

Unable to speak, the cowboy laid down the negro's body, removed the iron tabard and hurled it, angrily, as far as he could. The metal plates reflected moonlight, clanged to the ground and scraped across the stone. Startled horses whickered.

Brent hugged Patch Up to his chest.

"Is he okay?" Dolores's question echoed across the mountain wall.

The cowboy put his arms underneath the dead man, raised him from the ground and walked up the log ramp, across grit, through the west door and into the fort. His siblings and the dandy turned their anxious faces toward him.

"He's gone."

"No!" Dolores yelled from her stool. "No!"

The dandy slapped his palm against the stone wall. "Damnation!"

Stevie discarded his rifle, ran across the enclosure and looked down at Patch Up. "I…I can't believe it." His eyes filled with moonlight. "I can't believe it. I didn't think…I didn't think that he'd ever…ever…" He was unable to complete his sentence.

"Slide Pa over," Brent said, "Patch Up wants to be next to him."

Stevie nodded and went to the funereal bunk, where he was joined by Nathaniel. The two men slid the patriarch against the north wall, and Brent laid Patch Up beside the huge body. Without a word or a glance at anyone, the dandy walked away from the deceased.

Dolores gathered her crutches and hobbled beside her brothers.

To his siblings, Brent said, "He wants it to go Patch Up Plugford—on the tombstone."

The redheaded woman patted the dead man's hands. "It should." Tears dripped from her chin. "That's what he was."

Stevie began to sob.

Brent hugged his little brother tightly to his chest. "He said he was gonna haunt you forever."

"I hope...I hope he does it." Stevie withdrew, grinned sadly, wiped his eyes, sniffed and walked back toward his slit.

The cowboy hugged his sister.

"Brent?" asked Dolores.

"Yeah?"

"We're all gonna die out here, ain't we?"

Before Brent was able to reply, Long Clay said, "Deep Lakes is bringing the hostages."

"I'll rip their hearts out!" proclaimed Stevie. "I'll stomp their goddamn nuts and piss in—"

"You will listen to me," the gunfighter warned, "or you'll get another mark on your tally."

Stevie grumbled.

Brent helped Dolores back to her stool and returned to his position on the south wall. "Patch Up saw sixty others—not even includin' the ones we put down."

Dolores and Stevie and the dandy were silent.

"Sixty men," restated Long Clay.

"'At least sixty' were his words, exact precise," clarified Brent.

Long Clay announced, "We need to go all the way mean."

"Okay."

"My pleasure!" proclaimed the youngest Plugford. "The meaner the better!"

"Stevie," said Long Clay.

"Yessir."

"Get a fire going in the potbelly stove."

"Yessir."

Stevie set his rifle upon its stock, leaned it to the wall and opened the tinderbox earlier placed beside the molten potbelly stove.

The dandy stared at the gunfighter.

"Mr. Stromler," said Long Clay.

"Yes." Nathaniel's voice was hard with contempt.

"We're outnumbered ten to one. Or perhaps the ratio is worse. We must be ruthless."

"Do you intend to torture people?"

"If you can't stomach mean business, you should leave. If you lodge one complaint, Stevie and Brent will throw you in the cell and lock the door until it's all over. If you attempt to impede my tactics in any way, I will shoot you."

"Long Clay's got the reins," affirmed Stevie. "He's the tactician."

The gunfighter eyed the dandy. "Will you follow my lead?"

"I will." Nathaniel turned away and faced his slit.

"You've been warned."

"I have."

Long Clay looked meaningfully at Brent.

To the wraith that offered his dark services, the cowboy nodded.

The tall narrow man returned his gaze to his telescopic sight, and the moonlight captured within its lenses turned his right eye into an opalescent gem.

Chapter II
The End of Nathaniel Stromler

A match scratched and hissed. White light flared in the southeastern corner of the enclosure, turned orange, shrank and became an amber rectangle that was the opening of a potbelly stove. Wood shavings curled with serpentine life and crackled like a phonographic cylinder or a bowl of scorpions.

Nathaniel Stromler turned back to his west wall crenellation, looked outside and surveyed the cemetery in which tombstones and markers sprouted from the sere land like dull teeth. On the far side of the burial ground was the horse that carried the native, followed by a trio of steeds laden with blindfolded prisoners.

"Deep Lakes is thirty yards from the door," announced the gentleman.

"Mind your words when the captives are in," ordered Long Clay. "We don't want them to know the size of our crew."

"Understood," said Nathaniel.

"Okay," said the Plugfords.

Forty minutes before the first shot was fired, Nathaniel had crouched in the latrine and forced the last prickly scorpion through his bowels. Everything in his life, all of his relationships and hopes and ideals, had yielded to the agony of the bleeding orifice. He was a sweaty, unintelligent animal that was in intense pain, nothing more and he doubted it would be much easier for him to witness other people reduced to the same bestial state.

"Brent. Stromler," said Long Clay. "Help Deep Lakes with the captives. Mind the blindfolds."

"Okay," said the cowboy.

The gentleman slung his weapon over his shoulder and found that his hands were shaking.

"Leave your rifle here," said Brent. "Their hands're tied, but you don't wanna risk one of them grabbin' no gun."

Nathaniel set his rifle against the wall.

Brent pulled open the door and exited the fort.

The gentleman walked outside and felt the night—cool, vast and deadly—open up around his head. The halved moon was magnified by a thick gray cloudbank, upon which he saw an electric blue thread that was either distant lightning or a flaw in his retina.

Five yards away, Deep Lakes reined his purloined colt to a halt, leaped from the saddle, slung his strange bow and walked to the trio of horses that he had trailed. He grabbed the ankles of two captives and pulled. The men thudded against the ground and were dragged toward the fort like sacks of bad potatoes that were about to be turned into fertilizer.

Brent pointed to a redheaded man who wore a pinstriped brown suit and had arrows in his chest and right shoulder. "Grab that one." Like all of the captives, the individual was blindfolded and had his wrists bound together.

Nathaniel slid his arms underneath the injured man's back, heaved him from the horse and grunted.

"Draggin' is easier," remarked the cowboy.

While carrying the redheaded man toward the fort, the feathers of embedded arrows waggled in front of the gentleman man's nose and elicited a sneeze.

Nathaniel entered the edifice and laid his burden upon the floor, beside a stout Mexican who had a boyish face and the triumphant individual who had exclaimed, "¡Triunfo!" in both Castillo Elegante and the crimson stagecoach. Brent indelicately dropped his captive, a heavy fellow with a dark green suit and a thick handlebar mustache, next to the redheaded man, and Deep Lakes dragged the last hombre, who wore a black vaquero outfit decorated with silver fringes, across the stone until he laid alongside his peers. The amber glow of the potbelly stove shone obliquely upon the five bound and blindfolded men, only two of whom appeared to be conscious.

It was clear to Nathaniel that he could not remain indoors while the torturous endeavors occurred. "I shall wait outside," he said as he walked toward the west wall.

"Stay here," ordered Long Clay. "I need you to translate."

Nathaniel silently cursed.

Brent closed the west door.

To the brothers, the gunfighter said, "Watch the perimeters."

"Okay." Brent and Stevie returned to their slits.

Long Clay knelt beside the redheaded man and slapped his face.

"Don't!" protested the bound and blindfolded captive.

"How many men are in your posse?"

"A...a lot. We've got a big crew." The man's accent indicated that he was from the Midwest.

Long Clay swatted the man's throat. "Give me a number. If it doesn't match what the other captives say, I'll cut off your right hand."

The Midwesterner paled. "Uh...um...ninety, I believe."

A terrible dread flooded throughout Nathaniel's body. For the second time in two days, he was hopeless.

"Goddamn," muttered Stevie.

Dolores lowered her head, and Brent spat through his slit.

"Some horses got sick after we went through your campsite," the Midwesterner added, "and a few men too."

"Why're you out here?" asked Long Clay.

"I'm friends with Diego and Rosalinda. Was."

"Who're they?"

"Gris's son and daughter-in-law. Good, kind people that you folks murdered when you robbed Catacumbas."

Irked, Brent spun around. "We didn't rob that damn place or kill one woman."

"The pregnant woman," the Midwesterner said, "the one that the tall man shot in the hand, she went into shock and bled to death. And her little baby died too."

Long Clay seemed unaffected by the news that he had killed a pregnant woman and her child. "Are you close with Gris's family?"

"I…I know them." The Midwesterner's voice was weak.

The gunfighter looked at the cowboy. "This one goes on the wall."

At that moment, Nathaniel knew that Long Clay was the most immoral man he had ever known, and the single most odious individual on either side of this battle, including Gris himself.

The gunfighter knelt beside the only other conscious man, the stout Mexican with the boyish face, and inquired, "Do you speak English?"

"No Ingles." The fellow seemed very proud of this fact. "Soy Mejicano verdadero."

Long Clay looked over at Nathaniel. "Ask him how he's connected to Gris."

The gentleman restated the inquiry in Spanish.

A moment later, the boyish Mexican replied.

Nathaniel said, "He was hired by a third party to join the posse and does not personally know Gris."

"Perfect." The gunfighter looked at the native. "Separate this one from the other four. He's the messenger."

Deep Lakes grabbed the boyish Mexican by the left ankle and dragged him toward the west door.

Long Clay looked at Stevie. "Put five iron stakes into the stove. Just the tips."

"Gladly."

Nathaniel's skin tingled.

Stevie opened a green crate that was beside the table, grabbed five stakes, set their points into the luminous amber interior of the potbelly stove and returned his right eye to the telescopic sight above the gunfighter's rifle.

Long Clay looked at Brent. "Strip these four naked."

"Okay."

Queasy, Nathaniel walked toward the door.

"The dandy will help you."

A void opened up within the gentleman, and his vision narrowed.

"C'mon." Brent clasped Nathaniel's right elbow, pulled him to the bound quartet, opened the toolbox, withdrew two pairs of steel shears (one of which had a curl of sheep's wool in-between its heavy blades), knelt beside the captive who had earlier exclaimed, "¡Triunfo!" and clipped the jutting arrows.

"Pull off his shoes and pants," the cowboy said to his reluctant accomplice.

Nathaniel got on his knees, grabbed the captive's left boot, wrested it loose, claimed its sibling, undid four suspender tabs, unbuttoned the fellow's waist band, clutched both hems and pulled. A brass compass and a monocle clinked upon the stone, and burgundy underclothes were revealed.

Brent handed Nathaniel the second pair of shears. "Cut through his sleeves and then we can pull the whole thing off o' him." The men applied their flashing blades and rent three layers of clothing. "That'll work." The duo set down their shears and pulled the cleft jacket, shirt and union suit off of the unconscious Mexican. Emanating from the man's naked body were the smells of blood and excrement.

Stevie and Dolores furtively observed Brent.

A spool of barbed wire dropped to the ground beside the captive's feet. "Bind his ankles together," ordered Long Clay.

Nathaniel tasted cold dread.

"Hold his head good and tight," Brent said as he donned thick gloves, "so that he don't break his skull." The cowboy unwound two yards of wire and clipped it with his shears.

Nathaniel leaned forward and braced the triumphant man's head against the floor.

Brent pulled the gleaming wire around the captive's flush ankles, and four barbs pierced the skin. The triumphant man screamed. Throughout Nathaniel's body, the sound of another man's agony reverberated.

Hastily, the cowboy pulled the line through four more circuits, twisted its ends secure, released the bound limbs and withdrew. The captive's toes clutched the air like the webbed extremities of an amphibian.

"Don't kill me." The Midwestern captive began to sob. "Please. I have two young daughters back—"

Long Clay inserted a plum into the man's mouth. "I'll cut off your right hand if you spit that out."

No more pleas emerged from the Midwesterner.

Brent pointed to the unconscious captive who had the handlebar mustache. "Let's do him."

Myopically focusing his thoughts on each assigned task, Nathaniel nodded his head. He knelt. The cowboy clipped arrows, and the gentleman removed the unconscious fellow's shoes, green trousers and long john bottoms. Both men cut away the captive's jacket and blood-stained white shirt.

"I know that one." Dolores smoldered.

Brent's face darkened.

Nathaniel leaned forward and braced the captive's head.

"Hold it firm."

The cowboy pulled barbed wire in a quick circuit, and the captive yelled. Nathaniel's arms shook. Brent glanced at his sister and yanked the line. Barbs tore open the man's shins and calves, and he shrieked.

"Go easy for now," cautioned Long Clay.

Brent finished binding the man's legs and dropped them to the floor, where they twitched and dripped blood. Nathaniel released the captive's moaning head.

Dolores hobbled over and struck the captive's face with her crutch. "Disgusting!"

Brent and Nathaniel stripped the bloody vaquero, who had been shot by four arrows. The man was dying and did not awaken when his feet were bound.

Presently, the duo knelt beside the redheaded Midwesterner. The man whimpered when his trousers were removed, fell unconscious when his arrows were clipped and reawakened when the remainder of his clothing was ripped from his body. Brent wrapped freckled ankles with barbed wire, and Nathaniel felt warm tears upon his palms.

"Is the horizon clear?" asked Long Clay.

"Yessir," replied Stevie.

"It's clear," Deep Lakes said from outside.

Long Clay looked at Nathaniel and Brent. "Hang the captives from the stakes by their ankles."

Nathaniel's skin grew cold.

"Get 'em by the feet and stay in front, so they can't kick you," Brent advised, as if he were discussing the best way to handle a roped steer. He grabbed the right big toe of the plump man with the handlebar mustache and dragged him across the floor, through the west door and out of view.

Nathaniel similarly trailed his burden, the Midwesterner. The nude captive's back and buttocks sizzled across the ground.

"Wait until he comes back," ordered Long Clay.

Nathaniel paused, watched Brent and Deep Lakes walk past the southern crenellations and heard the creak of the stepladder, followed by a couple of grunts and a gurgling yell.

Presently, the cowboy returned.

Clasping a freckled foot, Nathaniel walked outside. Deep Lakes accompanied the lumbering and draggling Midwesterners through the vast night to the front of the fort.

"Jesus Christ." Nathaniel stared at previously hung captive, whose legs and inverted phallus were agleam with moonlit blood.

"Climb the stepladder," Deep Lakes said to the glassy-eyed gentleman. "I'll hand him up to you."

Nathaniel narrowed his thoughts, ascended three rungs, received the legs of the Midwesterner and guided them toward the wall. An iron stake poked into the barbed wire, slid between the captive's ankles and emerged on the near side of the metallic binding.

Deep Lakes released the man's torso.

The inverted Midwesterner dropped. Wires snapped taut against the stake, and barbs revealed yellow tissue, pink muscle and white tendons. The captive shrieked, and the plum fell out of his mouth.

Nathaniel tumbled from the stepladder and onto the ground. With shaking hands, he picked up the fallen fruit and—to silence the terrible wailing—reinserted it inside the Midwesterner's mouth. Covered with sweat and shaking, the gentleman hastened back inside the fort.

Trailing the Mexican vaquero, Brent departed.

Nathaniel could not stop trembling.

After an impossibly short period of time, Brent returned.

Nathaniel dragged the man who exclaimed, "¡Triunfo!" to the façade, where hung three nude hostages, bloody and inverted. The gentleman climbed the ladder, received the upended limbs from Deep Lakes, slid the wire binding along an iron stake and shut his eyes when the captive's weight pulled his ankles into the cold sharp barbs.

After an upside-down human being made terrible animal sounds, the tall empty thing that looked like Nathaniel Stromler walked back into the fort.

Deep Lakes shut the door.

Long Clay looked at Brent and Nathaniel. "Get back to your slits."

"Okay."

After a tiny nod, the gentleman moved his legs.

Long Clay strode toward the potbelly stove, from which sprouted the long ends of five iron stakes. "Ready the messenger."

Deep Lakes knelt beside the boyish Mexican, whose wrists were bound behind his back, and pulled a cord around his ankles.

Standing at the west wall, Nathaniel looked outside, over the mute tombstones and at the dark, empty horizon. The boy from Michigan who had traveled to Europe with his family, stayed in luxurious hotels and adventured was gone, as were the teenager who vowed never to turn a gun on another person, and the twenty-two-year-old gentleman who had fallen in love with Kathleen O'Corley. This current incarnation of Nathaniel Stromler was an unscrupulous animal that would do anything to preserve its own life—even torture innocent people. He was a corporeal shell that lived in the present, divorced from his former identity, obeying the threats of an evil gunfighter.

The gentleman from Michigan reviled what was left of himself—his spineless, quivering remainder.

Outside the fort, inverted hostages gargled and moaned like rheumatic haunts.

Nathaniel looked over his shoulder. In the southeast corner, Long Clay withdrew a stake from the molten potbelly stove. The luminous iron point traveled across the room like a fang pulled directly from the Devil's mouth.

The boyish Mexican pleaded.

Although he doubted that the poor man's words would change the gunfighter's itinerary, Nathaniel translated. "He said that his name is Alberto Querrera and that—"

"I'm not interested."

Deep Lakes tore open Alberto's brown shirt. Catapulted buttons skittered across the stones, clicking.

Long Clay stepped upon the captive's bound ankles and looked at Nathaniel. "How do you say, 'I work for Gris' in Spanish?"

"Yo trabajo para Gris," replied the gentleman.

"Spell it one word at a time."

"Y. O."

Long Clay pressed the luminous tip of the iron stake into the skin above Alberto's left pectoral muscle. Flesh sizzled.

The captive jerked and shrieked. "¡No! ¡Por favor! ¡No se nada!" Long Clay withdrew the iron stake. Upon Alberto's chest sat a lone diagonal line, red and swollen.

With a steady hand, the gunfighter reapplied the glowing metal, elicited a scream and added the mirror image of the first mark (to create a V) and a vertical scar that dropped down from the connection of its antecedents. Long Clay lifted the luminous point, set it down, summoned a groan and inscribed a sizzling circle next to the first symbol. Alberto squirmed like a live fish dropped into a frying pan, but the native and the gunfighter held him firmly in place.

Upon the captive's chest sat two bloody letters.

Yo

"Next word," prompted Long Clay.

Nathaniel turned away from the shuddering canvas. "T. R. A. B. A. J. O." Behind his back, skin sizzled, and the metallic smells of blood, urine and heated iron permeated the air.

"Por favor," pleaded Alberto, "por favor…"

Nathaniel's hands squeezed the barrel of his repeater rifle, and his heart raced. The cemetery outside his slit became blurry.

Alberto spoke of his crippled mother, Leticia, who was confined to her bed in Nueva Vida.

Long Clay set the red stake inside the potbelly stove, withdrew a bright orange replacement and returned. "Next word."

"P. A. R. A."

Skin sizzled. In between sobs, Alberto explained that he had taken the job with Gris so that he could buy Leticia new bedclothes.

The empty gentleman strangled his rifle.

Long Clay inquired, "G. R. I. S?"

Holding his breath, Nathaniel nodded.

Skin sizzled, but the Mexican made no sound.

"Did he pass out?" asked Brent.

"Yes."

"Too bad," remarked Stevie.

"Stromler," prompted Long Clay. "Look at this."

The gentleman turned around and looked down. Burned into the unconscious Mexican's chest was the message.

Yo trabajo
para Gris

The gunfighter inquired, "This reads, 'I work for Gris?'"

Unable to breath the tarnished air, Nathaniel nodded.

Long Clay walked to the potbelly stove, inserted his writing implement and withdrew an iron stake that had a bright white tip. Around the luminous fang, the night air warped.

Nathaniel's pulse pounded violently within his temples. He momentarily forgot his fiancé's name and the address of his mother's empty candy store in Michigan and where his father was buried.

The gunfighter strode across the room and extended the radiant point toward the captive's blindfold. Dolores and Brent turned away from the grim tableau.

"Please," Nathaniel pleaded, "you do not have to—"

Long Clay plunged the stake into Alberto's left eye.

The captive shrieked, but was held in place by the native.

As the gunfighter lifted the stake, Alberto's left eyelid stuck to the radiant metal, stretched and tore loose. Clear fluid bubbled within the ruined socket, and the blindfold sloughed to the ground. The captive was no longer conscious.

"The man is a hired hand," Nathaniel said, "you—"

Long Clay positioned the smoking iron above the captive's remaining eye.

"Stop! You have done enough." Nathaniel's voice was strong and hard. "I will—"

Long Clay thrust the stake.

"No!"

The gunfighter pulled the iron from the man's hissing eye socket and looked at the native. "Pull down his trousers."

Nathaniel raised his rifle.

A black circle appeared and flashed brilliantly. Nathaniel flew west and impacted the stone wall. Unused, the repeater rifle fell from the gentleman's hands and clattered upon the ground. Across the left side of his chest, a sharp and burning pain flared.

"You dumb idiot," remarked Stevie.

Long Clay claimed the fallen repeater rifle.

Nathaniel felt warm fluid pour from the bullet hole and run down his abdomen. The walls of the fort elongated.

Appalled and speechless, Dolores watched the gentleman sink.

Nathaniel's buttocks struck the floor. The world shook, and he keeled north. Suddenly, the back of his skull smacked against the stone, and he stared, glassy-eyed, at the ceiling.

Throughout the gentleman's collapsed body spread a blue chill.

A silhouetted man appeared and knelt upon the stone. "I'm…I'm so, so sorry." Nathaniel recognized the speaker as Brent. "You shouldn't be here at all." The cowboy pressed a cool cloth to the bullet hole.

"I t-told you that I should not…use a f-f-firearm."

"You were right. One hundred percent."

The narrow black wraith slid across the room, expanded and hissed.

"I hope that…most of you…survive." Nathaniel tasted blood in his throat.

"Thanks."

Deep Lakes removed Alberto's trousers and long johns. The glowing tip of the iron stake shone upon the dark curl that was the blinded Mexican's exposed phallus.

Blackness expanded before Nathaniel's eyes.

Skin sizzled and hissed.

"Goddamn," said Stevie. "Goddamn that's terrible."

Chapter III
The Torture Tactic

The circus dog growled meritorious accusations at Brent Plugford and his brother as they set the unconscious dandy upon the floor of the prisoners' cell, beside the collection of bones that was Yvette. Stevie mumbled ungraciously and left the dark room.

"Say one for Mr. Stromler," Brent whispered to his sleeping sister, "he don't deserve any of this." Troubled by guilt, the cowboy exited the dark, windowless chamber.

"Lock that door," Long Clay ordered from his position along the south wall.

Brent slid the iron bolt and turned around. He glanced at the bunk upon which laid the inert bodies of Patch Up and John Lawrence Plugford and quickly looked away. Any ruminations upon these dead men—or the pregnant woman and unborn child Long Clay had murdered—grew the cowboy's sadness and turned it into a debilitating, all-consuming despair. Now was not the time for self-recriminations or mourning.

"Hell."

Deep Lakes dragged the blinded and inscribed messenger toward the west door. Brent felt a pang of nausea when he noticed the blackened nub between the Mexican's legs.

"How's Mr. Stromler?" asked Dolores.

"I stopped the bleeding, but..." Brent shook his head. "I don't think he's gonna make it." He knew that Patch Up would have better tended the injury.

Dolores glared at Long Clay. "You shouldn't've shot him."

The remorseless gunfighter did not bother to defend himself.

Stevie said, "Who cares what happens to that dumb dandy."

"You should," barked Brent. "He helped us rescue our sisters and only got shot because he didn't want to see no hired gun get mutilated."

"He drew on Long Clay," Stevie rebutted, "and deserves what he got."

"I pray you ain't as stupid as your mouth advertises." The cowboy returned to the south wall, shouldered his repeater rifle and unscrewed his spyglass.

As if Long Clay were not in the room, the young man asked, "You wanted the dandy to win?"

The honest answer to that question was complicated. Brent knew that the gunfighter was the Plugfords' only chance for survival, but on a personal level, the cowboy would have preferred to see the dandy win the exchange. "I wish it didn't happen is all," he stated, equitably.

"Stevie," said the gunfighter.

"Yessir?"

"Take the position on the west wall."

"Okay."

The young man slung his rifle, gathered together his spare magazines and strode to the opening that had previously been monitored by the dandy.

Brent raised his spyglass and looked outside. The halved moon was sinking behind the southern mountains, and the landscape was darker than before.

"What time is it?" asked Stevie.

Skilled at divining the hour from heavenly bodies, Brent answered, "Half past four."

"Feels like next year."

"At least," remarked Dolores from the far side of the fort.

Long Clay said "Brent."

"Yeah?"

"Put two lanterns on the front wall so that the opposition can see our decorations whenever they charge."

"Okay."

Brent gathered two lanterns, went outside, hung them over the inverted men, lit the wicks and hastened indoors. Presently, he returned to his slit, picked up his spyglass and located Deep Lakes.

The Indian rode a purloined gray mustang and trailed a white colt, upon which laid the unconscious body of the inscribed, blinded and castrated messenger. For ten minutes, the cowboy watched the horses race south, toward the weedy terrain that laid in-between the woodlands and the sere incline.

The animals reached the halfway point and stopped. In the spyglass optics, the steeds were magnified to the size of mice. The Indian leaped from his horse, took the messenger from the second beast and stood him upright. Weak starlight glimmered upon the Mexican's inscribed chest and the dark dots that had replaced his eyes and phallus.

Deep Lakes leaned over, removed the messenger's fetters, turned him south and shoved him forward. The blind eunuch fell to his knees. Then, the Indian helped the man to his feet, slapped him twice, and shoved him south once more.

Toward the black forest, the mutilated man drifted.

"Brent. Stevie. Dolores."

"Yeah?"

"Yessir?"

"What?"

Long Clay adjusted the telescopic sight of his rifle, and weak moonlight glowed within his right eye like a cataract. "You need to understand our tactic."

"We trust you," said Stevie.

"You need to know it fully," the gunfighter replied, "in case I get put down."

"Okay," replied Stevie and Dolores.

"Go 'head." Brent was certain that he was about to hear the machinations of evil.

"On an instinctual level," Long Clay said, "a man fears torture and disfigurement more than he fears death. He can imagine what it's like to be branded, because he's burned himself; he can imagine what's its like to be blind, because he's been in a dark room stumbling into furniture; and if he's ever had any pain in his privates, he can imagine what being castrated might feel like.

"Death is very different to him, because it's an unknown. The man might even believe it's the beginning of some new type of existence—like those heaven fantasies your sister entertains.

"But the man doesn't have any delusions about what kind of life awaits a mutilated, blind fellow whose penis has been removed."

"A terrible one," opined Stevie. "I'd kill myself."

Brent tried not to picture Alberto's future.

Long Clay resumed, "After Gris's men see the messenger we sent over, the hired guns who're not personally invested in this battle will either ask Gris for more money-—a lot more—or they'll leave no matter what wage is proffered. Nobody wants to be the next messenger.

"Gris will lose one quarter to one third of his crew as a result of this tactic. Maybe more."

"Holy goddamn!" enthused Stevie. "They should've hired you for the Alamo."

Through the wooden spyglass, Brent watched the blind specter drift.

"The remaining men in Gris's crew will become angrier," Long Clay stated, "which is also to our advantage. Angry men don't think clearly and they make hasty decisions—like charging onto a field filled with land torpedoes."

"I sure hope it goes like that." Brent watched Deep Lakes hasten his gray mustang up the sere incline, toward the fort.

"If Gris's posse staged a siege, they would win," declared Long Clay. "They have superior numbers and could pin us, while accessing unlimited reinforcements and supplies. We need to hasten their attack, kill as many as we can, cow the rest and get Gris."

"I get to kill him," said Dolores. "And I want to make him suffer."

"We're not dragging things out for revenge," stated the gunfighter.

"Gris deserves to die slow."

Long Clay did not respond to Dolores's remark.

Ink spilled from the northern edge of the forest, toward the drifting snowflake that was the messenger. The distant particles that comprised the emergence were the riders and horses of the opposition, but in the heavy darkness they appeared to be a single entity, the arm of some gigantic black bear.

Suddenly, the messenger was seized by the extrusion and pulled into the woodlands.

"They snatched him up," Brent informed his siblings.

Long Clay said, "Dolores. Stevie."

"What?"

"Yessir?"

"Get on the south wall and put your guns forward."

Chapter IV
Blood Gathering

The high heels of two beige dress boots dangled an inch above the brown carpet that Daddy and Patch Up had installed throughout the house when Dolores Plugford and her twin brother were first learning to crawl. Sitting upon the edge of her bed, the twenty-seven-year-old woman stared at a dark blemish amongst the familiar fibers and recalled authoring the stain when she and Brent had inexpertly opened a purloined bottle of wine with a pocketknife.

The hallway floorboards creaked six times, and a huge fist gently knocked upon the closed bedroom door.

"Angel?"

"Yes Daddy?"

"Can I come in?"

"Okay."

The bedroom door opened and revealed Dolores's handsome, broad-shouldered father, who was dressed in a dark blue three-piece suit. His silver and brown hair was neatly combed, and his face, washed and shaved by the best barber in Shoulderstone, gleamed. "I know I said it at the church, but you look stunning pretty in that dress."

"Thanks. You look real handsome in that suit."

"Tell Patch Up—he picked it out for me." John Lawrence Plugford walked beside the green desk that Dolores had once used for her grammar school assignments and placed his hand upon its matching chair. "Mind if I sit?"

"Go 'head."

The patriarch set the chair beside the bed, seated himself and interlaced his big fingers. "I can understand why you're upset. Can't be easy watchin' your kid sister get married first."

Dolores looked through the window and down at the twilit celebration that occurred upon the festooned porch of the Plugford ranch. Sixty guests attended the wedding celebration, including a score of folks who had traveled all the way from San Francisco to watch Yvette change her last name to Upfield. Patch Up, wearing a tuxedo and a top hat, and Stevie, wearing a gray suit that was a little too small for him, argued beside the new phonograph that was to depart with the newlyweds, but their words and the sounds of the gay throng were muted by the thick pane of glass.

John Lawrence Plugford took Dolores's right hand. "You're still young and beautiful, and you got spark like your mother. A lady like you don't need to worry about findin' a man—only which one's good enough for her."

The compliment only grew the cancan dancer's melancholy. "I wanted to marry Aaron."

John Lawrence Plugford shook his head. "You'll find somebody better than him."

"I ain't so sure."

"You will. I've got perspective, and I know it definite certain." The patriarch kissed his daughter's hand. "You'll find yours. And he'll be better than Aaron Alders."

"I never told you the real reason why he ended it with me," confessed Dolores. "It had nothin' at all to do with me."

John Lawrence Plugford's face stiffened. "Who'd it have to do with?"

Aaron Alders had an uncle in northern Florida who had heard some very disconcerting rumors about John Lawrence Plugford. These crumbs of information were conveyed to Dolores's fiancé, and the oil man had inquired after their veracity. The cancan dancer was unable to lie to her betrothed, and he took the news very badly. "I still love you," said Aaron, tears shining his eyes, "but I cannot—in good conscience—legally connect my family to yours." After a long and heavy silence, the oil man added, "I know it's not your fault…but it's a fact and my uncle will raise an objection to my parents if I don't break things off." Too destroyed to get angry, Dolores nodded her head and asked the man to leave. She had never told anybody (excepting Brent) the real reason that the engagement had ended, and two years later she found that she still loved Aaron.

"Who'd it have to do with?" John Lawrence Plugford asked for the second time. The huge man looked intensely uncomfortable.

"Aaron found himself another woman. A secretary at one of his wells." Although she was usually candid with her father, Dolores could not bear to tell him that he was the cause of her great disappointment.

John Lawrence Plugford looked relieved. "I know it hurts, but it's better that you found out how he was before you two got married. You want your husband to be devoted steadfast. A man who thinks your smile is the most important thing in the world." His eyes sparkled, and he squeezed his daughter's hand.

The cancan dancer swung her boots back and forth. "Thanks."

"Lets get down there and have us a waltz." The huge man rose from his chair.

"I wanna be alone for a bit."

"Nope." John Lawrence Plugford leaned over and scooped his daughter up into his arms. "Moving and music will change your humors."

The room spun around Dolores's head, and a smile crept onto her face, despite herself. Once the revolutions stopped, she saw Brent, standing in her doorway. Presently, Patch Up appeared, wiping his forehead with a handkerchief.

Brent looked at Dolores. "You okay?"

"I'm okay. Your tuxedo's nice—I didn't see it good at the church."

"I borrowed it from Isaac Isaacs. And he should mind what he leaves in the pockets." Her brother grimaced.

The patriarch announced, "We're comin' down to waltz."

"I'll warn people," said Patch Up.

"I know two waltzes."

"Gigantic and huger."

"Daddy. Put me down—I can walk."

The floor rose, and the soles of Dolores's beige boots sank into the brown carpet. John Lawrence Plugford extended his right elbow.

Arm in arm, Father and daughter walked out of the room, across the second floor hallway, down the stairwell upon which Stevie had broken his right arm when he was seven, eight and twelve years old, through the oaken dining room wherein hung a portrait of the petite matriarch (rendered in the year eighteen seventy-five) and a singed painting of the Florida plantation, across the turquoise tiles of the kitchen, through the back entrance and onto the porch where the recently-married couple and their guests celebrated holy matrimony.

Dolores was cheered by the fresh air, the sounds of the throng and the music that emanated from the flower of the phonograph.

"Stevie!" shouted Patch Up.

"What?" The nineteen-year-old's lips were stained purplish-red with wine.

"Put on a waltz!"

"Which one?"

"'His Waves Shall Carry Us Home!'"

Stevie pulled the needle from the wax cylinder, and music was sucked from the air. The dancers awkwardly aborted their steps and threw unhappy looks at the youngest Plugford.

"Wait 'til the song's finished done," said Brent.

The chastened young man returned the needle to the groove from which it had been taken, and the music resumed, abruptly alive like a sleeper startled awake. After a few lurching steps, the dancers reclaimed their pulse. The phonograph attendant raised his glass of wine and drank.

John Lawrence Plugford walked Dolores around the guests, toward the eastern veranda, where the newlyweds stood and conversed with an older couple from Wyoming. Yvette's sky blue wedding gown modestly displayed her figure, which had become lush and womanly in recent years, and her blonde hair was arranged in an artful swirl that looked like liquid sunlight. Her face was joyful. Samuel C. Upfield IV's opalescent tuxedo scintillated, and his twilit eyes glowed as if they were made of gold.

When the older couple from Wyoming noted the approaching relations, they excused themselves from the newlyweds with a kiss and a handshake.

John Lawrence Plugford ducked his head underneath a blue and white festoon. "Mr. and Mrs. Upfield."

Samuel and Yvette turned into the sun and glowed.

"You look real good together." Dolores had her reservations about Samuel C. Upfield IV, but she could not deny how much he adored Yvette. "A real pretty couple."

Twilight coruscated within the bride's smiling eyes. "Thank you."

"That yellow dress and you have a wonderful partnership," Samuel remarked to Dolores over a glass of twilit gin. "My friend David has twice complimented the synergy."

The music reached its cadence and, before its final chord had naturally decayed, vanished.

"The man has an interest," clarified Yvette.

Dolores did not find the fawning banker from San Francisco at all appealing and had openly avoided his solicitations. "I've been apprised."

Concerned looks were exchanged between Yvette and Samuel.

"Today is 'bout you two gettin' together," remarked Dolores. "And making real long speeches with lots of words that nobody knows." This later remark was addressed to the groom.

"Sesquipedalians draw from the supernal lexicon."

A slow waltz emerged from the flower of the phonograph.

John Lawrence Plugford's shadow covered over his daughters. "Let's have us a dance."

"That is an exceedingly splendid idea." Samuel set his drink upon the banister that was once favored by the rotund tabby cat Pineapple, took Yvette's gloved hands and walked her toward the center of the porch. John Lawrence Plugford and Dolores followed after the newlyweds.

"Daddy," said Yvette.

"Angel?"

"This one's in a five-four time signature. It's complicated."

"J.L. practiced with the record," Patch Up said as he escorted the mulatto seamstress Jessica Jones into the dance area.

Yvette was surprised. "Daddy practiced dance steps?"

"Once the phonograph stopped laughing."

The patriarch frowned at his best friend.

Stevie pulled Rosemary Finley into the dance area, and Brent, holding the rugose right hand of the widow Mrs. Walters, followed after his younger brother. Overhead wheeled two birds that blazed with golden twilight.

John Lawrence Plugford took Dolores's hands and positioned his feet as if a boxing match were about to begin. His lips silently counted, 'one, two, three; one, two; one, two, three; one, two,' and on the third downbeat, the house, porch, guests and twilit ranch scrolled across his huge shoulders.

Right hand upraised, Dolores matched her father's deft footwork, twirling for three and two-beat durations. "You can do it good."

"Thanks." John Lawrence Plugford smiled. "And you're a better dancer than Patch Up."

"Bigot," said the negro.

The patriarch alternated the direction in which he twirled his daughter and fluidly guided her alongside his sons and their partners.

Brent looked away from his widow and appraised his father's footwork. "You've got it all the way correct."

"This ain't easy natural to a man like me," John Lawrence Plugford remarked, "but I learned how, and take real pleasure in doin' it proper."

Dolores knew that this comment was about more than just dancing.

Darkness expanded.

"Doloresssss."

Darkness thickened. The face of John Lawrence Plugford wailed and coughed up blood. Fluid dripped from his wrinkled eyes.

Darkness receded.

"Doloresssss."

Sitting upon Patch Up's stool with her face pressed to the wall, Dolores awakened. The molten potbelly stove was dark, and the fort was cold and dim. She lifted her head.

"They're riding toward us," said Long Clay. "Put your gun in the slit."

"Okay." The redheaded woman glanced at her father and Patch Up, both of whom had been alive in her dream only ten seconds earlier. They were still and filled with chill night.

"Let's get this goddamn Gris for permanent," Stevie remarked from the far side of the south wall.

Dolores raised her rifle, pointed the barrel outside and looked at the moonless night. "I can't see hardly anything."

Long Clay exhaled through his nose and aimed his telescopic rifle. "Neither can they."

Chapter V
The New Constellations

Brent Plugford watched a broad shadow emerge from the southern woodlands. Even with the powerful magnification of his spyglass, it was impossible for him to discern how many riders comprised the opposition, although it was clear that they rode at a full gallop, directly toward the fort.

"You don't like what we did to your amigo, do you?" taunted Stevie. "Don't like what we done to his tamale."

The dark mass poured across grasslands that were slick with dew.

Brent asked, "How does Deep Lakes fit into this plan?"

"He improvises."

"Okay."

Three stars that were muzzle flashes twinkled within the charging horde and shone light like a photographer's powder flash. Brent saw approximately fifty riders as well as several horse-drawn vehicles.

"Looks like nearly three score men are comin'."

The announcement poisoned the air.

"Goddamn."

Dolores swiveled upon her stool. "Brent?"

"Yeah?"

"When…when I was a whore in Catacumbas, I thought about…about ending it every day. You've got no idea of how bad it really was—'specially after I was crippled." The redheaded woman turned back to her opening and gazed out at the dark world. "But I didn't kill myself…'cause…well…it ain't easy, and 'cause I thought maybe you all would rescue me someday like you did. But if Gris got me again…I wouldn't even have that small hope." She paused, and the silence that filled the fort was heavier than the world. "I can't go back there. I can't. Never."

Unable to respond to his sister's terrible request, Brent stared through his spyglass at the charging enemy, who were three-and-a-half miles distant.

"They won't get you," Stevie said, "I won't let 'em."

"Brent," Dolores prompted, "you know what I'm askin' you to do."

"I know and I'll do it," agreed the cowboy, shuddering.

"Thank you."

Stevie looked over. "Brent?"

"Yeah?"

"I'm sorry for sayin' that stuff 'bout you. Please don't be angry with me."

"It's okay. This's a hard time for every Plugford."

The riders careered onto the pale weedy terrain and became sharp silhouettes. Galloping horses elongated and shortened twice per second, and vehicles vibrated upon invisible wooden wheels. The tattoo of hooves sounded like distant rain.

"If we survive," Stevie asked, "could I maybe come cowboy with you in your outfit? I ain't gonna run the ranch without Pa and Patch Up there with me."

"We gotta make sure Dolores and Yvette are situated good."

"After they're settled, can I come?"

Brent did not believe he would live to see any of these imagined scenarios, but he did not want to diminish his brother's hopes. "Okay. I'll hire you."

"Thanks. I'll work hard and behave, and I promise I won't drink."

Less than two miles south of the fort, horses and wagons sped across the terrain.

"Okay."

Long Clay squeezed his trigger, and light cracked. At the vanguard of the charging crew, a brown horse bucked. Even though the riders hunched forward in their saddles, their backs remained exposed because of the incline. The gunfighter flung his bolt, and a spinning shell clinked upon the stone.

"That's still well over a mile," remarked Stevie.

Long Clay adjusted his aim and fired. A man fell from a black colt to the ground, where his linear form was trampled until it became circular.

After a stentorian cry, the riders poked white holes into the night. Bullets hit the terrain far below the trench or climbed uselessly into the air.

Stevie fired.

"Save it," Brent said, "they're not in range of our guns yet."

Long Clay fired his telescopic rifle. A sombrero took flight, and a hatless rider tumbled into the dirt. Again, the gunfighter fired. A man grabbed his neck, fell from his saddle and struck the ground, where his head was kicked, cracked and crushed by hooves.

The riders extended their hands and conjured crackling white constellations. Plumes of dirt blossomed at the foot of the incline, and wild bullets whistled toward the sky.

Long Clay fired. A red dot burst upon the white neck of a horse, and the beast veered wildly, spilling its rider. The gunfighter emptied the chamber, loaded a new round and fired. A fallen man was trampled by a brace of horses and had his legs shorn at the knees by wagon wheels.

The opposition extended elongated arms and conjured crackling constellations. Dirt blossomed and wild rounds whistled.

Long Clay pulled the cartridge from the bottom of his rifle, slotted a fully-loaded replacement, drew a bullet into the chamber and fired. A man's hand turned into a red flower.

Half of a mile separated the charging crew from the fort.

"Start firing," ordered the gunfighter.

Brent set down his spyglass, raised his rifle, monitored the galloping opposition, pointed his barrel at its center and squeezed his trigger. White fire flashed before his eyes. A fleck that was too small to be a person dropped from the equine tide. Presently, Stevie and Dolores sent rounds.

Across the vanguard of the advancing horde, gunfire flashed.

Brent leaned back from the opening. Bullets struck brick or whistled into the sky or clicked against the mountain wall. From the ceiling of the fort, old dust sifted down.

The cowboy flung his trigger guard forward, and the spent shell clinked against the wall and floor. He leaned to the slit, aimed at the vanguard, and fired. The round whistled. A rider yelled, tumbled from his horse and was dismembered by hooves.

Thirty guns flashed.

Brent put his back to the stone wall, as did his siblings and the gunfighter. Bullets hissed overhead and cracked against the facade.

One of the captives shrieked, "¡No dispares, no dispares!"

The inverted Midwesterner yelled out, "We're still alive! Don't shoot us!"

"¡Ayudame, por favor, ayudame!" pleaded another inverted hostage.

The distant riders yelled and cursed.

"¡Diablos!"

"¡Animales!"

"¡Bárbaros!"

Although he did not know Spanish, Brent felt that he fully comprehended these imprecations. Presently, he heard the sound of crackling tinder that was Long Clay's ugly laugh.

Brent returned to the slit, aimed at the vanguard and fired. Atop the roof of a turquoise stagecoach, a rifle flashed. A bullet cracked into the stone directly beside the cowboy's opening.

"Hell." Brent leaned back from the opening and announced, "They've got a marksman." His heart was pounding. "Atop the turquoise stagecoach."

"I'll get him." Stevie pointed his rifle through the adjacent slit, fired, flung his trigger guard and aimed.

Brent slammed into his brother and knocked him west. A shot whistled through the slit and impacted the door of the prisoner's cell. The siblings struck the west wall, and their rifles clattered upon the floor.

"Double goddamn!"

"You gotta shoot and hide while they got that sharpshooter," Brent said as he retrieved their weapons.

On the far side of the fort, Dolores fired, leaned to the wall and flung her trigger guard. "Got somebody."

"Which one's the turquoise stagecoach?" asked Long Clay.

"The green-looking one," said Stevie.

"Tell me its position," clarified Long Clay, who was loath to admit that he could not see colors.

Brent surveyed the charging enemy, gleaned the turquoise stagecoach, fired his gun and hid. "On the right. The furthest on the right."

Long Clay shot, stepped away from his opening, jettisoned the spent shell, filled the chamber, went to a different slit, aimed and fired. "The sharpshooter's done."

Dolores fired and leaned back to the wall. "Got another."

"That's a Plugford woman!" Stevie fired.

Outside, fleet hooves thundered.

Brent raised his gun, aimed at the egg yolk that was the top of a yellow hat, pulled his trigger, blinked, flung his lever, watched the shot rider tumble and reveal a blonde man who wore a beige suit, fired, blinked and witnessed a gory corsage burgeon upon the man's left lapel.

Long Clay put down his telescopic weapon, raised his repeater rifle and sent bullets, alternately squeezing and fanning. Brent, Stevie and Dolores pulled magazines from their gunstocks, slotted replacements and sent three magazines at the enemy. Upon the stone floor, spent shells clinked like coins from a slot machine. Five members of the opposition tumbled to the sere terrain.

The siblings slotted new magazines.

"Hold fire," said the gunfighter. "Let them come."

All of the vehicles and five of the riders slowed their approach, but the remainder of the opposition, twenty-six horsemen who were hunched low in their saddles, hastened onward, toward the trench that laid one hundred and ten yards south of the fort.

The Plugfords and Long Clay watched.

Hiding behind the necks of their galloping steeds, the riders yelled obscenities at their enemies within the fort.

One of the inverted captives shouted, "¡Ayudame, por favor!"

"¡Nuestros amigos están aquí!" cried another hostage. "¡Triunfo, triunfo!"

The vanguard reached the line. Two hesitant animals tumbled into the trench and snapped their necks, but the majority of the horses hurdled the narrow gap. Hooves impacted the pregnant ground and the sun exploded from the earth. Steeds and men were hurled into the air, shrieking, atop a welter of white fire, shrapnel and dirt. Brent and his siblings were shoved from their slits by the blasts.

Myriad thunders echoed across the mountain wall.

"Go to Hell!" Dolores shouted from beside her toppled stool.

"They're on their way!" enthused Stevie. "Barbecued!"

A small amount of hope entered Brent's chest.

Beyond the cowboy's slit, the blackened pieces of steeds and men rained to the ground. A writhing vaquero struck the dirt, detonated another land torpedo and was wholly consumed by a bright white flash.

Five riders emerged from the cloud of smoke and continued their charge. Seared, deaf and blinded by grit, they fired wildly to the north, west and east.

Brent aimed his rifle at the nearest rider, fired and saw the dusty hombre fall. Long Clay shot two fellows from their saddles and sent an additional bullet into each man's skull when he landed. Stevie and Dolores fired upon and killed the remaining pair.

The cowboy surveyed the terrain that laid in-between the fort and the opaque curtain of smoke that hung seventy yards to the south. In that dark region, he saw no immediate threat.

"Guns forward," Long Clay ordered, "but hold until you've got something to shoot at."

Brent flung his trigger guard and snapped it back. In the eerie silence of the aftermath, the sound of the mechanism seemed especially loud and sharp. He looked at the sky and saw that the eastern horizon was a tiny bit brighter than the surrounding vault. Dawn approached.

Stevie and Dolores slotted new magazines.

One of the captives began to weep.

Brent raised his spyglass and inspected the terrain. The smoke dissipated, revealimg a score of jet-black craters that looked like holes in reality. Along the south side of the trench sat both stagecoaches and all three wagons. The vehicles were parked in a continuous line and had their sides forward.

"They made a wall with the wagons," announced Brent.

"Stevie," said Long Clay.

"Yessir?"

"Get to the west wall. Dolores."

"What?"

"Get to the east wall."

Stevie returned to the opening that overlooked the cemetery, and Dolores scooted her stool beside the slit that faced the well.

"Watch the ground," Long Clay advised, "there are probably survivors. Playing possum. Hiding."

"We will," said Stevie.

Brent monitored the terrain. Two blind horses stumbled amidst craters and incomplete corpses. South of the carnage, the line of vehicles sat still and quiet like an abandoned locomotive.

Immediately outside the fort, somebody sneezed. Brent stiffened—although none of the captives had their hands free, the sound had been muffled. "Back away from your slits," the cowboy whispered, "someone's out there."

The Plugfords and Long Clay leaned their backs to the wall. Silently, the gunfighter slung his rifle and drew a black revolver. The quartet waited, listening, for a very long minute.

Outside the fort, a pebble clicked.

Long Clay thrust his gun barrel through a slit and into an eyeball; he squeezed his trigger twice. The reports were dim, muted by the man's brainpan. As the gunfighter withdrew from the wall, and the man with the seared mind thudded to the ground outside. "Watch for them."

Brent returned to his opening and raised his spyglass. Through the lenses he saw the luminous dark blue teeth of a charred horse, the prostrated body of a dead man who had been pierced by shrapnel, a leg with no owner and the rim of the foremost crater.

Within the dark hole, something moved.

Brent adjusted his lenses and said, "I see—"

A muzzle flashed.

The cowboy flew backwards, and a gunshot resounded.

"Brent!" yelled Stevie.

"No, no, no!" shouted Dolores.

The floor slammed into Brent's shoulders, spine and buttocks. Fire flared across his shot left arm. "In the crater!"

In one fluid motion, Long Clay leaned to an opening, trained his rifle, fired twice and retreated.

Stevie ran to Brent.

"Stay on the wall," the cowboy said, "I ain't that bad off."

"No. You can't lose no more blood." Stevie knelt, withdrew a large handkerchief, folded it thrice and pulled it around his brother's left forearm.

"Hell!" The pain that burst from the wound almost knocked Brent unconscious. "Hell." His left hand twitched and clenched.

Stevie tightened the tourniquet and knotted its ends. "There."

Brent could not feel his left hand, but the wound was stanched. "Thanks."

"You're we—"

"Get to your slit," ordered Long Clay. "Now!"

"I'm goin.'" Stevie rose to his feet and glared at the gunfighter. "And you don't have to talk to me that way, neither. You can break all my limbs if that's real important to you, but if my brother or any of my kin get hurt, I'm helpin' them out no matter what."

A shadow covered the opening directly behind the young man.

Brent's stomach sank. "Stevie! Drop!"

Outside the darkened slit, a gun flashed.

The front of Stevie's forehead burst open.

Dolores shrieked.

"No!" yelled Brent.

The gun flashed a second time. Stevie lurched forward and dropped to his knees. Long Clay fired three shots through the slit, and the shadow outside screamed.

Stevie's face impacted the stone floor.

"Stevie!" Brent crawled to his brother and turned him over. "Stevie."

The young man's eyes were wide with horror and confusion. Gore filled his mouth and drained from the back of his head.

"We'll get you fixed," Brent said, "it ain't as bad as you think."

The terrified animal that was Stevie Plugford nodded. He moved his mouth and tried to say something.

"And after, you can come with me on the cattle trail. Okay?"

The young man nodded, relaxed and stopped breathing.

Brent looked away from his brother's piteous face.

"He's gone."

"No, no, no, no!" Dolores yelled from her stool. "None of this is fair—none of it is!" She looked up at the ceiling and yelled, "I hate you up there! Come on down so I can claw out your eyes and spit in the holes! I hate you all the way every bit!"

Long Clay looked at Brent. "We need you on the west wall."

The cowboy rested his brother's head upon the floor, concealed the young man's confused eyes with a handkerchief, focused his thoughts upon his living sisters and walked to the assigned slit. He saw the corpse outside and recognized the dead fellow as Jose Pastillo, an affable and kind vaquero with whom he had ridden and played checkers.

"Hell."

A wounded man who was covered so thoroughly with dirt that he looked wholly wrought from the substance crawled into the cemetery, dragging his detached right foot and long tubes that were his entrails. Brent aimed his gun and fired. The interior of the crawler's head splashed upon a tombstone that was previously unmarked. Atop dirt that covered old corpses, the dying man collapsed.

The cowboy focused his thoughts upon his sisters and killing the enemy, because all other ruminations had an undertow of despair that would pull him under.

"Roast in Hell!" Dolores fired and flung her trigger guard. The spent shell clinked against the floor, and a man groaned.

Long Clay fired two bullets. A man wept.

Brent saw a dirt-covered vaquero stumble toward the west side of the fort. The earthen being had a lopsided head and clutched a warped revolver with his lone remaining hand.

The cowboy shot him in the skull.

"Hell, Hell, Hell."

Chapter VI
We Ain't the Heroes

Something rapped upon the slanted roof of perdition. Brent Plugford pointed his rifle at the ceiling and flung his trigger guard.

"Don't fire," said Long Clay. "That's Deep Lakes."

"Where the hell's he been?" hissed Dolores.

"Guarding our back," said Long Clay. "Both of you get on the south wall and check the landscape."

Dolores scooted her stool across the floor.

"He's safe up there?" asked Brent.

"The roof's inclined away from the terrain so that defenders can go up top."

Brent walked to a forward slit and surveyed the foggy blue tapestry of corpses and craters that laid in-between the fort and the wall of vehicles.

"It's like the end of the world out there," remarked Dolores.

"Seems clear," said Brent. "And there can't be more than twenty of 'em left. Less, maybe."

"You're correct."

"Us Plugfords ain't easy huntin'," commented Dolores.

After a moment of silent surveillance, the gunfighter looked at the cowboy. "Get a pen and something to write on."

"Okay."

Brent circumnavigated the puddle that surrounded Stevie, walked to the bunk wherein laid Patch Up and John Lawrence Plugford, leaned over to retrieve his father's fountain pen and felt a painful burning in his head and left arm. Darkness expanded before his eyes, and in it he saw the wailing face of the patriarch, coughing up blood.

"Brent?" questioned Dolores. "You okay?"

The cowboy slammed his right palm to the north wall and regained his equilibrium. "Yeah." After a dizzy breath, he extracted the fountain pen from his father's pocket, grabbed a page of Samuel C. Upfield IV's confessional essay and walked toward the munitions table.

Long Clay strode to an eastern crenellation upon the south wall. "Midwestern Man."

There was no reply.

"Respond right now or the Indian will cut off one of your toes."

"I hear you," the Midwesterner replied from the façade.

Weak and dizzy, Brent reached the munitions table and leaned.

Long Clay asked the captive, "Do you speak Spanish?"

"Yes." The inverted man coughed and momentarily choked.

"You're going to translate a message for us to say to the opposition."

"Most of them speak English."

"I'd like for every single person to understand every single word."

"I'll translate your message."

Brent uncovered the fountain pen and touched its dripping tip to the blank side of the paper.

Long Clay said, "First part. 'Listen to me. You have lost.'"

"Escúchame. Usted ha perdido."

Brent wrote.

Escoochamay. Oosted a perdeedo.

Long Clay said, "Next part. 'Gris stole and raped my sisters. Gris is a bad man.'"

A heavy silence followed these declarations.

The Midwesterner said, "Gris wouldn't do that to a woman. He's—"

"It's true you dumb fool!" shouted Dolores. "That's what your amigo's father done to me and my sister—that's why all of this terrible stuff's happenin'!"

"I didn't know." The Midwesterner coughed. "I swear I didn't." Brent believed that the man was telling the truth.

"Translate," Long Clay said, "or the Indian will shove a stake through your scrotum."

"Gris robaton y violaron mi hermanas. Gris es un hombre malo."

"Again and slower."

The Midwesterner repeated himself, and Brent wrote.

Gris robaton ee beeolaron me ermanas. Gris es un ombray maloh.

"Next part," said Long Clay. "Give us Gris and we will let all of you live."

"Nos dan Gris y vamos a dejar a todos ustedes en vivo."

Brent wrote.

Nos don Gris ee bamos a dehar a todos oosteades en beebo.

"Last part. If you continue to fight, we will torture these men and kill all of you."

There was a momentary pause.

The Midwesterner cleared his throat. "Si continúa la lucha, vamos a la tortura a estos hombres y matar a todos ustedes."

See conteenewa la lewcha, bamos a la tortuda ah estos ombrays ee matar a todos oosteades.

Long Clay looked at Brent. “Say it back to the Midwestern Man so that he can correct your pronunciation.”

“Okay.” The cowboy walked over to the opening that was closest to the dangling Midwesterner and read the message aloud.

“Say, ‘tortura,’ with an ‘r’ sound at the end,” advised the captive. “What you said sounded like tortuga, which mean turtle.”

“Tortura,” repeated the cowboy.

“That’s right.”

~~tortuda~~
tortura

Long Clay raised his telescopic rifle and pointed it south. “Call that message through the slit as loud as you can.”

Brent put his left cheek to the stone bricks and yelled the message. ‘Listen to me! You have lost! Gris stole and raped my sisters! Gris is a bad man! Give us Gris and we will let all of you live! If you continue to fight, we will torture these men and kill all of you!’

Upon the façade, one of the inverted captives wailed, “¡Ayudame, por favor, ayudame!”

“Help us!” cried the Midwesterner. “Please, please help us!”

Brent peered through the slit. Outside, the ruined terrain was still, excepting two blind horses that struggled to escape from a deep crater into which they had fallen. The sounds of men engaged in a loud and hostile conversation emanated from behind the line of vehicles.

“Say again how he got me and Yvette,” suggested Dolores.

Brent yelled, “¡Gris beeolaron me ermanas!”

“He raped me!” cried his sister. “He raped me!”

The argument behind the vehicles grew louder, and the soft wings of hope fluttered within the cowboy’s chest.

Footsteps pounded south across the ceiling.

Long Clay looked at Brent. “Take his place on the roof. And bring a couple of iron stakes with you.”

“Okay.”

“Wear a tabard if you think you can manage the extra weight.”

“I can’t.”

“Get up there and stay low.” Long Clay eyed him sternly. “If they don’t yield, you’ll need to get mean.”

“I know we ain’t the heroes.”

The cowboy hung the wooden spyglass by its thong around his neck, slung his rifle over his good shoulder, slid magazines and two iron stakes into the sleeve of his left boot and walked toward the east door. His heart throbbed inside his chest, upon the side of his head and throughout his left arm.

"Brent!" shouted Dolores.

The cowboy looked over at his sister. "I'll get back safe."

"I've scolded you before 'bout not givin' a proper goodbye."

"I'm hopin' this ain't goodbye."

"Give me a goddamn hug!"

Brent walked to Dolores, leaned over and put his right arm around her shoulders. His gun swung forward and clacked against the stock of her weapon.

Into the cowboy's blood-soaked shirt, the woman said, "If you get shot…I…I'll…I'll—"

"I won't." Brent kissed her cheek. "I love you."

"I love you too." Dolores hugged him fiercely. "You're my favorite always."

"You too."

The cowboy withdrew from his sister and walked to the eastern door, through which the dandy, Stevie and Patch Up had recently carried supplies. Using the tip of his nickel-plated revolver, Brent slid the iron bolt north. He stepped aside, and a gentle wind pushed the door open. From the water well to the distant horizon, the azure terrain appeared tranquil.

Brent followed his outthrust pistol into the open world and hastened to the rear of the fort. No weapons were discharged during his beeline.

In the swath of dirt that laid in-between the edifice and the sunken stable stood Deep Lakes. The azure light of dawn shone eerily in his eyes. From the neck of his unique bow jutted the steel tips of five arrows and stuck into the ground around him like wooden topiary were one hundred more shafts.

Brent holstered his revolver, reached the iron ladder that led to the top of the fort, stepped onto the lowest rung and climbed, sliding his good hand along the outer bar. The north wall sank.

Pained and weak, the cowboy reached the inclined roof (the angle of which blocked his view of the opposition), clambered onto the desiccated wood and crawled. Sweat dripped from curls of his brown hair, and the spyglass that depended from his neck swung back and forth. Four yards from the southern edge, he lowered himself to his belly and slid, serpentine. Splinters pierced his chest and left cheek. "Hell."

Brent peered over the edge of the roof and saw a blue photograph that was the strange, funereal terrain. Chill winds carried the smells of charcoal, gunpowder, metal and burnt flesh, as well as the sound of the distant argument in which men shouted words that the cowboy did not understand. He considered removing the splinters from his face and body, but decided that they were not worth the effort.

A gunstock knocked thrice upon the ceiling.

"Next time I signal," Long Clay said from below, "shove a stake deep into a captive's rectum and leave it in."

"Not me!" shouted the inverted Midwesterner. "Please. I helped you and…and…I didn't know what Gris did to your sisters, I swear to—"

"It ain't gonna be you," said the cowboy.

"Thank you. Thank you."

Brent slid to the southwest corner of the roof and peered over the edge. Suspended from an iron stake were filthy feet, shredded ankles, a gory phallus and a pale belly that hid the inverted man's top half. The cowboy poked the captive's left heel with the tip of his revolver.

"¡No! ¡Por favor, no!"

The man jerked and twisted, and Brent glimpsed his very distinct handlebar mustache.

This creature had raped Dolores.

"I ain't gonna hesitate with you." The cowboy withdrew from the edge of the roof, prostrated himself behind the incline and arrayed his stakes, magazines, repeater rifle and spyglass. He knocked thrice upon the ceiling. "Ready."

"¡Escúchame!" shouted Long Clay. "¡Danos Gris!"

On the far side of the battlefield, the bickering opposition quietened.

A man with a heavy accent said, "We want our mens first. Trade."

"No," replied Long Clay. "Give us Gris and go home. After you're gone, we'll send the men. There will be no trade."

"Then no Gris."

Three knocks sounded upon the ceiling.

Brent thought of Dolores's agony, gripped the two-foot long iron stake, went to the edge of the roof, placed the narrow end in-between the captive's pale buttocks, poked his hairy rectum and thrust through rubbery guts until the sharp tip clicked against a hip bone.

The man's shriek was an inhuman skirl.

Repulsed, Brent released the rod, retreated to safety and prostrated himself upon the wood. His hands were shaking, and his heart was pounding. A moment later, the protruding half of the iron stake clanked against the stone façade, and the mortally-sodomized captive shrieked anew.

The opposition yelled across the nascent graveyard, "¡Diablo! ¡Eres el Diablo!"

"Barbarian!"

"Evil gringo!"

The captive's vocal cords ruptured, and his voice cut out.

Guns exploded. Bullets whistled over Brent's head and cracked into the mountain wall. He flung his trigger guard and inched forward on his belly. Invisible death whistled above his back, while below his chest, Long Clay and Dolores fired through their slits.

Brent reached the southern edge and looked for a clear shot.

The iron clanked against the façade, and the mute man hissed.

"I got one," Dolores called up from below.

Five arrows plummeted from the sky, directly behind the line of vehicles. A man screamed. Underneath the wagons and between the stagecoaches, guns thundered a reverberant polyrhythm.

Long Clay and Dolores fired continually.

A gun flashed inside of the turquoise stagecoach, and Brent aimed at the open window. He squeezed, flung his trigger guard and sent a second bullet after the first. A long rifle fell from the vehicle into the trench and was followed by the shootist.

Behind the cowboy, Deep Lakes released another quintet of arrows. The shafts flew into the sky, arced downward and fell behind enemy lines. A man yelled, "¡Puta, puta, puta!"

The wagons and stagecoaches shimmied upon their wheels.

Brent turned back to the Indian and yelled, "They've hid for cover in the vehicles!"

Deep Lakes adjusted his aim, sent arrows into the sky, notched five more and released.

The cowboy flung his trigger guard. As the spent shell clinked to the roof and rolled past his elbow, waist and feet he surveyed the vehicles through his spyglass, looking for a solid shot. In the middle of the line, the crimson stagecoach sank and rocked ponderously on its wheels.

"Watch the red one, far left," Brent shouted, "it's full up and I'm gonna tip it!" He aimed at the vehicle's large rear wheel, fired, expelled the used cartridge and sent a second shot. Wooden spokes shattered, and the hub cracked loose. The vehicle sagged, jerked like a living animal and tilted toward the trench.

The door swung open.

Into the gaping portal, Brent, Dolores and Long Clay sent a twenty shot barrage. Two men wearing dark cherry suits spilled outside and fell into the trench.

"¡Roberto!" cried a bereft man. "¡Francisco!"

"Those're Gris's sons," remarked Dolores from below. "We'll get your whole goddamn family!" she yelled across the terrain. "We'll kill all of you!"

Two shafts plummeted into the trench, five thudded into stagecoach roofs and three pierced wagon canopies. A man stumbled out into the open, unable to yell past the feathers of the arrow that he had swallowed.

"Hold fire," ordered Long Clay.

Brent flung his trigger guard. The ejected shell clinked to the roof and rolled north.

"¡Escúchame!" shouted Long Clay. "¡Danos Gris!" The demand echoed across the battlefield and smelled like gunpowder. "Give us Gris or we'll massacre all of you!"

"I will be out presently," said a man who spoke English as precisely as the dandy and Samuel C. Upfield IV.

"That's his voice," Dolores said through her opening. "That's Gris."

Chapter VII
The Deep Defeat

Dolores Plugford looked beyond the azure veil of gunpowder and at the crimson stagecoach that was parked one hundred and fifteen yards south of the fort. Inside that distant vehicle was the man who had defeated her.

Sitting at the far end of the oaken dining room table, the one-eyed Spaniard nodded his head in approbation. "Jorge Calao complimented your beauty and amenability. And Eduardo Ramirez, who described you as affectionate, prefers you over every other woman in Catacumbas."

"There ain't no pleasure in any of it. None at all—it's just..." Dolores rubbed her palms along the armrests of the stone chair in which she was seated. "It's just easier not to fight sometimes."

"That is exactly what I said to you three months earlier, when you first arrived."

"Roast in Hell."

"I ask for you to accept the fact that you are now my employee. If you do embrace your vocation, you will be treated well and granted the same privileges that—"

"I ain't no whore. Never."

A plate of shrimp and rice was set before the Spaniard and each of the six wraiths that sat beside him. Luminous eyes alternately observed the redheaded gringa and the steaming food.

"You are fucked by strangers," Gris said to Dolores. "You are from a lower class background and are poorly educated. Should I return you to society, no man would ever want to marry you, and cancan dancing will not provide you with very much income once you are middle-aged." The Spaniard unfolded his silk napkin and set it upon his lap. "The only thing that separates you from the other whores who work for me is that you have no say regarding what happens to you." He lifted a silver fork and speared a pink shrimp that looked like an embryo. "I would prefer to treat you well. But first, you must accept that you are my employee."

Gris put the shellfish into his mouth, chewed and swallowed.

The silent men picked up their forks, and the light from the candelabra flashed across polished silver.

Although Dolores knew that the quality of her life would be improved if she accepted Gris's offer, the thought of acquiescence filled her with shame.

A plate of real food landed on the table in front her, and the rich smells of butter, garlic, onions, peppers and shrimp caused her to salivate. Presently, a glass of aromatic red wine materialized. For three months Dolores had subsisted on sour chicken soup that was distributed by a pump through a pig's intestine.

Gris thrust four tines into a large pink shrimp. "I am pleased to see that you are taking my offer seriously."

Dolores ate the proffered meal and summarily accepted her forced vocation.

Three weeks later, she attacked one of her regular customers and had her foot shot off.

"You've got ten seconds!" warned Long Clay.

Dolores Plugford returned from her grim recollections and surveyed the world that opposed the barrel of her rifle. Horizontal rays of sunlight brightened the fog and turned charred corpses into obsidian abstractions. From the open portal of the crimson stagecoach emerged a man in a white suit that was spattered with blood.

"Go to the other animals!" yelled a man from within the turquoise stagecoach.

"Don't fire," Long Clay told the siblings. "We need to be sure."

"Okay," said Brent.

The gunfighter handed his telescopic sight to Dolores. "Identify him."

Holding the optical device before her right eye, the redheaded woman looked across the battlefield. The white-haired, one-eyed Spaniard stood at the edge of the trench, looking down at his dead progeny. Hatred filled the woman's belly. "That's him."

Dolores released the telescopic sight and grabbed her rifle.

Gris dropped into the trench, out of view.

Long Clay snatched the weapon from Dolores's hands and cast it across the fort. "A bad shot or an injury will prolong the engagement." He picked up his telescopic sight and reattached it to his long-range rifle. "Gris! Get out of the trench!"

"I want to shoot him," said Dolores. "After…after what he made me—I get to do it myself."

"Revenge isn't a tactic."

The crippled woman from Texas would not allow another man to take something from her ever again. With both hands, she seized the barrel of the telescopic rifle. "Give it over!"

The gunfighter grabbed the woman's left wrist and twisted. "Let go."

"Gris just bolted," Brent remarked from the roof.

Long Clay slapped Dolores.

The woman capsized her stool and fell to the ground. "Bastard!" The fort wobbled before her eyes, and her left cheek stung.

"What the hell's goin' on down there?!?" shouted Brent.

Long Clay threw a cold look at Dolores. "Don't make this worse."

If she told Brent what had happened, he would climb down from the roof, race into the fort and confront a man who could easily kill him. "Nothin'." This was not the first time she had lied for the benefit of a Plugford man.

"You sure?" asked Brent.

"I'm sure."

Long Clay pointed his gun through the crenellation. "Brent. Where is he?"

"He jumped into a crater."

"Which one?"

"On the west. I'm not sure which exactly—he moved fast."

Deep Lakes appeared in the east entrance, entered the fort, closed the door, slid the iron bolt north, strode beside Dolores and helped her onto her stool. His dark eyes noted the scarlet mark upon her left cheek, and his face grew grave. "Long Clay."

"Yeah."

"Don't ever hit J.L.'s daughter."

"I had a reason."

"No you didn't. Strike her again and our partnership will end."

"Fine. Take a look outside."

The Indian kissed the woman's stinging cheek, stood up and walked to the far side of the south wall.

Dolores looked though her slit. Pulled by hasty horses, the wagons and the turquoise stagecoach rolled downhill toward the woodlands. "They're leavin'," remarked the redheaded woman, perplexed. The significance of the opposition's descent struck her a moment later. "Brent!" A tingling hope electrified her nerves. "They're leavin'—they're runnin' off!"

"I see 'em!" her brother enthused from the roof. "Now it's only Gris we gotta get."

Hundreds of yards south of the fort, hooves thundered and wooden wheels spun. The opposing force retreated, careening.

"I don't like this," Long Clay said to the Indian.

"Nor do I." Deep Lakes fitted three arrows to his bow.

"But we won," opined Dolores, confused by the duo's concerns. "It's only Gris out there."

The triangular stock of a repeater rifle appeared before her face.

"Take it," said Long Clay.

Dolores reclaimed the weapon.

"Shoot him if you see him," the gunfighter announced, "it no longer matters if it's clean or in pieces."

"Okay," replied the siblings.

Dolores extracted the rifle's depleted magazine, dropped it to the ground, slotted a replacement, flung the trigger guard and pointed the barrel south. The retreating force was more than a mile away, and on the near side of the trench, the riven land was still. Three black cruciforms that were vultures wheeled in the dark blue sky.

Brent inquired, "Should we go out and hunt for—"

Two black lines shot up from a southern crater. The oblongs, each orbited by circle of white fire, spun end-over-end, landed fifty yards south of the fort, rolled two feet and exploded. Dolores squinted and was pushed back from her slit. Dawn sunlight turned the cloud of dust into a brilliant flower that obscured half of the horizon.

"Hell," remarked Brent from above.

Long Clay did not fire, nor did Deep Lakes release.

"Brent," the gunfighter asked, "can you see past that?"

"No."

Somewhere behind the brilliant flower, a gun resounded.

Deep Lakes stumbled back from his slit and clutched his gory throat. Three shafts thudded into the ceiling, and the Indian fell to the ground, gurgling.

"Oh God."

Dolores pointed her rifle in the general direction of the unseen report, fired, expelled the spent shell and sent another bullet. Four red oblongs flew from the opposite side of the brilliant white flower and landed less than ten yards from the fort.

"No," muttered Dolores.

The dynamite exploded. White fire and dirt flew through the slit, splashed Dolores's face and knocked her from her stool. The floor slammed into her back and concussed her head. Along the façade, the captives shrieked. Gunshots rang out.

Unable to see, Dolores discarded her rifle. She spat out a paste of gore and sand, scooped detritus from her tingling face and tugged upon a cord that was anchored to the back of her left eye socket.

"No."

Guns exploded pell-mell in the world of men.

"Your entire family shall perish!" The voice belonged to Gris.

Footsteps pounded across the fort. A hissing stick smacked Dolores Plugford's nose, bounced to the floor and rolled.

"Whore."

Chapter VIII
The Application of Hooked Beaks

Prone atop the southwest corner of the roof, Brent Plugford wiped grit from his face and ripped a splinter lose. "Hell." The brilliant limbo of sunlit dust enveloped him like heaven collapsed, and he could not see anything but light.

"Brent!" Dolores shouted from the opposite side of the fort. "Don't get killed! I love y—"

Thunder boomed. The eastern half of the roof erupted, and mortar, wood and bricks flew into the air. Brent was hurled from the west side into a bright white purgatory. Behind him, the fort shrank. The sere ground slammed into his left shoulder, and his right knee popped.

Brent lost consciousness and awakened a moment later, ears ringing and pains singing. On the far side of the blasted fort, stones and wood thudded against the ground. He prayed that Dolores had somehow survived the explosion. "Please," he said to the dirt.

The badly injured man knew that he would be physically incapable of chasing after Gris, and so he devised a simple tactic that he hoped would conclude the internecine engagement. He rolled onto his stomach and crawled, agonizingly, toward the body of Jose Pastillo, the vaquero who had killed Stevie. Brent surmised that the fellow (like the Midwesterner and others) had joined Gris's crew without knowing the real reason why the battle had first begun and what was at stake. "It's like a war," mumbled the cowboy as he reached the corpse.

Brent put his good hand underneath Jose Pastillo's nape, sat him upright and covered his gory head with a hat. "There." Presently, the cowboy claimed the fallen revolver, crawled into the graveyard, hid behind an unmarked stone, set the purloined weapon down and withdrew his own nickel-plated pistol. Twenty feet southwest of his position in the cemetery sat the corpse, hunched forward and ready to play checkers.

Shaking and dizzy, Brent monitored the riven land that laid south of the body. Nothing moved, excepting brilliant celestial smoke and vultures.

"¡Ayudame!" cried the cowboy.

An unseen man said, "¿Quién es ese?"

Brent waited in silence. He did not repeat his cry for help, which likely had some flaw in terms of enunciation, despite how many times he had heard the captives wail it from the façade.

Vultures applied their sharp beaks to obsidian corpses. Throughout the tableau, the hooked chisels of scavengers echoed.

A narrow shadow spilled from the southwest corner of the fort and inquired "¿Quién es ese?" Footsteps ground grit slowly, like the jaw of an old man eating peanuts.

Brent raised his nickel-plated pistol and aimed it at the elongate black stain, which was sixty feet away.

"I admit," the unseen man said from behind the fort, "that I imprisoned two women and forced them to work as whores so that they could pay off your family's debt. That was my crime." Hard shoes ground grit, and the shadow lengthened. "You killed and tortured innocent men. You murdered three of my sons. You murdered a pregnant woman, who was my daughter-in-law, and you murdered her baby, who was a beautiful girl. You murdered a baby girl!" The footsteps and the shadow stopped. "Face me with dignity if you have any, you vile, myopic and uneducated American!"

The cowboy could not contain his anger. "You stole and raped my sisters, you dumb hypocrite!" Vulture beaks chipped crystalline corpses. "You don't deserve no goddamn dign—"

Gris flung his left arm around the corner of the fort and fired twice.

Jose Pastillo's body fell over.

Brent squeezed rapidly. Two bullets cracked against the fort wall. The third shot impacted Gris's exposed forearm and knocked his gun into the air. When the cowboy's hammer clicked upon empty shells, he dropped his weapon.

Gris drew a second pistol.

Brent reached for Jose Pastillo's revolver.

A gunshot flashed within the west crenellation. The bullet cracked against the rock in Gris's face and sent it deep into his brain. His remaining eye bulged and gore squirted from his nose. The Spaniard stumbled forward, dropped to his knees and slammed to the ground. Three more bullets cracked his spinal column.

"Dolores?" Hope fluttered within Brent's chest. "That you?"

Trailing dark gray smoke and covered with black soot, Long Clay emerged from the fort. The overall shape of his body was somehow different, and he lacked his right hand.

Although the cowboy already knew the answer to his question, he asked, "Is Dolores okay?"

"She's dead."

Emptiness filled Brent.

Coughing up blood and dark bits, the misshapen gunfighter hobbled toward the sunken stable.

"Is Yvette okay?"

Long Clay slid into the ground.

"I need to check on Yvette," Brent said to himself. "See if she's still…see if she's okay." He clutched the top of a tombstone with his good arm and pulled himself to his feet. "I'm com—" His right knee buckled, and a grave marker struck the side of his head.

Lying upon the cemetery ground, Brent Plugford stared up at the blue sky, where not one cloud trespassed. "We didn't deserve none of this." He looked away from the empty vault. "We didn't." The hooked beaks of vultures clicked against crystalline corpses and unearthed red crystals.

Darkness consumed everything.

Part V

The Buried Phonographs

Chapter I
Their Small Purgatory

The four air holes on the west wall glowed with the golden light of sunset.

Yvette Upfield wiped flecks of dirt and dried blood from Mr. Stromler's blonde mustache, placed her fingertips upon his mouth, parted the two desiccated worms that were his lips, brought the nozzle of her canteen to the opening and watched the gentleman unconsciously swallow the water that she slowly poured into him.

Envious and with an idea, Henry stalked across the small chamber, sat beside the recumbent recipient of fluid, unfurled its long pink tongue and panted. The canine agendum was clear.

Yvette ignored the animal's request and poured a second tablespoon of water into Mr. Stromler's mouth. His fuzzy throat pulsated.

Frustrated, the beast reclaimed its tongue and whimpered. The immediate acoustics of the prisoners' cell turned the complaint into a sharp metallic sound.

"Silencio," commanded Yvette.

Henry eyed the woman, glanced at the canteen and tilted its head, perplexed.

"We're running out." The choirmaster liked dogs—and had a strong affinity for this particular creature—but she could not prioritize the life of an animal over the life of a man.

Yvette poured more water into Mr. Stromler's mouth. A long pink tongue lashed at the fluid, and the blonde woman laughed for the first time since she had heard the explosions. "You sneak."

Feigning innocence, the animal raised its left paw and unfurled its tongue.

"You've convinced me." Yvette took the lid from the top of the stew pot, set it upon the ground and poured out two tablespoons of water.

Henry walked directly across the gentleman—upon his head, chest and stomach—and lapped lustily.

Mr. Stromler opened his eyes and surveyed the dark enclosure. Upon his face was a look of utter bewilderment.

Yvette sat beside the man. "How are you feeling?"

"Why am—" The gentleman coughed and winced. "Why am I here? This is…the prisoners' cell, correct?" His voice creaked like dry wood.

"That's right. After you were shot, they brought you in here." Yvette hesitated for a moment. "We're locked in."

"Locked in?" the gentleman repeated with disbelief.

"Yes."

Mr. Stromler leaned forward, grimaced in pain and laid himself back down. "Damnation does my shoulder hurt." He placed his right palm to the bullet wound and grunted. "Is the bullet still inside?"

"It was removed before you were brought in. And the injury's healing up fine—doesn't seem to be infected."

"Thank you for tending to it."

"You're welcome." During the ministrations, Yvette had used only eleven tablespoons of water.

"How long have we been confined…here?"

"Three days."

"Jesus Christ." After a long silence, Mr. Stromler inquired, "What happened outside—with the engagement?"

"I don't know. I heard some gunfire and…and some explosions." Yvette had also heard Dolores scream out what were presumably her last words, but this was nothing that she could calmly discuss. "I don't know what happened."

"Nobody has come for us?"

"Not yet."

"Then your family must have been…" Mr. Stromler did not complete his awful surmise.

"That seems likely." As each day passed, Yvette's ability to believe that any of her family had survived was weakened by logic. What could possibly explain their absence, other than death or captivity? She stuffed away her morbid ruminations and raised the canteen to the gentleman's lips. "Drink some more."

"Why?" Mr. Stromler's question conveyed an immense despair.

"Because you should."

"Why?"

"Because," Yvette replied, "if you don't keep going through the bad times, things will never get better."

Tears leaked from the corners of Mr. Stromler's eyes, ran down his temples and disappeared within his blonde hair.

"Don't waste water." The choirmaster wiped the gentleman's face. "We're low."

Mr. Stromler nodded his head. "I am sorry."

"Drink some more." Yvette raised the canteen nozzle and saw Henry advance. "What's the Spanish for sit down? I forgot."

"Sientate."

The dog placed its rump upon the stone.

"I have an adversary," remarked Mr. Stromler.

"Henry won't hurt you."

The choirmaster drizzled two tablespoons of water into the gentleman's mouth, and he swallowed. "That's all I want to give you right now."

"Thank you."

Yvette placed a stopper into the nozzle, rose to her feet and set the vessel deep within the highest cubby, far beyond Henry's reach.

Mr. Stromler remarked, "You are looking far, far healthier than when last I saw you."

"Thank you. I've just been resting and eating—Patch Up's stew was real good, before it went sour." When Yvette said the negro's name, the gentleman's eyes sparkled. She could not yet bear to ask what had happened.

A moment of uncomfortable silence passed.

"Is there a place that I may…" inquired Mr. Stromler, sheepishly.

"To make water? There's hole over there." Yvette pointed to the northeast corner of the cell. "I won't look."

"Mrs. Upfield?"

Yvette opened her eyes and saw less. The chamber was black. In this drear perdition, she was a bodiless phantom, and her hideous memories were unconquerable.

"Are you awake?" inquired Mr. Stromler.

"Yes." The choirmaster was a blind and shivering wraith.

"There is somebody outside." The gentleman's voice had a hysterical edge.

"Might've been vultures or coyotes—they fooled me at first."

"I heard footsteps, a person walking, and also—"

Something rustled beyond the air holes. After a moment of quietude, metal scraped against stone.

A chill tingled Yvette's nape.

"Who's there?" inquired Mr. Stromler.

The coarse scraping grew louder and abruptly stopped.

Something clicked upon the stone bed, rolled and settled against Yvette's right shin. The woman reached down and felt a small hollow cylinder. "It's paper."

"A note?" inquired Mr. Stromler.

"Maybe." Through the air holes, Yvette said, "We don't got no—we don't have any light in here."

A guttural grunt was succeeded by the sound of metal scraping against stone.

Yvette cupped her hands near the air holes, and a sharp point pricked her left palm. "Ouch!" She withdrew her hands. "You poked me."

In the darkness outside, a muted vocalization that contained the letter 's' occurred. A crunching noise followed, which Yvette soon recognized as the sound of footsteps.

"He's leaving."

"See what he pushed through," suggested Mr. Stromler.

Yvette patted the area below the air holes until the tip of her right pinky landed upon an anomaly. She picked up the folded item and fingered its ribbed contents. "It's a matchbook—half of one."

"Good."

"Take them." The choirmaster pressed the matches into the gentleman's hands. "You light one when I say to."

"I shall."

Yvette rubbed her palm, unrolled the small scroll and pinched its top and bottom. "Okay."

A bright yellow arrow hissed beside the blue skirt that covered her legs, flared red and settled upon orange. Yvette squinted and looked directly at the bottom of the letter.

Sincerely,
Samuel C. Upfield IV

"Oh Lord Jesus." A wide array of conflicting emotions surged through Yvette and electrified her blood. "It's from my husband."

Mr. Stromler's face brightened.

Holding the curved letter in her tingling hands, Yvette read.

16, 17 or perhaps 18 August, 1902

Dear Yvette,

I will be brief.

My jaw was shattered, and thus I must communicate to you through the written word. I have very much work to do, and so I will only compose this letter during the brief respites that I am required—by my weakened condition—to take from my physical labors. (I do regret that I have not the time to write this communication in the calligraphic style that you so admire.)

I am currently excavating the rubble that blocks the door to the prison cell tenanted by you and Nathaniel Stromler.

As you must realize by now, most of your family has perished, including your father's house negro and the native. Although the current location of the evil gunfighter is unknown, I was told that he was badly wounded in the engagement—physically altered in a manner that is difficult to credit. Brent survived, but is currently incapacitated and in my care. After a period of

Darkness crowded the flame, and the match tip became a tiny red coal.

"Can you light another?" asked Yvette. "I didn't finish."

A flaming bug leapt across the darkness and became a glowing amber teardrop.

After a period of unconsciousness that lasted for one or two days, your brother crawled toward my residence, which was a trunk within the family wagon. He freed me and collapsed.

I had not eaten in several days (my cache of walnuts and raisins had dwindled two days earlier) and was too weak to walk uphill to the fortress, much less perform the menial labors that were required. After a necessary respite, I regained some strength and commenced the excavation.

I hope to reach you and Mr. Stromler in two days, but I dare not risk overexerting myself, since three lives now depend upon my efforts.

Although I occasionally suffer from hallucinations, I am fully aware that my current efforts will not balance out my odious crimes. You may dismiss me the very moment I am no longer of use to you, or you may have me jailed or hanged. I do not expect you to accept me back into your life, but I am grateful that I have an opportunity to aid you and your family in some way.

Sincerely,
Samuel C. Upfield IV

"Brent's still alive," said Yvette. "I didn't think that any of them—" She lost her words.

The flame neared Mr. Stromler's pinched fingers. "We are going to be rescued." A smile appeared beneath his thick mustache. "We are going to live."

Eyes stinging with joyful tears, Yvette nodded her head. "We're going to."

"And your husband is still alive."

Yvette nodded, but did not feign any joy.

The flame exhaled a plume of smoke and died. Against the outside of the cell door, the rubble shifted.

"That's my husband." Yvette was glad that the darkness hid her face from Mr. Stromler.

Chapter II
The Man Who is Samuel C. Upfield IV

When she opened her eyes, Yvette Upfield saw the four blue dots that declared dawn to the inhabitants of the prisoners' cell. Outside the door, the stones rumbled like a slow avalanche, although she felt more than heard their deep concussions. The dog sat before the sealed exit as if it expected a widely-heralded theater event.

Yvette raised her head and looked down her body. Upon her pelvis laid a tiny white tube. She seized the little scroll, sat upright and opened the communication. Wind blew through the luminous air holes, and the paper trembled.

Dear Yvette and Mr. Stromler,

I briefly interrupted the excavation so that I might raise a bucket of water from the well. I shall insert the muzzle of a rifle into an air hole and pour the gathered fluid into the weapon's open (and of course empty) chamber to facilitate its distribution.

Please call out to me whenever you are ready to receive a fresh supply of water.

In the near future, I shall be able to provide you with carrots, but currently their diameters are too large to transcend the air holes. I shall endeavor the auxiliary task of whittling roots during those regrettable moments that I am forced to recuperate from my exertions.

Sincerely,
Samuel C. Upfield IV

Yvette looked down at her slumbering cellmate, the mending gentleman, and decided not to call out for water until after he had awakened. Eight months of suffering in Catacumbas had taught her the value of sleep and dreams.

She rose to her feet, stretched, claimed the canteen from the cubby and poured water into the inverted pot lid. Henry's attention was diverted from the spectacle of the closed door.

The twenty-six-year-old woman who had been born in Shoulderstone, Texas and lived for seven years as a choirmaster in San Francisco summed and divided hundreds of beautiful and terrible memories in an attempt to determine what role Samuel C.

Upfield IV would have in her future. As the dog lashed the water Yvette envied the simplicity of its existence.

No matter what she decided, she would not have this conversation through an air hole, but when she finally saw her husband's face.

Although they were peppered with dust, the impossibly sweet and lush carrots that Yvette and Mr. Stromler devoured at twilight were the most delicious vegetables that she had ever eaten. (Eight months of wretched chicken soup certainly enhanced the flavor of all other comestibles.)

As the night progressed, the pair enjoyed water with abandon, although Yvette thought it tasted a little bit like rifle.

Cascading stones boomed and rumbled.

Yvette opened her eyes and found that she was adrift within the absolute darkness of an incorporeal hour. Rubble clicked and skipped upon itself and was succeeded by a heavy silence. She wondered if her husband had been injured or buried alive and was ashamed that thoughts of his agony elicited no small amount of joy. To the Savior, Yvette quietly prayed.

Presently, rocks shifted upon their siblings, and the sounds of Samuel C. Upfield IV's excavation resumed.

Illuminated by four circles of amber twilight, Yvette and Mr. Stromler unrolled the cylinders of bread that had passed through the air holes earlier that afternoon.

Stones rumbled outside the cell. The sentry barked, put its left forepaw to the door and scratched.

Yvette and Mr. Stromler observed the agitated dog.

A fist knocked upon the door.

The choirmaster started and dropped her cylinder of bread, as did the gentleman. Nearby, the canine proffered a delighted woof.

"Please do come in!" Mr. Stromler rose to his feet.

Yvette stood from her stone bed and pulled oily curls of blonde hair from her face.

Henry gamboled in excited circles.

A stone clanked against iron and startled all three of the cell's inhabitants. The metallic concussion resounded a second time.

"Perhaps the bolt is stuck?" suggested Mr. Stromler.

Yvette nodded. Her mouth and throat were dry, and her heart tugged. All of her lengthy ruminations had been fruitless, and she still did not know what she was going to say to her husband when they were finally reunited.

Stone clanked against metal.

Yvette imagined embracing her husband, and she felt a warm light permeate her body. She envisioned pushing him from the edge of an impossibly tall cliff, and she felt a just satisfaction. Her passions were a seesaw.

Henry snatched up, twice chewed and swallowed a cylinder of bread.

The metal bolt clanked, whined, cracked and clinked upon the ground. Suddenly, the thick door retreated half of an inch.

Yvette's muscles tightened.

The door was drawn open. Its bottom scraped across the stone floor, and its hinges creaked.

Leaning against the doorframe and wearing a baggy gold-and-brown striped suit that had once belonged to Patch Up was a five-foot-four-inch blonde man, limned by twilight rays, which shone through the exploded fort walls. The fellow's misshapen face was covered with dust, and his broken jaw was held in a silk sling that was stained with such an abundance of dried brown blood that it resembled a used diaper. Two blue marbles that were bleary eyes sparkled in the middle of the lumpy gray visage, and an embedded rock protruded from his forehead.

Yvette was immobilized by the piteous sight of Samuel C. Upfield IV.

Mr. Stromler cleared his throat. "I shall leave you two alone." He passed beside the small man—who was ten inches his inferior—and exited the fort through the exploded south wall.

No words came to Yvette. She stared at the miserable little betrayer who was her husband, and her internal war of hatred and sympathy did not abate. After a full minute of useless deliberation, the choirmaster regained the power of speech and announced, "I want to see Brent."

Samuel nodded his head, tightened the sash that fastened Patch Up's trousers to his narrow waist, turned and limped away.

Yvette walked through the door of the prisoners' cell and into the blasted fort, a blackened and shapeless enclosure that was wholly unrecognizable as the place wherein she had read the confessional essay, argued with Dolores and later apologized. She navigated piles of rubble that were taller than her husband and turned west.

After six days of dark confinement, Yvette stepped outside. Unseen hands release her spine, and she knew His presence in the twilight rays that turned her skin into gold. Tears that had many meanings came to her eyes, and the impossibly beautiful panorama scintillated. To God, the choirmaster quietly said, "Thank you."

The heels of Samuel's dilapidated loafers clicked upon a ramp that led down to the stable in which healthy horses stood amongst beasts that had starved to death. Yvette descended.

Presently, the mute prince stopped behind the family wagon and pointed a purple fingernail.

Yvette passed her husband, climbed into the canopy and walked over to Brent, who was bandaged and asleep inside a clean bedroll. She knelt beside an array of cups, which contained water, mashed carrots and wet bread, and touched her left wrist to her brother's forehead. His temperature felt normal. "No fever." The cowboy's respirations were even and his skin was dry. "Seems like he's doing okay."

A lumpy gray head tilted forward and back.

Yvette seated herself upon the wagon bed, directly beside her older brother.

The diminutive man turned away and walked south.

"Samuel," said Yvette.

The departing figure stopped, but did not turn around.

"I spent a lot of time thinking about what to tell you and how I feel," Yvette said, "but I still haven't figured it out." She looked deep within herself and admitted, "I don't know that I can ever look at you and see somebody other than the weak fool that got my family killed. The cringing coward that got me raped. A man who betrayed everything important."

The little man nodded his bandaged head.

"Maybe there was nothing else you could do once you got in deep with Gris," suggested Yvette. "If you went against him, you would've been killed by his gunmen like he said, and Dolores and I would still have been taken to Catacumbas."

Samuel's hands were trembling.

"Maybe that's the case—once Gris had you hooked, you had to do what you did." Yvette's heart was pounding. "But I don't believe that. Not right now and maybe... maybe not ever."

The little man nodded his bandaged head.

"But I know that I want to believe it," confessed Yvette. "I know that I want to believe you didn't have a choice so that I can have you back in my life. I just don't know that I can."

Samuel's back and shoulders were shaking.

"I want to sit here with my big brother." Yvette took Brent's left hand. "Alone."

Presently, the piteous man strode up the log ramp, reached the top and was struck by the horizontal rays of the setting sun. The southern sky was the exact same color as Samuel's illuminated right half, and Yvette was only able to see his shadowed remainder.

Chapter III
The Benign Specter

The man who could not remember his name saw a white pyramidal rock upon the ground, determined that he must reach that far-off destination, dug the fingers of his good hand into the sere dirt and pulled his agonized carcass forward. Across the dirt, three useless appendages draggled. Coarse grit abraded his skin, and the pyramidal rock moved one inch closer to his right eye.

Upon the other side of the stone and covered with dirt was a dead cowboy who gripped his large intestine as if it were a line to a sunken anchor.

The man who could not remember his name passed out and awakened in a dark place, lying upon his back. He knew that he must turn onto his stomach and continue toward his destination, the wagon, wherein sat the black trunk that contained his only hope.

"Are you awake?" asked somebody from somewhere.

An arrow of yellow fire flashed, flared red, traveled into a hanging lantern and became a radiant orb that illuminated the wagon canopy. The dandy shook the match and gazed upon the recumbent cowboy.

Brent Plugford croaked, "I believe it was…the other way 'round…last time."

"I prefer this arrangement."

"Yank."

The bushy blonde mustache atop the dandy's lips withdrew, revealing teeth. "How are you feeling?"

"Deep pain all over, but no fever anymore. And I got a little strength." Brent surveyed his surroundings. "Where's Yvette?"

The dandy's face became grave. "She is inside the fort."

Alarmed, Brent asked, "What's she doin' in there? Ain't no reason for her to go back inside that place."

"She is gathering together the remains of your family."

Brent leaned forward. Sharp blades skewered his wounds, and he collapsed. "Hell."

"Be mindful of your injuries."

"She shouldn't be in there—doin' that."

"I agree," the dandy replied, "but when Mr. Upfield and I offered to help her, she forbade us."

"Sounds like she's feeling better."

"She is unquestionably the halest member of our quartet."

"Yvette's always healed up quick," remarked Brent. "Like a lizard."

The cowboy and the dandy were quiet, and the scraping sounds that emanated from the fort unpleasantly filled the void. Although Brent could not offer his sister any physical assistance at this time, he desperately wanted to help her, and he ruminated on the matter while he drank water and ate mashed carrots.

Presently, an idea occurred to him. "There was a surprise that we brought down for the girls. I think it could help Yvette while she's doin' what she's doin'. Will you get it to her?"

"Certainly."

A painful journey brought Brent across the wagon bed and to its edge, where he could see the new moon and old stars that hung in the vault. Inside the fort, metal scraped against stone. Something cracked, and the cowboy wondered if it was a burnt part of somebody that he loved.

Nathaniel and Samuel carried the wooden box to the west wall and entered the blasted enclosure. Metal scraped against stone.

"Leave me alone." Yvette's voice was ragged with fatigue and grief.

"Brent asked us to bring this to you," stated the dandy. "If you do not want to use it, we shall take it away."

"What is—" Yvette stopped herself. "They brought this?" She sounded surprised. "I…I can't believe they brought it all the way here…from San Francisco."

"Brent thought it might make…your task…a little less dark."

"It might," said Yvette. "Please take it out of the box."

The cowboy heard the squeaks of four tiny hinges and the insectile clicks that the handle made when it was wound clockwise.

Yvette asked, "Did they bring, 'His Waves Shall Carry Us Home?'"

"Mr. Upfield has already readied that specific cylinder."

John Lawrence Plugford had planned to play music and dance with his daughters after they had been rescued, and although this was not to be, Brent hoped that the phonograph could at least give his sister some small comfort during her morbid endeavor.

"I'd like to hear it," said Yvette. "Please."

Henry barked.

The waltz that Brent had not heard since his sister's wedding celebration emanated from the lantern-illuminated openings of the fort. Like a benign specter, the music of strings, woodwinds and piano drifted across the riven land.

Hard-soled shoes traversed the rubble, and Brent looked to the blasted east side of the edifice. Yvette emerged, covered with soot, but looking far healthier than when last he had seen her.

"Thank you!" the choirmaster called down.

"You're welcome!" Although it hurt Brent to raise his voice, he added, "I'm sorry I ain't fit to help!"

"You just did!" Yvette reentered the fort and to the inhabitants said, "Please leave me alone."

Gentlemen, tall and short, emerged from the west wall.

The fifth time Yvette listened to the song, she sang along with the melodies.

"She has a beautiful voice," the dandy remarked over a cup of steaming tea.

"She does." Brent laid down upon his bedroll. "She always could sing pretty." He shut his eyes. "It's a gift."

The sounds of Yvette's sad labors were almost wholly obscured by the music, and on the eleventh repetition of the waltz, Brent Plugford fell asleep and had a dream in which his mother sang a beautiful lullaby about the expansive life of a cowboy who traveled the great landscape.

Chapter IV
The Embers of Nathaniel Stromler

The fort shrank.

On the left side of Nathaniel Stromler loomed the sheer mountain wall, the cyclopean barrier against which he had almost been crushed. Ahead of him was the eastern horizon, a black sky peppered with stars that he no longer recognized. He rode home, wounded, disenchanted and unsure.

The tan mare had not survived the engagement (the injured animal had died of thirst while tethered to a stable post), and so Nathaniel rode upon the spotted colt that had previously been owned by Stevie Plugford, whose incomplete remains were with those of his family inside the black trunk that Samuel C. Upfield IV had occupied for the major part of nineteen hundred-and-two.

Ten yards south of the tall gentleman, the green Plugford wagon rolled a parallel easterly course. Yvette drove the four horses with Patch Up's whip and Brent rested upon the bench directly beside her. Pressed to the cowboy's left thigh was the sparkling and sweaty black nose of the slumbering circus dog. A substantial distance away from the vehicle and traveling in the same direction was the diminutive blonde man, atop a little brown palfrey that had once belonged to a member of the opposition.

The unfamiliar celestial bodies dimmed, and, as the sky became royal blue, the land flattened. Nathaniel drank coffee from his flask and yawned the moment he was done.

Directly ahead of the caravan, the hidden sun showed its brilliant scalp.

"Mr. Stromler," Yvette said from the driver's bench.

Nathaniel reined his colt beside the vehicle. "Yes?"

The woman pointed her whip at the train of horses behind the family wagon, all of which had been owned by the opposition. "Brent and I would like to give you the extra animals."

"Thank you, but that is unnecessary."

"We don't have any more money," Yvette explained, "but we'd like to give you more than what was promised—especially considering all that happened to you."

Nathaniel could not accept any charity from the destroyed family.

"Each should fetch you a hundred and forty dollars," Yvette continued, "except that black mustang, who's pretty old and not very valuable."

Shaking his head, the gentleman replied, "I am afraid that—"

"Please take 'em," implored Brent. "Let my sister and me do one good thing for someone in all this horrible mess. Help you out with your hotel."

Nathaniel knew that he had no choice but to accept the gift. "Thank you."

Brent lifted the brim of his cowboy hat and looked at the gentleman. "If you ever need help—with anything—you get in touch with me. I'll be at the Plugford ranch with my sister over in Shoulderstone for a good long while. Maybe permanent, dependin' on how my injuries settle."

"Thank you for your offer."

"It's genuine true."

"I know."

Leesville emerged from the eastern horizon at half past five. Riding the spotted colt and trailing six additional horses, Nathaniel shook hands with Brent and Yvette and waved at Mr. Upfield. The little blonde man did not lift his gaze from the dirt.

The gentleman rode to the Sable ranch, which laid at the southwestern perimeter of town, and sold his motley train of steeds to the skinny, lavishly-bearded proprietor for eight hundred and fifty dollars, which was the very first offer. They spat in their hands, slapped palms together and shook thrice.

Isaac Sable picked a piece of corn from the waterfall of gray curls that comprised his beard and remarked, "Some folks said you'd taken a permanent weekend." He ate the kernel. "Glad to see you back in Leesville."

Although Nathaniel felt as if the major part of himself had not returned, he said, "Thank you."

The gentleman rode the spotted colt along the central avenue and passed by the blacksmith shop where he had met the Plugfords and first stared down the gunfighter who eventually shot him. Today the town seemed small and unreal—a child's toy of civilization in a huge and barbarous world.

Nathaniel guided his horse toward the southwestern part of Leesville, which was an area that he had avoided for many months. A few quizzical faces eyed his spotted colt, upon which there remained several brown bloodstains, and two customers from the cobbler shop called out to him, but he disregarded the citizens' solicitations and stared straight ahead.

The horse carried its introspective rider to the end of the avenue and was reined to a halt beside Stromler's Very High Quality Hotel. Silent and still, the gentleman studied the exposed rooms and warped halls of the incomplete hotel, a place that had been accosted by sand, rain, wind, tumbleweeds, coyotes, vagrants and six seasons.

Nathaniel Stromler looked at his destroyed dream, and he felt nothing.

He tugged upon his reins and guided his horse away from the sundered edifice. The shadow that he trailed was long.

Nathaniel hoped that the woman whom he had loved not so very long ago would better affect his dim embers. Directly at the setting sun, he hastened his tired animal.

The spotted colt appraised its whickering neighbors as it walked into the stall that the tan mare had previously tenanted. Nathaniel shut the beast inside, stepped back and wiped dust from his blue suit, which still smelled like horse and perspiration (and horse perspiration), but at least was not brown with blood, as was his yellow riding outfit, or saturated with noisome scorpion-wrought excreta, as was his black tuxedo. He shattered the wan visage that was reflected in the trough and splashed water upon his dry, dusty skin. Wiping his hands upon his trousers, he walked toward the door.

Nathaniel emerged from the stable and strode up the pebble pathway, toward the dark square that was the Footman's house. A silhouetted man whom he recognized as the yard negro, Sir, turned away from him without a salutation.

A distant voice boomed, "How many days go into a week?"

Nathaniel surveyed the façade and saw, upon the west porch, the telltale glow of Ezekiel's pipe.

"So that's the problem, eh? You don't know how many days go into a week?" The cattle rancher rocked in his chain-suspended bench, and the pipe bowl became an arc of red light. "I've overrated schools back east."

Nathaniel had no interest in squabbling with Ezekiel and thus ignored the jibe.

"The answer's seven," the cattle rancher stated, "not ten." The pipe bowl brightened and illuminated two angry eyebrows.

"Good evening, Mr. Footman," replied Nathaniel.

"Harriet!" cried Ezekiel.

"Yes?" the woman replied through the kitchen window.

"I think Mr. Stromler forgot something. A valuable pen or some gold cufflinks. Maybe an apple that's only been half-eaten."

"Why do you say that?"

The pipe glowed and darkened. "He's back."

Uninterested in defending himself, Nathaniel ascended two steps and landed upon the porch.

The cattle rancher's furry head sprouted from the southwest corner of the house and appraised his tenant. "You don't look too spectacular."

Nathaniel reached for the screen door.

"Kathleen's in the baby's room." Ezekiel's voice was gentle.

"Thank you."

"She started packing up this morning."

Although this news should have troubled him greatly, Nathaniel felt little more than a detached sense of concern. He nodded politely, opened the screen door, entered the Footman's wooden home (which smelled like savory pies), strode across the checkered rug, climbed the stairwell to the second floor, traversed the spotted carpet and in four more strides arrived at the closed door of the baby's room. His bullet wound throbbed, and he waited a moment for the pain to subside.

A door creaked behind Nathaniel, and he turned around. Orton, the pubescent son of Ezekiel and Harriet, poked his head from his room.

Nathaniel strode toward the youth and said, "Do not spy upon my fiancé ever again." He clenched his fists.

"I just—"

"Ever!"

The boy retreated into his room, slammed the door and turned the key. Nathaniel's pulse pounded in his shoulder and in his chest, as if he had two separate hearts. He was angry with Orton, but more upset by the terrible things that men did to women, and the fact that he was about to strike a thirteen-year-old boy. The gentleman shook his weary head and turned around. Standing in the open doorway of the baby's room and clothed in a green silk robe was his raven-haired fiancé, Kathleen O'Corley.

"Nathan?"

"I…I am sorry that I was delayed."

The stunned woman stared at the returned wraith to whom she was engaged, and he mirrored her gaze. Although Nathaniel no longer felt the warm light of love, he knew that he wanted to protect his fiancé from the mean world, and that desire was a tether that tied him to her.

"Let's talk in private," suggested Kathleen.

After following his fiancé into the baby's room, the gentleman shut the door to the world and turned the key until the lock clicked. The betrothed pair hugged. Silently, Nathaniel endured the pains that their embrace elicited.

"I'm so glad that you've returned," Kathleen said, "but I cannot believe that you are wearing a gun."

No words came to Nathaniel Stromler. He looked over his fiancé's shoulder and at the small warped window that sat upon the west wall of the baby's room. Superimposed on the dark gray landscape was the reflection of a translucent stranger.

About the Author

Florida-born New Yorker S. Craig Zahler worked for many years as a cinematographer and a catering chef, while playing heavy metal and creating some strange theater pieces. His debut western novel, *A Congregation of Jackals* was nominated for both the Peacemaker and the Spur awards, and his western screenplay, *The Brigands of Rattleborge*, garnered him a three-picture deal at Warner Brothers and topped the prestigious Black List. In 2011, a horror movie that he wrote in college called, *Asylum Blackout* (aka *The Incident*) was made and picked up by IFC Films after a couple of people fainted at its Toronto premiere. His directorial debut *Bone Tomahawk* will be in production in 2013.

A drummer, lyricist and songwriter, Zahler is half of the doomy epic metal band Realmbuilder (which is signed to I Hate Records of Sweden) and the black metal project Charnel Valley (whose two albums were released by Paragon Records). He studies kung-fu and is a longtime fan of animation (hand drawn and stop-motion), heavy metal (all types), soul music, genre books (especially, horror, crime and hard sci-fi), old movies, obese cats and asymmetrical robots.

To learn more about S. Craig Zahler, please visit scraigzahler.com and rawdogscreaming.com.

CPSIA information can be obtained at www.ICGtesting.com
Printed in the USA
BVOW000023170513

320936BV00001B/3/P